Praise For Brian O'Grady:

"I thoroughly loved reading *Hybrid* by Dr. Brian O' Grady! This well-written, suspenseful, thrilling novel will keep you on your toes waiting for what happens next. Move over Michael Crichton there is another medical thriller novelist on the block!"
— Gather

"This novel grabbed me from the first page and I just couldn't stop reading. It is terrifying and intriguing and I was drawn to the author's use of modern technology to give the plot a sense of realism."
— Simply Stacie on *Hybrid*

"*Amanda's Story* is the prequel to Hybrid and is just as exciting and terrifying."
— Single Titles

"*Amanda's Story* is a riveting and gripping novel that is a real page-turner."
— Hotchpotching

"Like Amanda, the reader is holding on to 'dear life' for this white-knuckle read. Chilling!"
— CMash Reads on *Amanda's Story*

The
Unyielding
Future

The Unyielding Future

Brian O'Grady

THE
ST●RY
PLANT

Studio Digital CT, LLC
P.O. Box 4331
Stamford, CT 06907

Story Plant Print ISBN-13: 978-1-61188-216-2
Fiction Studio Books E-book ISBN-13: 978-1-936558-87-2

Visit our website at www.TheStoryPlant.com

First Story Plant Printing: September 2015
Printed in The United States of America
0 9 8 7 6 5 4 3 2 1

To Margaret.
You are why I get out of bed every morning.

Note to the Reader

X X

FIRST LET ME APOLOGIZE. I am not a writer by profession, temperament, or talent. I have only a passing familiarity with grammar and would not recognize a conjunctive phrase if it bit me in the but (*sic*). My editor added the (*sic*). So, I am an unlikely and ill-equipped choice to be the chronicler of such important events. It was not my decision.

For the sake of honesty and accuracy let me revise that last sentence. It was never my decision to become a participant, but I take full responsibility for being the chronicler of these events. Weeks ago, I made a conscious decision to fill nearly every free moment with the telling of this story. It's almost become an obsession, and I can't tell you, Leah, my wife, or myself exactly why. Maybe it is a way of simply purging myself of the experience. It is not (unlike many in my profession) because I have a burning desire to write the great American novel, and it certainly is not because I feel I owe Adis anything. In fact, I spend more nights than not staring at the ceiling wishing he had never come into my life, because frankly he's complicated it beyond recovery. Before him I was happy in my cloistered world. For the most part I lived as I was raised and things made sense. I worked hard, did my homework, stuck to my principles and things generally turned my way. Not always, but enough to reinforce the belief that in most respects I was in control of my life and destiny. Please don't misunderstand me, I was not living an uneventful life or suffering from the delusion that I was immune to the vagaries of chance. Shit happens. Forrest Gump said it, sort of, and it's my wife's favorite phrase. I know shit happens, I see it almost every day at work, and sometimes it finds its way to me. I can't control that (shit) so I have to accept it and concentrate on what I can control. Only now, after Adis forced his way into my happy little bubble, I have to accept that instead of being the captain of my life's ship, romantically fighting rogue waves and rough seas, I am in fact only a pawn on someone else's chessboard. So, here I sit at 5:30 a.m. in front of my computer, while my wife and children sleep. My dog has curled up in the knee space of my desk, her head resting on my feet, and I wonder how cruel it would be if I could communicate to her all the realities of her life.

Okay, enough of that self-serving, depressing stuff. What follows is a chronology of events that occurred over a five month period, beginning last April. Most of these events of course involve Adis, a man who requires no introduction, either directly or indirectly. I first met the famous man a few hours after the incident at Northland High School, and at the start our relationship was purely professional. Unfortunately, it didn't stay that way. The evolution of our complex relationship forms the backbone of this story. I have been careful not to modify anything Adis said or did in any meaningful way; of course, I'm the one who decided what was meaningful. Beyond that I have taken full liberty to address any and all issues that are remotely related. Translation: I go off on a lot of tangents. Unfortunately, as my publisher tells me, tangents frustrate people, so to keep things moving I have included a few end notes (kind of like footnotes but at the end of the book instead of the bottom of the page).

One last thing. Most of what has appeared in the mainstream press about Adis (and to no less a degree about me) is either incomplete or completely inaccurate. It never seemed to bother him, but it bothers me. So, for my peace of mind, where it is necessary I have supplemented or directly refuted a fair amount of what is "known" about Adis. So here is my first correction. Adis's name is Adis. No title, just Adis. At first it was difficult for me not to add an honorific, but eventually I adjusted.

One last, last thing. At times this will be a hard story to follow, and not just because of my flight-of-ideas writing style. It is impossible to fully understand Adis, and most of the time I was forced to let go of the reins and allow him to take the lead. If I have faithfully reproduced these events, every "where is this leading" thought will have a corresponding "oh, I see" moment. Despite the long, seemingly unrelated and disconnected stories, in the end it all comes together.

Chapter One

X X

NBC NEWS INTERVIEW OF NATALIE TEWS. Recorded April 30, 2016. Unabridged. Comments added by me.

"We were about forty minutes into the third period when I heard the first shots. Several of the students also heard them and everything sort of froze. It was quiet for about a minute and we all stared at each other wondering what we had heard, then we heard the second volley. It was much longer, and closer."

Natalie Tews was twenty-four at the time of the shooting, and not much older than some of her students. Educated in a time when school shootings had become a depressingly known complication of the teaching profession, her quick reactions almost certainly saved lives. In my opinion, the petite brunette did not receive the attention and accolades that she deserved.

"At that point I slid my desk in front of the door. I tried to lock it but . . . I didn't have enough time. I probably should have gone for the lock first. I told the students to get down and then had them crawl towards the back of the room."

"And that was when one of the terrorists tried to force open the door?"

The reporter was Nina Gonzalez, one of the few Latino reporters working for NBC at the network level. Her questions seemed a little harsh, almost abrasive compared to the soft-spoken teacher's responses.

"Yes. At first the desk was working, but he kept ramming the door with his shoulder, and eventually he managed to open it a crack. I got in front of the desk and tried to block it with my body, but he kept slamming the door. I saw his face through the window. He had this look of wild, almost joyful . . . evil."

"Let me stop you for a moment,"

At this point in the interview Nina skews over to the terrorists and for the next several minutes she discusses their motivations. As this story has nothing to do with the motivations of the late Harold Leopolo and the three surviving members of the Righteous Thunder militia, I have chosen not to give them any more notoriety. It is my firm belief that anyone who murders children for political reasons deserves an eternity of roasting slowly on a spit in the depths of Hell. As Forrest Gump would say, "and that's all I have to say about that."

"He started calling my name as if he knew me, saying terrible disgusting things. I wanted to cover my ears with my hands, but I needed them to brace myself against the desk. The door was open about six inches when I heard him go down. A couple of the students helped me slam the door closed and this time I did manage to throw the lock."

"And that was when you first saw Adis?" Nina asked and Natalie noded. "Can you tell me what your first impressions were?"

Natalie's interview aired on an *NBC Special Report* May 1, 2016. The camera angle is a long shot with both ladies sitting in matching arm chairs. I sat in one of those same chairs when I visited Natalie in her apartment many months later.

"Most of what I remember about those few seconds is fragmentary. The terrorist's face was in the window then I heard a dull thump and he was gone. There were sounds of a scuffle and after a few moments I took a quick peek. The terrorist had his knee on the chest of an elderly man and he was hitting him in the face with his weapon. I didn't know who the older gentleman was or where he came from, he was just there. I don't even think I even consciously questioned why. I suppose a part of me assumed that he was a visitor, maybe a grandparent, or a janitor I hadn't met. What I do remember thinking was that this poor old guy was going to die for being in the wrong place at the wrong time."

"But that's not what happened," Nina said seriously, but if you study her beautiful face closely you can pick up on the hint of a smile.

"No, thank God. I heard them wrestling and punching, and then I heard something between a scream and a choking sound, and then it was quiet. The students heard it as well, and some of them started to cry while others tried to get them to be quiet, and with all the commotion I couldn't hear everything. After what seemed like hours but was probably only a couple seconds, I heard a voice at the door. I couldn't make out what he was saying even though I was right there. Then he gave a soft knock and I heard him say that everything was all right. He said it again, and that's when I found the courage to take another look out the window. Adis smiled back at me. He had a gash from his hairline down to his cheek and blood all over his shirt, but at that moment he was the best looking man I had ever seen." At this point both women are smiling openly.

"He told me to keep the door locked and to stay hidden and that he would be back," Natalie finished.

"And he did come back," Nina said brightly.

"Yes he did," Natalie answered just as brightly.

The historic details of April 20, 2016 are well known. What, where, when, and why have been codified by two police reviews, one Texas Department of Justice commission, one US Department of Justice commission and countless investigative reports (including the *NBC Special Report* above). The details are in stone, irrefutable, and beyond question. Now, I have no intention of complicating the prosecution of the remaining defendants (which at the time of this writing is months away), but some of the historic details are in fact open to reinterpretation.

At about 10:15 a.m. on Wednesday, April 20, 2016, six men drove into the south parking lot of Northland High School in Austin, Texas. The three-story structure was built in 2009 in a spoke-and-wheel pattern with three corridors emanating from a central administrative hub. It was heavily automated, with cameras and central locking mechanisms that could isolate individual rooms or corridors in an effort to prevent this very type of incursion. The men were not stopped or questioned at the gate and simply parked their 2010 Ford Expedition in the north parking lot adjacent to the football stadium and began to unload their equipment. Each man wore body armor (purchased illegally at a Phoenix gun and knife show three months earlier), carried two hand guns (all purchased legally), as well as an automatic weapon (the obligatory AK-47, origin unknown as they were obtained by Harold Leopolo and he wasn't doing much talking after April 20), and fifteen pounds each of a modified version of Semtex (a plastic explosive, some of which had been "obtained" earlier that morning at a quarry site). Each man also carried high-capacity rapid loaders, and combined the group had forty-two hundred rounds of ammunition.

Their first act was to lock from the outside all the accessible doors on the north, south, and west sides of the building (the eastside proved to be to difficult), but only after securing them with explosive trip wires (I'm sure there is a more accurate technical term for these booby-traps, but when it comes to exploding metal doors semantics aren't that important). Securing the eleven double doors took less than ten minutes and was witnessed by no less than a dozen people, all of whom failed to react or respond.

As a group they walked into the school's front door and encountered their first resistance in the form of sixty-four-year-old bus driver Ellen Boon. Harold Leopolo shot her three times with a silenced handgun before she could scream (for a short time the video of her murder was circulated on the Internet). Stepping over the dying woman, they entered the administrative offices of the high school and shot three more people, once again using sound suppressors. Vice Principal Mary Adams died at the scene, and administrative assistant Penny Roth was shot in the chest and abdomen but would survive. Student

Larry Fitzgerald was hit in the neck and head; he would live for three weeks before life support was discontinued, having never regained consciousness. The surviving administrative staff were herded into a windowless break room and the door was chained. James Monter, Harold Leopolo's cousin, the techie of the group, activated a cell phone scrambler, isolated each corridor, and then dialed 911 from a landline. It took only moments for the police to start arriving, and within a half hour the campus was surrounded by both the police and media.

It is clear that the group had expected their body count to be in the high hundreds. To accomplish this, the plan was to stampede the students and staff into the first-floor corridors that were blocked by the chained and booby-trapped doors, and when the world was watching, Righteous Thunder would detonate the explosives at regular intervals and stop only when the building collapsed around them, the explosives had been exhausted, or they themselves had been killed. To this point, they had moved with precision and perfect coordination (none of the witnesses remember even a single word exchanged amongst the terrorists). Records and testimony from the captured terrorists show that after the administrative offices had been secured and phone communication with the police had been established Harold Leopolo inexplicably deviated from their well-orchestrated plan.

Originally, they were to divide into three groups with one man (James Monter) watching the front door and monitoring the phones and equipment. Group two, comprised two men (Alan Locke and Eric Jaime), were to wire the main floor corridors with the remaining Semtex for final disposition and insure that none of the students escaped through the ground-floor windows . The members of group three (Leopolo, Casey Pinster, and Martin Heal) were to create panic by simultaneously entering second-floor classrooms with weapons firing. The goal was to allow most of the students to escape down the stairs, where some would be allowed out of the building but only after they forced their way through the shattered glass of the front doors.

The scene of bloodied and torn high school students running from their school was to be the image burned into every Americans mind. The remaining students were to be packed into the schools three main corridors to await destruction. Only Leopolo changed his mind at the last moment. He went to the third floor alone and signaled to Pinster and Heal to hold their attack until after he had started his (Alan Locke, the most talkative of the surviving terrorists, said that Leopolo had once mentioned the idea of forcing students to jump either from the windows of the third floor or from the roof).

These are the facts that everyone, including myself, can agree upon. Beyond this point things get a little fuzzy. Actually, more than a little fuzzy. What follows is an exchange I had with Detective John Sharpe on May 4, 2016. The circumstances surrounding this interview will in time become clear.

"What can you tell me about Adis?" John Sharpe asked me sharply. The context of the questioning was, to say the least, unfriendly, so his attitude and my circumspection were understandable. Again, more on this later; the important point is what he had to say about April 20.

"As his physician, not much."

"Do you know anything of his past?" He knew I wouldn't answer, but I give him credit for at least trying.

"Only what you already know."

"I know that he hasn't told me everything and neither have you. Do I have to get out the hot lights and phonebooks?"

"Now you're starting to sound like a detective in a pulp fiction novel." Okay, I added the last two parts.

"Up until April 20, Mr. Adis did not exist. No address, phone number, electric bill, social security number, bank account, driver's license, birth certificate, nothing. As far as anyone is concerned, this man still does not exist." By this point in my relationship with Adis, I had learned that there was a good deal more about him than what showed on his wrinkled face, but I hadn't suspected it went this far. "I can tell by the look on your face that this is somewhat of a surprise to you?" And that was the reason I went into neurosurgery as opposed to being a professional poker player.

"No, I mean yes, it is a surprise." I remember stumbling over my words.

"Did he ever tell you what really happened in that school?" He had, but I had the ultimate cloak of protection, the patient-doctor relationship.

"I can't talk with you about any of that." A degree of my confidence had been restored.

"I figured as much. I'm not a lawyer, but our attorney general is, and she is fairly certain we could compel you to answer that and a whole lot of other questions." He was bluffing and I knew it. Once again I had the ultimate cloak of protection, the patient-doctor relationship. I had operated on the attorney general of Texas two years earlier. "But I'm not going to do that. Instead, I'm going to level with you and tell you what I know about what really happened in that school.

"Adis says that he was walking along the running path just behind the school when he happened to look into the lobby just as the gunmen were dragging the body of Mrs. Boon away. It's possible, barely. I went and walked that path, and you can just make out the front lobby by looking all the way down the east corridor. I'll give him that, reluctantly. Next, he says he squeezed through a hole in the chain-link to get on to school grounds. Again, I found the gap in the fence. It was pretty small, and I needed someone else's help to get under and through it. I have no idea how a man in his late seventies did that on his own, but again I'll look past that. He then manages to walk into one of the only unlocked doors, down a 200-foot corridor, and up a flight of stairs without being detected by any of the six armed gunmen."

I had a number of sarcastic comments. Maybe he has really good eyes. Maybe you should lose some weight. Maybe he was wearing hush puppies that day. But my sarcasm would not change the fact that Adis's entire story was improbable at best, and the worst part of Sharpe's story was that it perfectly matched the story Adis had told me earlier.

"We have videotape evidence of him walking up the corridor and then up the stairs. One of the gunmen was within two feet of Adis and never alerted to his presence. But the most bizarre part, the thing we just can't explain, is how a man in his seventies disarms and kills three men less than half his age in eight minutes. Do you have any theories on how he could do that?"

"I thought that the snipers shot two of them." This was the official position and Adis never refuted it. In fact he never discussed any aspect of his more lethal heroics.

"The snipers did shoot, but only after one of the gunmen fired his weapon. He did that because someone had put a knife in his throat. Care to guess where Adis found the knife?"

I'll cover the rest of the interview sometime later when once again it becomes relevant.

Once the three gunmen had been dispatched (Pinster and Heal with stab wounds to the neck, and Leopolo with a fractured neck—the bastard suffocated to death: it probably took several long agonizing minutes, and it's likely he was conscious for most of it), Adis walked back down the two flights of stairs, dripping blood along the way, and back into view of the cameras. He looks a little woozy and actually slips slightly on the bloody floor before he reaches a stunned James Monter. The terrorist had been so absorbed with his electronic gadgets, monitors, and the growing police presence that when he turned and found an old man standing over him he slipped from his chair, lost his footing on the same bloody floor, and ended up on his butt.

Exactly what happens next is obscured by the front counter, but what we do see is Adis moving towards the fallen terrorist with a degree of speed that would challenge a much younger man. An instant later the fire doors, along with all the classroom doors in the west corridor, slam closed, trapping Alan Locke and

Eric Jaime. Later, Monter required surgery to remove the fragments of one of the four detonators from his broken hand.

Before I go on I have to confess that after I had the whole story of April 20, I was somewhat conflicted (I had a momentary break when I felt a twinge of sympathy for the three dead men) and more than a little confused. Like most people, I have a tendency to discount the elderly. We don't like to think of grandpa as Rambo (and if he starts to act like Rambo he gets put away after being started on some fairly powerful antipsychotics). Old men drive too slow, talk too loud, and generally have an unpleasant odor about them (I may be reaching here); they don't walk into a building full of armed men and violently kill three of them. I don't consider myself a wilting flower, but the thought of stabbing two men in the neck with the same knife (the *same knife* aspect bothers me, pulling it out of one man and then using it on another is so unsanitary) is disconcerting. I think if I found myself in that type of situation I could do it (I would at least wipe down the blade), but I'm not sure. What I am sure of is that I would not knowingly walk into a school being held hostage by armed men with the idea of killing some and capturing the rest, and if I ever do start to exhibit those tendencies I need to be put away after being started on some fairly powerful antipsychotics.

Chapter Two

Ӿ Ӿ

I FIRST MET ADIS IN THE EMERGENCY ROOM OF BRAND X HOS-
PITAL (SOUTH AUSTIN MEDICAL CENTER ASKED ME NOT TO USE
THEIR NAME). It was around noon on April 20, and he was delivered with a phalanx of uniformed officers. I had no idea what
was going on, and when faced with a patient that requires (or
in this case has earned) a police escort, I have learned not to
ask. I really had very little interest. I was between surgical cases
and was going to be late to clinic, which meant I would be late
going home. I was wrapped up in my own world, and the importance of the moment passed me by. To me he was a slightly
abnormal CAT scan of the brain (which meant no surgical procedure), an elderly man who required admission to the hospital
with a closed head injury, and a pile of paperwork. In short, Adis
meant work, nothing more, and I did it with all the enthusiasm
of a government worker. I took his history (he was quite vague
with his social history, like where he lived, his age, where he was
born) and physical exam (the ENT doctor was sewing up the
lacerations in his face), did the requisite paperwork, in which he
was described as a healthy elderly man with a mild concussion
and a confused mental state, possibly premorbid (meaning he
was like that before being struck in the head with the stock of an
automatic weapon), and got back to my real job.

When I finally made it to the office (which was filled with
impatient patients), my secretaries filled me in on the whole
story. I would like to tell you that my first thought was, "What a
brave, special, and heroic man Adis is." (I know I'm not allowed
to end a sentence with the word "is" but because it's an imaginary sentence it's OK) Unfortunately, before I could have a first

21

thought my secretaries informed me that the CEO of the hospital was in my office, which made my first thought "Why did Adis have to come here?"

I'm not a big fan of hospital CEOs in general, especially if the hospital is for profit, especially squared if the hospital is owned by a giant corporation (HCA, which does not stand for Hair Club of America) that has more MBAs than MDs making decisions. I realize that my opinion is more than a little disingenuous, because for me to do my job someone has to make the decisions that keep the lights on. Nick Latoris did that well. He had been Brand X's CEO for about six years, and for the most part was despised by the staff and tolerated by the physicians, which was probably the exact mixture for success. We had a cool, professional relationship, meaning we would politely nod our head to the other when passing in the halls and then wonder why.

"I know you're busy, so I'll come right to the point. Can you give the press a few minutes of your time this afternoon? There is a great deal of interest in Adis."

"I'll bet there is. Are you sure you want me to do that? Maybe your new chief medical officer should handle it. Last time we tried something like this it didn't work out so well." About seven years earlier, the governor of Texas had come to Brand X hospital to push for tort reform and I had been asked to stand next to him while he gave a press conference. Sort of a statement to the public that your hometown doctors are behind this effort. Halfway through the questioning the Governor reached back, grabbed me by the arm, and described me as his close personal friend (I had met the man fifteen minutes earlier). The look of incredulity on my face made the papers and, more importantly, was used as fodder by his competitors when he ran for the Republican presidential nomination two years later.

"No, I don't think it's a good idea, but the patient insists." The words stuck in his mouth, and it dawned on me that it must have taken a lot for Nick to come to my office and ask for my help.

"Wow, a direct answer. This must be really serious." I couldn't help but enjoy how uncomfortable he looked. I'm not above being a jerk.

"This is an opportunity for us all to shine here." Nick-the-Slick was back, and for the next several sentences he used the words 'we' and 'us' more than he used vowels. "We would like you to read a prepared statement and leave the questions to our media coordinator."

I can't remember if I laughed or not. I probably did. In the end I agreed to participate, but without preconditions. Later that afternoon I described Adis's degree of injury and answered several general questions from local and network reporters, then I raced home to watch myself on TV.

It took a few hours for the rest of Nick Latoris's statement to catch up: *The patient insists*. I know I'm extremely charismatic, a fact I remind my family of almost every day, but I don't remember my interaction with Adis being that significant. Adis's statement in Nick's voice stuck with me through the night (I'm pretty sure I had a dream about Adis, Nick Latoris, the governor of Texas and a llama—go figure), so I was up and out early the morning of April 21. Adis was in our step-down unit, partly for the slight possibility of a medical decline but mostly because the security of the unit could be better ensured. He had his own room, and I was a little surprised to find him dead to the world (meaning he was asleep) just after 6 a.m. It is rare for anyone to sleep so deeply in the hospital, especially on the first night, and I gently woke him with a tap.

"Mr. Adis. Sorry to wake you." He stirred quickly and his eyes opened without a trace of confusion. I remember thinking that he had only been feigning sleep. "How are you feeling this morning?"

"Good morning, Doctor. Please call me Adis. No mister, no first or last name, just Adis. In answer to your question, I am doing well, all things considered. How are you?" His gaze was piercing, and his question was more than just a perfunctory response. He expected an answer, which threw me off balance.

Usually, as the physician I set the tone, ask the questions, basically steer the conversation. Rarely will I have a patient who insists on being treated as an equal (the audacity) and attempts to direct our interaction according to their agenda as opposed to my schedule, but never as easily and as completely as Adis that first morning (and every subsequent morning we met).

"I am well." I gave him the stock answer, but his expression immediately registered displeasure with my dismissal of his question. "Your repeat CAT scan . . ." I prattled on for a few moments, technically doing my duty, but really trying to reestablish the usual, appropriate, and inequitable relationship between patient and physician. I had little success, as Adis waved me away from his bed before I could finish updating him on his condition and then stood unaided. He was wearing a new set of pajamas, not the usual one-sided hospital gown, and he proceeded to sit in the bedside chair.

"Why don't you sit down, Doctor? Tell me about yourself." He crossed his bare legs (which caused me a bit of concern, as he should have been wearing anti-blood clot stockings) and leaned back into the tall green chair, and suddenly I felt as if I were the patient and we were in a psychiatrist's office (I have never been in a psychiatrist's office, so I was only guessing at the degree of discomfort).

"Unfortunately, I really must be . . ." Again, a wave, and I was silenced.

"Nonsense. It's early. I can tell you're Irish, where does your family come from?"

"Chicago," I answered. He laughed. Adis was, for lack of a better word, vital. I know that for a lot of people that maybe an odd description. It certainly is a nonmedical description. We have all sorts of clever words with special meanings used to communicate secretly among medical professions when we describe patients: citizen, gomer, etc. None of them fully encompasses Adis. The elderly are a remarkably heterogeneous groups (unlike the other end of the spectrum—newborns are amazingly homogeneous); some are feeble in their sixties while others remain hale into their nineties and beyond, but I have never met an elderly person who radiated so much energy (I wanted to use the word life here but my editor told me not to).

"I'm guessing your family came from Galway." He nodded his head knowingly and I tried to hide the fact that he was exactly correct, both my parents' families emigrated from County Galway. "A long time ago I knew a priest from a little town just south of Galway . . ."

I have to stop here and again issue a warning. Adis tells a lot of stories, and I've only included a few here. I think that at some point in his long life he decided that the best way to make a point is allegorical, so he became a storyteller. Jesus Christ was allegorical and a storyteller, so I suppose Adis was in good company. Not all his tales are directly on point; in fact, as I recall, none of his stories were directly on point, and I invariably had to work out their meaning. You will as well—it's not hard. One more thing: this happened a long time ago and I think I have most of the important details correct. I have had to fill in some of the blank spots with my own contribution (remember in Jurassic Park they had to fill in the gaps of the dinosaur DNA with amphibian DNA, and that turned out all right).

"He lived in a town called Oranmore and spoke only Gaelic, and Latin of course, which worked out well as everyone in his small parish spoke Gaelic, this despite England's attempt to wipe out Gaelic by teaching only the King's English."

Once again I have to stop. For those of you who have any degree of familiarity with the British occupation of Ireland (or Eire) you will have surmised by now that Adis's timeline is impossible. My advice to you is to roll with it; in time all will become clear.

"He was a large man, even by today's standards, and when he was sermonizing, by God people paid attention. Back then the parish priest was more respected than the mayor, and certainly more than the local magistrate, who more often times than not was English, so it did not pay to be on Father Liam's bad side. He was stern and rigid as priests were back then, but

I got the impression he was basically a fair man and someone who would listen to reason." Adis's eye lost their focus and he began to idly twirl his intravenous line. I thought he was done reminiscing so I stood to leave, and instantly he snapped back into the moment. "Sorry, my mind wandered off there for a moment. Sit, sit, everyone is running late this morning, so you might as well spend the extra time learning something about where you came from instead of packing away a few Danishes."

Without a conscious thought I sat back down on to his hospital bed. My left knee was almost touching his right, and he leaned forward to pat mine.

"You were raised well and obey your elders." He smiled like a kind but slightly senile grandfather, and I felt like a seven-year-old.

My phone chirped three times, alerting me to an incoming text message. I reached for it with anticipation of escape. 'First case delayed. Patient ate breakfast. Next patient two hours away. Go have a long breakfast yourself.' It was from my surgical assistant, who was obviously in cahoots with Adis. I looked at him, and his slightly vacant smile had morphed into something bordering on omniscient.

"It was a reasonably quiet period in Irish history, and by that I mean they were between wars. It was just before the great famine . . ." He craned his neck and stared at the ceiling once he had confirmed that I had settled in for the duration.

"The potato famine," I added, with a desire to both speed up his story and to look like I was paying attention.

"No, long before that," he answered slowly. He turned his gaze back to me and I felt like I was getting a CAT scan. "They didn't teach you much history in your fancy schools." It was a cutting remark, so I will respond in kind by cutting some of this story. What followed was a primer on Irish history that has little to do with this story. For the sake of completeness I've included some of what I remember in the end notes.[1]

"Anyway, back to Father Liam, he lived and died many years before the potato arrived and the great migration began. When there was still magic in the air." Ok, I added that last part.

"Early one chilly spring morning, Father Liam found himself on his way to Galway from his home in Oranmore when a half dozen English soldiers overtook him on the road. Had he been anyone else, the soldiers would have stopped and robbed the poor individual in the name of the King of England, but the broad, burly priest was well known by all to have taken a vow of poverty. Besides, even the English would think twice about stealing from a priest. Instead, they warned Liam that they were chasing down a ruthless bandit who had come down from the north, and if by chance he spotted the criminal he was duty-bound to report it immediately. I doubt Liam answered, he could only speak Gaelic and Latin, so I'm guessing he nodded, and when they rounded the next corner he probably gave them the finger. A few miles up the road, Liam crossed over to a goat path to avoid a bend in the road that would have taken him miles out of his way. He looked twice for the soldiers, because anyone found off the road would, if they were lucky, be beaten and arrested. Ordinarily, the English would simply murder the offender on the spot and then toss his body back on the road as a warning. But the road was also a bad place for the English. Anything less than a squad of soldiers was likely to be attacked by the bandits and patriots that lived in the wilds. And as turnabout is fair play, their bodies would turn up on the road as a warning. Luck was with the good cleric that morning, and he disappeared down the hidden path and into the marshes of west Galway.

"A couple of miles down the path, Liam heard the muffled sounds of a man struggling. He stopped and listened, but he couldn't locate the source. Fearing for his own safety, Liam hurried on, but the struggling became less furtive and more desperate, which once again stopped him. He called out softly and the struggling stopped. All Liam could hear was the wind in the reeds and the buzzing of the insects; even the birds had become quiet. He called out a second time, and this time he was rewarded with an answer.

"'Who are you?' a voice asked in Gaelic, but it was muted, as if coming from under a thick blanket.

"'Father Liam of Oranmore. Who might you be, and where are you?' He tried to follow the voice, but it was impossible to locate. A pause followed. 'I said who are you, and where are you?'

"A bright beautiful Gaelic curse followed, and it finished with 'I am in a hole.'

"Liam understood immediately and after a few minutes of searching found the entrance to one of the many pits that had formed when the bogs were rechanneled. A dark and dirty man stood no less than a dozen feet below Liam's sandals. His head was turned up towards the priest. 'For the love of God, can you throw me a rope?' the stranger asked Liam, who of course had no rope.

"'I have no rope,' he answered, and then started to look for anything that would reach the stranger. He tried stripping the few local trees of their branches and then weaving them together, but they were not nearly strong enough to bear the weight of the trapped man. Next, Liam tried to weave some of the vines into a thicker rope but had an identical result. They broke the instant the man tried to climb. After much colorful exposition by the trapped man, Liam blessed himself, stripped off his cassock, lay on the gravel, leaned into the hole, and dropped one end of his only worldly possession down to the stranger. For a moment, it seemed to be working. The stranger was no more than a foot from Liam when a loud screech announced their third failure. As the garment split, Liam lunged for the man and for an instant they grasped hands, but then gravity took over. A nearly naked Father Liam of Oranmore fell on top of the stranded man. Now there were two men in a hole.

"After the two pushed and pried each other they were both able to regain their feet. Father Liam wrapped himself with what remained of his tunic, which was split down the middle, and unwittingly invented the bathrobe. He then took stock of his trapped companion. He was a thin, small man, under-fed but with no obvious contagious diseases or open sores that Liam should avoid in such close quarters. He looked to be in his early twenties, and in the semidarkness Liam thought that the younger man had the look of an Ulster native. 'Sorry about that, my son,' he said. The two could just stand without touch-ing; sitting or lying down was out of the question. The younger man wore a look far past exasperation, and Liam thought that once again the only thing that saved him from a beating was his priestly calling.

"The young man turned away from Father Liam and let loose with another long string of beautifully formed profanity while simultaneously beating the walls of soft dirt that would broach no purchase. After several moments the young profanity artist regained enough composure to turn back to Liam. 'Sha-mus Cormorach,' he said while offering his hand, which Liam accepted. 'Any thoughts on what we should do now?'

"The good Father turned around and in the process bumped Shamus into the wall. 'Not much room, but perhaps you could climb up on my shoulders and reach the edge.' Both looked up into the sunlight and the soft dirt that formed the rim of their prison. The pit was narrowest at the top and only opened the last six feet. 'Doesn't look very promising, but I see no other way. How did you get in here in the first place?'

"I was hiding from the English.' He slurred the last word derisively.

"So you're the man from the North they're looking for.' Sha-mus nodded his head while Father Liam tried to fit the young man before him into the description of a ruthless bandit. 'You don't look like a ruthless bandit.'

"Only to the English and Scots.' Without warning Shamus put his hands on Father Liam's shoulders and tried to squeeze his way up. It didn't work, and for the next hour they tried every con-ceivable position, but the cone-shaped hole prevented the needed acrobatics for escape. 'Will your absence be missed by anyone?' Shamus asked, finally accepting the futility of self-rescue.

"Not for many hours. I was on my way to the cathedral in Galway, but they would not expect me until after midday. They probably won't start looking until the morning, and I fear it will rain long before then.' Both men instinctively looked to the sky and found what little was available to them remained bright and blue. 'Still, I am confident someone will be along directly,' Father Liam added. 'So how long were you down here before I came along?'

"Shamus paused. His mood was dark and he didn't feel particularly chatty finding himself stuck in a hole with an oversized priest. 'Maybe an hour or two. I climbed in after the English spotted me. The walls gave way and I fell.'

"'Bad luck,' Liam said. 'Well, let us make the best use of our time. Tell me why you came to Galway?'

"'To find food and drive the English back to their . . .' Shamus bit off the rest of his remark. 'I have no need for confession, or priests, or for the God they serve. He has forgotten his people and turned a deaf ear to their suffering.' His tone was bitter and aggressive and for a time it was enough to stifle any conversation, so the two men simply stood and stared up the hole.

"Eventually Liam could stand the strained silence no longer. 'This is ridiculous, and my neck is starting to get sore. Do you like riddles?'

"'No,' Shamus answered sharply, but he too had dropped his head and started to massage the muscles of his neck. 'Why don't you wear anything under that, it's freezing outside?' Shamus pointed to Liam's torn cassock.

"'The discomfort brings me closer to Jesus. It reminds me of his suffering.'

"'He must have been Irish then,' Shamus sneered. 'But what would you know of suffering? You and your kind live like lap dogs for the English. Happy in your enslavement, so long as your masters occasionally throw you a bone.'

"Not many things could get old Liam's Irish up, but sure enough Shamus Cormorach had found one, and a moment later he found his feet dangling above the dirt floor and his head rammed into the soft ceiling. 'I don't think I appreciate that,' Liam said into the surprised face of Shamus. 'You have the luxury of freedom because you have no responsibilities beyond yourself. I have an entire village whose lives and souls are my responsibility.' Liam's words were liberally marinated with spittle.

"'That freedom was bought for the price of my family, lost to murder, the plague, and starvation all brought by the English,' Shamus spat back. Liam held him pinned to the wall a moment longer and then unceremoniously dropped the smaller man.

"'I'm sorry for your loss, but that doesn't give you the right to say things you know nothing about. You're a simple naïve boy in the body of a man who hasn't realized that others pay the price for your ill-conceived and completely futile acts. Two years ago, a band of you Northerners came to Galway and burned an English skiff. It wasn't even armed; it was little more than a raft with a sail. For that the English burned all the crops ten miles round, right up to the gates of my town. Dozens died over the winter and spring. When we get out of here I can take you to their families so you can see how happy they are.' Liam had rounded on Shamus again and had to restrain himself from throttling the smaller man. 'We don't want the English here anymore than you do, but we use the brains God gave us to not make the situation worse.'

"'Where was God when the English raped and slaughtered my sister, or while my children starved?' Shamus pushed Liam back, although their accommodations prevented it from being anything more than a gesture. 'Where is God when an entire country begs for deliverance?'

"Liam paused. He had no ready answer, or any answer at all. He had spent many nights pondering this very question and still couldn't explain God's seeming indifference. 'I don't know why God allows us to suffer. All I know is that He allowed the

Israelites to suffer under the Romans and never interceded. But I do believe with all my heart and soul that justice not delivered in this life will be more than repaid in the next.'

"'Then I shall find out soon enough. I have nothing left to give but my life, and when I get out of here I will offer that as well. No matter how futile, the best thing I can achieve in this life is a righteous death.' Shamus took a step back and rose to his full height, resolve steeling his spine.

"You would waste the very thing the English stole from your family? There can be no greater insult to their memory. Are you a coward, too afraid to live, or are you just to simple to see?'

"'I'm neither. I am a realist. It is only a matter of time before the English find me. I have nowhere to go and no way of getting there. I would already being dangling from the end of a rope if it wasn't for this hole. Soon I will find death, but it will be on my own terms, not theirs. I don't fear it, I have seen things far worse.'

"'I don't doubt that you have seen terrible things, but there is nothing worse than the death of an unredeemed soul.' Father Liam put his hand on Shamus's shoulder and an idea struck him with the force of a mule's kick. 'It may be that God needs you elsewhere.' Father Liam smiled as inspiration filled his heart.

"'What are you thinking, old man?' Shamus asked with suspicion, but Father Liam told me later that he recalled the slightest look of relief on the young man's face. A sort of last-second-call-from-the-governor expression. 'I won't become a priest.'

"'No, you are no priest, of that I am certain, but I'm thinking that maybe you need a boat ride to a new shore.' Before Father Liam could finish his thought a shovelful of foul-smelling dirt landed on his head. And then a second, followed closely by a third. Sputtering and coughing, he finally cried out. 'Hello up there, we need your help.'

"The dirt storm ceased and a tiny face blotted out the morning sun, which had just reached the lip of their hole. 'Hey what are you doing down there? This is my bog, and you're in my secret spot.'

"'We fell in. Do you have a rope?' Father Liam stayed in the light while Shamus tried to hide in the shadows.

"Of course I have a rope. Only a fool would go walking through a bog without a rope.' His voice was odd and high-pitched.

"Can you throw it to us?' Liam answered after spitting out some of the muck.

"The little man looked puzzled and muttered something to himself. 'How do I know you'll give it back?'

"Now Liam looked puzzled. 'What I mean is, can you throw an end down here and help us up? We really would like to get out.'

"The face disappeared for a moment and Liam swore that he heard the little man ask himself, 'Why did they get into the hole in the first place if all they wanted was to get out?' Several moments later a fine-threaded rope dropped between Liam and Shamus. 'I'll go first and look around a bit,' Liam said while testing the security of the rope. The large man climbed awkwardly out of the hole, scraping loose more dirt, which showered Shamus below. Finally, he emerged into the bright sunlight and rolled himself onto the damp moss. A half-sized man dressed in forest green stared down at him.

"'There's nothin' down that hole you know,' he said as an introduction. 'And you're robe's torn,' he added.

"Liam couldn't help but laugh. The little man was the epitome of Irish, always zeroing in on the obvious. 'I know that. I am Father Liam of Oranmore, and my colleague is . . . Father Shamus.' Lying didn't come easily to Liam.

"The little green man tilted his head and squinted his eyes. 'Didn't know priests were allowed to lie to strangers, but I guess a lie to a stranger is better than a lie to a friend. Now get Mr. Shamus, or whatever name he wants to use, and get out of my bog. The English will be returning soon enough."

"It only took a few minutes to pull Shamus to freedom, and Liam returned the rope to their rescuer after untying it from a stump that Liam had somehow missed earlier. The little man dressed in green was eyeing Shamus suspiciously. 'I've seen you before, out in the fields. You should be more discrete. Now get out of my bog.'

"Shamus led the way down the path and Liam followed. Both men stopped to relieve themselves, and when Liam looked back the little man was nowhere to be seen. They returned to the path in silence and Shamus waited another five minutes before returning to their conversation. 'You mentioned a boat ride earlier.'

"Liam was pleased that the young man had at least been listening, and more important was open to possibilities beyond murder and futile self-sacrifice. 'There is a ship arriving this afternoon in Galway. On the morning tide it will leave Ireland, and you should be on it.' Shamus remained quiet, which Father Liam took as a good sign. 'I believe I can pass you off as a young priest who has met some unfortunate characters on the road. This should get us into the town and as far as the abbey, where we can get you cleaned up and properly dressed, but getting passage . . . I haven't worked that out yet.'

"Shamus hesitated and then stopped. Liam turned to find his walking companion frozen in thought. The young man pulled his hand from his pocket and in it were ten solid gold pieces. 'I found them in the hole', he said almost dreamily, but I don't remember them being gold, or that I had so many of them. The two men stared at the fortune. It was more money than either had ever seen, and enough to feed every inhabitant of Oranmore for years. 'Why are you helping me, Father? I'm sure you can imagine all the things I've done.'

"'I can't push the English back into the sea, or stop them from hurting our people, but I can help you. As far as what you've done, I'm more interested in what you will do.'

"The following morning, April 20, 1691, Shamus Cormorach started his long journey to the new world, and Father Liam walked slowly back to his small church in Oranmore with a new cassock and seven gold pieces."

✗ ✗

Which brings me back to Adis's hospital room and the near-present. I was smiling not only because of his tale but because in the telling of his tale I had, for the moment, reached a point of clarity with Adis. A delusion is a fixed belief despite the impossibility of that belief. It is not an organic brain syndrome like Alzheimer's, nor is it related to trauma. You don't get hit in the head and wake up thinking you're Napoleon. Patients with delusions often appear normal and are capable of functioning in society if their delusion is mild and unobtrusive. It was clear that Adis's delusions were neither mild nor unobtrusive. His beliefs endangered his life and caused him to walk into a school occupied by heavily armed men without a second thought. My intention had been to discharge Adis this afternoon, but ethically I was bound to keep him until he no longer posed a danger to himself or others. But first I had some housekeeping.

"I loved the story, but I really do need to be going." I stood and he followed suit. "I need a few answers from you though."

"By all means, fire away."

"How old are you?" He stared at me as if he hadn't heard me. "Can you tell me your age?"

"I can, but it will only get us into trouble." His smile and demeanor radiated charm, but I wasn't going to be put off. He had yet to answer that question, or any of the questions normally asked when a person is admitted to the hospital, and it was my responsibility to get them. "I warn you that the more you know the more you will become involved. Fate has a way of doing that you know."

"The hospital needs some basic information so they can get paid, otherwise they will look to you." I tried a little charm of my own, but it fell flat.

"They needn't worry about getting paid. It will be taken care of. My question to you is, do you personally want to know my age?" He was closely appraising me, and I have to admit at that moment I felt like I was about to take the last step off of the high dive.

I looked at him funny. I was fairly certain that I could live the rest of my life without ever knowing his age, but now that he had made a point of it I was concerned, and a little curious. "Yes, I would really like to know your age. I am worried about your ability to take care of yourself and stay safe, because frankly what you did yesterday, while heroic, was distinctly unsafe."

"I will warn you one last time. It is still possible for you to walk away from this without becoming any more involved. You need to know nothing more about me aside from the fact that I pose no danger to myself or others. Is that enough for you?"

I remember thinking that this guy really had problems and that maybe I shouldn't push this and simply let Psych take it from here. I'm pretty sure I took half a step towards the door but then stopped. I'm not sure what stopped me, but I faced Adis and shook my head.

"I didn't think so." He answered ruefully. "I was born more than 2000 years ago. I can't be more specific as the manner of timekeeping has changed so much over the years."

I stared at him at first thinking that he was having me on, as the British say, but his expression never faltered, and as the moment began to stretch it dawned on me that he was telling what he believed to be the truth. "You do realize that is not possible?"

"For you, yes. But for me it is quite normal." We stood only inches apart, staring into the others eyes, neither gaze wavering, both of us completely comfortable with our individual concept of reality.

Chapter Three
X X

THE REST OF THE DAY PASSED IN A FOG. An Irish fog. Adis was never far from my thoughts, and before I left for the day I stopped by to check his chart, hoping that the psychological evaluation and consult had been completed. Not surprisingly, they hadn't. I called Nick Latoris and gave him a medically sanitized update, then walked by Adis's room. I waved and he waved back.

"Everything all right?" he asked me, and I got the impression he was more concerned about me than I was about him.

"Just checking on you. I'm on my way home." I remember that I didn't even enter his room, which was uncharacteristic of me. I simply addressed him from the hall.

"Drive carefully, and I will see you in the morning." He waved and turned back to the magazine he had been reading. I had been dismissed, but only after I'd been directed to drive carefully. It's a common phrase and on the surface it doesn't mean much beyond, *I'll be sad if you get burned up in a fiery car crash on the interstate,* but that evening it seemed more like an order, or a warning that had less to do with me and more about the guy next to me on the interstate who gets burned up because I caused a fiery crash. I remember my head was filled with all sorts of these bizarre thoughts as I walked to my car that evening. I also remember using the back streets all the way home.

When I made it home my son greeted me with the usual teenage response: *Hey.* My wife greeted me with a bill for the roof repair, and my dog greeted me with her Frisbee. Ah, the joys of coming home after hunting and gathering all day. At least, Mia, my youngest daughter, was excited to see me, but mostly so she could show someone else what she had created on her new laptop (a birthday present of five days earlier, the laptop would be lost and replaced, at greater cost, two weeks later after an Emmy-deserving demonstration of drama). After validating her abilities as a computer graphics genius, on a whim I asked if she could look up a couple of names for me. I gave her the name Adis and she immediately said that she had already Googled him but the search came up empty for the Hero of Northland High. I gave her the names of Shamus Cormorach and Father Liam of Oranmore. She typed those in and found nothing helpful.

"We could search the Irish National Data Bank." It was one of the hits that came up under Father Liam. "It will probably cost a few dollars." I nodded my approval and reached to give her my wallet. "It's OK. I'll just use Mom's card." I retreated to the safety of the couch intending to ask my wife how our eight-year-old daughter had our credit card number committed to memory, but then thought better of it.

Two hours later, I was stretched out on the couch slipping into a comfortable sleep when I was awoken by my lovely wife's raised voice. "Don't wake him, he's sleeping." I opened my eyes to find my daughter inches from my face, beaming with success.

"I found them," she said triumphantly. "I printed off their bios." She handed me three sheets of my good printing paper, which meant that she had abandoned her laptop to use MY computer in MY office. "The priest was the easiest. He became a bishop in 1698 and lived until he was 59, which was a long time back then. The guy was kind of famous; they built a statue of him." She took the copies from my hand, shuffled them until they were in correct order, and pointed at a picture of a bird-poop-stained statue that bore an uncanny resemblance to John Madden dressed as a monk. "The other guy, Shamus, he was a lot harder. There were more than two hundred Shamus Cormorachs in the 1600s. Our guy was a brigand. Do you know what a brigand is?" Children absolutely shine when they think they know something their parents don't.

"An outlaw," I said, yawning, and my daughter deflated, but not completely.

"Do you know what else he was?" This time it looked like she was going to explode. I shook my head.

"He was a murderer." She drew her last word out and beamed a smile that told me there was something more. "Do you know what else he was?" She began to bounce, and I watched her for a second longer than necessary just to tease her. "Okay, I'll tell you. He's your mother's great, great, great . . . like sixteen greats, grandfather. You come from a bunch of criminals."

I said, "If that's true, it explains you," and I poked her in the chest with my finger. We were having a family moment and I didn't want thoughts of Adis intruding; he had already done enough of that. An hour later, with all of us full of familial bliss, the three children were put to bed and my wife and I were on our way. Then, as if on cue, my phone rang. As a physician, I am always available for someone to reach out and touch me. Even on days when I'm not taking calls, more often than not an ER or referring physician with my phone number will call and chat about a patient, and again more often than not ask if I wouldn't mind swinging by and offering an opinion. Unless I am out of town, I am never truly free. I have to admit that sometimes I resent that, but most of the time I don't. It is a fact of life that my family and I have learned to accept.

This time it was Carl Saiki, a hospitalist (a physician that works for the hospital seeing all the inpatients, similar to the old house doctors) who also coordinated hospital consults. Carl spent the requisite two minutes with unimportant small talk and then launched into his real reason for calling, a seventy-nine-year-old woman with a spine fracture due to osteoporosis. He assured me that there was no rush and that I could see her first thing in the morning. It was then my turn to ask him for a favor.

"Before you go, Carl, did you get a chance to send off the psych consult and evaluation on Adis, the patient in step-down?"

"Yeah, I have that right here. I did the mental status exam this morning, and Joe Tyson did the formal psych consult. Didn't he call you?" Carl asked. He knew the answer already. Joe Tyson was a psychiatrist in his mid-sixties, and he thought he still lived in the mid-sixties. I have nothing against ponytails and tie-dye shirts in general, but not if you're mostly bald and fifty pounds overweight. If you could get past his appearance Joe was a pretty good psychiatrist; he was just painfully slow, and a consult could take several days.

"No, he didn't call and there were no notes in the chart."

"Your guy is good to go. Both of us agree. He's going to be a little concussed for a few weeks, but for an old guy he is still pretty sharp." Carl was an excellent physician and I fully trusted him. In the twenty years I'd known him he had never let me down. At least until today. Joe Tyson also was very solid. At least until today.

"You're kidding me." I was almost at a loss for words. "This morning he told me that he was 2000 years old. Straight to my face. Said it was normal for someone like him. The man is seriously delusional; I think it's why he went into that school yesterday."

Carl took a moment, and I'm sure he was having the same thoughts I had about him. "I think he was yanking your chain. The guy's a little odd, I'll grant you that, but not delusional."

"Did you ask him when he was born?"

"I can't remember, but I'm sure I did. If you're really worried about him, I would have social work look for a SNF bed, or you could just send him home." A SNF is a skilled nursing facility—a step up from a nursing home used for a short time while a patient convalesces, but I didn't think Adis would convalesce unless he received some form of treatment. And as far as sending him home, no one knew where the man lived.

I was going to ask Carl to recheck Adis in the morning, but thanked him and hung up instead. I had the strong impression that his opinion would be the same. "The Adis effect," I said to myself. The man had a strange permeating aura that was almost hypnotic, and a part of me was glad that I wasn't the only one affected by it.

The next morning, I discharged Adis to parts unknown. I had broached the subject of a SNF with him and he simply laughed. I gave him a follow-up appointment to see me in a week and gave him instructions to call me if he had any questions or problems. True to his cryptic nature, he asked if he should call if I was experiencing questions or problems.

Chapter Four

X X

WE NEED TO LEAVE ADIS FOR A WHILE AND TURN TO MATTERS
CONSIDERABLY MORE PERSONAL. As you have probably guessed
by now, I live in Austin, Texas, with my wife and three children.
We love Austin, and as far as we are concerned the hill country
is the only place in Texas fit for human habitation. Austin is the
live music capitol of the world. It's also the capitol of Texas. It
is home to the University of Texas (hook 'em horns). It's unof-
ficial motto is 'keep Austin weird.' You can't but love a city that
in every mayoral election features a homeless cross-dressing/
transvestite who regularly polls in the double digits. We have
lived in Austin most of our lives and watched it grow from a
quirky little city with an abundance of personality into a large
city that has managed to avoid the problems of most big cities.
However, all is not perfect. Absolutely the biggest problem in
Austin is the traffic. To imagine how bad it can be think of LA at
rush hour, now remove most of the public transport and roughly
half the freeways. Now you have Austin between the hours of 5
a.m. and 10 p.m.

Why is any of this relevant? Because for years now I have
fancied myself first as a runner and later as a triathlete. I'm
really not very good at either, but I've finished enough races to
lay claim to the titles, and to become addicted. Historically, my
one and only running course had been downtown, around Town
Lake, which is actually the lower Colorado River (the river has
recently changed its name to Lady Bird Lake in honor of Lady
Bird Johnson). Roughly a year and a half ago I reached the obvious conclusion that the soft dirt track was just not worth the
hour-long commute and started using the southern end of Aus-

tin's north-to-south corridor, MOPAC (named after the Missouri—Pacific railroad, which once owned the land). It's not a bad route, and in the early mornings it's really very pretty and usually quiet. The four-lane highway wraps around an extension of a long-standing planned community called Circle C. Years ago, we lived in Circle C, but after a while I got tired of living so close to my neighbors that I could turn off their television by reaching out my bathroom window, so we moved. Still, Circle C is a great place to raise a family, and that is why all of this becomes relevant.

Sometime during the early morning hours on April 25, 2016, five days after the school shooting a four-year-old girl named Maggie Dale disappeared from her bedroom, which was 200 feet from the Circle C fence, MOPAC Avenue, and my running course.

I do not possess the talent to describe the horror her parents must have felt. This is one of those situations in which words, no matter how carefully chosen and beautifully arranged, are completely inadequate.

I had no idea any of this had happened. That morning I ran, showered, drove to work, and came home blissfully ignorant of Maggie Dale's plight. My wife told me about it that evening, and like everyone else I watched the local news station spin what little information they had.

"Can you imagine what her parents are going through?" my wife asked after we had settled in bed for the night (only after both of us individually had checked on our children).

"I don't want to," I whispered back to her and to the universe. The closest we could relate was when our youngest child developed a pre-leukemic condition at eighteen months. For the next two years she required blood draws, transfusions, and bone marrow examinations. One morning, during a particularly bad patch, when she was about three and old enough to know what the nice doctor was about to do, she turned to me as I was holding her, tears filled her eyes, and with a pleading voice she said,

"Daddy, please don't let them hurt me again." Nothing in this world can make you more vulnerable than having children.

At first the thought was that the little girl had simply gone outside with the family dog (who was also missing) and gotten lost in the neighboring woods. A massive search began, and it wasn't long before the remains of the Dale's dog were found along the greenbelt that separated the subdivision from the highway. The search continued, but any hope that this was simply a case of a lost child was gone.

Months later as I sit here typing, I can tell you what really happened, but I'm not ready to divulge everything yet. You need more information to appreciate, or perhaps accept is a better word, the whole story. But, in the interest of moving things along, I'm going to encapsulate what was known at the time (plus a little of the behind-the-scenes stuff).

John and Brittany Dale were, and still are, both cops. They met in the police academy and married a year later. Margaret, AKA Maggie, arrived four years later. After shuffling schedules, the couple were able to care for Maggie themselves, a priority they had agreed upon before Maggie's arrival. John remained on patrol but worked a split shift that started at 7:00 p.m and ended at 3:30 a.m. Brittany worked a desk job, predominantly computer fraud at the South Austin substation, from 11:00 a.m to 5:00 p.m, and generally finished her work at home after John had left for the night and Maggie was put to bed. The toddler was last seen by John in her second-floor bedroom a little after 4:00 a.m. and was discovered missing by Brittany at 7:00 a.m. There were no signs of a forced entry or a struggle. Forensics at the crime scene were entirely negative.

Within an hour of finding the Dale's Boston Terrier, Detective John Sharpe from north Austin was assigned the case. He was a logical choice, as he had never met either of the Dales, which avoided any potential conflicts, and he had worked both of Austin's only two major child disappearances in the past ten years. Months later, he confided to me that he had never had so little to work with, and had initially put the probability of finding Maggie alive and unharmed in the low single digits. The only real leads came from two security cameras. One was located at the entrance to the subdivision and had a good view of vehicles entering or leaving Circle C from MOPAC, and another was a gas station camera roughly a quarter mile away that showed not only the gas pumps but also a long view of MOPAC. It took the police a day to secure the video from both cameras, another day to examine the tapes (both of which had an odd, unexplained gap), and, finally, a third day to identify and track down the thirty-seven vehicles that had been seen from four a.m. to seven a.m. It would take another week to fully vet the thirty-seven drivers, but all were eventually cleared. Three pedestrians were seen using MOPAC during those three hours, and it took APD four more days to put my name with my face.

May 4, 2016, was a Wednesday and a normal work day. I had only a single surgical case that morning and had the luxury of the rest of the morning to catch up on the paperwork that had been piling up on my desk. I made it to the office before ten and was greeted by the smiling face of Debbie, my receptionist. She always smiles when she has bad news.

"I know you were hoping for the morning to be clear, but I had to put your patient Mr. Adis in at ten-thirty." She was still smiling, so I knew there was more.

"It's Adis. Don't call him Mister. Why are you still smiling?" I answered gruffly. I like to play the grumpy old man at work.

Debbie stopped smiling and screwed her face into what looked like a very painful smirk. "There are two police detectives in your office." My initial reaction was that at least it's not the hospital CEO again. My second thought was that my receptionist has to stop putting people in my office. "I think it's about the lost baby." I nodded and walked back to my office, and nearly knocked on my own door. It's a little disconcerting when the police show up to your place of employment.

John Sharpe and his partner, Lewis Willis, were both at my window studying the large lion figurines that sat on either end of the sill. They were a matched set, and have a name that I can't remember. A Japanese patient had given them as a gift, and normally I would have taken them home, but my wife said no. She thought they were more scary than decorative. Sharpe was in his early sixties, and Willis was probably half that. Both were about six feet and dressed in suits that looked OK. As an aside, I know most authors describe by name and in detail what every character wears, but I will not, chiefly because my everyday wardrobe consists of scrubs (green, reversible with an irritating little tag on the back collar), running shorts (black, nonreversible with a little pocket on the inside), and jeans (blue, nonreversible and a little long in the inseam). I simply do not have the knowledge base to make it sound legitimate.

Introductions were made and Willis pulled out a laptop and wordlessly placed it on my cluttered desk. "We're here because of the child that disappeared last week," Sharpe said, and I nodded. "We have some video footage we would like your opinion on." His tone had shifted slightly, just enough to be detectable but not enough for me to make a comment. He went from being artificially friendly in a call center way ("Hi my name is Abhi, how can I help you have a great day?") to mildly imposing with an edge of accusation. "These came from cameras outside Circle C last Friday." Willis hit a few keys and turned the screen towards me. I watched a twenty-second loop of me running with my head down along MOPAC. I was running towards the camera, my eyes glued to the painted stripe that borders MOPAC's bike lane. Just as I was approaching the turn off to the subdivision, the clip ended. A second loop started and lasted only about five seconds. I could be seen running from right to left, and once again just before I hit the turnoff the clip froze. "That is you isn't it?"

"It is," I said and uncharacteristically added nothing more. My threat radar was pinging, and I took the advice a TV lawyer once gave his TV client: *The less you say, the better.* A part of me wanted to say that I had been running that route for a couple years now, that I run usually every other morning, etc., pretty much everything that I just wrote above, but I really did not like the vibe in the room.

"Did you know that Maggie Dale's house is just over that fence?" Willis joined in by tapping the screen with his pen, which was entirely unnecessary as the frozen image had only one fence visible.

"No, I didn't." I continued my less-is-more routine.

"Did you see anything unusual that morning? Someone you didn't recognize. A car parked off the street?" Back to Sharpe.

"Nothing, but I run with my head down and with an MP3 player."

"Did you go into the woods for any reason that morning?" Sharpe again.

"Not that I can remember." My two guests said nothing. They both stared in a silent and unnerving way. I have to admit that after several moments of the staring I was unnerved. "Look, is there something I'm missing here?" I finally asked.

They exchanged a very subtle glance that seemed to communicate that Sharpe would take it from here. "Do you remember what happened after this?" Once again the screen was tapped, this time by Sharpe.

I blinked in confusion. "I ran some more." Apparently that was the wrong answer, as both men shifted in their seats.

"The two cameras that gave us these images went blank for nine minutes just as you approached the intersection. Do you have any idea why or how that would happen?" Sharpe's tone was now purely professional and accusatory.

I blinked in confusion, again. "Was Richard Nixon around?" I smiled, but my attempt at nervous humor only bounced off of their stony faces. "I really have no idea," I said, but it was clear both Sharpe and Willis had an idea that didn't involve the late former president.

Sharpe turned the laptop back to himself and hit more keys. I could hear the hissing from the computer that told me he had hit the playback button. After several seconds he turned the screen back to me. "Do you know what that is?" He pointed at a zoomed image from the gas station. It was a quart-sized red bottle two to three hundred feet past the Circle C intersection.

"My PowerAde bottle. I put it there before I started to run that morning, but I'm guessing you already know that. That's my turnaround point; usually I pick it up and drink from it on the way back." A sudden realization hit me, but before I could explain Sharpe had changed the image.

"Isn't that your PowerAde bottle again?" It was, and the video's time stamp was more than an hour later.

"I blew by it on Friday, and when I realized that I had already passed it I just kept going. I had planned to pick it up on my way home." This looked bad and I knew it, but it was the truth. I didn't remember that I had left the bottle until two days later when I was dropping off another bottle and found Friday's still on the curb.

"So you went to all the trouble of dropping off a bottle only to run right past it, and then you forget to pick it up later."

"What does this prove except that I get forgetful when I run?" I remember getting more than a little defensive at this point. "Do you think I would leave a bottle on the curb just before I went and kidnapped a baby?"

"I'm not thinking anything, Doctor. I'm trying to understand what happened that morning, and these videos and that bottle of PowerAde are just about all we have to go on." Sharpe answered my defensiveness with aggression.

"Then that child has a problem." Now I was being aggressive. A tense moment followed.

"Do you know either John or Brittany Dale?" Sharpe finally asked, in a more civil but still hyper-professional tone.

"No," I said flatly, correctly assuming John and Brittany were the baby's parents.

"You've never been to their house?"

"Not that I know of." I managed to control my temper but not my frustration.

"You used to live in Circle C." I nodded and for a moment considered asking them to leave so I could call a lawyer. The fact that they had already researched my background sent a cold shiver down my back. "So it would be reasonable to assume that you were familiar with the area the Dales now reside in?"

"No, it would not be reasonable to assume that," I snapped back. Although I didn't know it at the time, John Sharpe knew very little about south Austin and less about Circle C.

"You once lived a mile from their home; surely you would have run by their house at least once." It was all so obvious to him.

"No, I did not live a mile from them, ever. That section of Circle C was built three years after we left." I wanted to add, *Take that, you unprepared flatfoot!* But I thought better of it; I still had a tiny remnant of respect for the police at that point.

My "gotcha moment" rocked both men. Willis immediately wrote something in his small note pad, and Sharpe had an unintentional, brief look of surprise. He recovered well but subtly retreated back into his chair. "I see." He nodded and tried a different approach. "Whoever took Maggie had to learn the routines of her parents, which means that they had to know how to blend in and not arouse suspicion. Somebody who runs a lot could do that."

"I don't run that much." I said but they appeared unconvinced. It was at this point that Detective Sharpe abruptly changed his line of questioning and asked about Adis. I covered that exchange a couple of chapters earlier, so I'll skip to the end.

"I would gather Adis either took the knife from one of the terrorists or brought it himself." As a reminder, Sharpe had just asked me where I thought Adis had gotten the knife he used to kill two of the Northland High School terrorists. I tried to keep the squeamish feeling out of my face, as I said earlier the thought of stabbing two men with the same knife was somewhat disconcerting.

"He did indeed take it from one of the terrorists. A man probably fifty years younger than him."

He waited for a response, but I really had nothing to say. Yes it was odd, but we already knew that the entire situation was odd. I tried to get us back on point. "What does any of that have to do with me or the kidnapping of this child?" I was flustered at this point, and I'm certain that was the intent of the rapid-fire questioning and the abrupt segues. My adrenergic nervous system was fully engaged (translation, my adrenaline was flowing, although technically it wasn't), which caused my pulse to race, my face to flush, and my IQ to drop about fifty points.

"We're not sure yet." Sharpe paused an instant and I felt another abrupt segue coming. "So, having never met the Dales, you would not know that they were both police officers?"

"No, I didn't know." This was really becoming tiresome, and again I thought of calling my lawyer.

"That makes Maggie Dale one of our own, and we take care of our own." He didn't need to complete his thought; his message was loud and clear.

"Are you trying to intimidate me in my own office?" I was on my feet now, seeing red. I can't remember my exact words, but our interview had come to a sudden and none-too-pleasant end. My next clear memory is of standing in my waiting room with my office staff asking me what just happened as the two detectives walked to their car. "Assholes," I said out loud. I rarely swear and never at work, but this was a special occasion. "Don't let them in again unless they have a warrant," I ordered as I turned back to my receptionist but found Adis instead.

Chapter Five
⚔ ⚔

To say that I was startled to find someone inches behind me, much less my famous patient, would be an understatement. I took a half step back and nearly swore a second time.

"Sorry," he said, and he reached for my shoulder to steady me. He had a bright smile and seemed to have enjoyed my performance. "I believe we have an appointment this morning." It was as much of an order as it was a statement.

"Adis, would you like to follow me?" Debbie appeared at his side and the two glided away to an exam room. It took a few seconds for my brain to catch up, and when it did they were gone. I stood there dumbly and wondered if time had begun to flow faster or slower. "He's all ready for you," Debbie said with a lilt after she had returned to her chair. "Do you need some help, sir?" she added with mock sincerity. Apparently, my immobility was cause for her amusement.

I wanted to say something clever, but between cops threatening me and Adis's sudden appearance, clever had abandoned me. "You know I'm from Texas, which gives me the right to shoot you," I said, which only made her laugh. I love having the respect of my staff. A moment later I was alone with Adis in my small exam room.

"Well, it looks like you have had an eventful morning." His smile and tone gave me the impression that he had expected to see exactly what he saw.

I was somewhat surprised that he had kept his appointment. Over the past week he had become a media darling. I had watched him give the local news and then the network news extended press conferences on two separate nights. On PBS, he chatted with the president, who called him a national hero. He was on the cover of every weekly magazine. What didn't surprise me, however, was that after all this attention Adis had artfully maintained his anonymity.

"You're here alone? No family?" He shook his head. "No one drove you? Not even the press?"

"No, they don't know I'm here. How is your family?" He managed to slip in his question almost subliminally.

"They are well." I gave him the stock answer, and he frowned. His disappointment affected me more than it should have. "Your face looks good." I tried to shake off the "Adis effect" and gain at least a modicum of control over our conversation and myself.

"I heal very fast. I've had a lot of experience. Were they here about Maggie Dale?" The question came suddenly, and I'm not sure if I actually asked him how he knew or if it was just my expression. "Detective Sharpe is the lead investigator in her disappearance. He's been on television almost as much as I have," he answered, and for a moment I was glad there was a normal, reasonable explanation, but then he ruined it. "I am surprised at how fast you became involved."

"I'm not involved; they were simply asking me some questions. I—er—run down by her house." I stammered as I realized that normal people don't swear at cops who are simply asking questions.

"For now, they're asking questions." His statement hung in the air as he fixed me with a stare. I have heard that expression before, *fixed me with a stare*, but I had never really felt fixed by anyone's stare until that moment.

"What does that mean?" My voice wavered just a little, and I felt icy fingers walk down my spine.

"Do you really want me to tell you?" I still felt fixed in place, and I struggled to tell myself that this man was, at a minimum, delusional.

But he seemed so rational.

But what he was saying was utter nonsense.

But it felt right.

Nothing but superstition.

Or a warning I shouldn't ignore.

"Are you telling me you know something about this?" I said suddenly, coming down on the side of sanity. I was a grown man. A father of three children. A neurologic surgeon. I couldn't be fixed by a stare. My life was rooted in reality, and Adis was up somewhere in the clouds. I chided myself for buying into his pathology.

"I know some things, but not everything. Not yet." At least he was consistently cryptic.

"Do you know where she is?" I had no real hope he would answer the question directly, but I suddenly had a strange and thoroughly uncharacteristic thought. More than a thought really, but less than a vision. I imagined myself finding young Brittany and heroically returning her to her parents. My long suppressed id began cheering in my mind. My superego, which is really where I live my life, clicked back in and squashed my id back into the dark recesses of my subconscious.

"That is a very dangerous question. Just asking it puts you in danger." His face became dark and serious, which scared the hell out of my id, which had managed to pop back into the light for a moment.

"If you know something, anything, you need to talk with the police," I stressed. I regretted opening this can of worms with Adis, but now that I had I was honor bound to see it through.

"That would only make matters worse." He dangled those six words. I told myself I wouldn't ask why. I wasn't going to reinforce his delusions or my superstition any more. For the next thirty seconds we silently regarded the other. He sat calmly, serenely, expectantly as I struggled to keep my vow. A half minute was about as long as I could restrain myself. The desire to follow Adis down his rabbit hole became an imperative, and the words were already on my tongue when he broke the silence. "Have you ever spent time in the northeast?"

It took a couple more moments for my mind to catch up to his abrupt segue. His trademark smile, more appropriate for a

Hallmark card than a discussion of kidnapped children, never dimmed. After a few more seconds of silence he tilted his head slightly to the left in an attempt to elicit a response, and for the first time I lost my temper with Adis and his impenetrable serenity. "Look, this is important." For reasons I can't explain, I started jabbing the table top with my finger (afterward it ached for days). "Whether or not I have ever been to the northeast is unimportant. If you know anything about Maggie Dale you need to come forward." I slapped the table for emphasis. I'm not usually so demonstrative, but a missing four-year-old was hitting close to home.

"I have already told you that it would be unwise for me to become involved."

"Unwise? Unwise?" I repeated. "We're talking about the life of a small child. To hell with what is unwise." My voice was loud enough to carry through the walls, and I half expected Debbie to knock on the door.

"What we are talking about is a good deal more than the life of young Maggie Dale, and before you ask the question that is forming in your mind I will again caution you. This is a very sensitive subject and pivotal period. Questions and answers will have consequences." The serenity in his face that I had begun to resent had completely disappeared. Adis looked fierce, determined, and above all, dangerous.

I have never been known for my restraint. I think most neurosurgeons lack that gene and I am no exception. Under different conditions, and by that I mean non-Adis conditions, I would have met his aggression with my own, the consequences be damned (yes, I can at times be a little self-destructive), but that morning a long-buried trace of discretion asserted itself and I made an uncharacteristic tactical retreat. I sat back in my chair and another long uncomfortable pause followed. Adis-the-avenger slowly morphed back into Adis-the-elder. "Why do you want to know if I've ever been to the northeast?" It was my turn to break the silence.

I was sullen, almost petulant, but Adis didn't seem to mind. He beamed as if I were a slow student who had just managed to answer a question correctly. "I was suddenly reminded of a wonderful story and I thought you might like to hear it."

I didn't want another Adis story; my daughter was still talking about my family's criminal background (in fact, Mia's teacher had cornered my wife in the grocery store and wanted details), but I only had two other options: renew our Maggie Dale discussion, or send Adis packing (politely). My first option I deemed unwise. As for my second, I have never been very good at abruptly ending a conversation or office visit (it will come as a surprise to some, but I have a hard time being intentionally rude). As a result, I have sat through countless hours listening to patients and friends drone on as I feign interest while psychically projecting the thought to leave me alone. This experience has led me to the incontrovertible fact that I am not psychic. "If it is a short one," I answered.

"It's a story set in New Hampshire. There aren't many stories about the Granite State, so you might learn something."

To be honest, while I knew New Hampshire was one of our fifty, and that Concord was its capital, I knew almost nothing more about it. "I have never been to New Hampshire," I answered in a voice that my mother would describe as sulky, which is in fact a step up from sullen, or petulant.

"Oh, that's too bad. If you ever get the chance, you should go, particularly in the early autumn. The hills and mountains are beautiful."

Once again, I have to admit that at that moment I was completely unaware that New Hampshire had mountains, and I apologize for my geographic ignorance. I have subsequently learned that the White Mountains cover about a third of the state, including a number of peaks named after US presidents. While I personally don't think Franklin Pierce's presidential record was distinguished enough to warrant an entire mountain bearing his name, he was the only US president born in New Hampshire, so I suppose they had to do something.

"The story is about a man named Jedidiah Woodman . . ."

I'm going to stop Adis here. He is a wonderful storyteller, and Jedidiah Woodman's story is quite a yarn, but it really has very little to do with this story, so I'll skip over it. Still, I think it's a good read, and like the stories that came before and after, it gives us a glimpse of the man behind those celebrated blue eyes. If you have the time, I'd recommend that you find it in the afternotes.[2]

Adis had talked for about twenty minutes when my phone began to vibrate and then ring. I had been so absorbed in Adis's story that I actually jumped. In the interest of full disclosure, I do have to confess that at the time I had just started wearing one of the new smart phones on my hip and really wasn't used to having anything attached to me suddenly start vibrating. What was surprising was Adis's response. The unexpected ringing caused him to jump every bit as much as I had. I fumbled with the phone, thinking that this was the first time I had seen Adis display a truly normal human reaction, which made me smile.

It was the hospital, someone asking for an urgent consult that would likely not only consume my entire day but also throw off my schedule for the rest of the week, but I continued to smile and had to consciously suppress a laugh. I finished the call by saying that I would be over as soon as possible, knowing that in all likelihood I would be working well into the evening, but at that moment I didn't care. I clumsily tried to reattach the phone to its holder on my waistband, feeling like the cat that had swallowed the canary.

"A good call?" Adis finally asked.

"No. Actually, it was a very bad call." A small guffaw escaped my control. "I'm sorry for laughing, but I just learned something about you." He gave me his Hallmark-grandfatherly smile and waited. "You don't control everything."

His smile changed into something that I can only describe as "knowing," which had the same effect as if someone had just thrown a bucket of cold water on my head. "No, I don't, and you may come to regret that." He stood suddenly, and I lagged behind trying to understand his quick retort. He looked down at me and his expression became serious and his smile faded. I was struck by the number of wrinkles that lined his face and wondered why I hadn't registered them earlier. "These next several days are going to be a little difficult for you and your family. It will be very easy to lose yourself. My only advice is to remember who you are." At some point he had put his hand on my shoulder. "I will see you soon. Good luck." He turned and left. A moment later I was alone, sitting in my exam room staring at the open door.

Chapter Six

X X

NOW WE COME TO MY PART IN THE STORY. So far I have really just been a peripheral player in the grand scheme of things, but this is where I take center stage. Let me start by saying that most of what you think you know about these events is inaccurate, incomplete, or purposefully misleading. I really am not some conspiracy nut, but after seeing my life unrecognizably twisted by every form of media, I can't help but be a little paranoid. Time and subsequent events have blessed me with a degree of perspective, and I realize now that the only real objective this sometimes malignant host of journalists has is self-interest. Either self-promotion or the desire to uncover only the facts that promote their personal point of view. I know this sounds self-evident but when you find yourself in the middle of a media storm it begins to feel very personal. Enough of this. Let me get started.

The next twenty-four hours were the last normal hours I spent for a very long time. I was simply a doctor, father, and husband continuing along the same familiar rut we as a family had dug together. Thursday, May 5, 2016, around two in the afternoon is when everything changed. I was in the office trying to see both the previous days' patients who had been rescheduled as well as those who were previously scheduled for that afternoon. I was trying to walk that fine line between being efficient and not rushing through anyone's appointment. Which of course meant that I was steadily losing ground and my waiting room was filling up. We must have had twenty people waiting when Detectives John Sharpe and Lewis Willis arrived with a cadre of Austin police officers and presented my office staff with a search warrant. They made a dramatic show of bringing in boxes of all sizes each with the word Evidence stenciled on the side. Detective Sharpe made it clear in a voice that could easily be heard through walls that they were not here to interrupt or interfere with anyone's visit, they were just looking for anything that would help them solve a kidnapping. A half hour later, when they left empty-handed, my waiting room was empty.

It took less than an hour before my office staff started to field calls from curious and friendly referring physicians. After two hours, all seven of our phone lines were ringing. At five o'clock, we finally turned the phones over to the answering service. My wife had tried to call the office and couldn't get through. She finally reached me on my cell phone and told me that Sharpe and his cohort had paid her a visit as well and had taken every pair of running shoes I owned. I had called our lawyer (actually he was a patient, but also a CPA and a tax attorney who had set up our office's 401K a few years earlier, making him ideally suited to deal with a potential criminal defense). Basically, after I had given him a rushed and emotional accounting of the afternoon's events, liberally mixed with words you shouldn't use in church, he told me not to interfere and not to say anything until he could find a lawyer who could help me. Which left me with my haggard office staff.

"What the hell was all that about?" asked Debbie. She was the newest employee, having worked for me for only eight years. She was responsible for about ninety percent of patient contacts and was truly the face of my practice. A true Texas girl, she effortlessly blended blunt, straight talk with irresistible charm. Linda and Melody, my billing department and contracting department, respectively, drifted into our reception area and waited for an explanation. Only, I really didn't have one.

"It's about the little girl who disappeared last week." The faces of the three ladies told me that they had already figured that part out. "I run by her house and a couple of video tapes showed me passing her house around the time that she was kidnapped. They think I had something to do with it."

A long uncomfortable silence fell as no one wanted to ask the obvious question. I knew these three women as well as anyone, and they in turn knew me. They knew my family, and I knew theirs. They had been to our house hundreds of times and knew just about every detail of my life and my family's life. I had worked too long and hard with each of them to have any secrets; still, the faintest shadow of doubt hung between us. "Did you?" Debbie finally asked. Linda and Melody both stiffened and shot Debbie a look that would turn a normal person to stone.

I actually smiled. I realized that the question had to be asked, and Debbie had done it so inoffensively that I was relieved. For a moment I thought of Walter White, the lead character in one of our favorite series, *Breaking Bad*. Walter was a high school chemistry teacher that in time morphed slowly and invisibly (at least to those around him) into a methamphetamine-cooking devil. For all they knew, I led the life of a surgeon and family man during the daylight hours but turned into a kidnapping monster at night. "No," I finally answered.

"I didn't think so." She dropped into her chair and ignored her coworkers continued glares. Of the three, Debbie was the only one to have young children, which gave her the greatest right to ask that question. Her son Travis, like Maggie Dale, had just turned four. "Well, we will see who shows up tomorrow." She gave me a sweet smile and began to gather her things, and just for a moment I wondered if she meant patients, police, or herself.

A half hour later I pulled into my driveway. We live in a cul-de-sac that ordinarily contains only our basketball hoop. That evening it was filled with cars, vans, and all sorts of people milling around the perimeter of our house. Several flashes blinded me as I maneuvered my car through the crowd, and I ignored the hundreds of shouted questions. As I waited for my garage door to open, I watched a couple of brave souls venture up my driveway. One was lugging a shoulder-mounted camera and another a microphone. I rolled down my window and shouted at them. They stopped mid-stride and shouted something unrecognizable back at me. I said something uncharitable and turned back to find that my wife had parked her Denali in both spots. I said something even less charitable, threw my car into park, and hurried inside to the relative safety of my castle.

The atmosphere of the house was, to say the least, charged with excitement and fear. Our dog was in dog jail (the laundry room) because she kept barking. In an unprecedented demonstration of family unity, all three of our children were in the kitchen with my wife, making sandwiches. This above all gave me a read on my wife. She knows that it is my firm belief that sandwiches, no matter how tasty or artfully prepared, are not appropriate for dinner. That night she didn't care. At least they were roast beef. All four looked at me and waited for me to say something. "I guess we're famous now."

"Do we have to go to school tomorrow?" Mia, our youngest, asked.

I deferred the question to our keeper of school schedules and my wife ignored it. "I had to disconnect the house phone. I don't think it will take them long to get our cell numbers." She looked tired and worried. I didn't dare tell her that, the last thing I needed now was a domestic dispute with an irritable spouse. She slid a sandwich across the counter in my general direction. "Have you seen the news?"

"No," I answered. My son took it upon himself to turn on the TV. *Jeopardy* was on, and before I could answer a single question he turned on the DVR.

"We recorded it," he said, hitting the rewind button (as he is blessed with a Y chromosome, he is the only other person in our house, aside from me, who can work the remote—I know it's a stereotype, but in this case it's an accurate one). "Check this out," he said, dropping into our sofa with his shoes on. Apparently, most of the house rules had been temporarily suspended.

I listened as the mayor and chief of police describe the ongoing investigation and the identification of a person of interest. The picture cut away to a view of our house with a reporter to one side giving all the world our name and general location (our address was clearly visible on the mailbox), and that search warrants had been served at our home and my office. At least they described me as a prominent local neurosurgeon.

For my wife and me, the rest of the evening passed in a surreal fog. My mind kept cycling through two questions: *Is this really happening?* and *How could this be happening?* We tried to watch TV, but that didn't help. The children stayed with us for a while and then drifted back into their normal routines of computers, homework, and cell phones, secure in their belief that nothing in their world had fundamentally changed. Frustrated with the inanity of television and the world in general, my wife and I finally went to bed and silently stared at the dark ceiling. "I don't think I'll run in the morning," I said, to break the tension.

She chuckled politely. "Did you let the dog out?" Apparently I hadn't changed her mood.

"Yes," I said, and we returned to watching the ceiling. "A person of interest," I said softly.

"A person of interest," she repeated. She rolled over and whispered "goodnight" in a voice usually reserved for nights when we have an unresolved issue (a nice way of saying when we are fighting).

I lay there listening to her trying to fall asleep and wondered how I was to blame for all of this.

Chapter Seven

XX

THE NEXT DAY WAS FRIDAY, NORMALLY MY LONG RUN DAY AND A CATCH UP DAY AT WORK. As usual, I was up early and peeked outside. A television van sat right in front of our sidewalk. I milled around the house at a loss for something to do. Our dog followed me for a time and then gave up and went back to her bed. I ended up in my office and without thinking turned on my computer, and there I was, just below a picture of Vladimir Putin. I turned off the monitor.

"Anything interesting?" a familiar voice said, interrupting the perfect silence.

"You scared the hell out of me," I snapped at Leah. "I'm going to put a bell around you so I'll know when you're sneaking up on me." She slipped into our old sofa, which was the only other piece of furniture in my office aside from my desk. I waited for her usual comment about how much she has always hated this sofa, or how much of a pack rat I am, but all I got from her was a deep sigh. Her hair was a mess; she had dark circles under her eyes and wore mismatched pajamas. If I had a camera I would have taken her picture and used it for blackmail.

"Are we in trouble?" she asked. It was her first direct question since all this had started.

"No. It's all a misunderstanding." I gave her the unabridged version of Wednesday's meeting with the two detectives.

"Why didn't you tell me this earlier?" She had rolled onto her back, stretching the length of the sofa.

"It didn't seem important. All of this over a forgotten bottle of PowerAde. It's absurd."

"What's absurd is your face below Vladimir Putin on MSNBC." She sat up and faced me. We were about to have one of those conversations. "You need to take this seriously . . ." She went on for a time about my practice, reputation, finances, the children, etc. Nothing that wasn't already eating away at me, but after more than twenty years of marriage I knew she needed to give voice to the concerns that were eating away at her. She really wasn't very good at holding things in.

"I'll talk with a lawyer today," I said gently. Another thing I've learned after being married to the same person for more than twenty years is that it really does take two to fight. Leah was sleep deprived, worried, and embarrassed; therefore, it was my turn to be the responsible one.

She glared at me. It was obvious that I was placating her, and I braced myself either for a verbal assault or, worse yet, the "whatever" response, which would be followed immediately by a cold silence. I got neither. "Sorry. I know this isn't your fault." She collapsed back into the cushions and ran her hands through her hair. "I must look like shit." As I mentioned earlier, shit is one of her favorite words.

"I have a bit of a dilemma," I said, steering the conversation away from our current predicament.

"You mean beyond this?" She reached for one of the curtains and pulled it back. I noticed a second van had appeared in the cul-de-sac. They were waiting for me to go for a run (I remember thinking, *Ha ha, the cops took all my shoes*) or go to work (*Ha ha, I'm staying home today*). It hadn't occurred to me at the time, but as I would learn later, the new arrival, the local NBC affiliate, was actually waiting for our kids to go to school. Ambush journalism with children.

"Yeah. Adis came by the office after the cops left, and he said something that has me concerned." I waited for Leah to close the drapes. I wanted her full attention. "He insinuated that he knew that all this was going to happen." I gestured towards the window and the waiting press corps. "He also gave me the impression that he knew more about Maggie Dale than he was willing to tell. I told him that he needed to go to the cops and tell them everything he knew, but he said that would be unwise. Things got a little heated and he warned me that for my sake I shouldn't force the issue."

"He threatened you?" Leah lowered her voice.

I had to think for a moment. "Not exactly. He said something like if I knew any more it would be dangerous." I was struggling again with the Adis effect. Every conversation I had with him felt more like a dream, as if we communicated more in whole concepts than individual words. "No. He said, 'questions and answers have consequences.'" The memory of a stern Adis suddenly snapped into focus.

"Sounds like a threat to me." She was sitting upright now.

"I took it more as a warning."

"But you already told me that he was unstable. Delusional."

"I did say that, and he probably is delusional." I hadn't told her what was really bothering me. I looked at her wild hair, tired face, and mismatched, rumpled pajamas and felt safe. "He insinuated that by asking him his age I had already "plucked a string" and that all this was a consequence. I know it's ludicrous, but I can't seem to shake the idea that maybe he was telling the truth, that maybe I wasn't supposed to peek behind the curtain."

Leah stared at me—actually she stared through me—and I waited. "So you think by asking a man his age you caused all of this? It made someone break into a little girl's house, kidnap her, and then frame you for it?"

"I know it's ridiculous, preposterous, but . . ." My voice trailed off and she gave me a moment to finish. "I don't know what I think." I was tired and didn't want to think anymore. "I decided to close the office today. The ladies can have a long weekend. I don't want to deal with patients, Adis, cops, reporters, or lost little girls. I'm going to hide in our little house and let the world sort itself out."

"That sounds like a plan. Let's go back to bed." She took my hand and I pulled her up. She kissed me on the cheek and we walked hand in hand back to our bedroom.

We got a little more than an hour of extra sleep before we were interrupted by a tentative knock on our open bedroom door. "I don't want to go to school today," our eight-year-old Mia announced. She was fully dressed, with her hands on her hips. I looked at the clock and found that it was after seven. "I tried to go outside and about a hundred of those idiots attacked me." Her face registered the highest level of frustration our little drama queen could generate.

"How did they attack you?" I asked with a smile.

"It's not funny," she yelled. "They all ran up to me, some of them grabbed me and asked me the stupidest questions ever." For the record, Mia's grammar is age appropriate. The word "stupidest" is used frequently in our house and derives from our son's description of his new little sister (who just happens to be Mia).

"Did they hurt you?" Leah asked, swinging her legs out of bed. I sensed no urgency in her question or movements.

"No. They just wouldn't let me pass." Her dramatic pose sagged a little, now that she had our attention. "I was going to let Nitrox out and let her chase them away." Nitrox is our 120-pound lab-greyhound mix. She is a powerfully built, beautiful brindle dog that is as fast as the Texas deer (which are small, overfed versions of real deer). She is fiercely protective of our children, especially Mia who has the responsibility of feeding her.

"Do not let Nitrox out," both Leah and I said in unison. The last thing we needed now was for Nitrox to dismember a few local reporters on television.

"Fine," our little angel said with a stamp of her foot.

"I guess we're all staying home today," I said after swinging my legs out of bed.

☒ ☒

The rest of the morning passed with a flurry of phone calls. I talked with Debbie and told her to stay home and enjoy the weekend. She would pass the message on to Linda and Melody, and reschedule any patient visits, so that took care of my professional responsibilities. I talked with a lawyer with criminal experience and was given exactly the same advice my tax lawyer gave me: Keep quiet and don't interfere with the police. Nick Latoris called me on my cell phone and we chatted amiably. I assured him that I would do my best to keep the hospital out of my current predicament. Neither one of us put much stock in that statement. Several colleagues called and offered emotional support, and that was nice.

The rest of the day was filled with movies and Xbox games. The crowd outside our house steadily thinned, and by evening we were once again alone in our little corner of the world. Just as we were getting ready to sit down to dinner, our doorbell rang. Nitrox was still on edge, and her booming bark literally shook the house. She easily hurdled the baby gate that had been erected to keep her away from the front door, and continued her verbal barrage. We wrestled her away from the door, and I remember thinking that anyone who would still be waiting on the other side of the door must be very brave or well-armed. I was at least half right.

I looked through our peephole and found two well-dressed men. They must have heard my approach, because they both immediately raised ID wallets to the tiny window. The letters *FBI* were emblazoned across the top of each badge. It hadn't dawned on me until that very minute that kidnapping was a federal crime, yet as far as I knew only the local cops had been involved to this point. As it turns out, kidnapping is only a federal crime under some circumstances: for instance, if it goes on for more than twenty-four hours (in which interstate flight is assumed), interstate flight is confirmed, or in especially egregious situations, like when babies are kidnapped. I opened the door with a sigh of relief. Certainly, FBI agents were more experienced and professional than the local law enforcement, and I was for the moment confident that they would see reason and put things right. All I had to do was to explain to these reasonable men that I had nothing to do with Maggie Dale's kidnapping—that all of this was a simple misunderstanding—and life would return to normal.

Only, I had forgotten that the FBI was a part of our wonderfully efficient federal government.

I invited the two agents (or maybe they were special agents, I don't remember) into our kitchen, where they were eyed with a mixture of suspicion and awe by our children. My wife was all out of awe and running strong on suspicion. She asked rather pointedly to examine their IDs and then wrote down each agent's name and badge number.

Kirby Valle and Gordon Anderson were both experienced agents. Kirby was the younger of the two and was in his mid-forties, with Anderson at least a decade older. Both had an aura of competence and charm that immediately put me at ease. I showed them to our kitchen table and the three of us sat. After a moment Leah quietly joined us, and a single glance told me that she was far from being at ease. Her forehead was furrowed and her eyebrows were nearly touching. I'd seen this look many times before.

"We just have a few questions for you," Agent Valle said.

"I have a question for you." My lovely, demure wife interrupted the armed federal agent. Reflexively, I leaned back to get clear of the blast zone. "Where have you people been? Isn't the FBI supposed to investigate the kidnapping of children?"

"We have been on the scene since the beginning." Agent Anderson answered my wife's accusation with politeness.

"I see. So you have allowed the local police, who couldn't find their butts with two hands and a flashlight, to focus on my husband and a forgotten bottle of PowerAde instead of looking for whoever really took the child?" Small patches of red began to appear across her face and throat.

"That's not entirely true, but yes your husband is a part of the investigation." Anderson was still polite, but all I heard was that I was still a part of the investigation. I suddenly felt betrayed and realized that that despite their fancy suits and practiced charm they were no more competent than the local cops.

"For God's sake, you work for the FBI! You're trained to think critically and should be able to see right through my coincidental involvement, instead of mindlessly following breadcrumbs." I wanted to add in a few expletives, but turned away instead. I had two thoughts at that moment. The first was that if this was the caliber of police work Maggie Dale and her parents could expect, there was no chance she would ever be found. The second, which to my shame caused more fear and concern, was much more personal. I was being railroaded. With all the resources available to the combined forces of the FBI and Austin police department, they had managed to uncover only two potential clues: a power failure (that was the logical conclusion for the gaps in the video surveillance—portions of Circle C and the nearby gas station were on the same electrical grid, which took me less than ten minutes on the computer to figure out), and a forgotten bottle of sports drink, and they were determined to make the most out of what they thought they had.

"I can't tell if you people are just stupid or malicious." Leah's face was mostly red now. All three of our children, who were pretending not to listen in the next room, suddenly hushed at their parents' open disrespect of an authority figure. I thought I could just hear our son whisper *Yes!* and I imagined him pumping his arm.

"I assure you we are neither," Anderson answered, without any visible evidence of having taken offense. He managed to maintain a completely impassive expression, but survived only a moment of Leah's withering stare. Abruptly, he turned back to me in an attempt to cut off any further comments from her. I smiled. In my mind I said *Yes!* and pumped my arm, as Leah's comment had indeed hit home. "I have read the statement you gave detectives Sharpe and Willis. I know that you say you didn't see anyone or anything . . ." His voice suddenly irritated me. It sounded like the character Lumbergh in the movie *Office Space*. Each time he paused, he drew out the last syllable of the last word. "Do you remember if you looked into the woods?"

Gary Cole is the actor who played Bill Lumbergh, and my mind had superimposed his picture on Anderson's face.

"Righhhht. Did I go see anything in the wooooddds?" I looked up at the ceiling and stroked my chin in a dramatic display of thought. I know it was puerile and an inappropriate thing to do, considering the gravity of the situation, which is exactly why I did it. When humans become stressed, a portion of the brain called the thalamus becomes activated. To be more specific, a portion of the thalamus, the reticular nucleus, becomes activated. The reticular nucleus is the thalamus' amplifier, and when stimulated every sensation, thought, and emotion is sharpened. For most people, it's why time seems to slow down. For some, it's why they think faster; for others, it means that they cry more readily; for me, it means that I laugh at inappropriate times. Okay, I'm odd. "Nooo. I can't say that I diiiid." My wife knew exactly what I was doing and threw me a wicked look.

"Is there any reason that you would have gone into the woods that morning?" Anderson ignored my Lumbergh impression and continued with his own.

My unusual affect did not impair my cognitive ability. I immediately made the connection between the Austin police asking if I had gone into the woods, then taking my shoes, and now the FBI asking me the same question. I actually did pause a moment and tried to remember that morning. On very rare occasions I will make a pit stop in the woods, to visit a tree, shall we say. But not so close to the fence line, and never so close to the gas station's bathroom (I like peeing outside as much as the next guy, but I do actually prefer indoor plumbing). "No, I did not go in the woods that morning." I tried to sound definitive, but, truth be told, I couldn't remember. "Let me guess. You found foot prints in the woods that match mine." I dropped my Lumbergh and shook my head.

"We did find a number of footprints, but we have not yet been able to make a definitive match." Anderson said. Kirby Valle silently sat at the table studying me. We made eye contact briefly, and I almost told him that compared to Adis his intimidation technique was laughable. "We were hoping you could help clear some of this up."

"How? I already told you that I didn't see anything and I didn't go into the woods." The way things had been going, it came as a shock that they hadn't found footprints with my name and address on them. I looked at Leah, and her expression was one of barely contained anger. It's a fact that after years of marriage you begin to adopt some of your spouse's habits and temperaments. Leah returned my gaze, and I felt her pull me towards the dark emotional side. For as long as I have known her she has always worn her emotions on her sleeve (I would insert a comment here about it being a consequence of her gender, but that would sound way to sexist), and over the years I have consciously tried to resist the tendency to react more with my heart than with my brain. Some days I'm more successful than others, but this wasn't one of those days. "Look, you clearly have a reason to be here, and it isn't about me going into the woods. Sharpe and the other guy . . ." At the moment I couldn't remember Lewis Willis's name. "They went through this already. I told them and now I'm telling you: I did not go into the woods! " My voice was raised, but not loud enough to obscure my inner voice that said *I think*. "Now, tell me that the two of you didn't drive down here just to ask me the same questions I've already answered."

Anderson remained impassive. "No, we didn't just drive down here to ask you the same questions. We were hoping that perhaps you remembered something that you didn't share with the detectives."

"I remember exactly what happened." Okay so in truth I didn't remember exactly what happened, but this was not the time to hedge. "I shared everything that happened with the detectives, nothing more and nothing less." I looked at my wife, whose expression had softened just a bit now that I was carrying some of the emotional load. "You can't possibly believe that just because I ran by that little girl's house I'm a suspect in her kidnapping?"

Anderson stared at me the same way I stare at an MRI of the brain. Leah and I waited for him to respond, but he kept right on staring. Finally, he shifted in his chair. "Noooo." his Lumbergh accent was more noticeable. "No, I don't think you are a suspect. But I also think that somehow you are involved."

Leah and I exchanged a look of *What the hell does that mean?* It was her turn to take the lead. "What the hell does that mean?" I heard another hush from our children and then some not so concealed giggling.

"It means I do not believe in coincidences, and I can't help but notice that in the last two weeks you, Doctor—" he was addressing me and trying to avoid my wife's glare "—have been involved, however peripherally, with both the incident at the high school and now the disappearance of Maggie Dale."

In a moment of clarity, I saw things from Anderson's point of view, and it did look suspicious, odd, and unexplained. Of course, those three adjectives perfectly describe Adis, who began to float through my mind and I'm sure Leah's as well. Possibly also Kirby Valle's; maybe that's why he just sat there staring at me. "That's true, but I still don't understand what you mean when you say you think that somehow I am involved."

"I haven't sorted that out yet. Call it an educated guess, or a hunch, if you like." He continued to study me, but not with so much intensity. I stared back. I understood hunches, or educated guesses. It may come as a surprise to many that more than a few important medical and even surgical decisions are made at a gut level. We try to project to the world that we physicians are driven only by data—that the practice of medicine is a science—but it's more of an art. I, too, will look at a situation and form a purely subjective opinion, and often that opinion will conflict with our objective science. Like Anderson, I had learned to trust my gut.

Leah's scowl, which until recently had been reserved only for me or our children, twisted into incredulity. "So, the Federal Bureau of Investigation has connected the wackos who tried to blow up a school to a kidnapper of a four-year-old girl because my husband is peripherally involved with both cases? I never realized he was that important." She patted my hand, and I smiled, relieved that she finally accepted what I had been telling her for years. "If this is the kind of thinking that my tax dollars are paying for, I want them back."

Anderson now smiled. "I will pass your request on to the IRS." He turned to Valle as if to communicate that he had seen enough, and it dawned on me that that was the real purpose of this evening's visit. Anderson and Valle needed to lay eyes on me, to size me up at a gut level.

Valle finally spoke. "Well, I think we've taken up enough of your evening." All four of us stood, which made Nitrox, who had been watching us from the laundry room, huff loudly.

"Did you get what you came for?" Leah's voice was hard. "Is my husband the most inept kidnapper in history or an evil mastermind?"

"I doubt he's either." Anderson answered. "And no, I did not get what I came for. To be honest, I had hoped for one or the other."

"So no more person of interest," I followed up.

"I wouldn't go that far." We locked eyes for a moment. "At some level, you are involved, whether you know it or not, but right now that's not important. Our only priority is bringing a little girl home, and I don't think you can help make that happen."

The memory of Anderson staring back at me has stuck with me for almost a year now. It wasn't what he said—he was merely stating the obvious; in fact, it probably had nothing at all do with the FBI agent at all—but as soon as he finished I felt something outside of my normal five senses shift. Remember that I routinely assess my psychic abilities and routinely find them nonexistent, but for the first time in my life a part of me had connected with something beyond my limited concept of reality. Something enormous. I could almost feel the giant gears of an impossibly large mechanism begin to spin because some imaginary trip wire had been triggered.

My adrenergic nervous system (the fight-or-flight system) must have been clicked into overdrive, because just after we closed the door on the FBI agents Leah turned to me and asked if I was OK. I had broken out into a light sweat, and goose-pimples ran down my back and both arms. I hesitated in our foyer as she rubbed my arms (for the record we are not foyer people; I always thought a foyer was an entrance way until a real estate agent corrected me; now I know that a foyer is the little space in front of the front door that doesn't have any carpet).

"Somebody just walked over my grave," I said, and Leah immediately understood. I had first heard that expression from her father when we were dating, but Leah had grown up with it. "One of the last things Anderson said, that I couldn't help bring the little girl home . . . Did that strike you in any way?"

"Like you weren't involved? I don't know what you mean." She looked up at me, and I was glad to see that her expression was one of concern and not the scowl she had worn for the last thirty-six hours.

"Something I can't easily put into words. If I were a character in a *Star Wars* movie I would have said that there was a disturbance in the force."

"Somebody did walk over your grave. I thought you didn't like *Star Wars*? " She kissed me on the cheek and turned back to the kitchen calling to the children to set the table. The moment was over.

Chapter Eight
X X

I WOULD LIKE TO GET BACK TO ADIS, BUT UNFORTUNATELY I CAN'T. The spot light has to remain on me for a little while longer. By way of introduction, let me say that this is the point where I really started to believe that all was not right with the world. Special Agent Anderson's suspicion that at some level the Northland High School shootings and the disappearance of Maggie Dale were connected was surprisingly prescient. I knew that the connection was a man named Adis (at that point Anderson didn't, which makes his suspicion all the more impressive), but it wasn't until the events of May 8 had completely unfolded that I realized just how prescient the FBI agent had been.

Finally, one more disclaimer: the events of May 8, like the Northland shootings and Maggie Dale's disappearance, were widely reported in the media. The same media that had camped out in front of my house, accosted my daughter, embarrassed my wife and children, chased away my patients, etc. You get the idea. We (the media and I) were not on speaking terms, and this dearth of information has led to some wild speculation and accusations concerning myself and the cluster of news stories coming out of Austin, Texas. I'm not going to spend time trying to refute these, my goal is only to set the record straight. So let me get started.

Saturday, May 7, passed uneventfully, and Sunday, May 8, dawned with a booming Texas thunderstorm. Nitrox the Fearless was cowering in the knee space of my desk as I watched the flashes of lightning from our front porch (which is just outside the foyer). I sat long enough for the sky to lighten, all the while trying to shake the sensation that, instead of our lives moving

back to the blessedly mundane, we were approaching a precipice. Leah had begun to sense it as well. Only the night before
she asked if I thought things would ever return to the way they
had been.

The front door opened quietly and Mia slipped out. She sat
down beside me and then cuddled up under my arm. I knew that
she would soon outgrow this, just as her brother and sister had,
and my heart dropped.

"Nitrox won't come out to eat. She's such a baby." Mia was
freshly bathed and smelled clean. I noticed that she was wearing her going-to-church Sunday dress. It was a gaudy shade of
purple, and she would soon outgrow it as well. "Mom wants you
to come in and get dressed for Mass." She had delivered her
message but wanted another minute. So did I. "Where do you
think Maggie Dale is this very moment?"

Her question was as unexpected as it was impressive for an
eight-year-old. "I think someone very evil has her locked away."
It was a horrible image, and the only thing that could make it
worse was the fact that this was the best-case scenario, and the
least likely.

"If I knew who took her I would kill them," she said in her
sweet, eight-year-old voice. A voice that not so long ago was
singing her version of the alphabet song. What she had just said
and how much thought she had put into it was more horrifying
to me than the image of a four-year-old child being locked away
somewhere. "I don't think that would be a sin."

I was speechless, a rare state indeed. "It would be, a mortal
sin. We don't get to make those decisions. We leave them up to
God." Leah and I would surely be discussing the fact that our
youngest child was developing homicidal ideations.

"God works through us, and if He wanted to stop the evil
man from kidnapping and murdering more children, it would be
one of us that would have to do it." I noticed that she had her
pink fuzzy slippers on as she debated the legitimacy of murder.
"If God wants us to do something, it can't be a sin."

I was proud and terrified at the same time. Those same words and the same logic had been used for eons to justify some of the worst human behavior possible. "If God wants to stop the evil person, He has better ways of doing it besides having you kill someone. God wants you pure, just like when you were born, and killing someone, no matter how evil will . . ." I wanted to use the word *defile* but then I remembered I was talking to an eight-year-old. "It will hurt you in His eyes."

"What about if it was him or Maggie Dale? What if she could only be saved if someone killed the bad guy? You can't really disagree with that can you?" It was like arguing with my wife. I shuddered to think what Mia would be like in ten or fifteen years. She would probably move to Waco and set up a cult.

"Don't you want to talk about where babies come from instead?"

She sat up and punched my shoulder as hard as she could. "Don't be gross."

"Okay I won't be gross," I said, and belched for a good five seconds. "Now, go and ask your mother those questions and then come back and tell me what she said."

"No. You have to go in and get ready for Mass." She obviously thought I could use as much church as possible so that one day I would catch up to her theological understanding.

Ten minutes later Leah brought me the clothes she wanted me to wear to Mass. If I understand the typical American marriage correctly, this is not an uncommon or unusual division of labor. She picks out the clothes and I wear them. "Did you talk with Mia?" I had just finished showering, and we only had a few minutes of alone time.

"She wants to kill the bastard that took that girl, and I don't blame her." Leah was busy fluffing, or combing or doing something with her hair and was giving me only a small fraction of her attention. "I told her to go talk to you."

"Thanks. By the way, I'm cancelling the automatic weapon I was going to buy for her birthday."

"Okay," she said, now hurrying into the closet.

"I'm going to buy her an elephant instead. One that can ride a tricycle and do taxes. What do you think?" I was now more dressed than she was.

She said, "All right," and then my sarcasm caught up to her. "Very funny. Can you hurry? I don't want to walk in late and give people even more of an opportunity to gawk." She rushed by me a little more than half-dressed.

"I'll wait for you in the car. As usual." I left our bathroom before I got an earful of how *hard it is to get all these people ready while I do is just get myself ready.*

Ten minutes later, all five of us were in the car, heading to church. Rain pounded the roof of the car, and we all listened to it quietly.

As a complete aside, I am reminded of a similar trip to St. Catherine Catholic Church on another rainy Sunday morning years earlier. It was also spring, and Mia, who is becoming the star of this chapter, was quietly sitting in her car seat. She was only about three at the time and being quiet was not her forte. We were enjoying the respite from her nonstop banter when she said very simply, "You shouldn't squeeze rolly-pollys." For those of you not familiar with rolly-pollys, they are small insects, sort of a cross between a beetle and a centipede. They are not the most attractive insect, but in spring they are one of the most abundant. "Yellow stuff comes out," she finished. I was driving, so I couldn't turn, but Leah spun in her seat to find her darling daughter squeezing small squirmy insects and then wiping their guts all over her dress. All five of us to some degree are reminded of that precious moment when we are driving in the rain. Telling that story always makes me feel better. Now back to a not-so-precious reality.

Our drive to church is a relatively short four miles (relatively short for Austin). Our route is straight and flat except for a single overpass just before our exit. Traffic on an early Sunday morning is generally light, again by Austin standards, and we can usually drive the speed limit, but on that morning the torrential downpour had reduced us to a snail's pace. I was having a hard time seeing even with the wipers on maximum. About a half mile before the bridge, a Porsche blew by us, literally blew by, in a rooster-tail of rain at least ten feet high. I just caught a glimpse of the driver's profile, and the most I could tell was that it was probably a male. Fully loaded, our Denali is about seven thousand pounds, and the small sports car's wake nearly pushed us into the median.

"What a jerk," I said, keeping my language clean for the children. Leah's comment was a little more colorful. My view was obscured for several moments, and I tapped the brakes. When I had regained control and my windshield finally cleared, I saw the most unusual sight. A flying tanker truck. To be more exact, it was just the tanker; the truck part had slammed into the bridge abutment. I watched with disbelief as the tanker spun in mid-air, its wheels spinning madly, and then flipped upside down landing astride a passing school bus. It was one of those surreal moments when everyone asks themselves if that really just happened. A second later, when the fuel inside the tanker ignited, there was no question whether it had just happened.

I have had very little previous personal experience with pyrotechnics and exploding tanker trucks. Like most Americans, my expectations were crafted in Hollywood, but the reality fell far short. The blast wasn't an ear-shattering explosion that makes everyone cover their ears; it was a deep, low-frequency "whoop" that I felt more in my bones. The flash, however, was worthy of an Academy Award, and like all the drivers around me I was completely blinded for an instant. I slammed on my brakes and skidded to a stop close enough to the burning tanker to feel the heat through our windows. I quickly backed away as far as I could, maneuvering around the half dozen or so cars that had also come to a screeching halt, when Leah screamed that there were people in the bus.

I looked up and saw that the front half of the bus was crushed under the weight of the burning tanker, but that the back half, though blackened by the flash and twisted by the impact, was still relatively intact. I also saw hands pounding at the windows and rear door.

I'm no hero, at least consciously, but a moment later I found myself outside in the rain trying to get as close to the bus as possible. I have no recollection of leaving my vehicle. Leah tells me that I had jammed the Denali into park and then jumped from the car before it had completely stopped moving (which of course is mechanically impossible, but she knows nothing about transmissions). I think it took a few seconds for my sensible, keep-me-alive-and-unburned mind to recover from the shock of the accident and my impulsive you-can't-be-hurt mind must have stepped in to fill the void. The heat from the burning fuel was baking the skin of my face and arms despite the rain. I took a step forward, but the heat forced me back. People were shouting something about the bus exploding and warning me to get out of there. I could see the faces of the people in the back of the bus. They were all old. It was a church bus that had been gathering the elderly and driving them to Mass. A downdraft of wind blew smoke and steam all around me, and in an instant the world behind me was obscured. It was just me and the dozen or so old people, who were probably already burning alive. I tried another step but couldn't get closer than ten feet. My lungs began to burn, and I dropped to my knees coughing uncontrollably. I was seeing stars when I felt a hand touch my shoulder and then help me to my feet. A familiar set of blue eyes stared back at me.

"I'll take care of this," Adis said into the howling of the rain, wind, steam and flames. Still, I heard him clear as a bell.

Without a trace of hesitation, he walked straight up to the emergency exit and wrenched it open. Splinters of the metal hinges flew by my head and the large door clattered to the asphalt. Immediately, bodies began to tumble out, burned, but alive. Adis jumped up into the bus, and more survivors found their way out. I screamed at them to move this way but they either couldn't hear me or couldn't move. Finally, I forced myself into the furnace and grabbed a couple of the fallen and dragged them away from the inferno. Burning wasn't as bad as I had imagined, and I was able to make three or four trips before I couldn't breathe or move anymore. By that time others had arrived and began to pull the fallen to safety. I was one of the fallen.

I know that there are different versions of this story, and you would have to have been living under a rock not to hear at least one, but this is what really happened. I did not drive the trucker off the road to deflect accusations that I was involved with the kidnapping of Maggie Dale. I am not a member of any radical group, and that includes, al-Qaeda of Austin, Righteous Thunder, the National Democratic Party, or the Republican National Committee. More important, I did not imagine Adis walking through an inferno and saving eighteen lives as a number of organizations and prominent individuals have suggested. This last point needs emphasis, so let me make it absolutely clear. It was not me who opened that door, and it was not me who saved those people. I would love to accept the acclaim and accolades, but I don't deserve it. If it had only been me out there every one of those people would have died. Period.

Chapter Nine
X X

"And in the News Hour today, the third breaking story from Austin, Texas, in as many weeks." I watched Gwen Ifill open the *PBS News Hour* on Monday, May 9, from the comfort of my hospital bed. I was a bit singed around the edges but essentially out of danger. I had been pumped full of medications to counteract the carbon monoxide and cyanide generated from the burning vehicles, and still needed a face mask and supplemental oxygen. My face burned like the worst sunburn I had ever had, which was a good sign. If I had lost all sensation, including pain, I would have been in real trouble. My hands and arms were a little worse, and in time I would need some rather unpleasant treatments to regain full use. Both my wife and I were happy that three months earlier we had updated my disability policy.

Everyone wanted to be my friend now. South Austin Medical Center was prominently displayed in a network broadcast hosted by my new close friend Nick Latoris, and I wondered if the governor would show up. Leah was alternating between being angry with me and proud of me. Our children had become instant celebrities at school.

Most of the survivors from the bus were doing well. Of the eighteen that made it out, four would ultimately succumb to a combination of injury and age. Six passengers and the bus driver never made it out. The truck driver also didn't survive. In the end, the most reliable eyewitness of the accident was an insurance salesman named Kevin Patter. Like us he had been driving his wife and two children to St. Catherine's. He was also the individual that pulled me to safety after I had lost consciousness. A video of Kevin pulling bodies out of the smoke, not once or twice but three times, had been shown on every news channel and network, and I had already seen it multiple times.

The driver of the Porsche was never found. He had side-swiped Kevin Patter, who had been behind us, and then apparently the crazy man took aim at our Denali. Once he had just about driven us off the road, he crossed two lanes to slice in front of the tractor-trailer. The trucker stood on his brakes and hydroplaned into the abutment of the overpass, and the rest was history.

It took a day before the Austin police were able to interview me. A captain, accompanied by a couple of lieutenants, took my statement, for what it was worth. It turned into a photo op for the cops as reporters had somehow managed to skirt hospital security. I was a little disappointed that detectives Sharpe and Willis weren't there to answer my question about still being a person of interest. I honestly don't remember much more of that day, as morphine goes a long way in my veins.

Leah woke me long after everyone had left and the TV had been turned off. She put her hand on my knee, afraid to touch any other part of my body. My mind was relatively clear, as I had asked and then ordered the nurses to stop the morphine. The pain was better than that floating, disconnected feeling.

"Hey," I whispered. "You okay?" She tried to hide the fact that she had recently been crying. I heard some voices outside my room and distinctly heard a male voice say, "family only." More words were exchanged and the conversation ended with the male voice saying "sorry"; only, he didn't sound sorry. "What's going on?" I looked up at the clock on the wall and it said 1:23. For a moment I wasn't certain if it was early afternoon or the middle of the night. I turned my head, painfully, to the window and found that the world was still dark. "What are you doing here? Where are the kids?" I wasn't firing on all eight cylinders, but I could tell something had happened.

"The kids are fine. We moved them to Jim's house." Her voice was weak, almost exhausted. I had seen this woman in every conceivable state in the twenty-five years I had known her, but I had never seen her like this. She was terrified, mortally afraid of something. Fear radiated from her, and now I was terrified. I waited for more, an explanation, something that would help me understand. I reached for her hand despite the pain. A searing bolt shot up my arm and I ignored it.

"Leah tell me what's going on. Why are the children at the Lees?" Jim Lee was an ENT surgeon we knew. He was one of the best technical surgeons I had ever seen. We were probably closer than just ordinary colleagues, but I couldn't see Leah calling them in the dead of the night to watch our children.

"We needed something, somewhere secure." Her voice was marginally stronger. I remembered that the Lees lived in a gated community with twenty-four-hour security. "And someone a little remote from us."

I started to shake, which probably hurt like hell, only I don't remember. "For God's sake, Leah, tell me what's going on." I raised my voice and I immediately concluded that that had been a mistake. My throat had been burned, and it responded to the stress by clamping down. I started to cough and couldn't catch my breath. I started to wheeze and reflexively began to hyperventilate, which dropped the amount of air that reached by damaged lungs. A nurse appeared, then another, and everyone was pushing things into my burned face. Through it all I watched the woman I loved with every fiber of my being pushed aside. Her face had gone ashen and she silently cried. A man appeared at her side and tried to guide her away but she resisted.

"I'm all right," I finally managed to get out. A rebreather mask had been strapped to my face, and I felt the cool flow of humidified oxygen. I started to breathe easier and pushed the hands away. I reached for Leah. "Tell me. Now!" In that moment I had never loved her more, or been more angry with her. "NOW!" I ordered. She cried harder. The man that had tried to restrain her stepped between us. He said something that I ignored. "No. Leah tell me what's going on!" I pushed the stranger's hand away and tried to reach my wife.

Everyone started to look at each other. They all had a secret. A terrible, horrible secret, and no one had the guts to tell me. The moment stretched, and I watched Leah transform into the woman that I had fallen in love with. She dried her face and took a deep breath. I could see the resolve, the steel return to her. She walked to my bedside and sat. "When we came home this evening, after visiting you—" she paused for a breath "—someone had broken in." Another pause. I felt a degree of relief. Things could be replaced; I just needed my family. "They left something." A shorter pause, but they were starting to stretch in my mind. "A shoe. A little girl's shoe. Maggie Dale's shoe. It was covered in blood." She swallowed several times and held my eyes. I could feel the love that we share secretly, something so deep and personal, something that is only meant for us. She held my burned hand and tightened her grip. "Next to it was a photograph of Mia. She was sitting in her desk at school."

"Is everyone . . ." I couldn't finish.

"Everyone is all right." Her grip remained tight, and I welcomed it despite the pain. It felt as if we were melding together. "They took Nitrox."

☒ ☒

Something was beeping and I wanted to tell Leah to answer her phone. I was cold but so relaxed that I didn't care. The beeping continued, but it seemed almost impossible to open my eyes, much less talk. Somebody moved beside me and the beeping stopped. My sleepy brain thanked them, and I dropped back into the most relaxing sleep I had ever experienced. Then someone rudely opened my left eye and flashed a bright light in it. I turned away, but then they did it to my right eye. "What are you doing?" I fended off my assailant and they went away for a moment. Then I felt something tighten around my right bicep and a brilliant burst of white pain exploded in my head. Instantly I was fully conscious, and I tried to use my bandaged left hand to tear off the blood pressure cuff. A tiny little girl dressed all in white stood next to me. She had a name tag that said 'Andrea R. N.' A little smiley face covered the South Austin Hospital emblem. Her attention was directed upward at the EKG monitor and she was busy transcribing my vital signs into a computer notebook. The cuff got tighter and tighter and I was certain that my arm would burst.

"No," she yelled when she realized what I was doing. We began to wrestle. I managed to hook my burned fingers into the Velcro and rip the cuff off my bicep. The Kerlix dressing that had been protecting my burned flesh caught and it came off as well, along with a two-inch strip of blackened skin. A pattern of red spots appeared across the front of her blouse and she screamed.

A real nurse appeared and immediately lifted my arm. "Sorry, she's new," she said while quickly disentangling my arm from the dressing and the blood pressure cuff. The skin over my elbow and bicep was in tatters, and a long strip of skin hung from my suspended arm. Blood dripped from the end. "We're gonna have to treat that," she said, stating the obvious. A second nurse appeared and together they managed to redress my wound. "I'll need to call Dr. Saiki," the first nurse said. "I don't suppose you want anything for pain?"

I had been adamant about minimizing my narcotic usage, but at that moment I was strongly reconsidering it. "What did I get last night?" A funny thing about pain is its ability to activate the brain, to turn the lights on a little brighter. I suddenly remembered everything Leah and I talked about last night, or actually this morning, including the plans we had made to keep our family safe. The FBI had suggested that we get as far from Austin as possible. She had called her mother, and they were working out details that would almost certainly include using my in-laws' mountain house in northern New Mexico. Leah's father and three brothers were marines (I almost wrote ex-marines, but once a marine, always a marine), and they owned a lot of guns. A lot of guns. There was no way I could join them. Austin is barely five hundred feet above sea level, and even in this oxygen-rich environment I could not be without a face mask and supplemental oxygen. I wouldn't last three minutes at nine thousand feet.

"You got morphine, Versed, and Benadryl." The nurse answered. A triple cocktail. Major league sedation, which explained why I felt like I had been poured into the bed. I don't remember asking for something so potent, but after Leah and her armed escort had left I probably didn't offer any resistance to chemically induced sleep.

"Two milligrams of morphine," I said, and tried not to grit my teeth.

"There are no badges for heroes, tough guy. This is going to be rough." I finally recognized the nurse. She was the unit supervisor, Sandy Fuller.

"Hi, Sandy. What are you doing delivering patient care? You're one of the important people." I grimaced as she lowered my arm and the veins began to re-expand.

"I'll tell you a secret if you won't let it go to your head." She smiled and I nodded. "They're lining up outside to help you." She winked. It was without a doubt the nicest thing anyone had said to me in a very long time. "Sorry about Andrea."

I spent an eternity in a treatment room that morning, with dressing changes and wound debridement (where the dead tissue is cut or scrubbed off). In the end I needed eight more milligrams of morphine to take the edge off. I guess I'm not so tough after all. I slept away the rest of the morning and early afternoon. Leah had visited but didn't wake me. She left me a note that simply said, *Love you.*

I finally opened my eyes around two thirty. I was disoriented and for several minutes thought that I was having a dream about work. I recognized our ICU, realized that I couldn't really move, and that I wasn't wearing any clothes. I looked around and found a clear plastic bag filled with fluid hanging above my bed. Morphine Sulfate was stamped across it. I followed an intravenous line down from the bag to my arm. "Wheee," I whispered.

I found Leah's note, and it took me roughly an hour to read and understand the words. I dropped it to the floor and tried to process what had been happening. Memories and random thoughts flowed through my thick mind, and I tried to arrange them into something that approximated a logical sequence, but my mind refused to stay on task. Like Mia, I wondered where Nitrox, our beloved dog, was this very moment. My brain was swimming in a pool of morphine about ten feet above my body, and from that height I could see both Nitrox and Maggie. The toddler was astride our dog like a jockey, and they were running home through a pine forest. *Good girl*, I thought. Nitrox must have followed the evil man back to his lair, killed him as Mia had instructed, and rescued Maggie. Suddenly, everything was right with the world. Leah and the kids wouldn't have to leave, and I would go home. I closed my eyes and it was suddenly evening.

I was more alert, and my narcotic-fueled hallucinations were now just a disorganized dream. I was sore and stiff and began to slowly stretch my arms and neck. As I turned to the left I found Adis smiling back at me.

"How are you?" My mind was clear enough to remember that when he asked this question he expected an answer.

"I hurt and my mind is still in a fog," I said through my oxygen mask, in a voice too raspy to be my own. "I saw what you did." My throat felt raw, and a tickle deep in my pharynx warned me of an impending cough.

"I know, and I think that you should keep that between us." He looked pink and healthy. No unsightly burns or scars. Even his wrinkled face had somehow smoothed out.

"Too late." I whispered. I tried to suppress the cough that I knew would lead to an episode of laryngospasm.

"Just leave it for now. No one else needs to know." His voice was soothing like a cool compress on my burned skin.

"Why aren't you burned?" I whispered. It didn't seem to matter that the strength of my voice was so poor that I could barely hear my own words.

"Why am I not burned?" he repeated in a soft voice. That was all he said for several long seconds, and then he leaned into my bed and stared at me. He studied my face long enough for me to feel uncomfortable. "At this point it's not important for you to know why I am not burned," he finally said. "Knowing won't help you. But there are things that are important for you to know." He waited for me to signal that I understood. I nodded. "I am a small cog in a vast machine that maintains balance."

"Balance?" I whispered, and my sluggish brain conjured up an image of Adis standing on a large exercise ball. I think I may have chuckled.

"Balance," he repeated. "Without balance there can be no free will. Without free will there can be no balance. We would be left with chaos."

"So, by extension, you work to maintain free will and prevent chaos." It took me almost a minute to work that out. "That's very noble." I wasn't trying to be sarcastic, but in retrospect it probably sounded that way. "Who's free will? Ours?"

"Everyone's." His face floated in front of me, which I know was only possible because I had been pumped full of more mind-altering drugs than were used at the last Grateful Dead concert.

"Well, thank you." I was slipping into narcotic-induced frivolity and I tried to fight it. "So you run into burning buses and kill terrorists so we can choose between cable or network TV? What a lousy job." His smiling face drifted in and out of focus. "Wait a minute. That's not right." The obvious contradiction energized my mind for a moment. "You interfered with those guys, those terrorists. You took away their free will." In fact he had taken away more than just their free will.

"All for the greater good."

"And helping Maggie Dale, that's not for the greater good?" I thought that I had just scored a point.

"Until I know more, as I have already told you, it would be unwise for me to become involved."

"Unwise," I whispered dramatically, or as dramatically as a burned man high on narcotics wearing a breathing mask can be. "But it wasn't unwise to run into that bus. You made that decision pretty quick." I should have asked him how he knew to be there at that moment, but words were getting lost in my head. "Why aren't you burned?" It dawned on me that he still hadn't answered the original question.

"I have a duty, a purpose for being, and for the most part I have been given the tools to do it."

"That's why you don't burn. You're made of asbestos. The asbestos man." I was really starting to slur my words as I began to sink back into the bed and oblivion. I fought to focus my thoughts. "How do you know . . ." I kept losing myself. "How do you know—" I really wanted an answer to this question, only I couldn't get the words out "—who tells you when you can do . . ." That was as much of my thought that I could piece together.

"No one tells me," he said simply.

I understood his words, but their implications were a little beyond my reach, so I asked the only question my slow brain could generate. "Are you God?"

He laughed loudly. Heartily. It was the same laugh I use when one of my children does or says something in complete innocence. He went on for a while, and I began to feel foolish and made a mental note to remind myself how this feels the next time the roles are reversed.

"Oh, goodness no." He could barely get the words out. "This is a discussion we need to have when you are feeling better." He smiled and shifted his position. "We do have an important matter to discuss."

I nearly cut him off by telling him that Leah had taken care of everything, but for the moment couldn't get my thoughts out fast enough.

He reached over the bed rail and took my bandaged hand. It should have hurt like hell, but all I felt was a tingling sensation (if I had been working I would have called it a paresthesia) that raced up my arm and into my brain. My eyes snapped open. In a millisecond I was awake and alert. "You need to listen to me now. This is important."

"I'm listening." My voice was unnaturally strong for my current condition. I was more than listening; it was as if a recorder had been turned on in my brain.

"I have to stay here in Austin." He spoke in short sentences that were easily digested. His face looked as if it were made of granite. "I can't go to New Mexico. Not even for a short time. Leah and your children must stay here." He let go of my hand and I suddenly felt unplugged, but I understood not only what he had said, but what he had left unsaid.

"All right." I felt somewhat hypnotized. Hypnotized, but afraid. His face began to soften back into Adis-the-grandfather, and a wave of exhaustion washed over me

"These recent events, the high school, the kidnapping, the bus . . ." He paused as he struggled to find the right words. "They are just the beginning. Somehow you and your family have become a focal point for something that remains undefined." This was the first time that I had ever seen Adis look truly worried. "If your family leaves, the situation will become more complicated. More unpredictable." He stood, and I was flagging so badly that I couldn't tell if he actually spoke those words aloud or inserted them directly into my brain.

"Okay," I said, in a voice that would surely warrant a field sobriety test had I been driving.

"Sleep now. I will see you again soon." He walked to the door and opened it. I saw an Imperial Guard that stood at least twelve feet tall guarding my room. In his mechanical voice he wished Adis a good night, and the door closed. "But I really don't like *Star Wars*," I said to myself.

Chapter Ten

X X

LEAH WAS AT MY BEDSIDE EARLY WEDNESDAY MORNING. She had spent almost an entire day and night making arrangements with her family, the children's schools, and the FBI. She was not exactly open to suddenly cancelling them on the request of a drugged-up husband and a mystery man that I had already described as delusional. In the midst of our "discussion," which had been interrupted by one of the nurses pointedly asking if everything was all right, Leah had called Special Agent Anderson so that I could explain to him why she and the kids should remain in harm's way simply because Adis insisted. He was no more impressed with my reasoning than Leah.

"You have to realize that your thinking is impaired. You're just going to have to let go and let me take care of things." She had finally put her phone away after having a hushed conversation with the FBI agent. "We really don't have a choice." She was all action and resolve now. She would not be dissuaded, no matter what I said. If I had Adis's cell phone number, and if Adis actually had had a cell phone, I would have called him and let him explain it to the immovable object that I had married more than two decades earlier. As it turned out, I didn't need a cell phone.

The door opened and I caught a glimpse of a police officer of normal dimensions, wearing only an APD uniform, guarding my room. He closed the door after Adis himself walked in. I am going to break with convention now and actually describe what I think Leah saw.

Adis was probably a little over six feet and around two hundred pounds. He had broad shoulders, a thick chest, and thicker arms. I was struck by the fact that Adis must actively work out and I wondered where. He wore a red-and-black short-sleeved flannel shirt that was much too warm for Austin in May. He had on a pair of tan pants and a pair of brown hiking boots that looked like they just came out of the box. Leah stood and gawked.

"You must be Leah." He closed the distance literally in the blink of an eye and swept up her hand to shake it.

"How do you do?" she answered mechanically. I can't ever remember her looking so dumbfounded or star struck.

"I do very well," he answered in typical Adis fashion. "We should sit, as I have very little time to convince you that I am not a fruitcake." His smile was the most charming I had ever seen it.

"I don't think you're really a fruitcake," she said slowly, which was a refreshing break from her usual torrent.

"Of course you do, or at least you should." He held her hand and she looked hypnotized, a state that had become thoroughly familiar to me.

"I'm just not sure we should stay in Austin. The FBI . . ."

He interrupted her. "The FBI cannot protect you or your children. As I was explaining to your husband, we have a bit of a serious situation here." I watched Leah as Adis worked his way around her natural suspicions. Her eyes were a fraction wider, her expression slightly vacant, and she allowed this total stranger to hold her hand. "And, for reasons that aren't yet clear, you and your family seem to be at the center of it."

She stared at Adis for a very long moment and then slowly pulled her hand back. "He has shared with me some of your unusual beliefs." Her gaze was beginning to refocus and her natural suspicion had crept back into her voice.

"Like how I believe that I am thousands of years old, and that my job is to bring balance to the world?" He smiled but Leah wasn't so easily seduced.

"You do know that you sound delusional. So why should I follow the advice of a delusional man, no matter how charming?" She folded her arms across her chest and gave him an I'm-not-so-easily-fooled look. So much for the Adis-effect.

"Excellent question." He leaned away from Leah and gave her space. "What would it take to convince you? Magic tricks? Do you want me to prove myself by making the diamond earring you lost at the Krietz's Christmas party last year reappear? Or would you like me to read your mind and tell you what Mia told you she did to Nitrox a week ago? Would that be enough to convince you?"

Leah had lost a single diamond earring at the Krietz's. We had been dancing rather vigorously, after a few to many glasses of holiday punch, on their boat dock when the earring flew off into the darkness of Lake Austin. I had no idea what Mia had confided to Leah about our missing dog, but I was convinced.

She eyed him suspiciously, and for a moment it looked like Adis's gambit had backfired. "Tell me where Nitrox is."

"With Maggie Dale." He answered almost as if he had expected the question. I had expected her to ask for the earring (okay I had hoped she would ask for the earring).

"Nice try. Where?" Her arms tightened across her chest. I remember thinking that maybe it was just men who were susceptible to the Adis-effect.

I sat up, suddenly very interested in his answer, as well as how Leah seemed to be working Adis. "I have no specifics, only generalities, nothing that would convince you that you need to do what I say."

"How do you know that they are still alive?"

"Because if they weren't I could tell you exactly where they are."

"Is the person who took Maggie and Nitrox going to try and take one of our children?" Her voice was strong. I couldn't detect even the slightest quiver.

"As things stand, yes," he said instantly.

"Will they succeed?" she fired back.

"That depends on what you do." They stared at each other, and I suddenly felt like the odd man out.

"Can you stop them?" Her voice broke very subtly.

"Only if the conditions are right," Adis answered. Leah had begun to lean forward almost plaintively.

"And if they aren't, you would let some bastard take one of our children?" Her voice rose half an octave.

"It wouldn't be my choice." Adis matched Leah's lean and the two were very nearly touching. "I promise you that I will do everything within my power to protect you and your family."

I didn't doubt his sincerity, but it was clear he had left a good deal unsaid "Everything within your power?" Leah questioned.

"As I told your husband, I am not God. I am not omnipotent. There are limits to what I can do. In time the situation will become clear." His tone was reassuring, but Leah was having none of it.

"What is clear is that a crazy person is threatening our baby. You can see that, can't you?" Leah had pulled back and raised her voice.

"Yes, I can see that, but I can also see that your family is a small part of a much larger process."

Leah stared back at Adis. I could see the internal struggle on her face. She was scared and fought hard to keep her head above the emotional waters that threatened to drown her. "Why can't you help the police find the Dales' child?" Leah asked after a long ten seconds.

"I have told them all they are capable of hearing. Unfortunately, most of them see me as a doddering old man that, after my recent exploits, is lucky to be alive."

"Not all of them," I finally added to the conversation.

"That is true. Some suspect that I am more than I seem." He smiled at the inside joke. "They see me as complicit, which colors any information I give them."

"Why can't you find her yourself? You tracked down those crackpots that attacked the high school." Leah asked.

Adis took a long breath, crossed his arms, and sat back up in his chair. "That was an entirely different situation." For a second Adis had let his façade drop, and both Leah and I could see that we had touched a nerve.

"What are you not telling us?" I asked.

"This is not the time to go into..." Adis started and Leah cut him off.

"This is the exact time," she said sharply. "If you want us to do what you say and ignore the advice of everyone around us you need to be straight with us."

It took Adis a half a minute to respond. He silently stared at the floor, and I couldn't tell if he was angry with Leah's sudden directness or if he was having difficulty finding the right words. "There are no rules that govern human behavior aside from those you impose upon yourselves. This is a fundamental principle. My existence, however, is very different. I have clear lines of responsibility and I cannot work outside them."

Leah and I exchanged a look. Even in my drug-addled mind I could tell that Adis had given us only half an answer.

"All right so your existence has rules that force you to color inside the lines. Are you saying that Maggie Dale and our family are outside those lines?" Leah's mind was clear and she was in no mood for half answers.

"The problem is that I can no longer see the lines clearly. Things have become fuzzy."

"Fuzzy?" I asked, which at the moment exactly described my thinking.

"Perhaps obscured would be a better term." He had more to say and made us wait for it. "What happened at the high school was something I should have seen coming, only I didn't until the last moment. It was very cleverly concealed. The bus fire I didn't see coming at all."

"You mean those wackos outsmarted you?" I whispered.

"No. It wasn't those wackos." He smiled briefly and then the serious version of Adis returned. "I am worried that someone ran interference for them, shielded them, and then when the time was right aimed them directly at me."

"So you think someone set you up. They drew you out in the open, to what, expose you?" Leah asked.

"That's one possibility. My greatest weapon has been anonymity."

"How do know that you're not being set up to keep us here?" Leah asked.

"I don't," he answered, with a degree of finality that signaled to both of us that he was done answering questions. I had about ten more, and he cut me off with a raised hand. "I have done all I can do to convince you. In the end it will be your decision." He stood suddenly. He stared down at Leah, and for the first time ever I watch my wife look away from someone's challenging stare. He looked at me and nodded slightly. A minute later Leah and I were alone.

"The photo that was left in our house was of Mia on Monday morning. It was taken from inside her school. Whoever took it got that close to her, and no one saw the bastard." She had started to cry silently. "He took that little girl from her locked bedroom without leaving a trace. He's a ghost. How do we protect our children from a ghost?" Leah hadn't moved. She remained frozen in the same position she was in when Adis left. "What are we going to do? I'm afraid of staying, and now I'm afraid of going."

"As strange as it sounds, I feel better with him than I do with the FBI," I answered.

Leah dropped her head and wiped her eyes, slowly nodding in agreement. "So do I," she said with resignation. She looked up and stared at me. "Where are we going to live? We can't go home."

In the end, Leah and the children made a show of packing up the car under the watchful eye and protection of both the FBI and APD (our son, the miniature detective, scoured the Denali for any tracking devices). Leah had already pulled all three kids from school. The year would be finished online for the older two, and Mia would get a pass. And then, for any and all who were watching, a three-car convoy left our house and neighborhood for parts unknown, presumably out of the state.

Gordon Anderson, who was driving the lead car, was anything but happy about our decision to stay local. The fact is, he was furious. He had called my hospital room earlier and berated me over the phone. He used words like reckless, ill-conceived, and the biggest mistake he had seen anyone make in twenty years of police work. I was unmoved, and as he became more strident I began to wonder if we would be better off without any sort of police or FBI involvement. When he finally realized that he had no chance of changing my mind (or Leah's), we had a rational discussion about Plan B.

He did win a concession when he convinced Leah to leave her cell phone at home. The children, each of whom had their own phone—ostensibly for safety reasons (a situation that I had always found to be so excessive as to be bordering on the obscene, at least up until recent events had proven me wrong)— had also been forced to leave their electronic lifelines at home, which in their minds changed the whole situation from mildly scary but very exciting to tedious, boring, and very inconvenient. After driving through the city, the trio of cars turned west and disappeared, we hoped, into the wilds of suburbia. To be more specific, a small house on Lake Travis (the lake was down about fifty feet and about a quarter mile away from the back yard, which did not improve our children's moods). The three-bedroom, two-bath house had been empty for two years, after the federal government had seized it from the previous owners who, like us, were now the guests of the federal government (only their accommodations came with orange jumpsuits, bars, guards with guns, and a twenty-year sentence). The bungalow had been sealed up for months, and it smelled like spoiled milk. It was infested with spiders and an odd assortment of other multilegged animals, which did not improve Leah's mood. Still, she and the children were safe. Or so we thought.

I, on the other hand, got to enjoy the benefits of a clean and sterile-smelling hospital bed with periodic burn debridement and morphine drips for another week. I probably could have left earlier, but I didn't really have a home to go back to. I talked with Leah three or four times a day via new disposable phones, courtesy of the FBI, and she regaled me with stories of exterminators, sullen children who were bored out of their minds, her new fast food diet, and the fact that it had taken almost a week for someone to get a stable Internet signal. I could have shared with her the joys of having burned skin scrubbed off, but I let her lean on me via cell phone signal.

I was saying good night to her when she suddenly told me to hold on for a moment. I could just make out a raised and excited voice in the background and then the sound of Mika screaming. Leah carried the phone and me along with it to our oldest child. Normally, Mika lives somewhere between reserved and sullen, but like her younger sister can, on a whim, demonstrate prodigious dramatic abilities. I kept whispering a prayer that this was just Mika being Mika and not some new development. God must have had his answering machine on, because the next thing I heard Leah say was *Oh, no*. She repeated it over and over again.

"What is it?" I screamed into the phone, but the only answer I got was the sound of Leah putting her phone down. Mika's cries were muffled but they still managed to freeze my blood. Finally, Tom, our son, picked up the forgotten phone.

"Dad?"

"Tom, what's going on?" Without thinking I had gotten out of bed and begun to look for something to wear.

"Mom's on the computer. Mika found something." His tone was even, and I could hear the strength he had inherited from his mother. "It's a picture of Nitrox on Facebook. It says that Mom sent it. She's all curled up and bloody." His voice finally broke. "She looks dead." He broke up the last word into two syllables. "The caption says, *See what I did.*" I could hear him swallow and try to master his twelve-year-old emotions. "There's a little girl next to Nitrox. I don't know if she's asleep, but she's wearing Mia's slippers." My mind flashed back to an image of

Mia snuggled up next to me wearing those pink, fuzzy slippers just ten days earlier.

"Put your mother on." I tried to sound like I was under control, that we had anticipated that something like this was going to happen, but Leah's repeated *oh, no*'s were undermining my effort.

"Dad," he paused. "This is weird and kinda scary but someone just signed in on Mika's page using Mom's account." I'm not a Facebook person, but as far as I know this isn't supposed to happen. "Mom just asked them why they are doing this." The smart thing would have been for me to tell him to hang up the phone and immediately call the FBI, the police, or even Ghostbusters (he probably wouldn't have known what that meant)— anyone. Only, I wasn't being smart at the moment, and I had to know what was happening with my family.

"What did they say?" I had waited as long as I could wait.

"It takes a minute," Tom answered with annoyance (he was at that age where it was okay to openly express his annoyance). "He's writing." Another pause. "He said, 'Because I can.' That's all. Mom just typed 'Who are you?'"

We waited, and waited. I looked at the clock above the door after what seemed like an hour, and then waited some more. "What's happening?" I knew he couldn't tell me, but I had to ask. I had to do something.

"It's only been a minute and twelve seconds." Tom's annoyance in the face of these terrible events was beginning to annoy me. I was just about to ask him if he had any concept of the gravity of this situation when he finally answered. "He said, 'A better question would be *What am I?*' Hold on there's more. 'Maybe this will help.' It's a picture of something. It's loading slowly." I didn't need to wait to know what it would be. "Oh, shit, Dad." He had inherited his fondness for the word *shit* from his mother as well. "It's a picture of the house we're in. He was right outside the house."

"I'm not surprised." I was almost resigned to the fact that whoever this guy was, or whatever this guy was, he was definitely one step ahead of us. "Put Mom on." My voice broached no argument.

"You heard?" she said simply. I could hear the resignation in her voice as well.

"Yeah. I can't say I'm surprised. I thought they had someone watching you,"

"They do, and they're still out there, I just checked. It's been clear all week except for this afternoon, and it's raining in the picture."

"You need to call them now. Are you armed?" In a complete role reversal, Leah is the protector of the family, at least when it comes to firearms. I have fired a gun maybe ten times in my life, but she grew up with them and is an excellent shot. To my knowledge she has never intentionally fired a weapon at another human, but if it came down to it I had every confidence that she would blow away anyone who threatened her or her family, without a trace of hesitation or regret. And it wouldn't be the Hollywood stereotype of a single dramatic shot that ends the scene (until the bad guy suddenly, dramatically jumps to his feet). Leah would use the entire clip. And then reload.

"Yes. I have the Sig." Years ago, Leah's father bought her a Sig Sauer P320 for Christmas (I don't remember what I got her that year, probably the earrings she lost). This is an intimidating weapon that is used primarily by law enforcement and made with the express intent of putting down whatever is hit. "I'll call you in a bit." She hung up, but through that ethereal connection long-married couples create I could imagine I felt her hand curl around the grip of her favorite gun.

Chapter Eleven

X X

THE FOLLOWING DAY, THURSDAY, MAY 19, WE WERE ALL BACK HOME. Protective custody and pretending to flee hadn't stopped this sicko (the term now adopted by all five of us that aptly described our tormenter) from reaching out and touching us. Leah and I purposefully avoided asking each other if we thought that events proved Adis right or wrong. We also didn't talk about Nitrox, although the kids did. She looked dead, or at a minimum badly injured. Maggie Dale looked just as bad.

My hands had started to work and I had fresh, raw pink skin up both my arms, meaning I wouldn't need any more debridements. Just dressing changes and physical therapy to maintain motion in my joints and flexibility in my skin. Our police protection, for what it's worth, had continued, but all of us derived more comfort from Leah's Sig sitting on the kitchen counter. The FBI was trying to track down how Mr. Sicko was able to sign in to Facebook as Leah. I didn't think that it was much of a mystery; the man (once again I was assuming it was a man, and as I sit here writing, and you sit there reading, we all know that it was a man) had been in our house. The press kept hounding us. Fortunately, they knew nothing of the latest development and simply wanted to know what it was like being back at home.

I was still pretty puny, and around noon I announced that I was going to take a nap. I slid my disposable, loaner phone across the kitchen counter and it lightly tapped the handgun. Leah gave me a that-wasn't-so-smart look, and I made my way to the bedroom. For the first time in a week and a half, I was going to drop into my own bed. I almost made it. My phone rang. Not my old smart phone that I had grown to hate (too big, too many apps, etc.), which had somehow managed to survive when its owner ran into a fire, but the smaller, simpler disposable phone. It chirped and vibrated next to the 9mm Sig. The phone that had a number known only to Leah. I turned and Leah was staring at it, and for an instant I thought she would pick up the Sig and shoot it. I wish she had.

Finally, it reached its requisite ten rings and stopped. I looked back at Leah, and she looked back at me. I was just about to say that it was probably just a telemarketer when her phone began to ring in her purse. Not her nice iPhone, which she loved, but the new disposable phone that had a number known only to me. Ten rings later, it stopped and mine rang again.

I had unconsciously walked back to the kitchen and watched the small device vibrate a few times before abruptly picking it up. "Hello." I'm not sure why I even said hello. I should have just asked Mr. Sicko what he wanted. It had to be him. The only other person we knew with "magical powers" was Adis, and calling wasn't his style. The police and FBI had anticipated that Mr. Sicko might accelerate his contact with us, and had put taps, or tracers, or some electronic means to monitor our house phone and our old cell phones. But no one had guessed that it would be this quick or that he would use the disposable phones we had no intention of ever using again.

"I didn't think you would pick up." His voice had an Adis quality. Behind his words was a subliminal sound track that slipped into my brain and set the mood. "I would have had to call all day, which would have taken me away from my work."

"I assume you're the deviant that kidnapped little Maggie and our dog." I turned the phone's speaker on so Leah could hear.

"You would assume correctly. I am also the deviant that made you famous. I will confess that at first I was a little upset with you. You did spoil my plans by giving the police and the FBI something to focus on, and I worked so hard to leave them only with shadows. You know dogs are happy even when they're barking up the wrong tree, or chasing their tails."

"So you like dogs?" I had no idea what to say or ask. "How is my dog?"

"Nitrox . . ." he paused for effect. His verbal mannerisms were very different from Adis's, much less polished. Less natural. He had to work to be charming. "I will admit that she has seen better days. She didn't seem to be very keen about going for a ride with me. On a positive note, she has taken quite a shine to Miss Margaret. But you interrupted me." He paused again to let his small rebuke resonate in my head, and it did. My only contact with psychopaths is through television and I expected him to say something like that would cost Nitrox or Maggie an appendage. "I congratulate you on your recent heroics. You seemed to have made the most of it."

"I haven't made the most of anything," I sputtered. "You did that! All of it! You killed all those people!"

"Now, now, let's not jump to conclusions," he said with a playful lilt.

"Is this all just a game to you? Do you place any value on human life?" Down deep, I felt something similar to the curiosity that affected me when I first met Adis. The depth of his psychosis was intriguing, and if conditions were different I would have liked to explore it a bit, but at that particular moment I wanted nothing more than to empty Leah's 9mm into him.

"I don't want to be drawn into a discussion of my psychopathology. They are quite boring. Suffice it to say that I am happy with myself and let's get back to what's important shall we?" I tried to place his accent and to keep track of his unusual mannerisms for the police and possibly Adis.

"What are you going to do with Maggie?" I wanted to keep the focus on the girl he had already taken, and away from my family.

"Nothing yet. It's not time." If voices could smile, his did.

"Look. I'm tired and hurting, and I don't have patience for games. If you're only calling to prove yourself I assure you it's unnecessary. We are very impressed with your abilities to move unseen and to manipulate cell phones and the Internet. Really, I speak for Leah as well, you are truly scary."

I had more to say, but he cut in. "Were you really going to go to New Mexico? Did the FBI convince you that you would be safe there?"

"Why are you doing this? Do you have some agenda? Do you hate the government, organized religion, the IRS, what? Are you being controlled by aliens? What is your deal?" At that moment I didn't care if I interrupted him again.

"I will tell you, but only if you do me the favor of relaying exactly what I say to the authorities." He gave me a moment to answer.

"I will," I said without hesitation. According to every television drama, when confronted by the unstable antagonist, get him to talk. Let him explain himself. Of course, that's useful in a scripted sixty-minute TV show, but not very helpful in real life.

"Tell them that I have no agenda. I am at peace with everyone and everything. What I do is completely natural for me. I am on a journey of discovery and this is my truest form of expression. I move through the world unseen, doing as I please. Sometimes I see myself as an artist, other times as a musician or a dancer, but never as an angry, hateful man metaphorically screaming out a window 'I'm angry as hell and I'm not going to take it anymore.' Does that surprise you?"

"Frankly, it scares me even more." I wondered what Leah thought at that moment. I was standing in our kitchen having a pleasant phone conversation with a psychopath that was threatening our family. It's moments like this when she thinks I don't display or express enough emotion, and it's moments like this that I tell her not to express emotions. "You went to a lot of trouble to reach us. Was it only so you could tell us that you really don't hate anyone and are just an artist?"

"Not entirely. I wanted to welcome you back home, but also to ask you about the man who calls himself Adis. He seems like a fascinating character, and I would love to meet him."

"I'm sure I can arrange it," I answered quickly. I imagined Adis sticking a nine-inch combat knife into the neck of Mr. Sicko.

"Oh, I'm sure you could, but I'd be concerned that there might be some complications along the way." He was chuckling, and at that moment I was struck by a sudden realization. For days now, ever since he had broken into our house, I had assumed that Mr. Sicko was somehow related to Adis, maybe the other side of the same coin. With Adis-like powers, you could sneak into the home of two police-people (police persons?) and steal their child without leaving anything behind. Or you could snap pictures of an elementary student while she was in class without anyone noticing. Or you could find a family hidden by the FBI. I could go on, but you get my point. Only, Mr. Sicko knew nothing of Adis, which implied that Mr. Sicko was probably just an ordinary man. Well, maybe an extraordinary man, but not on a par with Adis. "Someday soon I will meet the famous man. But tell me something. How did he convince you to stay? Did he offer you protection? Even the FBI couldn't keep you safe, so how do you expect an elderly, senile man to protect you? I am absolutely fascinated by this; please tell me what he said."

"Tell me why you are threatening our daughter and I will tell you about Adis." I thought it was a fair trade, and he did pause to consider it.

"I didn't know you or your beautiful wife and children even existed until you were drawn into poor Maggie's plight. You received a lot of attention. I'm not jealous, mind you. Take it while you can get it, I say. But to answer your question, I really didn't choose Mia." I flinched when I heard her name in his voice. "My muse did. Now, I'm not some nut that receives messages from Greek goddesses, or even my neighbor's dog. My muse is simply inspiration, an unconscious burst of creativity. A vision of what is possible. I found a picture of Mia on the Internet and suddenly I could see her as a part of an idea that needed exploration. Call it an experiment. When I am ready, Maggie

Dale will be the first and Mia will be the last." He stopped speaking and my powers of speech had abandoned me. "Are you still there? I'm sorry, but that must have been hard to hear. If it makes you feel any better, I am certain that what we discover and create will exceed anything I have accomplished before. A true masterpiece, something that will change mankind. It will take your breath away."

I knew what it was like to have your breath taken away. I was struggling to breathe. "How many pieces?" I finally asked.

"Good question! I'm not really sure yet; I've got some details that need ironing out, but I'm guessing no more than six." He paused, and I was grateful for it. "Now, before the police arrive and I am forced to get back into character, please tell me about Adis."

"He isn't human." I saw no point in lying, and although I wasn't quite certain what Adis was, I knew he didn't fit the generally accepted definition of human.

"Excellent!" Mr. Sicko seemed genuinely excited. "Does he know about me?"

"He knows what you've done, and what you're going to do."

"Wonderful, wonderful. I'm tingling all over with anticipation. He really knows what I'm going to do? I can't believe it! I'll let you in on a secret: even I don't know the exact specifics. I wish there was a way I could meet him. I would wager that he could appreciate my work. Has he told you whether he is going to try and stop me?"

"No." I turned to find that Tom had led two APD officers into our kitchen. Nearly a year later I don't know why I choose that moment to start lying to Mr. Sicko, but I think maybe it had to do with the sudden appearance of the cops. I can't explain why it was all right for Mr. Sicko to know the truth of Adis but not the police.

"Oh, dear, your tone suggests that the police have arrived." I felt the familiar weight of a hand on my shoulder. Tom had also let Adis in. "Pity that we will have to cut this short. Don't bother trying to track my position, I'll just tell you now. Leah will recognize the address; I am at 4509 Madison trail, and Jim Lee's cell service is AT&T. They will confirm it. I'll just leave his phone on." I heard him put the phone down and then suddenly pick it up. "My goodness, I almost forgot my message. Are you ready, are they listening?"

"Yes, you are on a speaker phone," I said.

"Good, good. Let me apologize in advance for my dramatics, but I can't help myself. Sometimes an audience is required for my work to reach its fullest potential." Once again Mr. Sicko struck me as odd. "Now, write this down." He waited a beat. "Two." The phone was put down a second time, and for a couple of seconds I could hear receding footsteps and then there was nothing but silence.

I looked over to Leah and she was white as a sheet. She backed into the sink and steadied herself with both hands. I was as confused with her reaction as I was with Mr. Sicko's message. "Amber Lee is eight years old," she said, and suddenly I understood.

By the time I put my phone down, both cops were on theirs in our dining room as the three remaining adults stared and waited for confirmation. Cop #1 walked back into the kitchen. "As best that we can tell right now he was telling the truth. The call is coming from the Sidewinder subdivision."

It took almost ten more minutes before Cop #2 confirmed the worst. Kim and Jim Lee were found sitting in their front porch swing, both dead from some unknown cause. Neither had a mark on them. Their daughter, Amber, was missing.

Chapter Twelve

X X

"ARE YOU ALL RIGHT?" LEAH ASKED ME. Her face was defiant. A madman had just threatened to take our daughter and then demonstrated his bona fides by killing two people and taking their daughter. She was determined that that was not going to happen to us. Leah is a complex person, to say the least, and although I personally will pay for what I'm about to say (if she ever reads this), just for a moment I want to share what twenty-five years has taught me about this woman.

Like most of us, she is a mixture of her parents, but not an amalgam. She is either her mother, the sweetest, most emotional person I have ever met, or she is her father, analytical and focused. Most of the time she favors her mother, but during those weeks and months when Adis and the outside world intruded upon our happy lives, she borrowed heavily from her father. She had mastered the art of sublimation. In chemistry, sublimation is the process in which a substance passes directly from the solid phase to the gas phase without passing through an intermediate liquid phase. In psychoanalytic theory, sublimation is the process in which a person diverts or modifies an instinctual impulse into a culturally higher or socially more acceptable activity (I borrowed the last sentence from Google). Mr. Sicko had forced Leah to pass from her more typical ethereal state of random thoughts and emotions into a more substantial, solid focused state (for those of you who are purists, this would in fact be a reverse sublimation), and at the same time forced her to redirect the fear and terror he was purposefully creating into a set of focused and determined actions.

I, on the other hand, had sublimated in the classic sense. Normally, I am the solid, focused one, but at that moment I was feeling so overwhelmed that I could barely think straight. My thoughts were flying through space, banging into each other, and ricocheting off in all directions. Just like the molecules of a gas.

"Oh, yeah, I'm just fine." My sarcasm wasn't directed at her, and I reached for her hand. I needed to hold something of substance. "Just peachy. I need to sit for a moment," I added, and we walked into the living room.

Adis had already settled into one of the two easy chairs that faced our sectional. His face and entire countenance was serene. Unfazed, unmoved, unaffected by the deaths of two people we had known and unwittingly put in the crosshairs of a madman. "Please, why don't both of you sit and let's talk."

I almost thanked him for inviting us to sit in our own sofa. "Do you know this . . . person?" I struggled with the description of Mr. Sicko as a person. "Is he one of . . . you?" I struggled with the description of Adis even more.

"No. He is definitely not like me. My guess is that he is just a man. A clever man." Adis uncrossed his legs and sat up in the chair.

"Well, can you do something now?" Leah's question was an undisguised accusation. I knew that she was blaming Adis's inaction as much as she blamed herself for the deaths of the Lees.

He stared at Leah and I realized that Adis rarely if ever blinked. The moment stretched, and finally he answered, "Not yet." Leah nearly catapulted out of the sofa, but before she started her rant Adis silenced her with a raised hand. "This is a very complex situation. As I told your husband, there is much more at stake than the lives of the two girls and the deaths of your friends." His voice was firm but not aggressive. Leah continued to stand but for the moment remained silent. "Please sit down and listen to all that I have to say." My wife slowly sat next to me. "I promise to level with you as much as I can, but allow me to do it in a manner that is most constructive."

"Let's start with who you are," Leah fired back, ignoring his request.

"Aside from a few peculiarities, I am not much different from either of you. I breathe, I eat, I sleep. I bleed." He nodded towards me, acknowledging how we first met. I remember being disappointed with his admission. I had pinned a great deal of hope on the chest of this strange man, and I wanted a superhero, or an alien, or possibly an angel. I didn't want someone with a few peculiarities. "I am the man nobody sees or remembers; at least, I had been until recently." He smiled, but his charm was once again lost on Leah.

"So, you are some kind of behind-the-scene angel that stops people from killing teenagers and burning old people," Leah said with impatience. "But the kidnapping of children is outside of your lines," she added.

"Only rarely," Adis answered, ignoring her sarcasm. "And I am certainly not an angel."

"Who do you work for?" Leah pressed.

"That is a good question, only I don't know the answer." I believed him, but then again I believed pretty much everything he said. Leah was a little more discriminating.

"You claim to have lived thousands of years, working behind the scenes for someone or something unknown? Do you expect me to believe that?"

Adis paused a beat and I watched him study my wife. "I know what I'm working for."

Leah returned his stare and I waited for her to ask the obvious question, but maybe it was only obvious to me because she went on to something else. "Who tells you what to do?"

They stared at each other for a moment, completely oblivious to my presence. Adis paused, and I watched Leah's right hand open and close. It was a sign I had learned to recognize years before we were married. A bad sign that foretold of the appearance of Angry Leah (similar to the Hulk, only prettier).

Adis's eyes drifted down to Leah's fidgeting hand. "Who tells me what to do?" he repeated. "That is a question that would take some time to answer, so let me say simply that no one directly tells me what to do."

I had the impression that he was about to expand on his answer, but Leah couldn't wait. "If no one tells you what to do, why don't you find Mr. Sicko and stick a knife in his neck? I think that most people would see that as an excellent utilization of your skill set." Apparently, Adis's celebrated execution style had struck a chord with her as well.

"There are a number of reasons why that could be a very significant mistake." Adis's expression became grave.

"How? How could killing a man who has kidnapped children and killed the innocent be a mistake?" Leah fired back.

"Because none of us know the consequences of that action. Our universe has only a few enduring truths, and one of the most important is that actions have consequences." Adis's voice lost all its usual soft, persuasive quality and now had an edge to it.

"That's obvious. No one can possibly predict all the consequences of any action. That is a defining characteristic of the human condition, but that can't excuse inaction in the face of a clear moral choice. That's another enduring truth."

"Maybe your eyes are better than mine, because I have always had a hard time seeing clear moral choices. If you stumble across a young man being attacked by a group of ruffians do you walk on by and ignore it? Or do you try and intervene by calling the police or perhaps taking a more direct approach?"

"I hope I would intervene," I said rejoining the conversation.

"And if that man is a lanky seventeen-year-old outside a bar in San Diego in 1957?"

I tried in vain to think of what historic figure I was or was not going to save. "I would, and you are about to tell me why that would be a mistake."

"It was a mistake." We waited for more but he moved on. "You asked me how killing this man would be a mistake and I've given you the answer, but it doesn't make much sense unless I put it in context." He spoke directly to Leah.

"All right, explain," she answered.

"There is a natural flow to all human events. A determinism that resists change."

"The obdurate future," I said almost unconsciously. It was a phrase from a Stephen King book that had stuck with me.

"An excellent description. The obdurate future." Adis repeated.

"What the hell does that mean?" my lovely wife asked.

"Imagine a mathematic equation so complex and inter-related that every time one variable is altered all the other variables are affected and the answer never changes," Adis answered, a smile starting to re-form.

"Determinism," I said. "The future defends itself."

"Precisely," Adis answered quickly, excited that I was catching on.

"Look, if you two want to have a private conversation I'll just go and find this son of a bitch myself, otherwise use plain English and tell me what math equations and determinism have to do with killing this bastard." Leah had shifted to the edge of her seat.

It may have been that Adis was beaming me psychic messages, but I suddenly saw the answer to Leah's question. "Because Adis may not be able to kill this bastard. The obdurate future would prevent it."

Adis nodded and Leah slapped her forehead with her hand.

"Of course, the obdurate future. I totally forgot that our destiny is predetermined. All of human history, the wars, famines, hatred, everything we do or have done, every decision we make has been scripted in advance by God. For a moment, I foolishly believed that we were all endowed with free will and self-determination, but then I remembered that we're all robots simply following our programming, and free will is merely an illusion." Leah's voice was pure derision.

"I understand your sarcasm. This is a difficult concept." Adis leaned towards Leah. "Let me make a couple of points and then hopefully things will begin to make sense." Thankfully, Leah held her tongue and simply nodded her assent. "I have come to believe that the ultimate destiny for humanity is a fixed point. Nothing you, I, or anyone else can do will change that."

"All right," Leah said tentatively.

"The path that is taken to reach that point is left for mankind to decide. Think of a boat carrying six billion people down a wide river. You decide whether to bounce off the rocky shoreline, to run the wild rapids, or to float calmly in the midstream."

"Go on," she said irritably, obviously frustrated with Adis's piecemeal approach.

"Your future is yours to determine, both individually and collectively, but no matter what that future is the boat still moves downstream."

"So now we are back to predestiny," Leah countered.

Adis shook his head. "Predestiny does not exist except at a level far beyond this discussion. Man must determine his own destiny." He shifted in his chair and tried a different approach. "Isaac Newton's third law of motion is that for every action there is an equal and opposite reaction. Perhaps it's not always obvious, but human actions are balanced by human reactions, and the result is balance, a straight line towards the inevitable. The beauty of the world, the majesty and magic of all this—" he swept his arms around the room "—is that it is all done naturally, fluidly, and without violating the principles of free will and self-determination. Your world is created largely by the free, unencumbered decisions and actions made by each of you."

"Unless of course some wacko decides to attack a high school, in which case someone like you may show up and violate their free will with extreme prejudice." Leah matched Adis's lean, but not in an attempt to close their philosophical differences.

"Free, unencumbered decisions and actions made by each of you," Adis repeated, with emphasis placed on his first two words. A light seemed to go on in Leah's mind, and she retreated back into the sofa. "I am prevented from interceding in most situations, no matter how heinous, by the laws that govern my existence and the universe's fail-safe mechanism, the obdurate future."

"The obdurate future," Leah said dramatically. "What does that even mean?"

"As you have rightly pointed out, any action I take has the potential to violate an individual's right to free-will . . ."

"And, as recent events have shown, the right to life and liberty," Leah said under her breath.

"Exactly. Anything that interferes with humanity's right to self-determination is met with resistance. In the case of the high school, I was that resistance."

"So that's your job. You are a tool of the obdurate future?" I asked.

"Think of it as a side job. My daytime job is to prevent small problems from becoming big problems. It's all rather innocuous and, until recently, anonymous. I redirect a person so that they miss a phone call, or buy the last magazine in a rack. Little things that in the course of time have great effect."

Leah eyed him suspiciously. "I thought you said that the future is decided by free and unencumbered decisions and actions. It sounds like you are stacking the deck. Steering us. Limiting our options and choices. That doesn't sound free or unencumbered."

Adis took a long breath. "On occasion an individual will do something that for this discussion I will label as unexpected, which will initiate a sequence of events that ultimately lead to, shall we say, an adverse, unintended outcome. My role is to interrupt that sequence."

"Unintended," Leah repeated as a challenge, but Adis simply stared at her.

"Which brings up two issues," I said interrupting their staring contest which had started to make me uncomfortable. "First, we are not truly the masters of our own destiny. You limit our options and choices. Second, your obdurate future has some holes. You, a nonhuman, are able to influence the future."

Again, Adis drew a frustrated long breath. "It is possible for me to influence the future by limiting your options and choices, but you must acknowledge that your choices are limited from the moment you first draw breath. Every day your choices are limited by the decisions of others, by chance, by the weather. It is another one of the defining characteristics of the human condition. What I do can be viewed as another example of random fate."

"Except it's not random," I answered.

"Without it, most of your species would not have survived the twentieth century." He answered so fast that I'm sure he had set me up.

"So if I understand correctly," Leah started after a long thoughtful moment, "you are saying that Mr. Sicko is just a human and therefore off-limits. He's making his own decisions and no matter what those decisions are the universe is okay with them. But over here we have someone else, someone like you, who is running around burning church busses and getting crazy people to attack schools, which is why you get to run in and save the day. Is that about it?"

Adis hesitated. "That is one possibility."

"Damn it," Leah screamed. "Do you know it's impossible to get a straight answer from you?"

"Yes I do," Adis answered quickly. His levity did little to appease my wife.

"You know, I am getting tired of this shit." I put my hand on hers and she tolerated it for exactly one second before she brushed away not just my hand but any attempt at nonverbal communication. "Don't! I'm angry. Two of our friends are dead, two girls are missing! The bastard took our dog and is threatening to take our daughter, and you and this—" she made a dismissive gesture towards Adis "—whatever you are, sit here calmly discussing philosophy." She glared at me and then turned to glare at Adis. "If you know who this bastard is, or where he is, and don't tell someone, even if that means violating your precious laws or pissing off the obdurate future, then you are responsible for whatever he does next!" Her finger jabbed the air in his direction. She was on her feet. Her face was a lovely shade of crimson and she was breathing as hard as our dog on a hot day.

It was my role to step in. I couldn't let this devolve into a screaming argument, and we were at least halfway there. It is probably true that the behavior of all wives is different when their spouse is present, and my wife is not an exception (I know this sounds sexist, so to make everyone feel better I also believe that this truism applies to husbands). Leah had allowed her emotions to outpace her intellect because she had the luxury of knowing that when she went too far I would reel her in. If it had just been the two of them she would have put on her cold, calculating face and they would have had a cold, calculating conversation. "Leah, please, calm down. This isn't helping." She turned away from Adis, gave me a withering look and then, just like one of our children, threw her hands in the air, whispered, "Fine," and stomped into the kitchen and began to pace.

I gave the air a moment to clear and then turned back to Adis. "So there are others like you?"

"There are others like me and others that are different," he answered in his frustratingly cryptic manner.

"You know, I'm starting to see Leah's point about straight answers," I said.

"You are making the assumption that I have all the answers. I don't. I do know that that there are beings similar to me and beings dissimilar to me. I have seen evidence of their handiwork, and there are times when I am called upon to address that handiwork."

"So we are talking about beings that are . . ." I hesitated because I knew the next word would set off Leah. Adis had no such qualms.

"Evil. It's Ok to say it out loud." Adis smiled at me.

Leah has always had a fairly wide liberal streak, and to my mind a tendency to embrace moral relativism (unless of course her family is threatened). Evil is a word that precludes any possibility of redemption, and she has trouble with that concept. A small but significant part of my professional life is devoted to picking up the pieces after inexplicable, and unfathomable acts of violence. Evil by any other name. It does exist, and unlike Leah I don't have the luxury of dismissing it as nothing more than a left wing punchline. After the Aurora, Colorado, shootings in 2012, a writer for *The New Yorker,* Rollo Romig, wrote an article titled 'What Do We Mean By *Evil*?' Anything I would say about evil he has already said so I would recommend finding the article and reading it.

"Evil?" She repeated with derision.

"As I was growing up, I tended to discount the idea as well. That all things were relative, that people just need to be understood. In time I found that even after being understood some people are simply evil, and that doesn't change when you are on my side of the divide. Until now, the closest you have ever been to true evil is a phone call. When you come face-to-face with it you may rethink your position."

That seemed to tame Leah for all of ten seconds. "Why don't we get back to your handiwork? Tell us about Lee Harvey Oswald?" Leah asked—or, more appropriately, accused—from the kitchen.

It took me a few seconds to catch on to her reference. "The lanky seventeen-year-old in San Diego," I said dumbly. I could feel Leah's irritated look on my neck. This was what we in our family call a 'unibrow moment.' When Tom, our son was about eight, we took him to a theater to see *Austin Powers*—I don't remember if this was the sequel or the original—and one of the characters is introduced as Uni Brow, and indeed she had one midline eyebrow. The theater chuckled and then became silent. About twenty seconds later, when it was dead quiet, Tom says in a voice that carried across the theater, "Oh, I get it. Unibrow!" The theater erupted in laughter and he has not lived it down since.

"That was a mistake on our part, and the world paid the price for it," Adis admitted after he gave my epiphany a few moments of silence. If you are wondering, as I was, in 1957 a very young Lee Harvey Oswald was involved in a drunken altercation outside a San Diego bar. He was very nearly beaten to death and would have been, save for the involvement of an unidentified man.

"Where was the obdurate future then?" Leah's voice was almost triumphant. "I thought that it was supposed to protect us from the likes of you?"

"That event should serve as a caution to all those who would act before thinking." Adis said without ever really answering Leah's question.

"So when shit happens do we look to you and those of your kind who act recklessly, or maybe to your evil boogiemen, or simply blame the obdurate future for not being obdurate enough? Or maybe because you forgot to realign the world's chakras?" I feel I need to explain my wife's aggressive and caustic behavior. In all the years we have been together, I have on very rare occasion been witness to this rather unattractive side of her personality. As a rule, she manages to hide it well, but the recent stress had begun to erode her control.

"No. Shit happens because the vast majority of time man keeps making shit happen," Adis shot back. It was clear that Leah had touched a sore subject. "It's not my role to stop it from happening."

"Why? If you can see what is going on and have the power to change it, why don't you?" Leah asked the ancient question of why bad things were allowed to happen. Of course, Adis had already explained why, but there was no way I was going to say that to Leah while her emotions were in overdrive.

"It is not my role to correct your mistakes," Adis said point-edly. "In fact, it is not my role to protect you from mistakes not of your own making." Those two sentences, spoken clearly and without a trace of emotion, completely changed my perspective of Adis. He really wasn't one of us.

"Then why are you here? It seems to me that your role should be finding your evil counterpart." She had walked back into the family room and sat on the arm of our sofa, something I am not allowed to do. "In fact, didn't you tell us that you didn't see the bus fire coming? Why were you at the bridge?"

"To keep you safe," he said, and then no one said anything for nearly a minute. "Why do you think he took your dog?"

If I could have turned to Leah I would have, but all I could do was blink at the whiplash-inducing shift in our conversation. "Why did he keep Nitrox alive?" I asked, completely perplexed. I will admit that I never once asked myself or anyone else why Mr. Sicko would kill the Dale's small, eminently portable dog and take our large, eminently unportable dog. "Why *did* he keep Nitrox alive?" I repeated as I suddenly realized the importance of that question. In retrospect, it was such an obvious question, one that should have been asked days earlier.

Chapter Thirteen

X X

"To induce terror," Leah answered with a questioning tone. "He sent the picture knowing that the children would see it." She didn't look or sound the least bit confident with her conclusion.

"I'm sure that's a part. Hope is a cruel weapon, and seeing Nitrox alive gives you hope that one day she will come home. But I think there's more," Adis continued with his far-off stare. "We're missing something important."

A small, prepubescent male voice emanating from the dining room interrupted the three of us. "Mr. Sicko wants you to look for him." I'm not sure who Tom had addressed his comment to, but we all looked at each other. I listened as our twelve-year-old walked tentatively into the kitchen with Mia and our oldest daughter Mika in tow. "He probably found out that Nitrox's collar is chipped. Did you forget?"

His question was clearly directed at me, but I had no idea what he was talking about. Adis looked just as puzzled. "What?" I asked Leah as our three children advanced as a unit into the living room.

"Remember when Nitrox was a puppy she kept getting out of the yard?" Mika asked. She was fourteen, and had evolved and devolved into every teenage stereotype, and held a firm belief that her younger siblings were borderline morons (especially her brother) and needed someone intelligent to speak for them, and that her father (me), while useful in some respects, needed an interpreter for all things "modern." "Mom got her a collar with a chip in it that would track her. If it's still working, all we have to do is to call the vet's office and they can give you the number of the chip. Then you call the tracking company and they can tell us where Nitrox is." She raised her cell phone. "Do you want me to get the number?"

"Hold on a minute," Leah announced, and indeed everyone did hold on. "That collar was broken when Tom tried to take it apart." A couple years earlier our son had gone through a phase of dismantling every electrical device he could get his hands on (including my cell phone, the television remote—which was now wrapped in duct tape following Tom's exploratory surgery—and both garage door remotes).

"I think I fixed it," he answered sheepishly. Both his sisters immediately scoffed in the manner of the day (meaning that the phrase "yeah right" was used by both).

"What do you mean, you fixed it?" Leah asked, and I could almost hear the silencing glare Tom shot his two sisters.

"I took the battery and some of the wires from the old Nintendo remote and soldered them into the collar. I got the light to come on, but I didn't have the code so I'm not sure it really works." He was undoubtedly telling the truth, because to admit to using Leah's soldering gun (yes, my wife has a soldering gun as well) was tantamount to suicide-by-mother.

A second followed and we all waited to see which way Leah was going to go. She shook her head. "You were in my workshop," Leah said slowly, menacingly, and yes, my wife also has a workshop.

"It was a long time ago," Tom pleaded, knowing that his mother had no statute of limitation on offenses that involved her workshop.

"Fine." Her answer was as sharp as a razor. "It doesn't matter, I got her a new collar for Christmas, and I threw the old one away," she said with finality. It seemed for the moment that Tom had thrown himself on his sword for nothing.

"I fixed it after you threw it away, then I changed it back around a month ago." Metaphorically, Tom had stood back up and impaled himself a second time. I imagined his sisters backing away from their doomed brother, and Mia thinking that she would finally get Tom's room, which had a tree next to its window.

"You changed it back?"

"I told Dad." Our children's ultimate excuse: place as much of the blame on inattentive Dad. "She didn't like the new collar; it was too fat and made her scratch . . ."

"Okay," I finally said. "We are way off point here. Can we get the number, or code, and find out if the damn thing is working?"

It took almost twenty minutes for Leah and Mika to get the number from the vet's office and exactly one minute to find out that we didn't need anything more than our cell phone to locate the chip. Our children then huddled together around my cell phone and downloaded the app to my Android device (I wanted it on Leah's iPhone, but Apple doesn't support the finding of lost dogs). It took another ten minutes for me to create a user ID and password and then get a confirmatory e-mail. My children and wife offered to do this for me about sixty-seven times after I kept typing in the wrong numbers and letters. At times I really hate cell phones, the Internet, and modern technology in general.

"All right, everyone needs to take a step backwards." I had four people breathing down my neck. Finally, the app pulled up a map of the United States and asked if I wanted to display the location of tracker 26596-01. I stifled my natural response to such an inane question and tapped *Yes*. I wondered who got paid to write that line of code, as a red dot flashed and then a local map appeared. "Oh my God, he really did fix it." I caught a glimpse of Tom, who grew a foot taller in that very instant. "We have a signal. It's only about five or six miles away." My family again surrounded me, trying to get a glimpse of the flashing dot. I was surprised the tracker was so close. A part of me expected that Mr. Sicko would have a longer commute from his evil lair to our sunlit world.

"I think we should call the FBI," Leah said, staring at the map on my phone.

"Probably. Let's use your phone; I don't want to do this again." I walked over to the breakfast bar and carefully put my phone down. Leah found Gordon Anderson's card and called him. I listened as she explained our "eureka" moment, and then as she gave him Nitrox's tracking number. He warned her not to try and follow the signal, and Leah ended the conversation in typical form with a "yeah right."

"He wants us to stay put," she said, collecting her purse and keys. Casually, she retrieved her Sig and slipped it into her purse.

"I heard. I gather we are not going to stay put." I stared as Leah draped the loaded purse across her shoulder.

"Hell no. What do we do with the kids?" Her question prompted all three to start pleading their case. Leah silenced them with a single look. They could read their mother's temperament as well as I.

"Mr. Sicko is out and about. We can't leave them alone. We all either stay here and leave it to the FBI and the police . . ." Instinctively, we both turned to look at the two uniformed officers in our dining room. Both were talking on their phones and neither gave us any degree of confidence. "Or we do it ourselves. Which means taking them."

"All right, but nobody gets out of the car." Normally, Leah is nearly four inches shorter than me, but today we were at eye level. She stared at me with pure determination.

"You know that this is reckless and dangerous." Once again we had flipped roles. Invariably it is Leah who uses those words.

"Being methodical and safe hasn't helped us so far," she said, and her stare was unwavering. She was going, and would not be dissuaded. In that moment, she was one hundred percent her father. "Besides, Anderson will probably get there before us."

"Mr. Sicko will recognize our car." I was feeling some of her recklessness and ready to follow her, but as I was playing her part today I had to say all my lines and state the obvious.

"Then God help him." She turned towards the garage. "Are you coming?" she asked Adis, who had silently watched our exchange.

"Of course."

Five minutes later, the six of us were situated in Leah's Denali and backing out of our driveway. Our three children had one of their typical discussions about who would sit next to Adis (Leah decreed that all three would sit together in the back seat while Adis would sit alone in the middle row, and if they continued to argue she would make them hold hands—the ultimate in punishments). I looked back at our house and found the two police officers running for their car.

Leah drove and kept muttering some variation of "I can't believe I didn't think of this." I navigated us through the familiar streets of south Austin and then out into the hill country. Everyone was quiet, respecting Leah's determined and hair-trigger mood.

"Nitrox is still wearing her collar in Mom's Facebook photograph," Mika said softly, and then passed her cell phone up to me. Our dog looked terrible, but her wide red collar was clear.

"Oh, shit," Leah said, after I told her to take a right-hand turn. The trees around us were fairly dense, and we nearly missed the sign announcing that we had arrived at Sidewinder Enclave, homes from the $800s. A gate stood open in front of us, and at least twenty police, CSI, and medical vehicles blocked our way.

"Goddamn it," I whispered.

"I was worried about this," Adis said.

"Isn't this where Amber lives?" Mia asked.

A uniformed officer rapped on Leah's window. "Yes, it's where the Lees live," she said, lowering the window.

My name, along with our very famous passenger, allowed us admittance. We were directed to park just in front of the Lees' house and we all piled out. Detective Sharpe appeared moments later and asked if he could have a word with Adis and me. My cell phone told me that we were feet from the GPS tracker.

I followed as Adis and Sharpe walked to a park bench. Adis sat and Sharpe stood over him, waiting for me to catch up.

"Following a dog collar," Sharpe said without any introduction. He motioned to a uniformed officer. "Get me the collar," he said gruffly. Sharpe was in a mood. "Does this belong to your dog?" Of course it did, and I nodded. "Do you want to sit down?" I must have looked like death warmed over (it's an expression my mother uses). I sat next to Adis; now Sharpe stood over both of us. "You could have let us know about this earlier."

I explained that we had just remembered that Nitrox had a tracker. I was thinking, and I'm sure everyone else had the same thought, that if we had remembered this earlier the Lees might still be alive.

"We found it on top of their daughter's dresser. He had taken it apart and put in a new battery. He even called the tracking service to make sure that it was still registered."

"So he knew about the tracker all along." Now Adis stated the obvious.

"One step ahead." Sharpe shook his head. "You are Mr. Adis?" He offered his hand.

"Just Adis." They shook.

"We met briefly a couple weeks ago." Sharpe shifted his feet. This had to be awkward for the detective. He had been trying to track down any information about Adis for weeks, suspecting all along that the old man was somehow involved with the high school shootings, these kidnappings, and quite possibly the Lindbergh baby kidnapping. My official police statement made things even more suspicious when I said that it was Adis who had opened the door to the burning bus, although very few people actually believed me. "You look surprisingly good. Surprisingly unburned." He smiled. "Can I ask what you are doing here?"

"I am a family friend." Adis offered nothing more.

"Are you a runner as well?" Sharpe was being a first rate asshole for my benefit.

"Only when I'm being chased." Adis smiled. "I'm guessing you haven't found any physical evidence, Detective?"

"None. Just the collar." There was a subtle shift in Sharpe's tone, an undercurrent of compliance.

"Can you show me where you found it? I will of course understand if you are unable." Adis voice was smooth and supple, and even though it wasn't directed at me I began to feel its narcotic effect.

"I don't see why not. I will ask that you not contaminate anything." Sharpe turned and started up the driveway. Adis followed, and I followed Adis after giving Leah and the kids a quick glance.

We stopped briefly on the porch. I expected to find tape outlining where the Lees had been found, but there was nothing. The same wooden swing I had seen on a half dozen occasions swung lazily in the spring breeze.

Adis silently stared at the swing. "They didn't die here," he finally said. I looked at him and half expected to see his hands suspended in a caricature of the TV detective Adrian Monk, but Adis's arms hung at his side. After a few more quiet moments I got the impression that he was trying to see through time and watch as Mr. Sicko placed each body. Sharpe seemed content to watch the elderly man. "Shall we?" Adis finally said, and he flipped his smile back on.

Sharpe led us through the house that I knew well. The Lees were people that I very much liked, and I physically felt their absence as I walked into their living room. For a moment I let Sharpe and Adis go on ahead as I paused by a Beladora lamp table (I actually researched the name of this piece of furniture in honor of the Lees). The Lees had a simple, elegant style, not garish or popular, just elegant. Every time we visited, I was struck by how different their house was from ours. We basically had all the same stuff—couches, chairs, knickknacks—but their stuff always seemed to be properly placed and new, while our stuff was usually a little askew and covered in a thin veneer of something I have come to call "children." I had worked with Jim

Lee on hundreds of different cases, and his steady hands and decades of experience had allowed us to do some extraordinary work (for which I was usually given an inordinate amount of credit). And I liked him. Genuinely. To this day I wish more had been done to avenge his death (he of course would counter with *To what end?*).

"Are you done in the child's room?" Sharpe asked an assembly of CSI technicians.

"We are done with the house," a bald man said after a moment's hesitation.

"Thank you," Adis answered, and the CSI team suddenly and collectively recognized the famous man. A few started towards him and others started to whisper. "Can I ask you gentlemen a favor?"

A jumble of *yes, certainly* and the like followed. The group of men began to encircle Adis. Sharpe and I stood outside it.

"I would like to borrow your watches for a small experiment." The eight men eagerly stripped off their watches, and Adis lead them to the fireplace mantel. "Now if each of you could lay your watch along here." Each man in turn arranged his watch until eight watches faced Adis. "Thank you. One last thing before I begin. Can you tell me how long you have been here, in this house?"

"We arrived—" I guessed the bald guy was the lead technician, because he again answered "—two hours and thirty-three minutes ago."

"You must have done a thorough job." Adis smiled and the eight men smiled back. I could have been hacking detective Sharpe to death and not one of them would have noticed. Adis turned back to the row of watches and withdrew his own watch from his pants pocket. For the next eight minutes he silently compared each watch with his own. All ten of us stared as he went from watch to watch never saying a word or giving any indication of what he was doing. "Thank you gentlemen. I'm all done." Adis walked over to where Sharpe and I were standing. "Can I see Amber's room?"

"Of course. Can I ask you what that was all about?" Sharpe was still suffering from the Adis-effect.

"I was looking for temporal irregularities on mechanical and electrical devices caused by recent quantum displacements. I just have one more test and then I'll be done. "

Sharpe nodded with a look of complete confusion and then led us through a hallway covered in family pictures. Adis touch a few in passing. "This is the little girl's room," Sharpe said after entering the neatest, cleanest, pinkest child's bedroom I had ever seen. I wanted to take a picture of it and show our eight-year-old that a child can exist in a clean environment without having her creativity stifled.

"Detective, her name is Amber Lee," Adis said without a trace of emotion. Had that been my comment it would likely have included at least one of the seven words you can't say on TV (unless you have cable).

"Of course." His voice was apologetic. "We found the dog's tracker here." He pointed to a desk that was more organized than my operating room.

Adis glanced at the desk and then walked to Amber's television and turned the set on. "How do we get an on-air channel?" I found the remote and hit several buttons until a car commercial popped on. The signal strength was poor and the image kept disappearing. "Can you put it on a channel that is not broadcasting?" I kept hitting the channel button until nothing but electrical snow appeared. As an aside, and completely unrelated to Amber Lee, her parents, Adis, or this story is the fact that the electric snow, or static, is largely produced by electromagnetic signals prompted by cosmic microwave background radiation, which as we all know is the residual thermal energy (heat) from the big bang that created the universe. So if you find yourself with some time, click on the television and watch the big bang.

"Is this the other test?" Sharpe asked, and he sounded a little, for lack of a better word, dumb.

Adis ignored him and studied the random pattern of dots. I told myself that if a little blonde girl appeared at the door saying "they're here," I was out of there.

After a minute Adis stood up. "All right. I think I've seen everything." He smiled and presented his hand to Sharpe, who reflexively shook it. "I will be getting out of your hair. It was nice to meet you again. I'm sure we will be seeing each other soon." Adis turned and worked his way out of the Lees' house and walked back to Leah and our children without once turning back. I hurried along behind him, and about halfway down the drive way we lost Sharpe. Gordon Anderson and a trio of black-suited men surrounded my family. Anderson looked like he was lecturing Leah, almost certainly about her rash behavior. She looked completely uninterested in his opinion.

Adis walked up to Leah and gave her cheek a peck and then climbed into the car. All three of our children started laughing. For about half a second Leah had the most adorable look of confusion, which was then replaced by a look of embarrassment, which immediately transformed into irritation with her chortling children. "Get in the car," she demanded. She glanced at me with a look that warned me not to say anything.

"Well?" Leah asked after we had driven past the police.

"Basically, we just looked the place over," I said after Adis had left the question hanging. I could feel her disappointment and frustration.

Mika and Tom both asked rapid-fire questions that went unanswered after Leah gave them a glare just before she turned on the highway. She floored the Denali, throwing everyone back into their seats. Fortunately, it was a short ride home.

As the garage door began its ascent, Adis spoke. "I wonder if I could have a few minutes alone with your parents?" He addressed the backseat, and our three children all agreed, uncharacteristically, without a single question.

Chapter Fourteen
X X

LEAH LED US TO MY STUDY AND THEN SAT IN MY DESK CHAIR. Her frustration filled the small room, but before she could launch into her rant I stopped her. "Leah, wait just a few minutes." I filled her in on everything Adis and I had done; basically, it was just what Adis had done. I turned to him. "All right, tell me what all the watch stuff and television stuff was about."

Adis sat next to me on my old favorite couch, taking the seat closest to the window. He ignored my question for several seconds and simply stared out at our front lawn. "The world was so much easier when I was younger. Simple. Clear. Maybe not as convenient, but easier to grasp and understand. We all saw things in black and white, and then color and shades came into the world."

Leah and I exchanged a glance. I mouthed the word *what?* and she shrugged her shoulders.

"You can both relax. I'm not losing it; I'm just trying to wrap my mind around—" he turned back to us—"Around every-thing." He took a deep breath and stared through Leah, who was in his direct line of sight. "I don't like the term Mr. Sicko. It makes him sound like a comic book villain."

"So you found out who he is? He's just a man?" Leah asked. Unfortunately, her questions did little to change Adis's pensive, introspective mood.

"The Greek goddess of strife and discord was called Eris. Centuries later it became a given name for males. Why don't we rename him Eris?" He looked at both of us and we nodded our agreement. Frankly, neither one of us cared what we called this guy. "I'm sorry, dear, but you asked me a question. Is Eris a man, or more properly, a human?" He seemed to refocus on Leah. "Oh, yes, he is most definitely human. But he is not the one we need to focus on." His words hung in the air.

"So you found the one responsible for the bus fire?" It was one of those rare times when I beat Leah to the punch.

"Responsible?" It sounded like he didn't understand the word. "Yes, ultimately he is responsible." He was at least responding directly to us, but he still seemed distant, distracted, and frustratingly cryptic. I glanced over at Leah, and as usual from her expression I could tell she was moments away from shaking Adis back to our reality.

"Come on, Adis. This is like pulling teeth. Tell us what you know, or at least what you think you know. What did all that stuff with the watches tell you?" I said just as Leah drew an audible, exasperated breath.

"How well do you understand the theory of relativity and quantum mechanics?" He turned to me and I was relieved to find that he had clued back into the moment, as his patented smile had returned.

"Oh, Christ! Skip the academic lesson and tell us what you know." My loving wife had reached the end of her rope and needed to shoot something.

"All right, but you'll be missing out on one of the universe's most beautiful secrets." His smile dropped a fraction, but I could understand Leah's impatience. Now was not the time for a science lecture. As an aside, I also understood his disappointment. I've had many similar moments when I wanted to explain some technical nuance to Leah or my parents, or on occasion to a patient, something that I think is truly fascinating, only to find that my audience is completely uninterested and annoyed with my attempt.

"I'll risk it," she answered sarcastically. "Just fast forward to the end and tell us what it all means."

"All right," he sounded a little disappointed. "What it means is that the situation is more complicated than what we had appreciated earlier. More complicated and more personal."

"It's always been personal to us. Can you simply tell us what you know in nontechnical terms?" Leah was gripping the arms of my desk chair hard enough to whiten her knuckles.

"Just like you, Eris is a man and as such could not create the temporal irregularities that I felt and then confirmed with the watches and television." He had turned to me at this point.

"What is a temporal irregularity?" Through gritted teeth, Leah enunciated each syllable slowly.

"I need to first give you some background." Leah immediately reacted and Adis cut her off. "I will be brief." She retreated, slightly. "A temporal irregularity, as its name implies, is an irregularity in time. To be a little more precise, in space-time, because as we all know they are in fact the same entity."

Leah was a humanities major in college. I would have been shocked if she could identify all the variables in Einstein's famous $e=mc^2$ equation. Her life did not exist in the very large scale of relativity or in the very small scale of quantum mechanics. In her world, space and time were two very separate entities. "Skip the physics, and tell me who this bastard is!"

Adis did something that I had not been able to do in twenty-five years: he ignored Leah. "Someone with the ability to manipulate quantum singularities was at the Lees' house today."

I was a science major and can name all the variables in Einstein's equation. Not only that, but I love reading about the ongoing struggle to unlock one of the last great scientific mysteries, how to link Einstein's equations, which describe the universe's very large objects (stars, galaxies, etc.) with quantum mechanics, which describes the universe at the subatomic level (it's a very weird theory that describes the nature of matter as both wave-like and particle-like; don't laugh, this theory is directly responsible for the development of most modern technology). A quantum singularity would not only bridge the gap between these two contradictory theories, but actually merge them into one theory of everything. "Quantum singularities?" I said with disbelief.

"Stop!" Leah yelled. "Stay on point. No esoteric discussions." Humanity majors use the word *esoteric* a lot.

"You told us earlier that you thought someone else was involved, someone like you, otherwise you wouldn't have been able to save those high school kids or those old people on the bus. Now, you're saying he's involved with Maggie Dale, and the Lees. With us." I wanted him to said it out loud because the implications were clear. "So you are certain he's someone like you?" Which, according to Adis' explanation of the rules should free him to go fetch Maggie Dale, Amber Lee and our dog, but only after he put a nine-inch combat blade into some soft part of Mr. Sicko. Both Leah and I exchanged a glance filled with hope.

Now Adis became thoughtful. "That remains to be seen. Let's say that it is someone with similar abilities." He looked away from Leah and his expression flipped. In an instant he changed from a pensive old man to someone capable of killing three men half his age. "Only once before have I met someone like this, and he was too young to be of any use. This person is different. This one is . . . formidable."

"So you're excited about this because he represents a challenge?" Leah reacted to both his statement and sudden transformation. "This isn't some pissing contest between superheroes. This is about our lives, and our children's lives!" Leah looked furious, but her tone was controlled and full of venom. "I need some air." She abruptly shot from her chair, which careened into the wall, and then stormed out of the room. A cloud of plaster fell from the wall to the carpet.

An awkward moment followed, and when it was clear she wasn't coming back I scooted over to the desk chair so I could face Adis. "Tell me this isn't a case of sibling rivalry."

"No, it's not. Leah misunderstood. This other person, let's call him Sida for the sake of convenience, creates the same temporal irregularity I create, which means that he is from my side of the divide."

"Do you have any idea why he's doing this?"

"I know nothing beyond the fact that he can produce the same temporal irregularities I use." He stared through me for a long moment, and when his eyes refocused Adis-the-avenger was gone. "The universe is far more complex than either of us could possibly understand, and most of its inner workings and secrets are hidden. For you and your kind, everything is open to discovery; you are only limited by your ingenuity. It is different for me. I live my life with blinders on, and learn only through experience. It has always been so." He sounded sad and lonely.

I almost said that I was sorry, but I wanted to get the conversation back on track. "So this is a new experience for you?"

"Oh, yes, this is a new experience for me." He did perk up a little.

"So it's possible he is just another one of 'you'?" I pride myself in how well I can communicate.

"It is definitely possible. Symmetry is a property woven through the fabric of the universe. I am here, why couldn't he be here?" Most of his answer was directed at me, but I think he was also trying to convince himself.

"Sida is Adis spelled backward. Is this your way of saying that he is your opposite? Yin to your yang."

He returned his gaze to our front yard. He wasn't being evasive, more contemplative. "No. I flipped my name around only to be clever." His smile was weak. "Although the property of polarity is also woven into the fabric of the universe." His voice trailed off, and I got the sense that my questions were bothering him. We sat in silence for an uncomfortable (at least for me) moment. "It is possible that he has a professional responsibility opposite my own. That would explain his interest in Eris." He finally answered the question I had asked a moment earlier, although he sounded less than convincing.

"But you don't believe that," I countered, but he had again retreated inside himself.

"I don't know what to think," he finally said after what seemed like minutes. Then, in an instant, his happy face dropped back into place, hiding all his inner workings, secrets, and turmoil.

Before I could follow up, the door opened and Leah walked back into the small study. She silently stared at me in my chair.

"Here, why don't you sit here." I rotated back to the couch. She took my chair and spun it towards Adis. It was obvious that she was still mad, but the small break had given her a chance to regain her equilibrium. "Better?" I asked, and she nodded.

"Sorry. I don't like losing control, especially in front of strangers." I'm not sure if she put emphasis on her last word or if I just heard it that way. "I need you to answer some questions, directly and as succinctly as possible. No stories, no lectures. Can you do that?" She held Adis's gaze.

"I will do my best." Adis slowly leaned towards Leah as he spoke. For a moment I thought he was going to reach for her hands.

"This person, the one who does this temporal stuff . . ."

"Let's call him Sida," Adis interrupted.

"You and your names," she sneered, and I thought that his small interruption was enough to push her over the edge again. "This Sida character is different from Eris, correct?"

"Yes."

"Is he the one responsible for the high school and the bus fire?"

"Probably." Adis seemed to be responding well to the rapid exchange.

"And now he's somehow hooked up with Mr. Sicko—"

"Eris," both Adis and I said in unison, which made Leah shake her head.

"Okay, Eris. They have some type of relationship?"

Now Adis paused. "Not in the traditional sense. In fact I doubt that they have even met. It's even possible that Eris is unaware of Sida."

"So Sida isn't helping him?" She sounded disappointed and confused.

"No, that doesn't necessarily follow. Sida could be working behind the scenes, creating opportunities for Eris, maybe cleaning up after him, but never actually influencing his decisions."

"Wait. If Sida is steering Eris, or allowing him to be successful, that should count for something."

"I'm afraid it doesn't. If Eris is acting freely, he is beyond my reach."

Under my breath I muttered half a dozen curse words aimed at Sida, Adis, the universe, and even God. "Do you know if he is acting freely? I mean, do you have anything tangible, or just impressions?"

Adis nodded. "If Sida was guiding Eris, I would have known. I would be free to act."

I dropped my head and now I wanted to shoot something. For two full minutes I thought that we had found our way out of this nightmare. That Adis would at any moment jump to his feet, say his final goodbye and be off to dispatch Eris and his master. I muttered a few more comments that would make my mother blush and then kicked the legs of the couch for good measure. The three of us sat in a strained silence until Leah had recovered enough of herself to restart the conversation.

"What could Sida hope to gain by helping a man like Eris kill and kidnap, not to mention attack schools and burn busses?"

"That's an excellent question, and one I will ask him when I find him, but right now I don't know." Adis looked out our window and I got the distinct impression that he was flirting around the edges of the truth. Leah must have had the same sense, because she looked at me intently.

We waited for a better answer, but once again Adis had checked out. "Adis," I finally said and he slowly turned back to us. "None of this makes sense. If what you've told us is true about the obdurate future and humanity's ultimate destination being a fixed point, this can't be about us. Unless this guy is just totally crazy, his motivation has to be personal, something unique to your kind. You told us a while ago that you thought the high school attack was aimed at you, to drag you out of the shadows. To limit your effectiveness." I turned to Adis. "I think we are just pawns." It was the only logical conclusion, a conclusion Adis should have tripped to long ago. I turned to Leah and she nodded. For a moment, we shared a glance and our suspicions about our guest.

"It is a possibility that he is using you as tools." He shook his head and turned back to our lawn. "As I said, my only means of knowledge is experience, and nothing like this has ever happened before."

"You mean like one of yours going off the reservation?" I asked.

AUTHOR'S NOTE: In this day of political correctness, I don't know if that expression is considered racist. I assure you I am not a racist, and if the expression *going off the reservation* bothers you, my advice is to get over it. If that bothers, you please discuss this with my wife, who is one-quarter Apache.

"That's not the phrase I would use, but it's close enough." Adis was apparently more politically correct than I had thought. "Eris is a curious fellow," Adis mused, and he effectively veered the conversation off track. "Unfortunately, I've seen his kind before. He isn't after attention, or accolades, or even to create fear. I think that he is bored and is simply looking for some mental stimulation. His world exists inside his mind. To Eris, our world is a stage and we are all just props. Conveniences. Toys. Mysteries that need to be solved." Adis was so lost in thought he looked like he had slipped into a hypnotic trance.

"He is a psychopath," I said as a medical professional.

"No, he's not a true psychopath," Leah responded. I looked at her with open incredulity.

"Yes, he is." I was shocked and a little offended by her contradicting me. I was the one with the medical degree.

"No, he is not." Leah was obviously unconcerned that I was offended. "A psychopath has poor impulse control. They need immediate gratification and have trouble with planning. This man demonstrates exactly the opposite. He has kept Maggie

Dale alive, and he told you himself that he won't hurt her until everything has been prepared." Adis nodded his head in agreement. "He is bold. That's a characteristic of a psychopath. The danger seems to entertain him, but it's not reckless. It's strategic. He wants to see how far he can go."

"Who are you?" I asked Leah. Suddenly, she had become an FBI profiler and a psychiatrist. I wondered if I should cancel her subscription to *Woman's Day* or start reading it myself.

"He's not cruel, either," Adis piled on.

"Sending us pictures, calling us, the tracking collar. That's not cruel? The man is taunting us. You asked the question yourself: Why did he keep Nitrox alive?" I tried to defend my losing position.

"I don't think that's our man. I think that's Sida. That's his way of calling me and saying 'Hey, lets you and I play.'" The three of us ruminated on that thought for a second.

"What if he is caught?" I asked. "Eris, I mean."

"What if he is killed?" Leah asked in a tone that immediately reminded me of her father

"I'm assuming we are still talking about Eris." Adis asked and both Leah and I nodded. "That would solve some problems, but not all." Adis answered. "Sida has his own agenda, and it is very different from Eris's. Deprived of his assistant, Sida will simply find another. In fact, I would be surprised if he isn't already developing a few more Eris.' Whatever Sida is planning it doesn't begin or end with Eris. Or with you."

"Wouldn't killing Eris solve our problems." Leah asked, always the pragmatist.

Adis hesitated, and then he made us wait for an answer. Finally, he shook his head. "I don't think so. I believe that Sida steered Eris to you for a reason, and that reason doesn't go away with the death of Eris."

"So the real problem is Sida," I said.

"The biggest problem is Sida, but Eris needs to be dealt with as well."

"How? What do we do?" I asked. "Maybe we should go to your father's cabin." I had turned to Leah.

"No," Adis answered strongly. "Even if you could elude Eris, Sida can always find you." Leah started to say something, but Adis cut her off. "I know that your family is well-armed and would be more than willing to create rings of defensive barriers around you, but in the end they won't protect you and will only put more people at risk."

"So what do we do, sit at home and wait?" Leah responded.

"For now." He softened his tone. "In time, the situation will declare itself."

"If we forced you, could you find Eris?" Leah asked softly. So soft that it almost didn't sound like a threat.

I started to laugh, until I realized that she was serious. "Are you crazy?" I asked my wife. The concept of forcing, or threatening, Adis had never entered my mind.

Adis and Leah both ignored me. "If you forced me," he repeated slowly. "Let's change that to a more civil question. How about, if I wanted to find Eris would I be able?"

"All right." Leah accepted her correction.

"No, I would not be able to find him. The obdurate future would prevent it."

"I'm not talking about killing him. Couldn't we exploit one of those holes in the obdurate future and just have you point him out . . ." She let her thought dangle.

"To you or the police?" Adis asked with a smile.

"Either," she quickly answered.

"I'm sorry, Leah, but you have to understand that anything I do, no matter how small, would only make things worse." Several very long moments of silence followed. I tried not to imagine how bad things could become.

"Why don't you go to the police and tell them all of this?" Leah finally asked.

"You asked me that question before, and my answer hasn't changed. I would ask you what you hope to achieve. Sida is far beyond their reach, and they already are using every resource to find Eris. Besides, have you met any one of them that would believe such a story?" Adis leaned forward, preparing to stand.

Leah apparently was unmoved by Adis's reasoning. She turned to me and said, "Then we need to go to the police ourselves and tell them everything we know. Everything." She glanced at Adis to make certain I understood her meaning.

I was about to say that they would almost certainly call child protective services and our three children would be raised in foster homes while we were medicated and created finger paintings between electroshock treatments, but Adis cut in.

"Of course you are free to do that. The probability that they would believe you is even less than if I told them myself. But I have a more compelling reason for you to keep your distance." Adis stood.

"And what is that?" Leah asked him, eye to eye.

"I believe that Eris is either a member of the FBI or the Austin police department."

"So you know who he is?" I asked, and then stood; I felt foolish being the only one seated in the small room.

"Not yet." His Cheshire cat smile was back. "Now, you will have to excuse me, but I have a bus to catch. Would either of you care to accompany me to the bus stop?"

Leah looked at me and communicated her thought quite clearly: *He's your responsibility.* "I'll walk with you," I said after the moment became awkward.

Chapter Fifteen

I WAS TIRED, DEAD TIRED, AND THE LAST THING I WANTED WAS TO GO FOR A WALK. I really just wanted to crawl into my own bed, pull the covers over my head, and dream away the next few weeks. Unfortunately, I knew that those dreams would be an unending loop of nightmares, so five minutes later I found myself following Adis out our front door.

"Why don't you fellas just stay and watch the girls," Adis ordered the two APD officers as we walked past their patrol car. They both nodded.

"Mom said I could come along." Tom suddenly appeared and inserted himself between us just as we reached the sidewalk. He was the hero of the day, and the fact that tracking the collar had led us nowhere did not diminish the fact that he had fixed it (of course only after he had broken it). "Where are we going?"

"Just up the hill to the bus stop," Adis said, slowing down to match my pace.

"Are you from the future?" Tom asked.

Adis laughed heartily and rested his hand on Tom's shoulder. "I am absolutely not from the future. I am, however, from the past."

Tom had lived with me long enough to understand and dislike word play, and his face darkened. He shot me a quick dirty look, as if I had given Adis his answer. "We all are from the past," he said testily.

"My past goes back a lot longer than yours," Adis said, undeterred by Tom's sudden change in tone.

"Then how do you know the things you know, and do the things that you do?" he fired back. I had started to trail them, allowing me to openly smile. Tom was his mother's son, unwilling to accept anything at face value.

"That is a very good question, and I wish I had a good answer, but I'm still struggling with it." To all the world the pair strolled through our cul-de-sac as grandfather and grandson. "It's not often I get to talk to twelve-year-olds, so let me ask you some questions. What's it like growing up in this day and age? What's your view of the world and the future?"

I nearly laughed. I was fairly certain that my son, who had mastered the art of living only in the moment, had never given a second's thought to such weighty matters. Once again one of my family surprised me.

"I have no way to compare what it was like to grow up in any other time but this one," he started. "I can imagine that a hundred years ago life was much different, much more difficult." I closed the distance just to make certain that it was my son who was talking. I had expected him to say something like *I dunno* and then ask Adis if he knew any of the cheat codes to *Grand Theft Auto*. "The world is a smaller place, and what happens all the way across the country or the world can affect us here at home."

"Very perceptive," Adis answered. "Do you think you would like it better if you were insulated from those events? If the world shrunk back down to Austin, or even just your neighborhood?"

Tom thought for several seconds, long enough for us to turn on to the main street. "I don't know. I don't see how you could take away the bad stuff without also taking away the good stuff."

Adis nodded his head and I shook mine in disbelief. My son was becoming a philosopher.

"Are you going to kill Mr. Sicko?" Tom asked after a moment. I will admit to being a little taken aback, more by Tom's directness with a relative stranger than the actual concept of a twelve-year-old contemplating murder. Maybe it was because my eight-year-old daughter had already introduced me to the concept of children regularly discussing homicide.

"Not if I can help it," Adis answered without hesitation. "That disappoints you?" Tom's face had dropped with Adis's answer. "If he can be stopped before he hurts anyone, else would you be satisfied?"

"What about the things that he has already done? He took our dog and killed Dad's friends, and took those girls, and stole things from our house." Tom began to plead and run on.

"Yes, he did all those things. Does that mean he should be killed?" Adis asked. He wasn't offering an argument, only asking Tom's opinion.

Tom was four years older than his sister Mia, who would have unhesitatingly answered in the affirmative. Only, his world had begun to take on the subtle shades of grey that come with the realization that not everything is as simple as it seems. He walked silently, studying the cracked sidewalk three feet ahead of him. "I don't know," he finally said, and a rush of pride filled my chest. He sounded defeated, and my pride was replaced with sadness as I realized that a small portion of Tom's childhood innocence had just died.

"Well, neither do I," Adis answered, partly to Tom and partly to himself.

"Did you have these problems when you were growing up?" Tom asked. I had never asked Adis about his youth, his childhood, or virtually anything of a personal nature. It's not that I had never thought to ask; in fact, I had thought often of where he had come from, but it never quite seemed to be the right time.

Adis hesitated. He hesitated long enough for us to reach the bus stop without answering or even acknowledging the question. "The bus won't be here for another twenty minutes or so." He had sat on the concrete bench and now stared up at me. "I know you're tired, so please don't feel obligated to wait." Once again he addressed his comment to me, and me alone.

"I can't leave Tom here alone. It's not safe." Considering my current state, it was a silly thing to say. If any type of confrontation arose, Tom would be of more use than me. In fact, he would probably be safer if I wasn't there.

"Well, then I suggest that you sit down." He turned to Tom, who remained standing just to Adis's left. "I can't remember ever growing up, Tom, and that's the truth. It was many lifetimes ago." I'm sure Tom thought that Adis was only being metaphorical (although I'm also sure he didn't know the word metaphorical). "But my world bore little resemblance to this one. That being said, people don't change. Mr. Sicko, whom I have taken to calling Eris, would have had a counterpart in my world." Adis slowly nodded and Tom continued to stand, waiting for more. "I do remember a story from when I was younger. It was about a young man not much older than you."

Tom signaled his interest by sitting next to Adis. We now flanked the elderly man.

"I was travelling through an area that is now called Romania on my way to the Black Sea." Tom nodded his understanding. "Good, you know Romania."

"That's where Transylvania is." Tom's interest was piqued. Hollywood, the popular press, and America's teens had rediscovered the undead, both zombies and vampires. It was almost impossible not to find at least one cable or network program playing at any time, day or night, that didn't feature one of them. Cable television had programs like *True Blood* and the *Walking Dead* on a continuous loop; writers of books and movies had invented stories about our sixteenth president hunting vampires. And then there were those terrible *Twilight* movies that never seem to go away (does that actress ever completely close her mouth?).

"Exactly. Now this was long before America was discovered by Europeans." Adis had leaned back, and I caught Tom's eye just before he was about to voice an objection to Adis being alive centuries earlier. I gave him "a roll with it" sign and he nodded back to me. "And as you said earlier, life was much different, much more difficult. Superstition, not logic, ruled the day. Christianity was mixed with mysticism and local legends, and the result was that most of the time what was unseen was more real than what was seen."

"When magic filled the air," Tom said, rolling his eyes towards me.

"You know Led Zeppelin?" Adis looked down at my son.

"We all do, we're forced to know it." Now he tipped his head towards me and I laughed. I had become my father, trying to expose my children to the virtues of good music.

"Well, it is an apt description." Adis had turned his head towards me and patted my knee as if I had written the line instead of Robert Plant. "I arrived in a small village named Corona on the last full moon of the summer in 1303. Years later its name was changed to Brasov, and it still stands today, only not as the small village I remember. It's a city now, and all the places that were so important those many years ago, the castles and churches, have become tourist sites. It's still very picturesque and I hope one day you get to see it for yourself, because there is still just a hint of that magic filling the air." Adis's expression was a little dreamy. "Anyway, Corona was a fortress city built on the east slope of the Carpathian Mountains. It was meant to defend the eastern border of the Hungarian empire, only in the end it didn't do so well, but that's another story. When I arrived there were several hundred settlers living around the small fortress, which at that time was really too small to accommodate any more than just the knights who had been sent to defend the city. It was, to say the least, an inopportune time to be visiting Corona, because along with the magic there was a good deal of fear and suspicion in the air."

"Vampires?" Tom guessed, and I could tell by his expression that he was hoping as well.

"Yes." Adis said with reservation. "But not as you would know them." He paused and looked down to study Tom. "You are quite taken with the legend of vampires." Tom looked a little embarrassed and sheepishly gave a small nod. "Do you know the origin of vampires?"

"Vlad the Impaler," Tom answered brightly.

"Actually, the legend began centuries before Vlad. Almost all cultures believed that spirits haunted the night; it helped to explain seemingly unexplainable events. In the Slavic regions of Europe, like Transylvania, these beliefs became as real as the changing of the seasons. They believed that the soul of the recent dead would wander around the village for forty days either performing good deeds or creating mischief. If there was a good harvest it was because of a benevolent soul; if there was an outbreak of an illness it was because a soul was unhappy with his former neighbors. After their period of wandering, the souls would depart forever, leaving behind their bodies, which could then be inhabited by unclean spirits, and by that I mean souls that were to evil or too restless to depart, or on occasion demons that had never walked the earth as humans. Some of these unclean spirits would drink the blood of animals or humans to sustain the body that they had stolen, and now you have vampires."

"So no Vlad?" Tom was clearly crestfallen.

"No, Vlad was very definitely real, and he did impale his enemies. Thousands of them, if that makes you feel better. He filled whole forests with impaled bodies to deter his enemies, but he never was accused of being a vampire. That legend started with a book written by an Irishman named Bram Stoker in 1897. Stoker had apparently read some old German pamphlets that extolled the virtues and cruelty of Vlad. His father was a member of the Order of Dragon, and carried the name Drac, so Vlad was the son of Drac, or Dracula, which was the name Stoker used for his vampire. Clear?"

"So no fangs or stakes in the heart?" I felt sorry for my disappointed son. I knew that he had no true belief in vampires, he just wanted to believe in the romantic idea of a world that included supernatural beings. I wanted to believe in a world that did not include supernatural beings.

Adis shook his head. "Stoker got that from the early Slavic tradition of driving a stake through the chest of a decomposing body to relieve the gases that result from decomposition. The fangs idea came from the fact that the gums recede after a person dies, giving an observer the impression that the teeth have grown."

"Well, *that* stinks," Tom said with irritation. His mind had shifted from disappointment to indignation.

"Okay, back to me." Adis crossed his legs. "Poor Corona had had more than its share of tragedies in the days that led up to my arrival. A month before, a fire had burned a number of buildings, including a communal barn and with it a fair amount of the community's stores. Two months earlier, a small contingent of soldiers had appeared in Corona demanding that the city produce a tribute for the King of Wallachia, the lands just south of Transylvania, or face a siege, and now most of that tribute was ash and smoke. To make matters worse, a number of Corona's inhabitants had come down with a brain fever and there were only a few able bodies capable of rebuilding the town and working the summer harvest."

"What's a brain fever?" Tom asked.

"In that time a brain fever could mean just about anything, but in this case it was an illness that came on quickly. It seemed to prefer the young and healthy and would start with a fever. Sometimes the afflicted would develop a yellow, sickly pallor and bizarre behaviors. They would dance naked under the summer moon and speak in languages no one could fathom. But what really worried the good people of Corona was the fact that most of the victims had developed sores on their limbs and blood had begun to ooze from their mouths. Everyone was convinced that an especially powerful vampire had taken up residence in the forests that surrounded Corona."

"I can see that," Tom said.

"On the evening I arrived not a soul would speak to me. I tried to find a bed for the night but all I got was closed doors and shuttered windows. Finally, I stumbled over, quite literally, a young man who had been sleeping in a dark corner of the burned-out barn. He told me of the town's recent troubles and fear of outsiders.

"He said his name was Constantin and that he was a man held in low esteem by all those who know him. He said that my arrival had caused quite a stir and that his fellow countrymen believed that I was either the vampire himself or was in league with him as I had arrived in the village unscathed.'

"I did assure young Constantin that I was not a vampire, nor was I in league with one, and he didn't look the least bit surprised.

"He answered,'Of course you are not a vampire.' I pressed him to tell me why he did not subscribe to the superstitions of his country. 'You appear to me a learned man, perhaps even of letters, so you will know that the local legends and myths apply only as far as a man can travel in one day. Then a whole new set of superstitions take over. How can any of them be true?'

"I asked his opinion on the source of the brain fever and he simply laughed. If I had seen a cask near him I would have thought that he had been drinking, but he was in fact as sober as Sunday.

"He whispered 'I will tell you only if you swear before all that you hold sacred to keep my secret.'

"I agreed, and he lowered his tone to a conspiratorial level. 'Mold,' he said simply. 'My own mold. I created it with moss, tree mold, and wild mushrooms. It grows on the wheat and the seeds.' He grinned madly, full of pride with his accomplishment. 'I am the keeper of the stores. It was no trouble for me to seed the spores through the grain.'

"I was about to ask him why—" Adis said, but Tom cut him off, proving that indeed he was Leah's son.

"He poisoned the tribute that was going to the other king, but the fire released it on his own people."

"Very good." Adis seemed genuinely surprised by my son's deductive reasoning, but not as surprised as I.

"Aflatoxins," I said. "Acute liver failure and encephalopathy."

"Boy, you two are right on top of this story." Adis took turns staring and smiling at each of us. "But have you figured out who started the fire?"

As there was only one other character in the story aside from Adis, our chances of answering his question correctly were pretty good.

"Constantin." Tom did the honors and Adis nodded.

"But why?" he quickly asked.

"You haven't told us enough about Constantin to answer that," I answered.

"What if I told you that Constantin and Eris are cut from the same cloth?" Adis stared off into the cedar trees that surrounded the bus stop.

"So you have met people like Mr. Sic—, Eris in the past," Tom said, jumping past Adis's question to the intent of the question.

"Societies may change, but men don't. People like Constantin march through history. Most of the time, circumstances limit their impact; occasionally, one comes to prominence." Adis continued his study of the forest across the street.

"So what do Constantin and all the other wackos you have met tell you about Eris?" I probably should have asked that question, but it came from Tom, and again his verbiage, complexity of thought, and maturity surprised me. Maybe watching TV and playing video games aren't as harmful as everyone thinks.

"It tells me that no matter how long I live I will never understand or relate to the man. I can better understand the motivations, thoughts, and desires of a terrorist that straps on a suicide vest than either Constantin or Eris. The terrorist has to learn to depersonalize his enemy, but Eris and his kind wouldn't understand the word depersonalize, because to them people are objects, things. Some things are interesting and fun to play with, but most are unimportant and disposable."

Tom shuddered very slightly. He would never admit it, but he was a fairly sensitive young man. Leah had told me about a time when she had watched Tom bury a sparrow that he had accidently shot out of a tree with a paintball gun. He had taken the bird to a dark corner of our yard, dug a hole deep enough to deter the neighbor's cat, and then carefully cover the sparrow with dirt. He never told anyone anything about the incident.

"What happened in Corona?" Tom finally asked.

"Well, I asked the young man why he would go to such lengths. Why burn down the barn and your only shelter when all you had to do was wait for . . ."

"He wanted to watch people get sick," Tom interjected. "It wasn't good enough to poison strangers."

"Well, that is the obvious answer isn't it? When I proposed that, he looked puzzled, as if he had misjudged my ability to understand the depth of his complexity. 'This isn't about those people,' he told me. 'It's about this.' He showed me a handful of grain covered with a light frosting of blue mold. 'I created this.' Now I know what you're thinking, that Constantin only found the mold, but he truly believed that by combining moss and tree mold with mushrooms he had created something new." Tom rolled his eyes. "Hey, remember that this was the fourteenth century." Adis smiled and playfully shouldered Tom. "Anyway, Constantin told me that he was on a 'voyage of discovery' that few would understand. He needed to test his creation to find out what his tiny spores were capable of and, by extension, what he was capable of. After much consideration, he decided to burn the barn and the spoiled oats with it, exposing the healthiest of the village to his creation."

"He sounds insane," Tom interjected. "How could those answers be more important than the lives of his neighbors?"

"He was the Josef Mengele of the fourteenth century," I answered. Tom looked puzzled and I debated telling him to what extent the physician of Auschwitz had gone to answer similar questions. "He was a Nazi that did some really bad things in World War II."

"What happened to him?" Tom asked.

"He died an old man in Brazil," I answered quickly.

"No, not the Nazi guy, Constantin," Tom said, irritated with my usual word play.

"As far as I know, he died in Brazil with Mengele," Adis said with a broad smile.

"OK, both of you can stop it now." Tom had leaned forward to glare at us. "So you didn't kill Constantin? After he had poisoned his neighbors you just let him go."

"I didn't say that, but you're right, I did not kill the young man. If you're interested, I didn't kill Mengele either." I could tell that Adis enjoyed yanking Tom's chain.

"Enough of the Nazi." Tom pretended to be frustrated, but he had a hint of a smile. "Tell me what happened to Constantin."

"I'm not certain you would understand the entirety of it, and I'm quite certain that your father would not approve of me telling the story." Both Adis and Tom turned to me.

"He's heard worse." I shrugged my shoulders. The little boy who once had nightmares of a disembodied hand for a week after watching the movie *The Addams Family* had grown up fast over the past month.

Adis turned to me. "Do you remember what the three of us were talking about earlier?" His voice had dropped, and I knew he meant our earlier discussion with Leah. I nodded my understanding. "This was a situation I should have stayed out of."

"Isn't that why you told this particular story. To make a point?"

My directness caught Adis a little off guard, a rarity indeed, and he leaned away from me. "I will try and not be so transparent in the future." After a moment he turned to his right and found Tom waiting for an answer. "I did try and stop Constantin, but the fates decided that at that moment he was more important than I."

"The obdurate future," Tom said, once again proving that no matter how secretive we thought we were, the children were always listening. "We looked up obdurate. It means stubbornly refusing to change." He obviously felt comfortable revealing his clandestine activities because Mom was nowhere in sight.

Adis nodded again. "The future does not like to be rewritten. It is quite obdurate."

"So what happened?" Tom demonstrated some of his famous impatience.

"After our discussion, we sat in the darkness and I watched Constantin's future roll through my mind. He would spend his life in the solitary pursuit of his selfish desires. He would ruin and take lives everywhere he went without a thought, just as he had taken lives in Corona. Yet I knew that he was not my responsibility. To the very core of my being I knew that I should leave that very moment."

"Why? God would expect you to stop him."

"No, He didn't. Nor did He want me to." Adis offered no further explanation, but that was not good enough for Tom.

"Why would God allow him to commit more evil?" Tom asked the question that had haunted humans from the moment a divine being was imagined or sensed. "He could have told you to stop him right then and there."

"I have spent a lifetime trying to understand why some evils are addressed and others are allowed to flourish." Adis said sadly. "If there is an answer, it's been hidden from me."

"Why is any evil allowed to exist?" Tom asked us both. I was about to answer but Adis cut me off.

"That's a much easier question. Evil lives in all of us. It is a part of who we are. A coin can't have one side. You do understand that?"

I was a getting a little uneasy that Adis had weighed into the realm of theology and was putting Tom's six years of Catholic education at risk. "I understand that we are judged and defined by the choices we make," Tom answered in perfect CCD form.

"Well said," Adis said simply and with a finality that made me happy our conversation was moving back to solid ground. "Despite knowing better I dragged the boy, because that's really all he was, out into the town square with the intent of having his countrymen decide his fate, but just as I reached the light of the town's signal fire I was struck by an arrow. A second arrow brought me to my knees, and Constantin ran. To the villagers of Corona, I was the vampire they feared and Constantin was my next victim." Adis paused to allow Tom to react. When Tom simply stared, Adis rolled up the back of his shirt to reveal a pale scar just below his right twelfth rib. "I have a matching scar right here." He pointed to a spot in his abdomen just below the liver. It should have been a lethal injury in 1303, and without immediate attention, in 2016 as well. "The fact that I had survived the arrows and their subsequent rough treatment only convinced the villagers of my evil intent and associations. When I was finally subdued, they tied me to a post and set a watch of three men. Several of Constantin's victims were paraded in front of me, and at least one of them was convinced that I was the demon that had very nearly drained the life from her. That was what passed for a trial back then. The town elders met in the same small inn that had refused me earlier, and I could hear them debating the safest way to dispose of a vampire. Constantin, who despite his age and appearance was generally agreed upon to be the most intelligent and well-read man in the village, insisted that my head needed to be removed from my body with a single blow from an axe that had just been forged and who's blade had never touched the heart of a tree. My body was then to be burned to dust and thrown in the river far downstream."

"Obviously that didn't happen," Tom said.

"Obviously," Adis confirmed.

"So how did you escape?"

"With difficulty." Adis settled back into the uncomfortable concrete bench. "As I sat there listening to the villagers decide on the exact ritual by which I should be destroyed, I could feel that something had changed; it was as if the very bonds of time began to strain. I wasn't the only one; my guards felt something as well. They started whispering amongst themselves, and then one by one they ran off. A cold wind had begun to blow from the mountains and it was the only thing that disturbed the unnatural silence. Even the birds and insects that hours earlier had been so noisy that I was able to walk into the village unheard had suddenly become still. Then even the wind stopped. The air became thick and stagnant and it was hard to draw a breath. Before dawn, the elders finished their discussion and my manner of death had been decided. As each man stepped from the building, the oppressive heaviness struck them. They all hurried home, save one. I watched Constantin skulk from the back of the building. Before disappearing into the darkness he stopped and stared at me for a moment. I have always wondered what he was thinking."

"I'll bet he was thinking that he should kill you before you told anyone what he had done," Tom offered.

"Perhaps." Adis slowly nodded his head. "I never saw Constantin again." He stopped and turned to me. "At this point in the story things become quite violent and graphic."

I looked at Tom and thought that he had had enough. With the mention of graphic violence he had retreated ever so subtly. "I think the sanitized version would be better, besides it is getting late."

Tom offered some resistance, but his heart really wasn't in it.

"A couple of hours later our friend attacked the local priest, who stumbled out into the mid-morning sun, bleeding. He fell across me, and as the villagers were attending to the old man the church began to burn. Within minutes, most of the town was aflame as the fire followed a line of pitch from building to building. The fire moved much too fast for any caught inside to survive. I worked my way loose and did what I could, which wasn't much. In the end not only did I fail to stop Constantin, but by trying to reveal his true identity I forced his hand. My actions were directly responsible for scores of deaths." Adis finished, and I was surprised that I couldn't detect even a shred of remorse.

Tom had crossed his arms and was staring at some crawling insect in the gutter. "Well, that sucked," he said, and I didn't know if he was referring to the story itself or how it ended. If history was any indicator, Tom would mull Adis story over for a couple days and then come to me with questions. "You should have just killed him," he said softly as he stood. The bus was cresting the hill.

"Maybe," Adis said, and then he turned to me. "Don't look now, but there are a pair of photographers in the woods across the street." Of course I immediately looked to the woods. "They are harmless, but I do expect that Eris, or perhaps Sida himself, will direct them your way while they prepare for what comes next."

"I don't suppose you know what that is?" I asked with no hope.

The bus arrived in a cloud of dust and squealing brakes. The door opened with a loud hiss and I could hear the passengers exclaim when they saw the famous Adis. "Not yet, but I'm fairly sure that we won't have to wait long. I am also fairly sure it will be dramatic." He stood and stared into my eyes. Maybe in that moment he was trying to see what lay behind my façade, but I doubt it. He put his hand on my shoulder. It was an odd gesture, and again I braced myself for a hug. His expression was serious, and I wondered if he was trying to communicate to me psychically.

"What?" I finally asked him.

"Just be careful," he said seriously. He looked down at Tom, patted his back, and then turned to the steps of the bus. In the blink of an eye, Adis the Grandfather reappeared. He accepted the helping hand of the bus driver and waved to the half dozen riders. "Hello, my friends." The doors closed and the bus was away in a soft whoosh.

Chapter Sixteen
ጀ ጀ

THE NEXT MORNING, THE *AUSTIN AMERICAN STATESMEN* RAN AN
ABOVE THE FOLD HEADLINE THAT READ "LOCAL SURGEON AND
WIFE MURDERED. CHILD TAKEN." The heading above the story
read "APD Confirms Connection with Dale Kidnapping." Below
the fold was a picture of Jim and Kim Lee in happier times. Next
to that was a photo of Adis and myself sitting on a concrete
bench; they had cropped Tom out of the picture. We were both
mentioned in the story as "contributing to the investigation."
For my part that represented a significant upgrade from being
"a person of interest." There were several more candid photos
of us posted to the Internet, each with an accompanying story
or tag line.

The police had restricted access to the Sidewinder subdivision, and Adis was nowhere to be found, making us the sole
focus of the media circus. By midmorning our cul-de-sac was
once again filled with satellite vans and on-air personalities.
Our neighbors love us.

For the next several days the five of us laid low, hiding out in
our besieged residence, watching TV and movies, occasionally
surfing the Internet for news beyond Austin, and collectively
becoming bored to tears. The only moment of drama came
when one astute reporter asked Mika where we were keeping
our dog. The two of us were hauling out our garbage and recy-
cling, and I froze the second I realized that she was going to
violate the house rule that reporters were to be ignored. She, of
course, knew that Nitrox's abduction was to remain a secret, but
Mika can be somewhat mercurial and the absence of our dog
had been keenly felt, if rarely spoken of.

"The big brown dog. I haven't seen her," the man asked. He was a tall, thin man, and I was guessing that he was in his early twenties. I was also guessing that more than half his interest was in fact our fourteen-year-old daughter, who could easily be mistaken for her early twenties.

Mika stopped and stared at the young man. It was the stare every pretty girl I have ever met has mastered. "You do know you are standing in dog poop," she said, and then she turned back for the garage. I followed her, but only after I watched the poor, defeated young man lift one foot and then the other and utter a string of words that were unlikely to be printed.

For the next two weeks our lives slowly began to return to some semblance of normality. Adis and his friends were never far from our minds but at least they weren't in our living room.

Just before noon on Friday June 3 all that ended. A fifty-seven-year-old mortgage broker named Mabelle Lopez stopped by the HEB in east Austin to do a little shopping. For those of you not from Texas, HEB is a supermarket. As far as I am concerned it is THE supermarket, as in the only supermarket (sorry Randall's and Albertsons) we frequent. I could go on about why, but suffice it to say that both Leah and I love HEB for a number of reasons, none of which are pertinent to this story, which makes what happened all the more difficult.

Mabelle had just bought a new crock pot and was looking for something to stew. She had five children and a husband that loved pot roast, so she headed for the meat aisle. The butcher had been busy that morning, and she had more than a dozen cuts to choose from. She sorted through the selection until she found the largest rump roast and was about to toss it into her cart when she noticed that it was more than just cold, it was frozen. Her indecision caught the attention of the butcher, who asked her if she had any questions, and the soft-spoken woman asked if they had switched to frozen meats. The butcher was somewhat offended and assured her that their beef was fresh and never frozen, and that he personally had cut each one of the steaks and roasts just this morning. He asked to see the offending roast and Mabelle passed it over the counter. The butcher examined the beef and confirmed that it was indeed frozen solid. He called over another butcher and the pair examined the anomaly. The second man remarked that the label, although similar to all the others, was just a little different. It had the obligatory bar code, and was stamped with the day's date, but the font and printing were off. The description was also unusual: "rump" was all it said. They set the block of meat aside and then with Mabelle's help they searched the shelves. In ten minutes they had six more suspicious packages, including three filet cuts that were labeled "back strap." At this point the store manager was called, who called his manager in San Antonio, who called the police in Austin, who called the US Department of Agriculture in Dallas, who called the Texas Department of Safety, who finally determined that the meat was not bovine in origin and was most likely human. By then it was after five in the afternoon and hundreds of pounds of HEB meat had been sold in the greater Austin area.

HEB put out a press statement that foreign and potentially dangerous material had been found in one of their stores and that they were issuing an immediate and emergent voluntary recall of all meat, not just beef, bought within the last forty-eight hours. All four network news programs were alerted and each ran a hastily assembled story that was light on the facts and long on speculation. Within a day, four other HEB stores were found to have human meat mixed in with their usual fare.

It took two days to track down the origin of the meat. It turned out to be a man named Carlos Gallegos, a sixty-six-year-old homeless man that had panhandled on the corner of Highway 290 and Texas Road 71 for many years. He was locally famous for his candid approach; his cardboard sign simply said: Why Lie? Need Money for Booze. His intersection, the busiest in south Austin, was only about four miles from our house, and one we used several times a day. On a number of occasions we had bought Carlos a meal from McDonald's (which probably did him more harm than the booze). It was not unusual for him to disappear for a time, so nobody noticed his absence, but most of the city heard of his dramatic return.

The 5th of June was a warm day for a triathlon, but that was part of the allure. The "Heat and Hills" race was a ten-year tradition in downtown Austin. It was limited to the first 3000 participants, and the race typically sold out in less than a day. Like most races it was well supported by the city and most of its residents (although a vocal minority complained bitterly of the traffic disruptions), with volunteers routinely outnumbering competitors. To the uninitiated, the finish line appeared chaotic but was in fact as well organized as any factory assembly line. Racers would cross, receive a medal, have their picture taken, and then be guided to the finishers' tent, where they would have their pick of food and drinks. Four hours into the race, just as the bulk of competitors were crossing or had crossed the finish line, a twenty-seven-year-old woman named Natalie Price reached into the large ice trough for a post-race beer and instead grabbed a handful of frozen hair. For less than an instant Natalie stared at the dead face of Carlos Gallegos, not quite comprehending what she was seeing. When realization struck, she dropped the dead man's head and screamed. And screamed. And screamed. One of the local film crews (who had recently moved out of our cul-de-sac) caught most of the incident on tape, including a brave soul retrieving the head and setting it on a table. Apparently, it sat in full view of a few hundred people before someone finally covered it with a towel.

Up the street and a few hours earlier the city editor of the Austin American had received a FedEx parcel that contained three items. The first was a bloodstained cardboard sign that read: Why Lie? Need Money for Booze. The package also contained a photograph of former city councilwoman Mindy Rashard-Tyler. A year earlier, Mindy had become a minor celebrity by pushing through the city council a measure that symbolically made Austin an open city to all legal and illegal immigrants. Three months later, she was forced to resign when her husband was indicted for laundering drug money through his BMW dealership. The last item in the parcel was a set of BMW car keys. The express package had been sent locally and paid for with an HEB corporate account.

That night, along with most of the country, I watched the edited version of Natalie Price meeting Carlos Gallegos on network news, and along with most of the country immediately got on the Internet to find the unedited version, only I did it for reasons not so macabre. Behind poor Natalie, standing by the entrance, was a figure silhouetted by the sun that just before the end of the clip walked into plain view. He was a tall, well-built man in his seventies with piercing blue eyes. My first thought was Adis, but when I finally found the Internet version I realized that the slightly fuzzy face belonged to someone else. Somebody who could have passed for Adis's brother; somebody wearing a race number that was clearly visible despite the low quality picture: #1130. A medal dangled from his neck, and he made no effort to hide himself from the camera. As Natalie started to scream, #1130 barely turned to look at the young girl and then continued out of the tent into a sun so bright that he was quickly lost.

"You saw him, too," Leah said behind me, and I jumped.

"Damn it! I really am going to buy you a bell." I zoomed a frame of the picture and Mr. 1130 became bigger, and a good deal fuzzier. "It's not Adis," I said as my pulse began to slow. "But it could be his brother." I didn't want to say the name Sida, but both of us were fairly certain we had just gotten our first look at Adis's evil twin. "You think he knows? Adis I mean." Leah gave me a 'how stupid can you be' look.

"Yeah, I'm pretty sure he knows," she said sarcastically. "Sorry, that was uncalled for." She gave my shoulders a squeeze. "Maybe these guys have moved on to bigger fish." We both stared at the image, which had started to look a little like a Rorschach chart.

"I doubt it," I said softly.

"But they're being so high profile. Killing and kidnapping people in flamboyant ways. I know Adis said they would do this, but maybe this is what they intended all along. Think about it. They have practically shut down the biggest supermarket chain in the city. They've made hundreds of people go to the hospital because they were convinced that they had eaten human flesh. They have taken a well-known council woman." I could see her point, and that despite her earlier skepticism she had bought into the Adis-story, as she had so derisively labeled it.

"That's what he wants," I said slowly. "Sida, I mean. I've given this a lot of thought, and I think Adis was right. Sida probably has a lot of other Erises running around. His minions are going to do things like this over and over again. He'll burn through them as fast as he can find them. He'll indulge every sick, twisted fantasy and wreak so much havoc that something will have to give." I turned my chair and she slid into my lap. Her arms naturally wrapped around my neck. "The Dales. The Lees. Us. We are all just a small part of what's happening."

"So where was Adis and his 'obdurate future' in all of this?" She nodded towards the screen, which displayed a fuzzy image of Carlos Gallegos's frozen head. "I can't believe anyone could do all this without help."

"Do you trust him, Adis, I mean?" I asked. It had been more than two weeks since we last saw him, and the doubts that were planted during that conversation had begun to grow.

"Not fully. He certainly isn't telling us everything he knows, so I'm not sure I can believe anything he has told us. He's also got a dark side. A really dark side.

"So you think Sida has a stable full of Erises?" Her head had dropped to my shoulder and she stared out the window at a large patch of yellow grass in our yard. A TV van had driven over a sprinkler head, forcing us to temporarily turn off the water. That had been four days ago.

"Yeah, I do." I shifted our combined weight off of my right leg and got comfortable. "I think Sida is the puppetmaster, and Eris and his kind are all dancing to their own individual tunes." Despite our chosen subject matter, I wanted the moment to last.

It had been a while since we were simply a couple. Unfortunately, we were not simply a couple.

"Oh, God. Really?" Tom had come looking for dinner and discovered us. He stomped away and the moment was gone.

Chapter Seventeen

☩ ☩

EVAN GRAND IS A NAME FEW PEOPLE WILL REMEMBER. He was a man with ideas that in his mind would make the world a better place. In that regard I have the smallest modicum of respect. His sole motivation was the greater good and, as far as I know, never for personal gain. I wonder if the Evan Grands of history all started out with noble but warped intentions. Visions born out of the ideal that JFK touched on when he challenged a generation to ask what they could do for their country. But I digress.

In truth, Evan Grand was a small man caught up in the midst of great events not of his making (a condition that I myself have been forced to accept). He was arrested in Temple, Texas, ten days after Carlos Gallegos's head was found by Natalie Price (if you are keeping track, that would have been June 15) after his Econo Van was pulled over by a Texas state trooper because a yellow liquid was observed leaking from between the two rear doors and leaving a trail down I-35. Six barrels of ammonium nitrate were found safely secured to the walls of the van, but the top seal on one had loosened, and in the Texas heat and humidity the typically granular material absorbed enough water from the air to expand and liquefy. Normally, ammonium nitrate is a fertilizer. Occasionally, it is mixed with fuel oil to create ANFO, a powerful explosive used by homegrown and foreign terrorists to bring down buildings, including the federal building in Oklahoma City in 1995, which killed 168 people (including nineteen children and three pregnant women) and injured more than 680 others. As it turned out, Evan had greater aspirations.

Why is Evan important to this tale? For a few reasons. First, he confirmed our suspicion that Sida was something more than just a theory dreamed up by Adis. Second, it showed that Sida was fallible, that he was just as susceptible to the *shit-happens* principal as the rest of us. Finally, it showed us that Sida had no regard for human life if that life stood between him and his objective, which at that time remained unclear.

Almost everything I know of Evan comes from Detective John Sharpe, who was one of the last people to talk with Evan. Detective Sharpe and I came to an understanding a few months ago, long after the conclusion of these matters, and began to share information on a variety of topics. Evan Grand was one of them. For the sake of simplicity, I am going to take a page from Adis and tell the tale of Evan Grand as a narrative story, so I will be forced to take some minor liberties. I will try and stay objective and in the third person, and once we're done I'll be back.

In the real world, Evan Grand was an unmarried man of twenty-six who lived in an upscale apartment in central Austin. He drove a two-year-old Camry, was cordial to his neighbors, and visited his mother once a month. He was raised as an only child in Brady, Texas, a small town northwest of Austin. His father was an auto parts manager who died under suspicious circumstances when Evan was fifteen. He attended Texas State University in San Marcos, and, after graduating with a degree in accounting and passing the CPA exam, he was hired by the IRS in Austin. He was an auditor, but preferred the term *examiner*. At the time of his arrest he had four years of experience, which put him near the middle of the seniority ladder, but had always scored high on the yearly employee reviews. Very few of his decisions were reversed, and to the entire world it appeared as if Evan would slowly work his way to the top. On the surface, Evan was a quiet, efficient, stable young man that would in time find a wife, start a family, and live his life in anonymity.

Except that below the surface Evan was also a closet Nazi. I don't mean that in the generic, small 'n' sort of way. I mean that in the goose-stepping, Hitler-loving, capital N sort of way. Evan was more of a Nazi than Martin Bormann (head of the German Nazi Party during the 1930s and 1940s). Only, he was a New-

Age Nazi that took racial purity and American nationalism to the very heights of lunacy. Indoctrinated by his father from a small age, Evan in a different time and place would have been perfect for the KKK. Born with an intelligence that flirted with genius, an utter lack of personal loyalty, and an innate ability to disappear even in the smallest of crowds, he probably would have been building and planting bombs that blew up dozens of Southern churches and little girls (if you don't understand this reference you need to look it up; it's important) within weeks of becoming a member. Fortunately, for all those involved, the KKK had a vanishingly slight presence in central Texas, so Evan did what most wackos do when they are trying to connect with other wackos, he got on the Internet. By the time he had finished college, he had an extensive but secret network of social misfits that subscribed to his way of thinking, and a smaller group of confidants that had already proven the courage of their convictions through acts of violence. As you have probably guessed, I really dislike this man. Sorry about that; I'm supposed to be dispassionate when I'm in the third person.

Despite the Bill of Rights, being a Nazi is not something that is going to jumpstart your career in the federal government, so Evan, as always, blended in. Having the confidence of your boss and coworkers is a great way of maintaining employment and, in Evan's case, continued access to some of the most personal information the citizens of Texas possess. Despite the official position that the IRS computers are guarded by firewalls so secure that unauthorized access is impossible, Evan had no difficulty scaling those very walls and taking all he wanted from the hard drives of his coworkers and the servers of the entire IRS network without ever arousing suspicion. Working from within, he eventually gained access to the computers of Homeland Security and the FBI (as an aside, after Evan's arrest his personal computer was decrypted and the FBI recovered the files of over six hundred Americans; files that included names, address, social security numbers, driver's license numbers, employment, income, medical records, marital records, phone records, arrest records, etc.; this inconvenient fact was never made public). After countless hours of research, he pared the list down to eighty-nine names. His list wasn't a who's who of liberal thinkers and policy makers. He wasn't after the Hillary Clintons, Al Sharptons, or Nancy Pelosis of the world; he was looking for their support staff. People close enough to the power to influence it and tarnish it. Guilt by association was the American way. His methods were simple. Through as many websites as he could reach, he would disseminate the private secrets of his targets and let nature take its course.

A year into his project, Evan had accomplished very little. The Internet is a wonderful thing, but exciting a few hundred people who spent most of their time surfing it and doing little else was proving an ineffective tool. He needed crossover to the mainstream media, which meant massive Internet saturation, or an entirely different approach. The logistics of maintaining a low profile, as well as employment, severely limited what he as an individual could accomplish. It was clear he needed help, and so he reluctantly reached out to the small cadre of confidants that he had first encountered online while he was still in school. He vetted his team in the same way he vetted his victims: the various databases of the US Federal government. In the end he choose six men, all in major population centers scattered across the country. He met with each of them individually and explained his plan and his vision. He was a pragmatist and held no illusions of remaking America in his image overnight, a concept that several of his new recruits found hard to accept. There would be no direct violence, as that was certain to prompt a response. They would instead use the weapon most suited to the destruction of ideas: information. It would be a slow, gradual process that in the end would neutralize the various liberal influences that to his mind steered the political agenda and the social landscape. As the hypocrisy of each of the remaining eighty-nine was revealed, mainstream America would slowly awaken to the fact that their country and the natural order had been actively perverted by pedophiles, sodomites, and miscreants since the election of Kennedy.

Even with help, progress remained frustratingly slow. The group focused on a single individual at a time, beginning with blogs and chat-room comments designed to capture the interest of the Internet's faceless masses, and on occasion to motivate its more extreme elements. Addresses, phone numbers, license plate numbers, and names of children came next, and usually the process became self-sustaining. In some cases, more personal information was deemed necessary and entire court records or medical records were dumped into Internet sites catering to the unstable. Two years into the process and halfway through the list they had some minor successes, including the implosion of the American Center for Justice (an organization dedicated to the appointment of progressive or liberal federal judges) after it was revealed that the founder and chief spokesman, Chauncey Lyon, had been arrested for solicitation three times and had contracted at least one sexually transmitted disease that he then passed on to his wife. The Appleton Research Center (a small but influential California-based think tank that professed to address the inherent inequities of American society—ironically, it was founded by six billionaires) also took a hit when their vice president was audited and found to have not declared hundreds of thousands in income. He was convicted of tax evasion, and Evan made certain that his partially obscured face was plastered over the Internet. Still, Evan and company were not having the impact anyone was hoping for. Several of the members began offering different, more active and aggressive ideas.

Three months before his arrest, just about the time his group was on the verge of disintegration, Evan received an e-mail without an address. The subject line stated simply: You can do better.

Evan deleted the e-mail without ever opening it. Before he could delete another message, his phone vibrated. A text message from a phone number with only six numbers again admonished him: You can do better. Evan stared at the words and nearly jumped when it vibrated a second time. An Internet address was listed on the screen below the first message. He touched the screen, and through the magic of cell phone technology he found himself at a website aptly named You Can Do Better. Only now the name Evan was added to the message. After a moment, a security video of him sitting at his desk opened. He watched the live feed of himself for several seconds, and then the image faded to black. The screen remained blank only for an instant, and then letters and words began to fill the small screen like snowflakes. They organized themselves into a new message. *Now that I have your attention* was all it said. It too faded to black, only to be replaced by a second video an instant later. A man shackled to a metal table stared into the camera. His face was puffy and swollen, clearly the victim of a recent beating. His complexion was dark.

"Sand nigger," Evan said to himself and then quickly looked around to make certain none of his coworkers overheard his indiscretion. He was alone.

"State your name," a voice off-camera demanded. The man hesitated and then jerked violently. His arms became rigid and his metal handcuffs cut into his wrist as he thrust his arms forward. His face froze in agony and he started making a strangled sound. Suddenly, he collapsed back onto the table, and Evan imagined a slight pall of smoke obscuring the man's face.

"Let us try that again, shall we?" the voice asked with false sincerity.

"John Emmitt." His voice was just above a whisper.

"That is the name you currently use, but that is not your real name is it?" The voice was soft but still communicated an undeniable threat. John Emmitt shook his head. "Good. Now will you please tell us your real name and where you were born." This was not a question.

"I was born Hashmi Kassan in Muscat, Oman," he answered quickly.

"Are you in the United States legally?"

Hashmi hesitated a fraction of a second and was again subjected to the electrical shock. As the man convulsed, Evan felt the smallest twinge of envy.

"No," he said after recovering. "I entered the United States through Mexico six years ago."

"Good. Please continue. Tell us why you came such a long way to sell water purification systems to the good people of Phoenix." The voice was almost playful now.

"To raise money and recruit for an organization . . ." Hashmi hesitated and Evan waited for the disciplinary shock, but the off-camera voice cut in.

"An organization based in Yemen that the US government has found to be a terrorist front?" the voice asked in a leading tone. Hashmi nodded again. "Are you planning, or have you ever committed, a crime on US soil?" The voice was again firm and demanding.

"No!" Hashmi suddenly sat up straight, and even Evan believed his sincerity, which disappointed him. "I swear."

"I believe you," the voice replied. "Still, you are a member of an organization that actively works against American interests, isn't that correct?" Hashmi slowly nodded. "An organization that has taken up arms against this country." His nod now was almost imperceptible. "So let me ask you a hypothetical question. If I was found in Yemen posing as a water purification salesmen but was in fact a spy for the US government, how would your organization react? Would they ask me to collect my things and put me on a plane?"

"Probably not." Hashmi's voice was low. He looked off camera, presumably to his questioner, and stared with the eyes of a condemned man that had finally accepted his fate.

"Probably not," the voice repeated. "Would they video tape me handcuffed to a table as electric shocks were administered to my genitals?" The voice received no answer.

I'm going to stop this part of the story now as I don't think I need to narrate what came next. The last several seconds of the video was the disembodied voice telling Evan that this was not a time for half measures, and that if he was truly interested in making a difference and had the stones to do what was necessary that he should be at Barton Springs pool at seven that evening.

Evan did of course prove himself by going to the huge, natural pool in the heart of Austin. He arrived well before seven and at first meandered through the large summer-evening crowd looking for signs of anything unnatural, and then stripped down to his bathing suit and climbed into the cool, crowded water to maintain the appearance of normality. He was fairly confident that this wasn't a law enforcement sting, but the possibility that his actions had been discovered and that this was an elaborate act of retribution resonated in his mind. After all, this is exactly what he would have done. After thirty minutes of wading through the water and scanning the crowd he was comfortable that no one was paying him any undue scrutiny, so he drifted towards the shallow end of the pool and climbed out. He dried himself, spread a towel on a dry patch of grass far from anyone, and waited.

After his arrest, Evan told Detective Sharpe that his first thought upon seeing the man we had named Sida was his striking similarity to Adis. "He appeared out of nowhere," he said and then regaled the police with stories too fantastic to believe (at least to them). The mystery man offered no name. His credentials came in the form of personal information. He knew every last detail of Evan's life, from the date and with whom he lost his virginity to how he had tapped into the computers of the FBI, Homeland Security, and a dozen private firms. He said that he had watched from a distance as Evan and his cohort proceeded with their smear campaigns until he could no longer abide such a tepid approach. Considering the information and access at Evan's disposal, they should have been much more successful. The mystery man (for the sake of simplicity and consistently, I am going to use his given name of Sida) outlined a more aggressive and at times violent approach that would in the end effect the social change that Evan, his crew, and Sida wanted.

"You will have to get your hands dirty," Sida told the younger man. "But I will protect you."

Within a week Evan had sold the idea to his six confederates of pivoting from Internet attacks to a more active approach. It was an easy sell. Over the coming months Sida met with Evan on several other occasions and each time supplied the younger man with an assignment for one of the group. The targets were seemingly random: a bridge in Tennessee, a mosque in St. Louis, a synagogue in Chicago, a state senator from California, but Sida assured Evan, who in turn assured the others that in the end everything would become clear. On that point he proved to be telling the truth. Despite not having any prior experience, each of Evan's six hackers proved to be spectacularly proficient in the tasks assigned them. The handling of explosives and the use of high-powered weapons seemed to come strangely natural to each of them. In a twelve-week period the group had successfully completed eight missions, and not a single law enforcement agency had made a connection. Then it came time for Evan to get his hands dirty.

The rest of the story is really rather simple. Sida briefed Evan in personal. He was given an address that he was told to memorize and instructed to arrange for the delivery of two hundred gallons of fuel oil. A week later he received an email giving him explicit instructions that explained how to mix fuel oil and ammonium nitrate. The day before his arrest Evan drove to a ramshackle farm in Bell County and found a large white Ryder truck (this was especially ironic as Timothy McVeigh used a Ryder truck in the Oklahoma City bombing) filled with six barrels of ammonium nitrate. It took him nearly an entire Sunday to carefully titrate and mix the exact amount of oil with fertilizer. When he was done, he double and triple checked the seals on each of the six barrels and then closed and locked the van. All that was left was to drive the truck to the JJ Pickle Federal Building in downtown Austin, park it on the south side of the building, and walk away. An hour later he was to call a specific number and then Boom! The ten-story building, along with most of the surrounding area, would be decimated. Only a broken seal and a relative humidity of seventy-four percent prevented the deaths of perhaps a thousand individuals. Or perhaps there was something more.

I have always found it unusual that Evan Grand spilled his guts so quickly and completely. He sung like a bird, as they say in the old black-and-white movies. Maybe it was the shock of arrest, or the effective interrogation techniques of the various law enforcement agencies that interviewed him. Maybe it was a sudden change of heart, a resurgent conscience? I doubt that. Evan was found dead in his cell before he was even arraigned. Like the Lees, the cause of his death was never determined. In my simple determination this man, as Adis put it, was evil, and I don't mourn his fate. How Christian of me.

In the end, only three of Evan's cohort were captured, and as of today they are awaiting trial. I presume the rest slipped back under slimy rocks, or perhaps they had a visit from a tall, well-built elderly man who had more than a passing familiarity to Adis, and perhaps with their last breath found a nine-inch combat knife in their neck. Sida, of course, had a different fate, but we'll get to that.

Chapter Eighteen

X X

EVAN GRAND AND HIS ACCOMPLICES WERE NEWS FOR A LITTLE LESS THAN A WEEK, AND THEN THEY FADED INTO THE RECESSES OF OUR COLLECTIVE MEMORY. His death was never solved or even explained, and that mystery, as opposed to why he had been arrested in the first place, was the only thing that gave the story its limited staying power. In mid-July, interest in the story briefly rebounded when the *Austin American Statesman* published a two-page article in the Sunday edition that traced the conspiracy all the way back to Evan's college days, but by then our collective attention had turned to other things.

Our smaller world had slowly begun to turn again. I returned to work on July 28, after a nearly three-month hiatus, and the kids had started to plan for their imminent return to school. Two out of three were excited, with Tom the holdout. Once again, we declined his request for home schooling. We had managed to stay out of the news for more than two months, and Leah had been able to make several trips to HEB without furtive glances, whispers, or finger pointing. We had become old news, just like Evan Grand. Still, we remained on guard. Reluctantly, I had taken shooting lessons, and with even more reluctance I took a concealed handgun class and bought my own Sig Sauer P320. I usually left it in my car, as it's hard to conceal a large handgun when all you're wearing are surgical scrubs. Leah's remained in her purse or on the kitchen counter. The kids were never left alone, which severely impacted on their God-given right to enjoy the summer as they saw fit. Leah's response to the almost daily complaint had been memorized by all: "It will give you something to talk about with your therapist."

The media remained consumed by the continued disappearance of the two children and the former city councilperson, Mindy Rashard-Tyler. Early on, it was assumed by most that the two cases were related, but the FBI and APD issued a statement in late June that in their opinion they were two separate events. Eris had taken to sending pictures of the two girls to the papers or the local TV stations on a regular but unpredictable schedule. They were never published, of course, but Eris had been kind enough to include us in his e-mailing. Occasionally, we got a glimpse of Nitrox, who seemed to have recovered some of her former health. The kidnappers of Mindy, however, remained completely silent, and I'm sure everyone was bracing for body parts to suddenly turn up in novel locations. Her husband made an impassioned plea from the Federal Correction Institute in Bastrop, Texas, but nothing came of it. The murders of Carlos Gallegos and the Lees were occasionally mentioned, but only in passing and usually only in relation to the disappearances. There was a brief flurry of news reports about the vulnerability of the homeless, and even a small organized march to the state capitol building, but nothing changed, and Carlos Gallegos faded away as well.

Adis had also dropped off the radar. I hadn't seen him since Tom and I watched him climb aboard a Cap City Metro bus more than two months earlier.

For a time it seemed as if everyone (with the possible exception of Eris) had taken a vacation. But as we all know, vacations come to an end.

You may recall that in the summer of 2016 the United States was struggling with a massive influx of unaccompanied illegal immigrant children, most fleeing poverty and gang wars throughout Central America. No matter what your politics and who you want to blame, it was hard to ignore the images of small, scared children standing in lines waiting for a meal or a place to sleep. It quickly became a humanitarian crisis as more than 50,000 unaccompanied minors overwhelmed resources from Texas to California. Faced with no good options, the government started shipping bus and planeloads of the children to distant locations. Unoccupied schools and government warehouses were quickly refurbished and turned into temporary living quarters until a more permanent solution could be found. There was considerable resistance to what many considered to be back-door amnesty, and even more resistance by several accepting communities. Organized protests were often successful in blocking the final disembarkation of the children, and the press corps was there to film it all. I will dip a toe into this political morass and say that I agree and disagree with both sides of this issue. As hints of widespread amnesty coming from the administration probably contributed to the mass immigration, we had to do something once it happened, and I think the government came up with the solution that was the least bad (my editor will put another [sic] notation here). This was a "shit happens" moment and we had to deal with it in the best way possible. Okay, enough of that.

On Sunday, August 14, McAllen Independent School bus #5863 left the McAllen US Immigration and Customs Enforcement detention facility carrying thirty-seven children between the ages of five and eleven. All were recent and illegal immigrants to the US from Guatemala. Leased by the federal government, the bus and its occupants were destined for a school complex outside Dallas. The sprawling facility had been on the brink of receivership for a year and the trustees jumped at the chance to rent the property to the government for as long as they needed it. The five-hundred-mile route would take seven and a half hours, most of it up I-35 through San Antonio and Austin. They pulled out just before 4 a.m. in hopes of both avoiding most of the daytime heat but also the two dozen protestors who had camped out in front of the detention centers gates after they had promised to block them. They did catch most of the protestors asleep, but unfortunately that was not the end of the story. For the first two hundred miles everything went smoothly, but just before San Antonio a rolling blockade of cars and semis intercepted the bus and slowed it to a crawl.

Larger vehicles and tractor trailers carried banners that decried the president's decisions and "open door" policy. More banners were draped from overpasses, each with a tag line written in English letters three feet tall for maximal TV exposure. Cars were honking and the big rigs sounded their air horns. To the children it all seemed like great fun, and they waved at all the colorfully draped vehicles. Inexplicably, they had become the main attraction in an American parade. They had little fear even as a man no one had noticed before began walking up the bus's aisle taking pictures of them as well as all the commotion outside the bus's dirty windows. A number of cameras outside the bus also captured images of a middle-aged man with a beard snapping photos, presumably with a cell phone. Just after the parade had passed through San Antonio, the bus began to slow and eventually coasted to a stop. The protestors also slowed and stopped, but a moment later the bus lurched back to a crawl and the convoy got moving again. The man with the beard was now driving, and the children, presumably exhausted from their early start and all the excitement, had disappeared from the windows. For the next thirty miles the bus and convoy rolled on. The cars and trucks began to thin, and by the time the bus reached New Braunfels they were once again alone and driving close to the speed limit. It was about here that the GPS failed and the bus disappeared.

Four hours later, the bus had yet to reach Austin and a second rolling convoy of protestors. The organizers of the protest contacted the Immigration Service in McAllen, in part out of concern but also to see if a last-minute route change had been made. They were politely told that this type of information was not available to the public and that they would look into the overdue bus. In fact, they had been looking for the bus for almost four hours. As soon as the GPS signal was lost, the Texas State Patrol was notified, and with each passing hour the search widened and became more intense. Helicopters from four different municipalities and armed services were flying racetrack patterns over a 500-square-mile portion of central Texas, all searching for bus #5863. Which would never be found.

To this day, even with everything that happened later, even with my Adis connection I can't tell you what happened to the bus, the driver, the four volunteers, and thirty-six of the thirty-seven children. With the exception of five-year-old Hector Gomez (not his real name), not one of them was heard from again. Attention and suspicion naturally fell on the confederation of small groups that had organized the rolling convoy, but after the FBI expended thousands of man-hours investigating the forty-six individuals they concluded that the rolling blockade, although well-coordinated, represented the organizational limit of the grass-roots movement, and that making a forty-five-foot bus and forty-one people disappear without a trace was well beyond their capabilities. Evan Grand's remaining three confederates were also bandied about, but like the bus they too were never heard from again. At this point almost every possible scenario has been debated in every possible venue, from network television programs to drunks in bars, but I don't believe any of them have got it right. Without a shred of evidence, I am convinced that either directly or indirectly this was the work of Sida.

Hector Gomez was of course found sleeping on a picnic table the following morning at Canyon Lake Park (about twenty miles west of New Braunfels and I-35). His discovery helped localize the search some, or perhaps it purposefully deflected it. Nobody really knows. Hector has a severe learning disability and was only able to communicate that a man came out of the light and told him to stay away from the water. Despite a concerted effort by a number of child psychologists, Hector has never been able to give anything more.

Monday, August 15 was a surgical day for me, and I learned of Hector as I was finishing up a small back operation. My scrub nurse came back from her break and filled us in. The discussion naturally swung to the weekend's event, and the consensus was that the rest of the children would be found in short order.

Maybe it was my long dormant psychic ability finally asserting itself, but I knew that Hector would be the one and only survivor of the bus trip. When I got home that afternoon Leah told me that she had had the same feeling all day. An hour later, the five o'clock news at least for the moment proved us right.

I managed to watch about half of the program before I drifted off to sleep with the idea that I would awaken for the network news. I was only vaguely aware that Leah's phone had begun ringing and have no recollection of what she said before I was rudely shrugged out of the most relaxing sleep I had had in hours. Leah had planted herself on the arm of our sofa and her butt nudged me into semi-consciousness.

"You do know that this phone is tapped?" she asked in her Mother-Bear's voice. I recognized the tone and the intent and was instantly awake. A small, tinny voice that could only be Eris answered.

"I just want to talk, to get your opinion on recent events." He sounded somewhat sincere, or perhaps less like he was playing with us. "I'm concerned about those people on the bus. I don't think any more will be found. Do you have that same feeling?"

"Is your concern more for their welfare or for the fact that you have been bumped off of the front page?" I asked.

"A fair question, and I will admit that I don't like to share." He paused long enough for Leah and me to share a glance. "I have been thinking lately that we have something in common. Have you seen your friend Adis recently?"

"No," Leah answered definitively. She was correct, as I said earlier we hadn't seen or talked with Adis in weeks, but even if he had been sitting next to her Leah would have given the same answer. There was no way she would ever share anything with this crazy man.

"That's too bad. I wanted to ask him a question." He sounded pensive and not the least bit threatening. "If you see him, can you ask him if he has any relatives?"

"Certainly. How do I reach you with his answer?" Now I was being cordial. Sneaky cordial. Obvious, but still cordial.

"Clever." He laughed and I felt a trace of his menace. "How about if I just pop by your house one day and I ask one of your children?"

"How about if I . . ." I pulled the phone from Leah's hand and cut off her response. I was more interested in knowing why he had developed a sudden interest in Adis than I was in her threat. We struggled for a moment but I won. She punched me in the shoulder.

"Now why would you start that?" I asked with an aggrieved voice. "You ask a favor and then issue a threat. That is rude. What would Hannibal Lecter say?"

"Only what Thomas Harris would have him say. But you are right, and I apologize to both you and to Leah." Now he was being cordial. "I have met someone similar to Adis, and this concerns me."

"What concerns you?" I asked, and wondered how long it took to get a trace on a cell phone call, or even if the police were aware that Eris had called to chat.

It took him several seconds to respond. "I think that I am being manipulated. Perhaps directed would be a better term. I'm not certain I appreciate it." He was being pensive again, but more important he was confirming the suspicions Adis had shared with us two months earlier. "For instance, why would this cell phone have Leah's number in it?" Leah went pale, and I'm sure I did as well. We both shared the same thought that he had done it again. Someone else we had known had been murdered, and quite possibly their child was now locked in a basement. We waited for more but all we heard was the electronic hiss of her iPhone speaker.

We both sat and listened for two, maybe three, minutes more before either of us moved.

"We need to call someone," I whispered, worried that I would be overheard, but I knew that Eris was gone. He wanted the phone and his recent horror to be found, not to eavesdrop on us.

"Who?" Leah matched my whisper. We quietly debated and in the end we settled on Special Agent Gordon Anderson. Leah retrieved his card and I dialed his cell but got his voice mail instead. "Great," she said. "Try Detective Sharpe. He'll find out soon enough; it might as well be from us." Sharpe answered on the second ring and ten minutes later we had police streaming into our kitchen.

The kids were ordered to gather around the kitchen table and be quiet. Their predictable resistance to being pulled away from computers, the Internet, and TV was countered by Leah's withering glare and six words. "I am in no mood for this." Each child demonstrated varying degrees of petulance as the adults went about their business. The spectacle generated very little interest now that a police presence had become a semiregular occurrence in their lives.

"I thought all this was over," Mika said to no one and everyone, carefully balancing her frustration and boredom.

"I suppose we're having sandwiches for dinner," Tom surmised. "I hate sandwiches for dinner," he added, and he slumped into a chair.

I caught Mia's eye and we shared a conspiratorial moment that communicated volumes. All of us knew that she was the focal point of her mother's concern, and that she had done nothing to make herself a target aside from existing. We had told her a hundred times that none of this was her fault, something that her brother and sister understood, but that understanding was being eroded away by their mother's increasingly harsh words and attitude. I put my hand on Leah's elbow and was about to guide her to a quiet spot so we could talk about it when John Sharpe called to us.

"The signal cut out before we could get a trace," he said dismissively. He didn't look up at either of us as his fingers flew across his phone's keyboard. "You need to tell me everything that he said."

Reflexively, I took a step back the instant I heard Leah take the breath that precedes unpleasantness. "Excuse me, Detective, but you can at least have the courtesy to look at me when you demand something from us in our house." Her voice carried through the room, and the half-dozen policemen standing in the kitchen suddenly looked very busy. Our children, on the other hand, suddenly looked very interested. "It was my understanding that you had placed electronic taps on our phones. I know that because we signed releases authorizing you to record our conversations, which means that if you were doing your jobs you would already know what he said and quite possibly where he called from. Wasn't that the purpose for all this?" She waved her cell phone in the air.

Sharpe took a step back, Leah's rebuke having the same effect as a slap in the face. "The, ah, authorizations were only good for forty-five days. No one has been monitoring your phones for a while now."

"You mean for a month now," she clarified. "And, you didn't think that this man, who has been two steps ahead of you all along, would figure that out?" She waited for an answer but got only silence. She shook her head, and I heard her whisper the word "Great" under her breath.

Sharpe looked over at me and we shared a conspiratorial moment that communicated his disdain for my habit of allowing my wife to speak for us. I smiled and purposefully took a full step back, isolating the two in the middle of the room.

He turned back to Leah. "Can you please tell us everything that this man told you?" He was much more civil. Leah eyeballed him for a long moment and then began to relay the two-minute phone conversation while he took notes. "So it was your understanding that this guy, who you're now calling Eris, has met someone like Adis, but not Adis himself, and Eris feels that this new individual is manipulating him."

"Directing him," I clarified. "I also got the impression that he wasn't particularly happy about it."

Sharpe nodded, but didn't look the least bit surprised about the sudden addition of a new character that had more than a passing similarity to Adis. I would later learn what you learned only a chapter ago, that Sharpe had recently heard a similar story from the late Evan Grand. "Have you had any recent contact with Adis?" He used his professional "cop" voice, but beneath it was a slight tremulous undercurrent. At first I thought it was just the excitement that a hunter gets after a brief glimpse of his prey, but the break in his voice and the tension that radiated from him told us that there was something more. He looked desperate. Both Leah and I stared at him, and it was clear that the pressure of this case had aged him. He was all out of ideas, capable only of reacting, and exhausted from the relentless demands for progress. I think that was the first time I saw him as a man, not as an asshole who recklessly used his authority.

Now I shared a conspiratorial moment with Leah that communicated the question of whether we should tell him what we had found. "Come with me," I said after Leah had given me an imperceptible nod. I led him to my study and my very fancy, state-of-the-art six-year-old computer. "We found this on the Internet. It was also on the news, but you had to look closely." I found the clip of Natalie Price's grisly discovery and played it at normal speed. Sharpe looked at me and his expression said, "So?" "Watch this figure." I pointed at Sida and then played the clip at normal speed and then slow speed. The lights suddenly came on in Sharpe's head.

"He didn't turn. He just kept walking." He nodded his head slowly. "How do you know that's not Adis?" It was a good question, and neither Leah nor I had an answer, just an impression. A really, really strong impression.

"It's not," Leah said flatly. "It's a man we call Sida." Leah sat in my sofa and for five minutes finally told the police everything, or her version of everything. In truth, it was more of a sanitized version of her everything. She skimmed over the depth of our relationship with Adis and some of his strange ideas. She left the more unusual ones for me. Sharpe remained standing but listened quietly, his ever-present notebook tucked away in his suit jacket. I had the strong impression that none of this would find its way into a police report. When Leah finished he slowly, robotically sat down next to her.

"That is quite a story." Now his tone was flat, and I had no idea on which side of the fence he would plant his feet. For almost a minute we watched him think. I'm sure at the time, which was before I really got to know the man, I was probably looking for smoke escaping from his ears. "I'm going to state the obvious," he started. "A lot of weird shit has happened around here these last few months. The high school, the kidnappings, the murders, the human remains, Evan Grand and his band of neo-Nazis. Hell, throw in the bus down south . . ."

"The bus fire," I added and raised my wrists. That had become a point of contention with me. My official statement and those of the other witnesses had been politely discarded for the more reasonable explanation that the accident was just that, an accident triggered by the weather and an unsafe, unknown driver, who remained at large. Sharpe looked at my pink fore-arms for a moment. "Okay, the bus fire as well," he conceded. "Adis or his friend seem to be around most of it. Only, where do they fit in with the kidnappings, or the threats to you?"

I looked at Leah, and her expression made it clear that it was now my turn. "In for a penny, in for a pound," I whispered. "Adis is not in the strictest sense human." Now I was stating the obvious.

"That much I gathered," Sharpe said with more humor than sarcasm, but the trace of the latter still irked me.

"We think that Adis and Sida are, for lack of a better term, siblings." I couldn't bring myself to start using sci-fi terms like *beings*, or *entities*. "Aside from a few peculiarities, they aren't that much different from us. They are—" I snuck a peek at Leah "—guardians of our future." I'm pretty sure I closed my eyes as I said that out loud.

"Have a hard time believing in anything that can't be measured or weighed?" he asked as a small dig.

I hesitated for a moment and had to stifle my urge to respond in kind. "Yes, I'll admit that I do, but what surprises me is that a police detective trained to think objectively would so eagerly accept such an outlandish story," I retorted, more stridently than necessary.

We stared at each other for a moment and I'm guessing that he too decided not to respond in kind. "From the beginning, I have suspected that Adis was something more than he seems, and after months of looking at the man from every conceivable angle I have finally concluded that he defies any reasonable, rational explanation." He looked at Leah for a moment and their eyes locked. "Who was it that said 'once you eliminate the probable, whatever remains, no matter how improbable, must be the truth'? Was it Sherlock Holmes?" Now he turned back to me.

I wanted to say that it really was Sir Arthur Conan Doyle and that Sherlock Holmes was nothing more than a fictional character, and that was not the actual quote, but it would have sounded petty, and a little like Eris. "Well, all I can say is that you are accepting this improbable truth a whole lot faster than either one of us did." I paused for him to comment, but all he did was shrug so I went on. "Adis and Sida, along with the rest of their family, keep humanity on the straight and narrow. Apparently, the final destiny of humanity has already been written, but written only in generalities. All of the specifics are still to be determined. Determined by people like us." I spoke quickly, as if the words had a bad taste. I turned to Leah, in part to have her take over, but she gave me a look that told me that I would be taking it from here.

"These specifics—" he leaned forward "—they're what? The choices we make, like whether I get gas now or before I go to work in the morning?" Sharpe asked with a disbelieving inflection.

"In most cases. Pretty much all cases. Rarely, someone will make a decision that will start a cascade of events that, I guess, threatens humanity. That's when Adis steps in." Giving voice to Adis's ideas, or theories, or construct of the universe—I didn't even know what to call it anymore—made me queasy. "It's very complicated, but basically they act behind the scenes to nip things in the bud."

"Running into a school held by armed men is nipping things in the bud?" Sharpe asked a logical question, but I didn't feel like delving deeper into the Adis-files, so I simply shrugged my shoulders. "So, if these guys are siblings, how did they find themselves on opposite sides?" That was a good question.

Leah returned to the conversation. "That is the sixty four thousand dollar question. Nothing this man is doing makes sense. We think that he's doing it for his own reasons that have nothing to do with us. It's possible that Sida has a number of little Erises running around creating all this grief. He uses them as tools."

"I see," he said, and we waited for more. "So Sida is like a control agent, running a number of operatives, and Eris is only one." It wasn't really a question, more of a verbal thought. "The homeless man's murder and dismemberment. Evan Grand and his group. The high school terrorists. The kidnappings and murders." With each statement, Leah and I nodded. "Probably the old people on the bus," he half-pointed at me. "Maybe the children's bus down in San Antonio. And those are just the ones we know about." A knock on the door interrupted his tally. "I'll be out in a minute," he said gruffly, and the old John Sharpe that we had come to love returned.

"Detective? It's the chief. He just drove up," the voice on the other side of the closed door said.

Sharpe responded with something that should only be said behind a closed door. "I'm coming," he said with resignation and then stood. "I need to deal with him before I get fired. I would like to talk with Adis. Can you make that happen?" he asked me, as civil as I have ever seen him. "We are getting a lot of pressure to solve these cases, and I'm under a good deal of scrutiny. I can't be found looking into Adis and his magical buddy Sida, so if you could please keep this between us, otherwise the chief will take great pleasure in firing me." He left my office like a man late for his own hanging.

I looked at Leah as a burst of inspiration filled my head. "Maybe Sida wants to get fired?"

Chapter Nineteen

IT TOOK THE AUSTIN POLICE DEPARTMENT LESS THAN AN HOUR
TO PUT OUR PHONE CALL TOGETHER WITH A HYSTERICAL WOMAN
AT ZILKER PARK (THE GIANT AUSTIN DOWNTOWN PARK). Yasmin Highton is a forty-four-year-old hairdresser. In fact, she is
Leah's hairdresser, which is why Eris was able to call us from
her phone. Yasmin is the mother of twin seven-year-old boys,
and on this hot Monday afternoon she finally relented to their
pleas to swim at the park. If you are familiar with Austin, or
have been reading closely, you will realize that this is the very
place that Evan Grand first met Sida. How coincidental that fact
is I will leave to you. Anyway, after a long day of swimming and
sleeping in the grass, Yasmin's two boys were climbing the small
hill to their minivan when they simply vanished. One minute
they were running up the hill to the parking lot and the next
minute, after Yasmin had crested the rise behind them, they
were gone. At first she thought it was just a game and called for
them loudly. It took her several minutes to realize that her kids
were not hiding, they were gone. Her first instinct was to call the
police, but she had given her purse to one of her sons, and now
that along with her cell phone was missing as well. She started
to run back down the hill toward the crowded pool but then
reversed herself, knowing that she couldn't leave the parking
lot. She started to scream for help. It took several more minutes
before anyone responded, and by then her children were miles
away and we were talking with Detective Sharpe. By ten that
night we received a new e-mail from an impossible address that
included a picture of two bound and gagged boys. The message
was simply the number four.

Despite the sleepless night, I still had to work in the morning. Fortunately, I wouldn't be digging around in somebody's brain or spine, I just had to see patients and try to stay awake as I recited the same instructions and comments I had been reciting for more than twenty years. The media was all abuzz with the latest development in the "Kid-Napper" case, and the Highton twins' picture was on every front page, every lead news story, and every web page from coast to coast. Eris had managed to bump the disappearance of forty-one individuals to page two. He must have been very happy.

My third patient of the morning canceled at the last minute, and by all rights I should have had a forty-minute break. Just as I had eased all the way back into my chair, Debbie, my usually smiling receptionist/secretary magically appeared at my door. She looked befuddled.

"Not so fast. We have a new patient that just walked in." She paused, which by itself was unusual. "He has an appointment—at least it's in the computer." She looked at a loss for words, at least coherent words, which was more than unusual. She shook her head. "I guess I don't remember scheduling it, but he's there, and now he's here," she continued to ramble. "Anyway—" her composure suddenly rebounded and she dropped a small pile of medical forms on my desk. "I put him in the room." she said, and she was off. I whispered Leah's favorite word to myself and reached for the forms, which were completely blank. In my office, this was an absolute no-no. I hate going in to see a patient without knowing at least what they are here for.

I followed Debbie to her desk. "Okay, what gives?" I showed her the blank forms. She smiled and pointed at the wall that separated her office from the exam room.

"He wouldn't fill them out," she mouthed. I repeated Leah's favorite word. This guy was going to be one of *those* patients (suspicious, controlling, questioning, etc.). Debbie nodded, sharing my thought.

I took the empty forms and walked to the exam room, knocked, and opened the door. Sitting at the desk was a man

I guessed to be in his mid-seventies. His face was minimally lined but his thick hair was pure white. Physically he could have passed for a man half his age. There was no need for introductions as the man we had named Sida smiled up at me.

"Hello," he said. He stood and offered his hand. I shook it out of reflex. We both sat down, and it dawned on me that I had just shaken hands with the devil. "I am not the devil," he said quickly, and the expression on my face prompted his next comment. "Adis never told you that we can sense your thoughts? Shame on him." His smile was just as charming as Adis's. "I am here to help you. That's all, so relax." He drew out the last word the same way I did when I was trying to calm a nervous patient. It didn't really work. "I just want to talk."

"Why don't you talk to the police?" Even to my own ears I sounded like a petulant adolescent.

"Let's not do this back and forth commentary. It is so tedious. I realize that you have some ideas of who and what I am, and enough of them are correct to make me comfortable that you have a working knowledge of the situation that confronts us both." He leaned back and crossed his legs just as Adis would have done, and I almost expected him to launch into a story. "Our mutual friend has been quite busy lately."

"Which mutual friend, Adis, or the one who keeps taking children?" I couldn't get the petulant tone out of my voice.

"Actually, both have been busy, but I was more referring to the man who calls himself Adis. And by the way, I do like the name he has given me: Sida. The anti-Adis. It's a little obvious and theatrical, but I like the sound of it. Sida." His smile broadened as he tried out the name. "But I'm not here about that. We need to talk about Adis."

"All right, so talk." I deepened my voice to sound a little less like a prepubescent teenager.

"Adis is suffering from the misconception that we are enemies, which is not true." He paused long enough for me to jump in.

"How could you say that you aren't enemies? Everything that you do is contrary to his purpose. Everything that you do involves death and destruction." I had no trouble sounding like myself now.

"If you define the word enemy as someone who works contrary to your purpose, then Adis and I are not enemies, because we both want the same thing. Which, considering our divergent beginnings, is quite remarkable. Only our methods differ. He is content to wait as things unfold, while I feel that a more direct approach is required." He leaned back in my chair, waiting for me to decipher his enigmatic response.

"How . . . where did you start out?" Sida frowned as if I had asked the wrong question.

"Adis started life much like you, as a human. My beginnings were very different. Despite that, we find ourselves as allies."

"I don't think Adis sees himself as your ally," I countered.

"Nevertheless we are. Now, you and I, well, that is a different story." He leaned forward, and I saw that just like Adis he could be remarkably intimidating for a senior citizen. "You and your kind live your short lives unaware of the complex machinery that makes that possible. Blissful ignorance." His face turned dark, ugly, mean. He was the antithesis of Adis. "I am not like Adis, and I have always found it difficult to relate to you. In fact, a long time ago I stopped trying. I simply don't care what happens to man at an individual or collective level. I see no difference between you dying now, next week, next year, or a hundred years from now. You play your role and then are gone in a blink of an eye. So if some of you want to kill others and it serves my purpose to facilitate that, then I will." He slowly leaned back in his chair, and even that looked menacing.

"So what is your purpose?" I asked after several moments. I wish I had thought of a profound retort, something about the nobility of man, the beauty of society, of all the things we had created from nothing. But it would have fallen flat. The nobility of man is so rare that we write books and stories about it, and how could I even speak of the beauty of society? He would negate anything I could say with the very real and stark statistics of infant mortality, childhood hunger, the millions of homeless, or any of a dozen depressing but very real conditions that gutted any notion of beauty. And as far as what we have created from nothing, he would simply tell me that we had help all along. As I told you at the beginning of this book, I am not the right person for any of this.

"Ahh, the *why* question. Humans thirst for knowledge and their need to understand. It all stems from a deep desire to be significant, meaningful. It's rather pathetic." He was staring at the ceiling, and I had to stifle a strong urge to look up. "It is not for you to understand my intentions. Adis understands them, and for reasons known only to him he has elected to keep them secret, so I will honor his decision.

"But we are getting off on the wrong foot." His countenance changed and he started to morph into a pleasant old man. "I want you to convince Adis to meet me. It won't be easy. He has been very active these past several weeks trying to undo all my work, and if I don't miss my guess he is probably quite upset with me."

This was the second time in two days someone had requested that I arrange a meeting with Adis. "I am not his social secretary. And besides, I have no way of reaching him."

"I know who and what you are probably better than you know who and what you are. After all, I have expended a good deal of energy so that the two of us could be at this very place at this very time." He stared back at me, challenging me to respond.

"Why would I do anything for you?" I stared back.

"How about the opportunity to make all this stop. No more attacks on schools. No more kidnapped children. No more bus fires. No more Sida. No more Adis. You could go back to your quiet life and try and find some meaning in what's left of your brief existence." His stare was less challenging. His proposal was on the table and now it was up to me to accept or reject it. Only, he wasn't quite done yet.

"Even if I could convince him to meet you, he would never go along with any of this. Adis is a company man. He will always do his job."

"I agree with you, but that is my problem, not yours. All you have to do is convince him to talk with me."

"Why can't you do this yourself? I'd guess you could find him without my help." This was starting to feel contrived, a little too convenient.

"It would be in no one's best interest for the two of us to confront each other." He smiled broadly, and for a moment I wondered what that meeting would look like. Would it be like matter and antimatter annihilating each other in a cataclysmic explosion? Or two septuagenarians wrestling on the floor? "It is very simple. The next time you see Adis, and I believe that it will be sooner than you think, I would like you to convince him to see me. Just for a discussion. A little chat." He played with the pronunciation of the last word.

The idea of me convincing Adis to do anything against his will or nature was ludicrous. "It won't work," I said simply.

"You need the proper motivation," he said. He hadn't moved a muscle as far as I could tell, but the menacing Sida had returned. "The man you call Eris is rather intriguing." He smiled like the devil and he knew he had every bit of my attention. "He is a very curious man, always searching for answers to questions no one would think to ask. His current fixation is innocence. That's why he keeps taking young children, and of course your dog. He has some unique thoughts on the subject, and I think very soon he will . . . try some out. Are you at all familiar with the pattern of serial killers?" I shook my head, not wanting him to finish his thought. "After they have established themselves and have achieved a degree of success, they typically enter a phase the experts call *acceleration*. They begin to take risks, and their level of violence increases. Despite my best efforts, Eris has begun to slide down that path." He paused for effect. "He is very definitely a bad man that has developed an unnatural interest in your daughter," he finished with mock solemnity.

"He knows about you." He had laid me bare and I was reduced to an adolescent tattling on someone.

"I know that." He was toying with me. "He has become troublesome, and if it weren't for his unique hold on you, and your unique relationship with Adis, I would cut him loose, shall we say." He truly smiled the smile of Satan. "So I propose that we cut the two of you out of the equation." He waited for me to respond.

"How?" I asked, as eloquent as always.

"I will deliver him to you as soon as you convince Adis to meet me. If you do it quickly, I believe that everyone will go home, safe and intact. Delay, and there will be consequences." His evil smile had dropped a notch. "It would be very simple for Eris to stumble across your daughter." Now the smile clicked back up to eleven.

"I don't want you to deliver him to anyone except the police." I realized that I had just agreed in principal to his deal and that we were just negotiating the details.

Surprisingly, he shook his head. "I'm afraid that won't work for me. In fact, I have a few conditions. Demands would be a better term. First, you have three days, after which another child will be taken. After seven days, it will be your daughter. I will also convince Eris to begin to express himself immediately after that." He paused for effect. "Second, you will tell no one, including your wife and especially Adis, that we have this agreement. You must hide it from him." He tapped his forehead. "Third, when I deliver Eris to you, it will be at a prescribed location. A location that is suitable for . . . what is that term? 'Enhanced interrogation.' You, yourself will need to extract from Eris the information you require." More pause and more smiling. "Lastly, when you have all you need from the man, you will end his life and I will dispose of the body. Eris will cease to exist and will never be found, and no one will ever know the part you played." He stared at me with eyes that should have been red, but were in fact light blue. "If for any reason you are incapable of completing these duties, I will be forced to take matters into my own hands."

"Why? Why would you have me do this? If all you are interested in is meeting with Adis, be done with it and go."

"Figure it out on your own." He stood and I joined him. "I will contact you with details when Adis has agreed. Until then the clock is running." He left without offering me his hand.

Chapter Twenty

X X

SIXTEEN AND A HALF HOURS LATER, I STEPPED OUT FROM MY GARAGE INTO THE COOL MORNING. The rest of Tuesday passed in a blur of "why are you so grumpy" and "are you all rights," but I stuck to my schedule, met my familial responsibility, and went to bed early so I could stare at the ceiling. I had no one I could talk to, so I didn't want to talk to anyone. Two thoughts battled in my head. Where was Adis? And could I really do this—could I torture a human and then kill in cold blood, all while Sida stood by and watched? I had no idea about the first question, but as Adis had never let us down before, I was certain that he would show up. As far as the second question I vacillated. After spending most of the evening watching Mia I was certain that I would kill to protect her. But kill a defenseless man strapped to a table (I had envisioned Dexter Morgan's kill room from the series *Dexter*)? I was kind of okay with the idea of enhanced interrogation. As a surgeon I could easily devise a half dozen ways to torture someone without actually endangering their life, at least until it came time to end it. Around 1:00 a.m., I started to wonder if what the pundits say about torture not working was correct. Would someone in extreme pain say anything to make the pain stop? Probably. So what was Sida's reason to have me torture Eris until he spilled the beans? Around 2:00 a.m., it dawned on me that with Sida present any lie that Eris told would be immediately discovered. I think I fell asleep with that thought. Around 4:00 a.m., I awoke with the question of what would Sida do if I didn't kill Eris, or if I told Adis, or the police? That answer was easy, and it kept me up until 5:00 a.m., when I finally got up. He would likely take Mia himself, or worse.

I walked out to our cul-de-sac in the early morning twilight and looked for Adis. He wasn't there, so I started my slow jog. I had a new route now, one that kept me away from MOPAC and Maggie Dale's house. It was considerably hillier, and I started the first climb. I passed the bus stop where I last saw Adis, but the bench was empty. Disappointed, I pushed on. An hour later, I made it back to our cul-de-sac and found an orange Mercury Capri sitting in our driveway. Just for a moment, I wondered why Nitrox wasn't barking her fool head off. I slowed to a walk and stared at the car. It was the exact make, model, and color as the first car I had ever owned. A grey-haired man sat in the driver's seat.

"Please be Adis," I whispered to myself. I bent down and Adis cranked down the window.

"Get in," he said brusquely. No smile. No happy countenance. No pleasant elderly man. I walked to the passenger side and dropped into the too-low bucket seats. I had forgotten how uncomfortable they were. He put the car in gear and silently glided out to the main street, then the highway, and finally to the HEB parking lot that I knew well. "You had a visitor yesterday," he finally said.

"I met Sida in my office," I answered, put off by his distant and mildly irritated attitude. "He wants me to convince you to meet with him." I felt myself dripping sweat onto the cloth seats.

Adis alternated between staring at me and looking out the windshield at the rising sun. I almost asked him if that hurt his eyes, but the time wasn't right. "He will ask me to join with him." His voice was closer to his usual, but remained somewhat strained. "He threatened you, didn't he?"

There was no point in lying. "Yes. He gave me three days to convince you before he gets Eris to take someone else and a week before he takes our Mia." Unexpectedly, my voice broke and I very nearly came to tears. "He told me not to tell anyone, including you." Hot tears ran down my cheeks.

"He was testing you. He knew that I would know as soon as I saw you. It's not possible for you to hide something like this from us."

I felt the floating, almost narcotic effect that to this point I had called the "Adis-Effect," only now I knew its origin. "That's you, inside my head, isn't it?" He nodded. "He said that he would deliver—" Adis raised his right hand to get me to stop, and suddenly I felt calm. Tranquil, as if everything were preordained to be all right, no matter how bad things looked now.

"I know what he told you. Some of it is the truth and the rest are artful lies." His voice drifted off and I felt like drifting off as well. The Adis-Effect was as strong as I had ever felt it. For a moment, I was certain that I had fallen into a restful sleep, and the next moment Adis was speaking. "He will carry out his threat, of that I am certain."

"Which threat?" I said dumbly.

"He will force you to kill Eris," Adis said after a very long pause. I wasn't certain if he was answering my question or simply speaking out loud, lost in his own thoughts.

"Can you stop him?" I became more alert as he retreated from my mind. "I'm guessing that there is some way of killing him. Can't we shoot him, or something?" I felt a little like a child offering advice that was all too obvious.

"No, I cannot stop him, any more than he can stop me. You could shoot him, if he allowed it, but it would only make him mad." He spoke with a little more patience, but was clearly annoyed with my interruption.

"What if you destroyed Eris?" Adis slowly shook his head and returned his gaze to the parking lot. A twenty-something brunette woman suddenly pulled her Explorer into the parking spot next to us. She jumped from her car and quickly dashed into the store. Adis opened his door and without a word climbed out. I watched as he walked around the front of the Capri to the young woman's car. It was then that I saw the woman's keys hanging from the ignition. Adis touched the driver's door handle and all four locks suddenly popped up. He retraced his steps and slid back into the Capri's driver's seat.

"No. I cannot interrupt Eris's timeline. The consequences would be significant." He placed emphasis on the last word. "I have been able to deal with Sida's other accomplices, but Eris is beyond my reach."

"That's what you have been doing for the last few weeks," I said, and Adis nodded.

He paused and stared at the entrance to the HEB. In less than a minute, the brunette hurried out the automatic doors, walking as fast as her short dress and high heels would allow. She crossed the parking lot, and both of us watched as she opened her door, pausing only a moment after finding where she had left her keys. She started her SUV and was gone an instant later. Adis started the Capri. "The obdurate future demands that responsibility for the disposal of Mr. Sicko resides elsewhere." He turned to me and his gaze made it clear who had that responsibility. "I would guess that Sida tripped to this quite a while ago. He has spent a good deal of time and trouble to find someone beyond my reach and then maneuver you into this position. It is clear that he hopes to gain some advantage by having you—specifically you—kill the man."

"Why would he want the man that he has been protecting and helping all these weeks to be killed by anyone? Was Sida just raising a pig for slaughter? Could all of this be about me taking this man's life?" All my life I have hated mysteries. Books. Movies. Medical conditions. They frustrate me to a point beyond irritability, and now I was living one.

"It could be that simple. It may also be much more complex. It's even possible that Eris has served his purpose and now is more of a liability than an asset. It could be that Eris is about to take things too far even for Sida. Or it may be as simple as Detective Sharpe and his suspicions." Adis turned towards me and my mood lifted slightly when I saw his smile. "I will see him soon." Now he winked.

"Wait," I said as Adis reached for the shifter. "What if I don't kill him, but just get him to talk, and then turn him over to the police? Do you have any idea how Sida would respond?" This had been my plan all along, or at least for the last few hours.

"I doubt very seriously if Sida has ever failed to follow through on anything, especially a threat." He had turned to me and held my eyes with his.

"Could you protect us?" Adis shook his head again, and I suddenly became very angry and cursed loudly. "Why? What weird rule of the universe would you violate if you just kept him away from us? At some point he would lose interest."

"There are things that you don't understand. We are not bound by your concept of linear space. It is no more difficult for any of us to slip into the folds of space and appear anywhere we want than it is for you to walk across a room. She would be gone in the blink of an eye. Even if we could protect Mia, Sida would simply choose another of your family. And there is no possibility that he would never lose interest."

I folded my arms across my chest and said Leah's favorite word over and over again, almost as a mantra. "All right," I said after having my little tantrum. "What possible advantage can Sida gain by having me torture and kill a man?"

His hand dropped from the shifter. "A lot of lines are beginning to intersect. Yours. Eris. Mine. Sida. Your daughters. The children he has taken. Their families. The children he will take in the future. The people he will murder in the future. The list goes on. This is an important moment. A defining moment."

"A defining moment," I repeated. "Are you saying that it is preordained that I kill this man?"

"Absolutely not. Only that you have a pivotal role to play. I can already feel the tension in the web of time. It's as if a bow has been drawn and your decision will not only release the arrow but aim it as well. "

We sat in silence as I listened to the oil in the engine cool and flow back into the pan. My imagination conjured up images of arrows flying through a crowd of people I loved. "Why us?" I finally asked. "What makes us so important or interesting that you stop me from running into a burning bus and Sida points Eris at our child?"

Adis shook his head, and maybe I imagined that his affect was just a touch insincere, or maybe subsequent events have colored my memory. "Just as you told Sida, I am a company man, and the company tells me what to do, not why I am to do it." He started the Capri. "Right now I need to get you home." Just as I remembered, the old car lurched into reverse, and then into first gear .

We drove home in silence. "Sida said that you were once human," I said as we pulled into the driveway.

"That is true, but that is a conversation for another time."

I unbuckled my seatbelt, either out of reflex or because of a subliminal command. "Hold on," I said. "Tell me why Sida thinks you are reluctant to meet with him?"

"Because I am. Very reluctant."

"I don't understand. Maybe the two of you can sit and talk things out. Come up with a plan that doesn't involve anybody getting killed." I realized that my voice had a pleading quality, but to my ear it sounded like a pretty good option.

"We are not allowed to meet. It is expressly prohibited. Sida knows this." Adis slid the automatic transmission into park. "Years ago, I met a colleague by pure chance, and even though there was no fault on anyone's part there was still a price to be paid." He looked old again. Sad and old. He could have passed for an elderly man confessing a lifetime of sins and mistakes.

"That hardly sounds fair."

He smiled ruefully. "Maybe. Maybe not." He had turned to face the windshield and for a long moment he simply stared at my front yard. "To willfully meet with Sida will invite a response. It will negate a large amount of my life's work, maybe all of it, but it seems as if I have no choice. Like you, I find myself in a no-win situation. Sida will continue to escalate, and Eris will . . ." His voice trailed off. The rest of his sentence obvious.

I knew next to nothing about his bosses, or overseers, or whatever they were, but I assumed that they were fair-minded and could appreciate Adis's situation. "You can't be disciplined for trying to do what's right." Once again I felt like a child offering advice that was much too obvious. He simply smiled.

"What is or isn't right is not important." He turned back to me. "Tell Sida that I will meet with him. We will talk," he said reluctantly.

At some level I knew our conversation was over. I reached for the door and it squeaked on its hinges. I climbed out of my old car and looked back at the wet spot. "Sorry about that," I said as his eyes followed mine to the damp seat. He waved his hand over it and the stain faded to nothing. His magic trick looked as tired as his face.

I stood up and found Leah staring at me from the living room window. Adis backed out of the driveway and drove off. She didn't wave. I stared at her for a second. There was no way I could share the entirety of this with her. I motioned that I would go through the garage, which would give me a few moments to come up with a suitable answer to her inevitable question. I hit the keypad for the garage door and as it slowly rolled upward I suddenly felt responsible for Adis' plight. I knew that it was an irrational reaction, but guilt filled my heart, and before I could really work through it my loving wife appeared at the door to the house.

"What did he want?" She hadn't seen him for weeks but was still suspicious of the man who was about to sacrifice so much. Her attitude made my anger flare.

"To help us," I said directly. She took it as the rebuke I had meant. "Only to help us, at an unimaginable cost." I sidestepped her and walked into the house. A moment later, she found me in the bathroom.

"What does that mean?" Her choice of words was poor but her tone was distinctly chastened.

"He is going to meet with Sida and try and help with Eris. It's going to cost him a great deal." I had had less than a minute to process the guilt I felt for putting Adis in this position, and

Leah's intransigently hostile attitude towards him made things worse. For months she had been irritable with me and the kids, and it had taken its toll on my emotional state. I knew that she was stressed, but I was stressed. The kids were stressed, and we weren't going around biting the heads off of anyone who annoyed us. We had been walking on eggshells for months, and this morning's attitude was the last straw. I turned and faced her, drew a long irritated breath and was about to vent when she interrupted me.

"I'm sorry," she said, and those two words immediately defused the moment. She wrapped her arms around my wet chest, and I felt a bit better. "How . . . what . . ." It was rare indeed for Leah to be so tongue-tied.

"If he meets with Sida he breaks one of their cardinal laws. It will destroy a lot of his life's work. He didn't tell me any more, but it sounds very serious." I stripped off my wet clothes and made it clear that I didn't want any more discussion. She hovered for a moment and then drifted back to our bedroom.

The rest of the morning passed in ill humor. I heard some of the OR staff whisper that I was in one of those moods, and they were right. I was short and impatient with everyone as I struggled through a relatively simple procedure. At the end of the case, just to improve my mood the computer crashed, taking all my orders and notes with it. I used a few words that children shouldn't hear and then waited for IT to fix the problem. I strummed my fingers and waited until I could wait no more, then decided to go and talk with the patient's family. I painted a smile on my face and mimed my usual palaver about everything going well. Before I finished the stock speech my phone buzzed. It was just an incoming text so I ignored it. I knew it would be Sida, and I needed another moment to prepare myself. When I finished my happy talk I found a corner and looked at my phone. The text came from a number I knew well. It was my home phone number, from forty years earlier. The message was a string of ten digits, a one followed by the local area code and then a seven-digit number. I was surprised that I didn't recognize it. I put my phone away and returned to my computer paperwork. Ten minutes later, I found myself alone in the doctor's lounge facing a phone.

Sida answered before the first ring was completed. "I instructed you not to share any of this with Adis."

"Technically, I shared nothing." I stressed the second to last word. "He took it from me." Sida started to laugh.

"I knew he would." His laughter was absolutely genuine, and for a moment I wondered if it was Adis on the other end. "No one, absolutely no one else must know, otherwise our deal is off and I take matters into my own hands. Clear?"

The funny thing about threats is that no matter how dire, at some point they lose their sting. Your defenses collapse and you almost become numb. "Yeah, sure," I said dismissing it. "Adis has agreed to meet with you."

"Interesting that he agreed so quickly." Now Sida sounded thoughtful. Suspicious.

"It's not a trick, so just tell me the details and the next time I see him I will pass them on." As I had proven all morning, I was in no mood for discussion. I still had half a day's work ahead of me, then afternoon rounds, probably some consults to do, and then I had to torture and kill Eris, rescue the children, and then find a way of getting Sida and his kind out of our lives. I was swamped. But at least I had my health (*Princess Bride* reference).

"Of course it is a trick, but that doesn't involve you." He chuckled in Adis's voice. "You have been surprisingly effective. Maybe I should keep you on the hook to control Adis?" His tone remained light, but his words had a malicious undercurrent. He suddenly laughed. "I'm just kidding. Like I told you yesterday, I want you and Eris out of the picture. So let's make some plans." My mind suddenly started to float above me. "Hmmm, I like the concept. A kill room with lots of plastic and duct tape." He had snatched an image of Dexter Morgan's kill room from my memory. "Are you really up for this? It seems a little hardcore."

"Tell me what you hope to gain by having me kill Eris?" I had a vague trace of pity for the kidnapping/killing son-of-a-bitch.

He made me wait long enough that I had a thought of asking him again. "Hmm. I can't give you a direct answer. That wouldn't be the Adis-way. I have to be cryptic. A little puzzle for your little mind to work out." The insult aside, I was excited that he was about to give me a peek at his cards. "When you find the point where vindication, retribution, and redemption meet, you will know my reasons." I could hear his smile. "Now back to what we were discussing. There is a question of timing." He paused and I could hear him humming deep in thought. "Do I meet with Adis first or do you and I conclude our business first? I'm a little embarrassed to admit that I hadn't expected you to be so efficient, and presently I'm right in the middle of something important." He started humming again, and I took the phone from my ear. "I'm afraid I'm going to need a few more days before we conclude our business."

"What about Eris?" I said quickly, afraid he was going to hang up precipitously.

He started his damnable humming again. "He has become rather inconvenient hasn't he? Can't really reason with a rabid dog off the leash. I won't make any promises, but I will try and put him on ice for a while."

He paused and waited for my acceptance, but no matter what promise he made or nearly made I probably wouldn't believe it. "Did you ever have any honor?" The words were out of my mouth before I even registered the thought that created them.

"You mean like Adis?" He chuckled knowingly. "Our friend Adis is not nearly as honorable as you have been led to believe. Like me, his only interest is self-interest. He just hides it better." I imagined a silly smirk on his face, followed by a wink. "I will be in touch soon," he said, and then he abruptly hung up.

Sometime that afternoon a crack developed in the containment vessel of Fukushima Daiichi Nuclear Power Plant, Unit 3

Reactor. If you recall, this was the reactor damaged by the 2013 earthquake and tsunami off the coast of Japan. Unbeknownst to anyone, at least for several hours, more than a metric ton of highly contaminated water (predominantly seawater that had been used initially to cool the containment vessel) reached the subsurface strata and poured into the Pacific. We all know what happened next.

Sometime that evening a magnitude 8.1 earthquake leveled most of Mexico City. More than 20,000 people were killed.

When I heard about the earthquake (the containment breach in Japan wouldn't be announced for three more days) I immediately thought of Sida, and then of the obdurate future. I could only guess at the limits of Sida's abilities. Was he capable of shifting tectonic plates or the cracking of reinforced concrete half a world away? Or was this the obdurate future asserting itself, accommodating in advance to the decision I would in time make regarding Eris? Was our world so complex and interrelated that the relatively small doings in Austin, Texas, caused the deaths of thousands of Mexicans and the contamination of millions of square miles of the Pacific Ocean? Or perhaps it was completely unrelated. Purely coincidental. The proverbial act of God. Was there even such a thing as an act of God, or was everything a result of the will of God? Which of course raises the issue of God's character? As you can probably guess, it didn't take me long for my mind to wrap itself into a Gordian knot. A knot I'm still trying to untie.

Chapter Twenty-One
✕ ✕

THE NEXT TWO DAYS PASSED BOTH SLOWLY AND FLEW BY (SORT OF LIKE A MIDDLE-AGED MAN'S LIFE, THE DAYS DRAG ON BUT THE YEARS FLY BY), AT LEAST FOR ME. I was angry with everyone, especially with God. I don't want this to turn into a religious rant, but His indifference seemed intentional. I felt like I had been tossed into a deep lake and He kept tossing me lead weights to string around my neck. In my mind I railed against the ridiculous nature of the world. Every time something happened, I started debating whether this was the obdurate future responding to something else Sida had done, a random act of fate, or the will of God. I needed a break from my own mind.

Finally, I decided that I had to cut myself off from the outside world while trying to maintain the appearance of normality in the world inside my walls. In the early morning hours of Friday, August 19, I decided that I needed to avoid every conceivable news source. No TV, no Internet, not even e-mail. I tried to put my head down, do what I had to do, and not think of the bigger picture, at least until I heard from Sida again. Alas, the harder I tried to avoid the world the harder it tried to crack my protective cocoon.

Friday morning a traffic helicopter lost power and crashed into a busy freeway in Dallas. Seventeen lives lost. The television in a patient's room brought me that information. Reluctantly, I watched the live TV feed from the crash site, hoping I wouldn't see a smiling, well-built elderly man, until my patient and his family asked me if I was all right.

I told myself that things like this happen all the time and not to read anything into it, but the knot in my head only tightened.

A few hours later, a tornado tore through what was left of West, Texas. Those poor people just couldn't catch a break. A couple of years earlier an explosion blew up most of the town. Now, with rebuilding almost complete, an F5 twister all but erased the city. Twenty-three souls lost or missing. I found out about that from my office staff just as the tornado siren outside my office began to wail. West, Texas, was a little more than halfway between Austin and Dallas.

Getting a little closer, I thought, but it was August in Texas. Tornados happen.

Fortunately, all other calamities that affected the world that day were turned back by my protective wall. Except for one. Around 2:00 a.m., our new roof failed. Unfortunately, the storm system that had spawned the West tornado had centered itself directly over our house. A portion of Mika's upstairs bedroom was suddenly converted into our fourth shower, and our stairwell into a water slide. Both the State Farm appraiser and our roofer would later say that they had never seen such a sudden and catastrophic failure. We were asked several times if anyone had been walking across the 40-degree pitched roof. Both Leah and Mika gave sarcastic and physically impossible answers.

After a mostly sleepless night filled with mops, towels, and buckets, I finally made it to Saturday morning. I drove to the hospital to see a couple patients and had every expectation of Adis popping up somewhere along the way, or perhaps of receiving a text message from Sida, but both seemed to have slept in. I turned off the televisions of all the patients I saw, did my work as unobtrusively as possible, and drove home in blessed silence. I toyed with the idea of going for a long quiet drive, but I couldn't leave Leah to deal with the roof alone. Although I wanted to.

After the insurance agent and the roofer had done their walk around, I found myself free and went to my one hideout.

Beneath my little red 1971 Corvette convertible. It was my project car, and I had been trying to restore it for the last two years (by restore I mean that I tried to fix whatever broke the last time I drove it). This was my haven. No one would come out and bother me while I was working on the car (chiefly because the ineptitude of the GM engineers reliably turned me into someone no one wanted to be around, or I would press them into servitude and they would spend the rest of the day running and fetching for me). Around five o'clock I was flat on my back trying to reattach the speedometer cable to the transmission for the eighth time when someone very brave kicked my leg.

"Whoever you are, you must have a death wish." I'm guessing that my voice betrayed some of my frustration. The car was so low that when I turned my head to see who I was about to murder I rapped my forehead on the drive shaft. "Son of a . . ." I don't think I need to finish that sentence.

"Dad! You will never guess what just happened." I could see Mika's skinny legs in the afternoon light, and could feel the vibration of her excitement through our concrete floor. She is not our most demonstrative child; that honor belongs to Mia, so this must have been important.

"Then I probably shouldn't guess and you should just tell me." I remember thinking that I wasn't even safe hiding under my car.

"I was just on television!" She spoke in exclamation points (at least metaphorically).

That news was both unexpected and unwelcome. I slid out from beneath the car.

"Dad, you are covered in black stuff." Her face wrinkled up just like Leah's. "It's all in your hair!" She pointed at my head and took a step backward as if I were going to rub it all over the purple bathing suit she wore (actually, had she been a couple of steps closer that's probably exactly what I would have done).

"Okay, it's in my hair. The next time it rains, I'll run up to your room and rinse off." I raised my eyebrows to complete my "get on with it" look.

"This morning Ashley and I went to the lake with her Dad," she started. After last night's deluge remodeled Mika's bedroom, Leah had decided that Mika would be better off spending the rest of the weekend at her friend's house. It was a major concession, one made only after we had talked at length with Mika and Ashley's parents. They too had concerns that there was still a wacko out there kidnapping children, but Ashley's dad just happened to be an occasional shooting buddy of Leah's, so off she went. And now she was back. "They wanted to go tubing, but the water was full of all sorts of junk so we had to go to . . ." She continued on, and I wondered if I had time for a sandwich before she got to anything important. "I didn't know what it was, so we got closer and then I touched it. It was a body! That lady who got kidnapped . . ."

I interrupted her. "Do you mean Mindy Rashard-Tyler?" If you remember, she was the former Austin city council woman that disappeared two months earlier.

"Yep, and I found her!" She beamed with pride.

I wondered for a moment why my extremely squeamish daughter would approach something so gross, touch it, and then brag about it. "You touched a dead body? You?"

"It was disgusting. There were weeds and bugs . . ." She went on, and I started to scratch my head thinking that this is a conversation that was better suited to Tom. He enjoys gross stuff, as evidenced by his room and bathing habits. Her excited voice drew first Mia and then their mother. Mika started the story over again and finally got to the part where a TV reporter interviewed her about the "grisly discovery." "I'm going in to watch the news." Mika ran into the house with her little sister trailing behind.

Leah stood over me. "You have black stuff all over you."

"So I've been told." I raised a hand for her to help me up and she shook her head and backed away.

"It's in your hair," she said with a wrinkled face that reminded me of Mika.

I climbed to my feet and stared at my wife. We had bigger concerns than grease in my hair. "What are the odds?" I asked.

"About 1.2 million to one." Leah answered, quoting the population of the greater Austin area. "Shit," Leah said shaking her head. "Don't tell her. She thinks she's queen for the day, and I don't want to take that from her."

"It clearly didn't have the desired effect. Who would have guessed? Maybe she'll become a pathologist."

"Did you hear about the fire downtown?"

I stretched my sore back. I was done for the day. The speedometer cable would have to wait. I didn't think the Corvette would leak that much transmission fluid (if you are wondering, a disconnected speedometer cable does in fact leak a lot of transmission fluid). "No, and don't tell me." I shook like a dog and small black flecks suddenly appeared on Leah's blouse.

She looked at me with frustration. "Thanks." She carefully started to pick off the small greasy particulates.

"You don't like that shirt anyway." I took a couple off her sleeve.

"It's a blouse, and that's not the point." She gave up and unbuttoned the blouse and stripped it off. I was disappointed to see that she was wearing a sports bra. "The Alamo burned down this afternoon."

Our Alamo is not the real Alamo of historical significance. It is a downtown theater that serves reasonably good food right in the theatre. It's a family favorite, and in fact, is an Austin institution that has now franchised itself all over the country. "Shit," I exclaimed. "The downtown one?" Leah nodded. "Shit," I repeated. I had been toying with the idea of going to the Alamo for dinner.

"That's what I said." She draped her blouse over her shoulder. "It started just after the first show and the theaters were packed. It's going to be bad."

I wondered if the ER had tried to reach me. I wasn't on call, but that had never stopped them before. Then in a rush I realized that Sida may have also tried to reach me. I had gotten so caught up in trying to isolate myself that I had forgotten why. I started to look around for my phone, and, as if she had been reading my mind, she pulled it from her back pocket. "You left it on the counter."

I checked, but there were no messages, either from the ER, Sida, or even Adis. "Probably shouldn't have done that," I said softly.

Leah looked at me with a knowing expression. I stared back, wondering how much she actually did know. "No, you probably shouldn't." She continued to stare at me, and I couldn't tell if we were having a hidden conversation or were still talking about the ER. "When is Adis going to see Sida?" Now it was clear.

"I don't think they've set a time." Even to my ears my voice sounded strange. Artificial. I don't lie well, and I wasn't much better with half answers.

"Are you going to tell me what's going on?" She stood there looking suspicious, and I was surprised by how similar her suspicious look was to her seductive look. If our neighbors peeked into our garage, her expression and distinct lack of clothes probably would have given them the wrong impression.

"No. I am not." I stared down at her. My tone was clear. I was admitting that there was indeed something going on— something that I would not, or could not, share with her. "You are going to have to trust me. That's all I can say." This was the first time I had knowingly withheld something important from her, but at least it was out in the open. That did make me feel better.

"All right," she finally said, and then she walked into the house.

"Well, that went better than I thought," I said to myself, and I followed her inside.

Chapter Twenty-Two
X X

AT 3:00 A.M. ON SUNDAY MORNING, MY PHONE RANG. I read long ago that 0300 is the time of day that human reactions are at their slowest. Maybe that's right, I don't know, but I can tell you with a great deal of certainty that at 0300 on Sunday, August 21, I was not at my best. My phone starts out with a low tone that progressively gets louder. Normally, I answer before the second ring, but for a variety of reasons I would have slept right through all the rings had it not been for my gentle and understanding wife, who pushed me in the back several times before I heard the deafening rings and shut them up.

"Hello," I said in a semipanicked voice. I rolled out of bed and went into our bathroom and shut the door.

"Sorry to wake you, but this is the first free moment I've had."

I was still fairly groggy, and it took me several moments to place the voice. It really should have been automatic. There were only two possibilities: Adis or Sida, and Adis didn't call. "I was beginning to wonder if you had forgotten me." I sat at Leah's make up table. A night light in the shape of a fish cast weird shadows in the mirror, which was kind of apropos.

"No, just busy."

"Was that you today? With our daughter and the movie theater?" I was wide awake now.

"With the theater, yes; with your daughter no. But I will admit that was quite a coincidence, wouldn't you say?" He sounded so much like Adis that I nearly forgot who I was talking to.

I forced myself to focus. "I would if I could trust you."

"Well, maybe I did have a little to do with that." Once again the similarity with Adis was disarming. "But that's not why I called. If you would be so kind as to inform Adis that I would like to meet him Monday at 10:00 a.m. at the capitol building's rotunda. That is, if he is available."

"The rotunda is closed for the next week." I knew this because my scrub tech's husband was the general contractor for the remodel.

"Once again, you needn't worry about those details. I assure you that we will have access and as much privacy as we require." His verbiage had begun to deviate slightly from Adis's, which was a relief. "Now on to our matter. What are you doing now?"

"Now? Sleeping?" My heart jumped in to my throat. In the last two days I had actively avoided thinking about Eris. I wasn't mentally prepared, and now there was no time. "Does it have to be now?"

"Well, I have gone to a lot of trouble preparing things just as you want. You could just hang up the phone and go back to sleep, but I would be remiss if I didn't tell you that Eris is at this very moment about to add to his collection in a most brutal manner."

I started to run from the bathroom but caught my foot on Leah's grease-stained blouse. She had thrown it on the floor earlier, and now it wrapped around my ankle. I shook it off and bumped into the bathroom door. It fell open and I nearly fell to the floor. I glanced at Leah after regaining my balance, and she continued to snore, blissfully unaware. I quietly ran to the kitchen counter and Leah's Sig and paused just for a moment. The house was completely silent. I ran to Mia's bedroom and found her asleep, wrapped in a tangle of pillows and blankets. I ran upstairs and Tom was equally asleep and safe.

"Everything where it should be?" Sida said after I raised the phone back to my ear.

"Yes," I said a little breathlessly. There was no point in trying to hide the fact that Sida could make me dance around like one of his puppets on a string. Ready or not, I really had no choice in the matter. "I need some things from my office." Being a physician has its advantages in securing medications and surgical instruments.

"Well, that poses a bit of a problem for the Hancocks, because if I don't miss my guess Eris is going to be inside long before that."

"You fucking bastard!" I sneered.

"I understand that Mika is having a sleepover. That girl. She is quite a pistol. I'll bet she gives Eris all he can handle." He chuckled in his mocking fashion. "But," he said loudly, "all is not lost."

I felt a rush of wind blow across my body, and suddenly I was not alone. A man of my height, wearing a flannel shirt, stood next to me. I dropped my phone. Sida did the same.

"Remember? Adis told you how we get around. It's a little like Harry Potter. Take my hand . . ." He looked at how I was dressed in a simple pair of shorts. "On second thought, run and get some clothes."

I stared at him. I have never really liked the word dumbfounded, but that was how I felt. I ran back to the bathroom and quickly donned a pair of running shorts and a T-shirt. I started to run back, but when I turned he was standing behind me. He picked at my sleeve and gave me a look worthy of Leah.

"I guess it will have to do." Before he finished the last word we were three blocks away, looking up at a dark two-story contemporary home. There was no spinning. No sensation of movement. Just as Adis had said, it happened in the blink of an eye.

The Hancock's home looked different at night, and it took me a moment to regain my bearings. Adis pointed at a dark figure slipping into a side window. "Oh dear, he's moving faster than I thought," he said, and again I found myself translocated or disapparated, this time into the living room of Patrick and Kelly Hancock's home. I lurched forward. Maybe Sida misjudged the landing a little, because he slipped as well. "Sorry about that; it's a little tricky with two people."

He spoke in full voice, and I jumped. I raised a finger to my lips to admonish him to be quiet, but he only laughed.

"He can't see or hear us unless I want him to. We aren't quite synched in time. We are just a millisecond or two ahead of him. It's not much, but it's all that's needed to create a separate reality."

Eris deftly walked around the messy family room. He was quiet, but not completely silent. "How come we can hear him?" I still whispered.

"Interesting, huh? Time moves in only one direction. Forward, never backward. When he makes noise, it moves forward through time and we hear it a moment or two later. The sounds we make also move forward through time, but the difference is that he will never catch up to them."

I nodded as if it all made sense, which it didn't. I guess I hadn't watched enough *Star Trek*. Sida walked into the family room and I followed, not knowing if it was the right thing to do or not.

"Now." He turned to me once he had advanced within feet of the dark figure, who seemed to have been frozen in place. The grandfather clock that had been ticking ever so softly also stopped. "I've sped us up a little, which has the effect of slowing everything around us down. I want to make certain that we are in complete agreement. I don't want there to be any misunderstandings." I could see Sida much better than Eris, who despite being only inches away remained dark and indistinguishable. "I will deliver him to a suitable location, and when you have all the information you require, you will end his life. I will take care of the rest. Agreed?"

I nodded.

"No. You say it out loud so I can hear it," he demanded.

"I agree," I said in full voice.

"Excellent." Now he smiled. He had the look of a man pausing to savor the moment just before biting into his favorite dessert. "Ready?" Just as I had begun to nod, the lights of the room switched on, temporarily blinding me. I bumped into a dining room chair and saw a form that could only be Eris fall back into the couch. After a second I could see, and the first thing I could make out was the smirk on Sida's face. His head swiveled between us. "Surprise!" he yelled. "We're all synched up again. Say hello to Eris!" His voice boomed through the house, and I heard movement on the floor above us.

Eris's hood had dropped and I recognized him as the twenty-something reporter who had asked Mika about our dog. The one she had so effectively brushed off. For a moment I was stunned, not by who Eris was in the sunlit world, but by the fact that Adis had misidentified him. Eris wasn't a member of the FBI or the APD. He didn't carry a badge or a gun. He was just a reporter, and judging by his age I wasn't certain he was even a full-fledged reporter. I was at first shocked, then disappointed. *This is the guy who has caused us all the heartache?* I asked myself. I looked at Sida with that question written across my face.

"Meet Eris. Born William Hartenstein on June 2, 1989, in Georgetown, Texas. Son of Abraham and Lucinda Hartenstein. Graduate of the University Of Texas School of Journalism." Sida had slid across the family room and put his left arm around Eris as if they were close friends.

I'm pretty sure that my mouth was hanging open, but emotions quickly took over. Anger, rage, and fury replaced disillusionment. A sudden realization filled my mind. "You knew Mika was here, didn't you?" I started to rush the bastard.

Sida raised an open hand to stop my advance. "No. Nothing happens here. We must do this correctly." He used an affectation when pronouncing *correctly*. He gave Eris's shoulders a squeeze. "Answer the man." Eris tried to squirm away, but Sida simply increased the pressure. Two syringes, each filled with a white fluid, dropped to the floor. "Whoops," Sida said. "Did you bring enough for everyone?" He shook Eris playfully.

I realized that Sida was enjoying this way too much, but filed that thought away. I heard multiple footsteps on the floors above, and then on the stairs behind, but I filed that thought away as well. A series of images began to form in my mind, all courtesy of Sida. I watched as Eris's plans for my daughter were acted out. Her punishment for embarrassing him, her violation, and finally her murder. Then, as the four of us grieved Mika's loss, Eris would come for our youngest daughter. "What are you doing," I asked Sida.

"Knowing what he had in mind is one thing, but seeing it is entirely another." He became serious. Sida continued to fill my mind with scenes that I won't relive or relate here. It was all too much, and I tried to close my mind as a wave of nausea bent me over.

"Who the hell are you?" demanded Patrick Hancock. The room was silent for several long seconds. Eris was incapable of answering, as Sida's grip was squeezing the air from his lungs. I was incapable of answering, as my mind was trying to squeeze dinner from my stomach, and Sida just smiled up at the man. "Answer me!" Hancock screamed.

"Dad?" I heard Mika's voice from the second-floor railing.

I managed to stand straight and said a really dumb thing. "Mika, we're a little busy here, can you go back to bed?" I looked up at Mika, and then at Patrick Hancock and the handgun in his right hand.

"We've called the police," Patrick said as he took two steps down the stairs.

"Good," I said. I wanted to say more but suddenly found myself on the set of *Dexter*. Sida stood opposite me, a table between us. He had recreated the kill room perfectly. Plastic sheets hung from the ceiling and covered the tiled floor. Two surgical stands, each covered in green towels, flanked the table.

Eris was lying naked on the stainless steel table. Clear duct table bound every part of his body except for his face. He was awake but confused. "What are you doing?" His eyes shifted to Sida.

"What I promised you at the beginning." He reached down and touched the tip of Eris's nose. "Consequences," he sang. He looked up at me and assumed a formal and dramatic pose. "Would you like me to read the charges?"

I was still adjusting to the rapid-fire scene changes. "What?" I returned his stare. "None of this is funny," I said after re-establishing a degree of mental equilibrium. "It is the unfunniest thing that could possibly be."

Eris said something that was immediately stifled by the rag Sida stuffed into his mouth. "I think it's important to enjoy your work," he said with mock sincerity.

I waved a hand at his inanity and stepped towards the bound man. Thoughts and images from Eris's sick imagination still assaulted me, and they hadn't dulled an iota with the change in our location, or with the change in his condition. I turned to Sida and was about to tell him a second time that I needed some things from my office when he slipped a sheet off the stand next to him and there was everything I needed.

I looked into the eyes of Eris, and his lingering confusion, mixed with disbelief, a sense of betrayal, and fear, made me smile (in truth I probably imagined most of this). I pulled the rag from his mouth. "Tell me everything," I said, inches from his face.

"No," he sneered. "I've watched you for months. You don't have it in you." He tried to turn his head towards Sida but the tape across his forehead prevented it. "And he can't touch me." He tried to spit but the spittle only fell back onto his face.

In my entire life I had never experienced such a hatred for anything or anyone. I was determined to make him suffer for as long as he had a pulse. I walked around the table and found everything that I needed to start an IV line. I jabbed his cephalic vein with a 16-gauge needle (trust me, this is a big needle, and no, I did not swab the site with alcohol first) and threaded in the silastic catheter. I started an intravenous drip, and when it was running nicely I taped the line to his arm. "I was going to just give you a little cocktail to lower your resistance, but now I'm having second thoughts." Visions of both my daughters having their innocence and lives ripped from them pulsed through my brain. It took everything I had not to beat or stab him to death. I created my own visions of unrestrained violence with Eris as the star, and they competed with the vile images of my daughters.

Just for a moment, I'm going to interrupt my story. One of the most disturbing and interesting movies I have seen in the last twenty or so years was *Man on Fire*. Denzel Washington plays the part of a little girl's body guard, and after she is kidnapped and presumed killed he goes on what is described as a "masterpiece of death." I've watched this movie a number of times and with a number of different people, and inevitably the post-movie discussion turns to whether we could do that. Could we go on a cold, merciless crusade of killing, the only point of which is retribution? I have always answered yes, believing that anyone, no matter how pious, could be maneuvered into a situation in which they could kill. Obviously, to that point those discussions had simply been hypothetical. Now it was real, and suddenly those earlier declarations seemed embarrassingly foolish.

At some point I had picked up a trocar (basically a sharp, pointed metal stick). I spun it in my right hand and imagined plunging the instrument into Eris's chest. I could almost feel the rush of exhilaration that would come when his face registered that he had been wrong about me. I found myself at the edge of the table, picking the perfect spot.

"Are you sure you want to do that right now?" Sida had switched sides and was again opposite me. "Don't you need something from him first?" Sida reminded me of my chief reason for being here.

Some of the murderous fog lifted in my mind, but enough remained for me to wonder if I was quick enough to bury the trocar far enough into Sida to eliminate the chiefest of my calamities. After a moment I pushed away from the table. He gave me a smile.

"Kill the son of a bitch! Now!" Eris screamed.

"Which son of a bitch?" I said, turning back to my immediate problem.

"You fool. No matter what he's promised you, he will fuck you over." I reached for the rag to ram between his teeth, but paused.

"He promised to deliver you." I patted his cheek, and my murderous desires moderated to sadistic desires.

"You are such an idiot. You don't get any of this do you?" The stress in his voice was like music to my ears. "Haven't you wondered how I could do what I did? Did you ever ask yourself why he wants you to kill me? Why he set this whole thing up in the first place?"

Only about a thousand times, I answered to myself. "The only thing I want to hear from you is where you have taken the children you kidnapped. And my dog."

"Your dog?" He laughed. "You want to know where your precious Nitrox and all the children went? Ask him." He tried to nod toward Sida. "He's got them."

There are a lot of times when I am pretty dense, but this wasn't one of them. My heart may have been pounding and my brain racing, but I knew the truth when I heard it. "You have them?" I looked at Sida.

"Do you have what you need?" Sida was completely unfazed by Eris's revelation.

"Did you take them?" I shifted back to Sida and demanded an answer.

"I haven't touched a hair on their heads. Mr. Hartenstein did that all by himself. Isn't that right William?" Sida had discarded his jovial, hypomaniac persona in favor of his more natural menacing persona.

"Fuck you!" William screamed.

"The children have been removed from William's care and are for the moment safe and secure." He placed emphasis on his last word. "Let me remind you that we have an agreement, and I expect you to meet your responsibility." He had taken half a step back from the table and rose to his full height. "If you are thinking about testing my resolve I would suggest you talk with Mr. Hartenstein."

"Do it!" Eris screamed.

For a second my attention was so focused on Sida that I had no idea what Eris was talking about. Then I began to register the weight of the trocar in my right hand. Sida was just within my reach. If I was fast enough, accurate enough, and lucky enough, I could sink the trocar in his chest. I considered it for only half a heartbeat and then took a step back from the table. The probability of missing was near one hundred percent, and the consequences of missing would be incalculable. "No. Adis will take care of you. I'm not playing your games anymore." I glanced down at Eris. We weren't allies except against Sida. "The police can take care of you." I turned around and tried to push through the vinyl sheets hanging from the ceiling and immediately knocked my hand against a solid wall. I followed the wall around the circumference of the room. I began to tear down the sheets and found that we were in a square room with four solid cinder block walls. There was no way out.

"You can leave when he is dead," Sida said.

"Do it yourself," I screamed at him, frantically looking for something Sida had overlooked.

"He can't, it's—" Sida stuffed the discarded rag back into Eris's mouth.

"That is the last we will hear from you." Sida had leaned towards Eris, and then turned back towards me.

"This is not what we agreed to," I said after giving up my search and returning to the small room's focal point. Sida was standing boldly in the light, his smirk bordering on a laugh. I squared my shoulders and faced him.

"I agreed to deliver this man to you. Here he is." Sida pointed at the struggling Eris. "You promised to take his life after you had everything you needed from him. Do you need more time to question him?" He was now mocking me with pseudosincerity.

"What about the children?" I yelled, but my voice seemed to be absorbed by the solid walls.

"The only children you should be worried about are your own. Destroy him and they are safe." He leaned across Eris, tantalizingly close to the trocar in my hand. "Fail to do so and I will make the same promise to John and Brittany Dale. If they fail, I will move on to Yasmin Highton."

I was trapped in more ways than just one. Even though I hadn't met the Dales or Yasmin, I had no doubt that to recover their children they would gladly thrust a trocar into Eris's chest, leaving my children open to Sida's retribution.

"You are a son of a bitch," I said to Sida.

"It's possible." Playful Sida had returned now that he knew he had me right where he wanted. "Take as much time as you need."

I slid up to the top of the table and pulled the rag from Eris's mouth. I had not a shred of pity for the young man. He had murdered Jim and Kim Lee without a moment's thought (in reality I had no idea how much thought he had put into it). He had stolen four children, and with it a good deal of their innocence. He had turned our lives inside out. He had taken my dog!

"Stop! There are things you don't know." He was scared now, maybe not as much as I wanted, but it was a start. For a while, I let him talk.

Chapter Twenty-Three
X X

I STUMBLED TO THE ASPHALT RIGHT BEHIND A POLICE CRUISER, LOST MY BALANCE, AND RAPPED MY FOREHEAD AGAINST ITS CHROME BUMPER. I saw a whole constellation of stars and reflexively used Leah's favorite word. I now had another reason to despise Sida.

"Put your hands on your head," an impossibly deep voice said. I managed to look up and found a giant of a man pointing a gun at me. "I will not tell you again. Put your hands on your head!"

I complied as fast as my dazed brain allowed, and half a moment later I was handcuffed, trussed up to my feet, and unceremoniously deposited in the back of the very police cruiser that now had an imprint of my forehead on its rear bumper. I had recovered enough to recognize that I was outside the home of the Hancocks, which was now crawling with Austin's finest. The sun was just peeking over the horizon, so I put the time at around 6:00 a.m., which made no sense. Sida had called me at 3:00 a.m., and the trip to the Hancocks' and Dexter's kill room couldn't have accounted for three hours.

A loud voice interrupted my attempt to get a peek at the dashboard clock. John Sharpe was on the Hancocks' porch dressing down Officer Gigantor (not his real name, probably) as Pat Hancock looked on. A moment later the trio hurried down the porch. All three of them stared at me as they crossed the small yard, and I tried not to look like a desperate criminal, which is a little difficult when your hands are cuffed behind you and you're sitting in the back of a police car.

Pat Hancock reached my window first but hesitated to open the door. Sharpe gave Gigantor an order, and seconds later I was on my feet rubbing my sore wrists.

"Good morning, again," Hancock started. "Would you like to tell me what's going on?" He was more cordial than I could have been had I caught him in my living room with two other men three hours earlier. I snuck a peek at Sharpe, who gave me an imperceptible shake of the head.

I hesitated a long second, which I'm certain did nothing to convince Hancock or Gigantor that my involvement was purely accidental ("sorry, wrong house," or, "I was sleep walking"). "I would love to tell you what's going on, but not right now." I tried for a friendly persuasive neighborly tone, but to my ear it came out somewhat terse and dismissive. He followed my eyes to Sharpe.

Pat Hancock was nearly as tall as Officer Gigantor, and he silently stared down at me for several moments. "All right. Give your statement to the detective," he finally said, and then looked over to Sharpe and then back to me. Hancock was a US federal judge and nobody's fool. "Before you go, I want a straight answer. Is this about the kidnappings?"

I stared back at Hancock and was careful not to look at Sharpe. "Yes, and that's all I can say."

He silently appraised me and then slowly nodded his head. "Okay." I heard the unstated "for now" in his tone. "Leah came and picked up Mika an hour ago. They were both pretty upset." He turned away from me and addressed Sharpe. "You might want to swing him by his house before you take him downtown," he ordered, and then he walked away without another word. Gigantor followed.

"What did he tell you?" I asked Sharpe once they were clear.

"That he found you in his dining room with another guy," he answered and to both of us that sounded completely wrong. "I mean you were with . . . Forget it, you know what I mean." Sharpe was in a mood.

"You mean two guys? Both Sida and Eris," I corrected.

Sharpe looked confused. "No. All the witnesses say that it was you and—" he referred to his ubiquitous notepad "—some guy named—"

"William Hartenstein," I finished, and Sharpe nodded. "He was a reporter. He was also Eris." That was the first time I had referred to Eris in the past tense. Sharpe stared at me, waiting for more.

"The children?" He surprised me by not pushing for a clear, declarative, indictable statement, but remained focused on what was important.

"Sida has them. I think he's had them for a while. I have no idea where they are." My answer rocked Sharpe. He slapped his thigh with the small note pad and made a comment about Sida's parentage that probably wasn't true.

"All right," he said after recovering his composure. "I will run you by your house, but after that I need to take you in and get a statement." We both thought about that for a second.

"So now you're okay with the chief knowing the truth?" I asked.

"A federal judge and two other witnesses just saw you and a felon disappear into a beam of light, and then an officer saw you materialize out of one. I think that gives us a little super-natural leeway." He gave me a small, pained smile, turned, and started up the sidewalk.

I followed him to his unmarked sedan. Less than a minute later, we were in my cul-de-sac weaving through television vans. The word was out and the circus was back in town. I would learn later that Ashley Hancock—Mika's friend and the third person to witness my disappearing act—had posted on Facebook a detailed description of this morning's events, complete with my name and the fact that two syringes had been found on the floor. You gotta love social media.

It took about twelve seconds for someone to recognize me, and then Sharpe's car was mobbed. I caught scraps of questions: Were you kidnapped? Are you the kidnapper? What was in the syringes? Are you being taken into custody? Sharpe laid on his horn and gradually forced his way through to our driveway. An orange Mercury Capri was parked just in front of our open garage door. I swore quietly to myself. With Eris's words ringing in my ears, Adis was very nearly the last person I wanted to see (I know this reference means nothing yet, but it will). Sharpe parked next to the Capri and I led him through our garage.

"Nice car," he said, running his finger along the raised wheel well of my Corvette.

I nearly yelled at him for touching my car, but then decided that I had bigger issues at the moment. "Don't be impressed, it keeps breaking," I said and then promptly stepped into a puddle of transmission fluid. Sharpe had already tracked his way through it. "You better take your shoes—" I never finished the sentence, because just then Leah flung open the laundry room door and, after a moment of hesitation long enough to make me wonder if I was going to get a kiss or a slap, she wrapped her arms around me and I got a tight hug as well as a kiss.

"Don't ever do that again," she whispered.

"I won't," I whispered back, fairly confident I could keep this promise. I looked over her shoulder and saw Adis leaning on our dryer. "I see we have company." If Leah recognized the venom in my voice, she didn't react to it.

"He was here after I picked up Mika. He's been helpful." I wondered how much it hurt to say those words. "He told me everything."

Not everything, I thought, but this wasn't the moment to correct her. "It's not something we will ever speak of," I said still whispering. That is a promise that I have kept.

Leah began to pull away, and I noticed that Adis was now close enough to hear our exchange. Sharpe was allowing us to have our moment and pretended to be busy checking out my car.

"We need to speak," Adis said. I'm sure to Leah's ear he sounded like the usual affable Adis, but to my ear his subtle conspiratorial tone was more than I could handle.

"What more do you and your kind want from us?!" I had taken Leah by both shoulders and not so gingerly moved her aside so I could face Adis. "Whatever it is, we are done with you! Use someone else."

"Can we do this somewhere a little more private?" Sharpe suggested, and I was so universally angry that I rounded on him. "Hey! You can air your dirty laundry all you want, just don't be surprised if it winds up on the front pages in the morning." He pointed, and I saw that several people had scaled our neighbor's fence and had an unobstructed view of the four of us standing in our garage.

Once again I used Leah's favorite word and punched the garage door opener on the wall. In a matter of moments we were plunged into darkness.

"Well, this is a little awkward," Sharpe said. "Don't garages usually have lights?" I, too, had yet to acclimate to the dim garage, and like the detective was basically blind.

I felt a slight tug on my chest and then the four of us were standing in a bright clearing, surrounded by tall pines. We had traded the smell of transmission fluid for mountain air. Sharpe and Leah both stumbled slightly and used an expression not usually heard in mixed company.

"This will do nicely," Adis said, and then he sat in a camp chair that appeared out of a beam of light. I found three more arranged around us. "Sit, unless you prefer to stand." I choose to stand. Anger and sitting don't mix. Leah and Sharpe slowly rotated, acclimating to their new surroundings.

"What the hell just happened?" Sharpe demanded after he had turned back to Adis.

"A quantum shift," Leah answered, her eyes fixed on Adis. "That's how you do it. You slip behind the curtains."

You may recognize that this is the exact phrase Adis had used earlier. I'm not certain whether this was pure coincidence or that my wife has some psychic ability than she has managed to hide all these years.

"A good analogy." He nodded his head. "I would love to explain it further but we have very little time, so let me get right to it." I almost made a comment about brevity, directness, and honesty not being his strong suit but let it pass. "Now that Eris is out of the picture . . ."

Both Leah and I reflexively looked at Sharpe, who had decided to test the camp chair. "Out of the picture?" he repeated. This was the second time in ten minutes that someone had alluded to the untimely demise of Eris, and I'm guessing that he wanted something more definitive. I really was in no mood for small matters so I simply gave a confirmatory nod and turned back to Adis. "What exactly does that mean?" Sharpe demanded.

"In eleven days a partially decomposed and dismembered body will be found in a shallow grave in a corn field outside of Springfield, Illinois. DNA evidence will confirm it to be William Hartenstein and fingerprint analysis will match a print on a syringe left at the Hancocks' home." Adis answered the detective's question as he stared at me. "In the pocket of his jacket will be a folded kerchief that has a small drop of Amber Lee's blood. A surgical trocar, which was intended to be recovered with the body, has been removed." I'm not certain if Leah or Sharpe were privy to Adis's last sentence. It certainly seemed as if he intended it for my ears alone.

"Am I supposed to thank you for that?" I asked with a raised voice. Leah looked confused, either because she wasn't privy to Adis's comment or because of my sudden hostility. "I mean, you and your friend Sida set this whole thing up, didn't you?" I didn't wait for an answer and turned to my wife. "I don't know how he did it, but Eris—no, Eris is his puppet name—William Hartenstein figured this whole thing out." I was practically yelling in Leah's face. "He's responsible for this." I raised my scarred forearms. "They're made in pairs." I realized that I wasn't making sense.

"Stop," she said. "You're not making sense."

"He"—I swallowed, took a breath and pointed at Adis—"knew about Sida all along. All that crap he shoveled us about the obdurate universe and rules he has to live by was a lie. It's all been an act. He and Sida engineered this whole scenario." I turned back to Adis. "Tell them why! Tell them who and what you are."

The echoes of my voice faded, and Adis sat impassively in his chair. Legs crossed, arms comfortably folded across his chest. It was a good thing I didn't have a surgical trocar. "Actually, very little of what I told you was a lie. The future is obdurate. Also, there can be little doubt about the rules that dictate our lives. As far as knowing Sida all along, it is a matter open to interpretation. I have never actually met the man."

"He's not a man, and neither are you, at least not anymore." I was back to yelling. It felt like I was suffering from dysprosody, a very rare neurologic condition that affects a person's ability to control the volume and tone of one's voice. "Tell them who and what you are. Tell them what all this is about."

"In time . . ." He was back to his controlling, grandfatherly affect.

"Fuck time!" I said, loud enough for the trees to blush. "Both he and Sida are prisoners, forced to serve humanity for the crimes they committed against humanity." All three of us turned to Adis who, gave no verbal or visible response. No acquiescence. No denial. I could sense Leah weighing what I said against his imperturbable demeanor.

Finally, tired of waiting for Adis to respond, she turned to me. "Start at the beginning and go slow." It was one of her trademark lines that she used when one of the kids was overexcited. She took me by the hand and guided me a couple of steps out of the circle of chairs and away from Adis. Sharpe joined us. "Eris—or Hartenstein—told you this?"

"Yes," was all I said. "Freely." I will admit that perhaps "freely" was a bit of a stretch. He was fairly compromised at the time. "Sida was standing right there." Leah and Sharpe exchanged a quick glance.

"Go on," the detective said, for the moment content with my credibility.

"I met Sida in my office." I gave the two of them the short and sanitized version of my interactions with Sida. "Normally, he lies so much you don't know what to believe, but tonight it seemed as if he wanted me to know the truth."

"All right, get to the truth, I'm freezing," Leah said, trying to pull the sleeves of her blouse (shirt by any other name) over her exposed arms. It took me a second to realize that I too was a little chilly. "So this is their purgatory," she encouraged me on.

"Yes. Sida would never tell me who he was, or what he had done to deserve such a punishment, but he was all too happy to tell me who Adis was." I paused for dramatic effect. We were touching history, and jumping right into it felt wrong. "Ladounis Drusilla, cousin of Livia Drusilla, wife of Tiberius Julius Caesar. Captain of the Guard. Exiled to Judea for offenses unknown." I turned back to Adis.

He gave me an exaggerated sweep of his hand and I expected him to say "At your service." "You are correct, but you failed to mention that simple assault and murder does not condemn you to this life. It takes oh so much more." He smiled, and for once it seemed genuine, and cruel. I saw the subtle rise of his eyebrow, the slight tilt of his head, and the glimmer of self-satisfaction in his eyes. I saw the possibility of brutality. A flash of the real Adis, Ladounis Drusilla, and not the affectation that had been wrought over two millennia.

"Sida showed me what you did," I said to Adis alone. For the moment, Leah and Sharpe would have to wait for an explanation.

"That was a very long time ago. How long should I pay for that mistake?" He asked me my opinion. That was the moment when Adis climbed down from the pedestal that society and I had raised in his honor.

"You knew what you were doing. I can understand the others . . ." I hesitated. "At least to a degree. They were following orders. Orders that you gave with full knowledge." The image of a young man, stripped to the waist and chained to a stone column, filled my mind. Ladounis, dressed in full Roman battle gear, sitting in the shade just outside the courtyard, idly twirling his sword in the dirt and periodically screaming, "Again!" To this day, this scene, courtesy of Sida, haunts me. At least once a week I wake up to the imagined sound of a whip snapping through the air faster than the speed of sound just before it tears into flesh, and some nights it's my flesh.

I felt a fleeting sense of weightlessness and tried to close my mind to Adis's intrusion, but had no idea how to actually close my mind.

"Full knowledge? How self-righteous, especially considering tonight's activities. How can you possibly know what it was like to be twenty years old and an officer in an army responsible for maintaining order? An army whose most effective tools were assault, theft, rape, and murder. What was another man's torture and death to me? We tortured and killed men by the score. What did I care who he thought he was? I had no god. An animal has no need for god."

A tense moment followed and I realized that at some point Adis had gotten to his feet. His face was flushed and he was breathing hard. We stared at each other, oblivious to the presence of Leah and Sharpe.

"Yes, Eris and I are cut from the same cloth." He stole the very words I had said to Sida only an hour ago (roughly an hour ago). "But there is a difference. What I did had to happen," he said, without a trace of emotion.

"You had a choice. You made the decision . . ."

"And if it wasn't me it would have been someone else. Prophesy and fulfillment. Can you appreciate the inherent inequity of the situation? This was a moment that had to happen as it happened. Human history required it. This was the purest example of the obdurate future. What would have happened if I had said no, and so did every other person down the line?"

"But you didn't say no."

"No, I did not say no. Like Eris, I succumbed to the weakness that is a part of all of us, including you. I take responsibility for that, but I have also paid for that mistake many times over."

It was a debate that Leah and I had had several times over the years, usually around Easter, and invariably I was the one taking Adis's side, only then we had been talking about Judas Iscariot.

I felt Leah stir behind me; she was catching on to our conversation. "Jesus Christ!" she exclaimed.

"That's not what he was called," Adis answered quickly. I never asked her, but I was fairly certain Leah's exclamation was just that, an exclamation of surprise and not a proper, specific name.

"Oh, my God," Sharpe said, slowly catching on as well. He appeared at my side and the three of us stood in judgment over Adis.

If this had been a television show, we would have cut to a commercial, but instead the silent moment began to stretch and eventually became awkward.

"Why are we here?" Sharpe brought us back to the immediate situation.

"Because, contrary to what you believe, I am trying to help." He addressed his answer to me and I remember thinking, *I wish I could believe you.*

"God draws good from evil," Leah said, almost as if she had read my thoughts. This was something I heard her father say on several occasions and maybe this was the first time I actually understood.

"Before we get to the good, I want to go back to the evil." The words and accusations of Eris and Sida still echoed in my ears, and no matter his logic, or the fact that he could be viewed as a victim of circumstance, I wasn't willing to trust him. "I want some answers. Simple answers. Nonqualified answers." I didn't wait for him to respond. "Are you Sida's twin?"

"Yes."

"So you knew about him, and all that speculating about who and what he was, that was all an act?"

"I knew of his existence and surmised that he had engineered most of the recent troubles." He smiled like the Adis I remembered, the one I could trust. He also didn't completely answer my question.

"But he's the passive twin, the devil that whispers in my ear. He couldn't, for instance, pick up a knife and stab someone in the throat. That's your job, correct?"

"That is correct. Sida has other talents, but a very limited capacity when it comes to impeding or injuring a human being." He nodded more vigorously and then answered my next question. "Which is why he manipulated you."

"And why he couldn't take care of Eris himself. But you could have taken care of him. All that crap you fed us about not being able to see him, about being blind, was a lie." Even before I finished, I felt Leah start with surprise and anger. In large part, I was guessing here. Neither Sida nor Eris told me anything about Adis's limitations. Despite being completely incorrect, I was still glad I asked the question.

"No, that is not correct. As I told you earlier, Sida did his homework well. Like it or not, the acts and decisions of William Hartenstein were of his own volition, and as such were protected just as any act or decision you have ever made," Adis answered, and his pointed meaning was clear.

"Except Hartenstein was under the influence of Sida, which calls into question whether they were made freely, or were the end result of Sida's manipulation." Sharpe now joined the inquisition. He, too, looked at Adis with suspicion.

"Hartenstein's decisions and actions were his own. All Sida did was create opportunities. He set the stage. It is only subtly different than what I do on a daily basis," Adis responded with growing frustration.

"If I give a known child molester directions to a grammar school, I am responsible for his acts." Sharpe was angry. "In my world it is called depraved indifference and makes you just as guilty."

"Not in my world," Adis shot back. "Sida was very careful not to change any substantive portion of Eris's time line, right down to the timing of his death."

This statement caught me off guard. "Explain that," I demanded.

"The whole of William Hartenstein's short, tragic life, and how it was to play out, is clear to me, as I am sure it was clear to Sida. He was to die at the hands of Patrick Hancock early this morning." Adis turned and focused on Leah. "Please don't ask me for any of the details."

I had a brief image of our oldest daughter standing at the Hancock's second floor railing, staring down at us. As I said earlier, at times I can be rather dense, but there are times when I know the truth and this was another one.

"Doesn't that change the time line of the judge, and the other people involved?" Sharpe asked.

"For most, the changes will cancel out." Adis was now staring at me. His expression told me that switching places with Pat Hancock perhaps wasn't such a good idea.

"What is all of this about? Not just the children, but all of this. What does he want?" Leah had assumed the role of the calm, analytic spouse, as I had already usurped the emotional role.

Adis took a deep breath. "That is a fair question, one that deserves more time than we have allotted to us, but briefly, as your husband already told you, Sida and I want the same thing." Now he turned back to me. "But that doesn't mean that we are working together." His voice was hard and defensive, a rare state for Adis. "We are both tired and want to lay down our burdens. We want to move on."

"You want to die," Leah clarified. "So why don't you step in front of a bus? Hell, I'll put two in Sida's head and he won't even have to thank me."

Adis smiled ruefully. "That would be easy, wouldn't it? We are all owed one death. Only one death. You can't do it twice. We must see this through to the end, only no one told us when that would be." The unused chair behind him flashed briefly and was gone. "Now back to more pressing matters. We still have four unaccounted children, who as the detective has already surmised have been affected by recent events. We have very little time. Sida has them in a small ranch house just east of Austin."

"Well, go get them," both Leah and Sharpe said as one (actually I wasn't completely certain what Sharpe said as Leah was so loud).

"I've tried. Twice. As I've told you."

"We know, the future is obdurate," Leah said sarcastically.

"We don't have time for a debate, Leah," Adis said sternly, which stopped my wife in her tracks. "My last attempt has triggered a series of events which puts the children at great risk. The price for my involvement from the start was their deaths and the passing of Eris has not changed that situation." He looked determined—determined and angry. "I will not allow the deaths of four children to be one of the last things I do on this planet. My mistake must be corrected." He directed his comment to Sharpe. "I will take you there and you will overcome the three men at the ranch and get the children to safety before they are hurt. This is important, do you understand?" Sharpe's expression was slightly vacant, and he nodded dutifully.

"Why don't you just call the police?" I asked. "Get a whole SWAT team over there."

"No. No one else can know and no one else can be involved. It would alert Sida, and if he is challenged he will engineer the destruction of the ranch and everyone on it. If we don't hurry, it may happen anyway." He put his hand on Sharpe's shoulder. "I can't force or coerce you to do this. This has to be of your own free will."

"Just get me there," Sharpe said. In retrospect, I would like to say that he sounded like John Wayne, a confident hero who had earned his swagger, but in reality he sounded more like a man tired of being asked to do things. That being said, you can't take anything from the man. Even if I had known what this decision would cost him, I'm certain he would still have gone.

"Unfortunately, I have no time to explain, but both of you will need to come with me now, without questions or debate." Adis, as one could have guessed, addressed this comment to Leah. Before either of us could respond, we found ourselves in the rectory of St. Catherine's church. Adis was gone, and in front of us sat a nun who appeared to have been expecting us.

"What the—" Leah censored herself the instant she realized where we were.

"Hell just happened?" The smirking nun finished.

Chapter Twenty-Four
X X

ONCE AGAIN, I'M GOING TO USE SOME LITERARY LICENSE AND CREATE A NARRATIVE OUT OF WHAT JOHN SHARPE, ADIS (TO A DEGREE), AND THE MANOR POLICE FOUND AT 2314 MONKEY ROAD, MANOR, TEXAS. I'll try to use the third-person perspective as much as possible, but occasionally I'll slip in some first-person commentary, so it may get a little confusing. Finally, you the reader will have to roll with some of this because I've had to fill in some pretty big gaps.

After Leah and I were dispatched to the safety of Sister Celeste (the name she gave us), Adis and John Sharpe apparated (I borrowed the term from Harry Potter) to the small, isolated ranch just east of Austin. Sharpe's first surprise was the presence of a Porsche 911 Turbo S sitting in the gravel driveway. He would comment later that the car was worth more than the house and property. I would later remind him that this was probably the car that very nearly drove us off the road and was responsible for the conflagration on the bridge. By then it was a moot point, but I'll get to that.

"This is as far as I can go," Adis explained to Sharpe, who would later remark that he too could feel that they were on the edge of some invisible boundary. They had slipped into a small clump of Texas cedars, and Adis motioned towards the house. "Right now there are three men." Adis paused long enough for Sharpe to work his way through the branches and get a glimpse of the clapboard house, which was decades beyond needing some repairs. "Benny Meeks is the youngest." A young man in his late teens was clearly visible in the front window. His gaze was directed at the horizon and the rising sun. He had a coffee cup in one hand and a sawed-off shotgun in the other.

"You have to be kidding." Sharpe slipped back into the small depression that offered them a degree of cover. "There's fifty feet of open ground between me and that door. I'll never make it, and if I do it's my Glock against that shotgun."

"His shotgun won't work, and in about ten seconds he is going to close the drapes. Four minutes after that he will walk back to the kitchen and turn on the television. That's when you need to move." Sharpe turned back towards the house, and just as Adis had said, Benny Meeks reached for the drapes and pulled them closed. "Aldo Caberra is asleep in the bedroom to the left. He's the ring leader and Benny Meeks's uncle. He is a very bad man."

"I'm guessing his shotgun won't work either," Sharpe said.

"The only firearm that will function is the one that you carry. Unfortunately, I can do nothing about Mr. Caberra's knife. Do not underestimate his skill or his ruthlessness."

"Never bring a knife to a gun fight," Sharpe answered.

"Put him down the moment you see him. Do not hesitate," Adis warned.

"Are you trying to tell me something?" Sharpe asked.

"You have never shot a man before. Your natural tendency will be to revert to your training, which is not something you can afford. If you don't unflinchingly kill these three men, you will not survive and neither will the children."

"Tell me why this is so important. Lots of children die. What makes these four any different?" Sharpe demanded, but Adis remained silent. "Look, if I'm about to get shot, I want to know why."

"They are all important," was all Adis said.

"But not equally," Sharpe answered quickly. Adis hesitated again. "Look, you don't have to be a brain surgeon to recognize that you have focused a great of attention on the Lees' daughter and the doc's daughter, Mia."

"They are focal points that warrant the special attention." Adis admitted. "When this is over I will answer all your questions, but right now we have a more urgent matter. The third man in the house is Mark Dane. You probably recognize the name."

Three years earlier, Mark Dane was a University of Texas engineering student accused of a number of on campus sexual assaults. Unfortunately, there was never enough evidence to justify legal action against Dane, but more than enough to prompt an illegal action. The father of a fifteen-year-old girl that had identified Dane as her assailant had used a nightstick to break Dane's arms and legs. Sharpe had the unfortunate task of arresting the father.

"Good," Sharpe said. The poor girl's father had offered a defense that became known as "Texas Justice." Unfortunately, it was no match for American justice, and he was convicted of aggravated assault.

"Dane is in the basement with the children. They have been drugged and chained to an eye bolt on the wall. Dane has the keys you will need. Now, listen closely. Early this morning, one of the chains caught around a gas pipe that leads to the hot water heater, and the joint has separated. The basement is slowly filling with gas. If you don't get to them quickly, the children will die of asphyxiation."

"Let me guess, the obdurate future and your mistake?" Sharpe asked, and Adis nodded. "Okay, so no firearms in the basement. How are we doing on time?"

"About ninety sec—" Before Adis could finish, a loud bark rattled the house and shook the ground. On a good day, Nitrox could register a 3.0 on the Richter scale. "She knows I'm here. If you can get to her, she will take care of Dane all by herself. They are not the best of friends."

"One more question. Why did he keep the children alive? Sida, I mean. The dog, too."

"I have no idea why he kept the dog alive—that completely baffles me—but the children were to be used for ransom."

Apparently, Adis's answer caused Sharpe's face to twist in disappointment. "Not ransom as you understand the word. He's not interested in money. He will use the children to pervert and destroy their families. He will use them for acts so terrible that the Elders will be forced to respond."

"The Elders are your bosses."

"Guards is a more accurate term. They have already begun to gather. All Sida needs is to give them a little push." Adis turned to face the sun. Sharpe remembered latter wondering if Adis could count the passing seconds by marking the slow rise of the sun. "It's time."

I have struggled with how to describe what happened over the next eight minutes. On the one hand, I have tried not to sensationalize the deaths. I am sure that John Sharpe would agree with me that the taking of a life diminishes you, and no amount of justification mitigates that. Still, I owe him an accurate accounting of what happened in that farm house.

Sharpe made the fifty foot run undetected, but just as he eased open the front door Nitrox boomed again, which prompted Aldo Caberra to roll out of bed and start for the basement. Sharpe saw Caberra first, and as Adis predicted, he hesitated. It took half a second for Caberra to register the open door and an armed figure in the shadows. Aldo was a big man, maybe six feet tall and approximately six and a half feet wide. He bull-rushed the detective, who had managed to raise his weapon only to chest level before Caberra slammed him into the door. A moment later, the knife meant for our dog flashed in Caberra's hand and Sharpe managed to deflect some of the blow by twisting his torso. The blade glanced off of Sharpe's shoulder and sunk into the soft wood of the door. Sharpe managed to pull the trigger of his Glock a half second after Nitrox boomed again. Unfortunately, the initial impact with Caberra had turned his hand upward, and the bullet passed through the fat man's abdomen without causing any vital injury. It drilled through the relatively soft adipose tissue without deflection and then exited Caberra and struck Sharpe in the jaw. Aldo staggered just enough for Sharpe to rotate the gun and fire a second bullet into Caberra's right pelvis. He staggered again but didn't go down. Again the bullet found mostly non-vital soft tissue but it did create enough space for Sharpe to finally raise his weapon and take a proper shot. The third bullet passed through Caberra's trachea, esophagus, fifth cervical disc space, and cervical spinal cord, and finally buried itself in the ample fat of Aldo's neck. He dropped to the floor paralyzed from the shoulders down. He survived long enough for paramedics to arrive and preserve his airway, but not his spinal cord.

As the echoes of Nitrox managed to conceal the initial struggle and the first two of the three shots, the third was unmuffled by Caberra's pannus and Benny Meeks came flying out of the kitchen with his shotgun three-quarters raised. Sharpe didn't hesitate, and Meeks went down with one shot to the head. He had been promised twenty-five hundred dollars to simply sit in the house and feed the children. He had in fact tried to make the children as comfortable as possible. He had rigged a shower curtain over the ten-gallon bucket that served as a toilet to allow them a degree of privacy, and snuck in several graphic novels (comic books) for when the children were allowed to remain awake. He was a lost eighteen-year-old kid who had nothing better to do than to help his uncle, and it cost him his life. There's nothing sensational about that.

Mark Dane had heard most of what was happening on the floor above. Instead of following the natural instinct to rush up the stairs, he managed to control the adrenaline coursing through his veins and think the situation through. Quietly, he snuck out the basement door and circled the house. Instead of finding a horde of police cars and flashing lights, he found, well, nothing. He continued to circle the house and found the front door ajar. A quick peek revealed Aldo on his back, gurgling, and the crumpled form of Benny, his shotgun a mere six feet away.

I am surprised by the fact that Dane didn't just jump in the Porsche and hightail it out of there. Someone had just taken out two of his confederates. Later investigations would find that he had already received fifteen thousand dollars. A car worth twelve times that was at his disposal, yet he choose to retrieve the shotgun and stalk the intruder. I am actually glad that he did. Unlike Benny Meeks, and just like Evan Grand, Mark Dane was a bad man and in my mind deserved his fate.

After Meeks fell, Sharpe slipped into the kitchen and then slowly worked his way down the stairs to the basement. He found four doors. The furthest door stood open and led to the backyard, so he turned to the nearest. The hinges creaked softly, and Sharpe found a small bedroom. He waded through the porn magazines and checked the empty, unmade bed. Finding nothing of interest, like a set of keys, he returned to the hallway and the second door. A scratch and a whine told him what he would find. Nitrox had been locked in a dog carrier that was two sizes too small, inside a filthy shower. A sink, medicine cabinet, and commode completed the small bathroom. Sharpe told us later that Nitrox simply stared at him, quietly waiting as he untwisted the wire used to secure the carrier. When the door was finally opened she slunk out, stretched, and gave Sharpe one last look that told him to take care of the children and she would do the rest. She silently padded up the stairs and waited at the landing.

Sharpe turned to the last door and found it locked. Dane had the keys. He turned and found that Nitrox was gone from the landing, and then a strangled cry filtered down from above. Sharpe ran up the stairs and found that Nitrox had found Mark Dane. She had latched on to a part of his anatomy that every man I know instinctively protects when faced with a 120-pound dog. Dane was so paralyzed by the shock of her attack that all he could manage was the strangled cry. Our dog shook her head, violently sawing through clothes and tissue until Dane lost his balance and fell to the floor. He tried to bring the shotgun to bear, but she swung her body into the weapon and he lost his grip. After a full minute of savagery, Nitrox finally let go of Dane's mutilated groin and stared up at Sharpe, panting heavily. He described her as having a look of unnatural awareness and knowledge.

Give me just another moment and all of this will be over, he imagined her saying, and then she turned to Dane's throat and it was over in a moment.

Mark Dane. Age 27. Race: Caucasian. Date of Death: August 21, 2016. Time of Death: 0710 (estimate). Cause of death: Exsanguination due to trauma. Secondary cause of death: Poetic justice. I would amend the last to read Texas Justice.

Sharpe rifled through the dead man's pockets and after finding a ring of keys finally clued into the smell of gas that had been tickling his nose from the moment he opened the front door. Nitrox chuffed at him and then sprinted down the stairs. It took him several tries to find the right key, and he opened the door to a pitch black room filled with the smell of mercaptan (the additive that gives natural gas that rotten egg smell). He reached for the light switch and Nitrox barked so loud that Sharpe's ears rang. She grabbed a cuff of his pants and tried to pull him back into the light of the hallway. He resisted, and she barked even louder, and then began to growl. Wisely, Sharpe backed into the hallway and Nitrox squeezed passed him and went into the small bedroom. She stood staring at a shelf over the television and again chuffed at a flashlight.

"Adis?" Sharpe asked the dog who answered with a small "Woof." "All right, I can deal with that," he said, and he retrieved the flashlight.

The pair returned to the room and found the four children chained and unconscious. He fumbled with the keys and light for several minutes and finally turned to the dog and said, "This would be so much easier if I turn on the light." He panned the flashlight beam to the ceiling and found a naked bulb. A broken naked bulb. With the electrical contacts still intact. "Holy shit," Sharpe said. It took him ten minutes to find the correct keys, free the children from the heavy iron chains, and carry them one by one into the backyard. All four were unconscious but breathing. As Sharpe was carrying the last of the children into the light, he saw that Nitrox had dragged the other three down into the dry creek that dominated the backyard. He stared at her odd behavior for a moment and then was lifted off his feet as the house behind him exploded.

Obviously, there has been much speculation regarding the cause of the explosion. Officially, it was determined to be an electrical short, and technically that is probably correct. However, even before the detective and the child he was carrying, Maggie Dale, hit the ground, my phone received a text. It was a simple one-word message: *Boom*. Sida probably should have just signed his name; instead, the originating number was my office's back line.

In the end, the Manor police, EMS, and Fire Department had enough warning (I assume from Adis) that they arrived in time to save Aldo Caberra, Sharpe, and the four children. The scent of blood was in the air, so naturally the media showed up in droves. Amber Lee and the Highton twins would ultimately make a full physical recovery, but I doubt that psychologically they will ever be the same. In that respect, Sida had achieved at least one goal, but more on that later. Maggie Dale, despite being the smallest and the frailest, survived with only a number of contusions and a broken arm after John Sharpe's body absorbed most of the concussive blast. She had few memories of her nearly 115 days of captivity, and most of them were about the "big brown dog."

John Sharpe had been shot, stabbed, and blown up. I could go through the long list of physical injuries, but I don't think many would find that interesting. For a long time I had real concerns that he would survive, much less live an independent life. In the end though, he not only survived but to great fanfare would return to work in a limited capacity. I doubt he will last to retirement; I just don't see him as a desk kind of guy. Surprisingly, few questions were ever asked about how he knew where to find the children, and his stock answer of following up on a lead seemed to suffice. The children were found, the bad guys had been dealt with, and the public had its hero. Case closed.

As Adis had predicted, the body of William Hartenstein was found in Illinois in late August. Forensics would link him back to Austin and the kidnappings, so now the case was really closed. The question of how he ended up in a field almost a thousand miles away remains unanswered officially, but I don't think many have an interest in pulling that string.

Which leaves us with Sida.

Chapter Twenty Five

I'M GOING TO TAKE US BACK ABOUT A HALF HOUR TO WHEN LEAH AND I FOUND OURSELVES IN THE COMPANY OF SISTER CELESTE. She was a pleasant-faced woman in her sixties that radiated . . . I guess the best word would be serenity. Leah and I sat in the two chairs that faced the nun. To be clear, she was not dressed as a nun. She wore regular clothes. Had no habit. In fact, I don't even remember her wearing a crucifix, but both of us immediately assumed she was a nun.

"I thought you would be more comfortable here." Her gaze seemed to hold each of us individually at the same moment. She was more Adis-like than Adis. "Mika and Tom are safe. They are with a colleague." Later, as I thought about our conversation and situation, it dawned on me that we had never once questioned if they were safe. Some father.

"Who are you?" Leah asked in a voice that respected her station.

The Sister smiled. "Sometimes the simplest questions are the hardest to answer. Why don't you call me Sister Celeste."

"Can you tell us what's going on, Sister?" I said in my church voice. I almost asked her if she was an angel.

"We are in the process of realigning the world's chakras," Sister said, and then she laughed. Leah shrunk back into her chair after having her long forgotten words tossed back at her. "Oh, don't be embarrassed, I thought it was very clever." She reached over to Leah and playfully swatted her knee. "Mostly, we are waiting for the situation on Monkey Road to resolve itself."

This was the first time I had heard the street name. Despite Monkey Road being more than twenty miles from our house, I knew the poorly maintained lane-and-a-half road well. It was one of the worse parts of Ironman Austin, a race I had done every year since its inception so I had a pretty good idea which house the children were being held. "Monkey road," I repeated.

"It's not a coincidence," Sister Celeste started. "There are no real coincidences in this entire affair. The man you call Sida has quite a talent for engineering irony. I only wish he could have redirected his considerable energy in other directions."

"Is that why you are here? To deal with him." Leah, thankfully, remained respectful. "You are a different . . ." She struggled to define Adis and Sida.

"Yes to both. I am here to deal with Sida, as well as Adis, and yes I am a different sort of soul." Her smile, in fact her entire aura, was inviting.

"Why did you allow him to do the things that he did?" I asked, and almost sprained my tongue with my eloquence.

"You mean why did I allow them to do the things that they did?" I nodded and she nodded.

"Why did you allow things to get so out of control?" Leah asked, and I stiffened.

"It's OK," she addressed my concern. She sat back and steepled her fingers in front of her nose, an affectation that would have been right at home with Adis. "That's not a question I can answer for you. I can tell you that there is an answer, but it is your responsibility to find it. If you don't discover it in this lifetime, you will in the next."

"Why our . . .?" Leah started haltingly.

"Why your daughter? Don't be shy, honey. It's perfectly normal for you to focus on your child." Sister finished, and then she leaned into us as if she were sharing a secret. "Because Sida knew it would lead to this." She shared some of Adis's cryptic nature, and his talent for not fully answering a question.

We waited for more, but the Sister simply smiled at us. "I can see that you work with Adis." I tried a different approach but her expression immediately changed.

"We don't actually work together," she corrected. "But you want to know why he has 'attached himself to you'?" She borrowed my air quotes, which was appropriate because they came along with the question that was taking shape in my mind.

I wanted to answer her with something that sounded a little less self-centered, but all I could come up with was a single word. "Yes."

"Our friend Adis should have been more discrete, but that is a discussion for another time." Her expression betrayed the stern taskmaster that lived beneath the serenity. "He has shared some things with you that should have remained hidden. However, not everything you have been told is accurate."

I felt Leah stir. Sister Celeste paused and focused all her attention on Leah. "I don't think he was being malicious," Sister said. "Reckless perhaps, but not malicious." She paused again, and it became obvious that the two ladies were having an unspoken conversation, once again proving that I was not the least bit psychic. "It can be a bit confusing, and in all fairness, he isn't allowed to see everything. Even I don't see everything."

Leah glanced over at me realizing that they had been excluding me, but then her eyes snapped back to the sister. "Are you an angel?" Leah asked in a voice that reminded me of Mia.

"Oh no. Definitely not an angel." She shook her head and smiled. "A parole officer?" She turned back to Leah. "That's part of what I do." She steepled her fingers again and for a moment studied us. "Adis once told you that it wasn't necessary for you to understand his inner workings, and if I can draw on that thought I would add that it's not necessary for you two to understand my inner workings, or the inner workings of the unseen world around you. Only that each and every one of you is cherished."

Leah began to shake her head. For as long as I have known her she has always harbored doubts. "I don't see how you can say that after all—"

"After all that you have seen and all that's happened? How can I say that you are cherished and turn a blind eye to your fate?" Sister began to rock slowly, thoughtfully, in her chair. "Can I give you a morally permissible reason that accommodates the existence of suffering and evil in the context of a benevolent and engaged God? I can, but I won't. As I said earlier, that has been left for you to discover. But please believe me when I say that all of you are cherished."

"Adis has a funny way of showing it." I tried for a little humor, but it fell flat.

"Yes, he does," Sister said, and then she turned to me and hit me so hard with her next sentence that it wiped away any thoughts of humor. "Even those who are guilty of unspeakable acts are cherished."

An image of William Hartenstein strapped to a table filled my mind. I wanted to argue that the life of a madman who would defile and slaughter our daughters had, in my opinion, voided his earth pass, and that his life was not worth the dust beneath our feet. I probably even opened my mouth, but the words as I rehearsed them in my head sounded more like an excuse than an argument.

"Some lives are more important than others," Leah said after a long, uncomfortable moment.

I'm fairly certain that at the moment I knew that she was headed in a different direction, but I used her comment to try and deflect some of the guilt that had begun to creep into my mind. "Like Jonas Salk or Alexander Fleming. By any metric they were more important than any hypothetical or metaphorical child dying of starvation in Somalia." Only the words *hypothetical* and *metaphorical* echoed in my mind. They weren't hypothetical or metaphorical. They were real. Still, I plowed on. "How could a child living and dying in obscurity be compared to men whose work touched the lives of billions?" It was a fair question, but only if it had been a different time and place.

"I believe your wife was concerned about the lives a little closer to home," Sister said, ignoring the transparency of my question. "Why Mia?"

"Why any of them?" Leah answered.

"That's a difficult question to answer without making the same mistakes Adis and Sida have." She sat back and gave us a radiant smile. "Your species has a wonderful future ahead of it. A thousand years from now humans will have completely transformed themselves. Some of that will be the result of simple evolution, but the vast majority of that transformation will be because you will have chosen to change. The things you will accomplish once you realize your combined potential. When you learn that you are not six billion individuals living on the same planet, but one organism composed of six billion interdependent parts.

"Unfortunately, your path to enlightenment will not be smooth. There will be many setbacks, many days when good people will question whether they have been abandoned. A number of you will stray from the path, and others will turn back to the old ways when the road becomes rough, finding safety in the familiar. In the end, each of you will have to make your own decision. We can guide you, help you make the right turns, but in the end each of you will have to decide whether to take our advice or to strike out on your own."

Leah and I exchanged a look as Sister Celeste became a little vague and lost in her own thoughts.

"But—" her eyes snapped back into focus "—before any of that can happen, you must first survive." Now she paused. "Much will be asked from a few. Your child and Amber Lee will in time be presented with opportunities that are important to this process."

"That's why Sida targeted them," I said.

"Not exactly. The man you call Sida has no interest in humanity. He has his own personal agenda."

"He wants to move on. And you are here to ensure that," I said.

"In a fashion," she said, nodding her head. "But that no longer involves you. In a very short while, your role in this tragic little drama will be over."

"And we are to return to our lives as if nothing happened?" Leah's emotions had swung towards the teary end of the spectrum.

"Your lives will never be the same." Sister Celeste ignored Leah's change in demeanor. "This experience will shape the rest of your lives." She abruptly paused and closed her eyes. A moment later, she opened them, and I knew that something somewhere had just changed. My phone vibrated with a message. "Go ahead and read it," she said. "It's from Sida."

I shared the text with Leah. "Boom?" She asked and we both looked to Sister Celeste.

"It means that Amber Lee's life will never be the same." I imagined I saw a fleeting look of fury in the Sister's expression. "It's a good thing that Mia is a very resourceful young lady."

Leah and I exchanged a glance and the two-word phrase *obdurate future* floated between us. I really hate the word obdurate.

I tried to visualize my eight-year-old daughter, a child who just a few months earlier was arguing the religious merits of murder, finding a cure for the common cold or becoming president of the United States. I hope at her inauguration she wears something other than fuzzy pink slippers.

"I'm certain she will be perfect," Sister Celeste said, and I clued into the fact that she was staring into me. "I will confess that I don't like the word obdurate either. It's so arcane. How about *unyielding*. The unyielding future rolls off the tongue a lot better than the obdurate future. Don't you think?"

I nodded, and out of the corner of my eye I saw Leah nod as well.

The break in the conversation was suddenly broken by a flash of light and the arrival of Adis, looking none the worse for wear.

"It is over," he said with great deference. I almost expected him to bow, and then to my surprise he did.

"Please, sit." Adis sat between us in a chair that a moment earlier was simply air. Sister Celeste closed her eyes and took a deep breath. "You have made a number of mistakes, penitent. Mistakes that demonstrate your lack of faith in the process. In us."

"I am not perfect," Adis said with a bowed head. I'm guessing he would have been more comfortable on his knees.

"No, you're not." Sister Celeste sounded both loving and harsh. "Nor do we have an expectation of perfection. Only obedience, and in that you failed."

In the last few hours, my opinion of Adis had run the gamut, but now I felt as if he were being judged unfairly. I was about to come to his defense when a glance by Sister Celeste silenced me.

"It is possible in some respect to view this entire affair as a test of your willingness to abide by the oaths that you have taken to avoid judgment." Sister allowed Adis to nod his agreement. "You are too old, penitent, and have come too far to have placed yourself in this position."

I snuck a peak at Leah and found her just as confused as I was. I was starting to worry that this was an I-see-dead-people moment and that Sister Celeste was about to turn to us and announce that Adis had been Sida all along, but she didn't.

"That is true," Adis said, and his transformation was nothing short of magical. Gone was the vigorous man in his seventies; in his place was a frail man in his late twenties, maybe early thirties. His arms had shriveled to mere skin and bones, and his blue eyes had yellowed and receded into dark sockets. He had the look of a man who had only days to live.

"No one needed to die at the high school, but they did. Their deaths are a direct result of your dereliction. You then compounded your sin by adding to the death toll," she admonished.

"I didn't recognize the signs earl—"

The Sister cut him off. Had this been a Hollywood movie, the lights would have dimmed, fog would have enveloped us, and thunder and lightning would have filled our ears as the Sister transformed into the very embodiment of God's wrath. But none of that happened. "You didn't recognize the signs because you had stopped looking for them. You were completely self-absorbed with your condition, a condition of your own making, and when you recovered you acted precipitously, recklessly, and overtly."

"Yes, ma'am," he answered. Leah and I watched as he slid from the chair and dropped to his knees. Given his current condition, I had a fleeting concern that the impact would break something.

"And that was just one example of your disobedience."

"The children . . ." Adis interrupted her, which was probably a bad idea.

Her voice rose, and I imagined a slight reverberation sound effect. "The children were never your responsibility. You endangered them, and the consequences now hang around your neck." Her voice had enough power behind it that I wished I wasn't sitting so close. It took several moments for the echoes to fade. "You had one responsibility."

"I understand." Now he sounded like the penitent she kept calling him.

Leah and I shared a glance over the nearly prostrate form of Adis. "One responsibility?" Leah mouthed and I just shrugged my shoulders.

"I would like to believe that your involvement was for the greater good, and for the moment I will set aside the fact that that presupposes that you know better than us. However, you are not our hit man, no matter the situation. We do not condone the taking of life. You have been given talents and gifts that were to be used to avoid it, yet you choose to end your service by perverting those talents.

"There has been much discussion about your motives. Whether you, like your brother, are trying to force our hand. Or whether your old sadistic tendencies have resurfaced. Possibly you have grown tired and find the taking of lives to be expedient and effective." She waited for him to respond.

"I have been worn thin," was all he said in his defense.

"I can understand that," she said after studying him for a long moment. "You are of no further use to us. The question now becomes, what do we do with you?" She continued to stare at him, and I was pretty certain she was staring into him as well. For his part, Adis didn't move. His head remained on his chest and he balanced himself on wobbly knees. "Justice would demand that you be sent for judgment, but I will concede that perhaps we left you out in the cold too long and that we bear some of the responsibility." I looked at Adis and watched as he transformed back into the man we knew. "Leave. Leave now as a man. Live the remainder of your years in anticipation of having the One you hurt so grievously decide your fate. I give you the opportunity to redeem yourself in His eyes."

His head rose from his chest, but he still wouldn't met the Sisters eyes. "I don't know . . ."

"I don't want you to say anything. I give you your name back Ladounis, or if you prefer, Adis." Sister Celeste rose from her seat and offered Adis her hand, which he kissed. "I wish you peace."

Adis scrambled to his feet and in a moment was gone. Without a word, he simply walked out the rectory door and our lives. I didn't know what to say, and by her look neither did Leah. I thought one of us should have said something, at least a goodbye. I stared at the door, but when it was clear he wasn't coming back I turned back to Sister Celeste, who obviously was more than just a nun.

"Well, that's done," she said, staring down at us.

"Should we have seen that?" I asked, uncomfortable at several levels with Adis's dismissal.

"Airing our dirty laundry?" Sister Celeste said, borrowing a term from Leah's lexicon. "If it makes you uncomfortable, I could take you home, but I thought that you deserve the right to witness the resolution of this affair. We still have one more unresolved issue."

"Sida," I said, always in tune with the obvious. "There are others more deserving. People he's hurt far more than us." Off the top of my head, I could think of a half-dozen people whose lives were affected to a greater degree than ours.

"But they are not here," the Sister answered, and I'm pretty sure she was referring to more than just our physical location.

"I would like to stay," Leah said sharply.

"Well, that may pose a problem, as we have to go to Sida." Sister smiled at Leah, who stood. They both looked at me and I stood as well (I'm not sure why it was necessary to stand— maybe it was for the same reason that when an airplane lands we have to bring our tray tables and seatbacks to an upright and locked position).

In the blink of an eye, the room around us changed into the Texas Capitol building. We stood in the middle of the rotunda, beneath the massive dome. I looked down to find that I was standing on the seal of Mexico, one of the seven nations whose flag has flown over Texas. I took a respectful step backward and looked up to find that the morning sun was creating oblique beams of light in the dust-filled air. The upper vaults of the dome were being refinished, and a light patina of dust covered just about everything.

Sida was sitting quietly on a wooden bench just beneath the portrait of George W. Bush. "Hello," he said, as friendly as anyone could say the word. Only, like pretty much everything he said, it had a menacing undercurrent.

Sister Celeste, who was standing on the United States seal, turned and faced him. For a second, they stared. "Is this how you address me, penitent?" An unseen force pulled Sida to his knees and then across the floor.

"That tickles." Sida laughed as he slid to a stop at the Sister's feet. He tried to stand, but his knees seemed to have been glued to the polished marble floor. "I promise you I have no thoughts of running away." He regained his balance and stared up at Sister Celeste. "So they sent you. I must really be in trouble. I see you brought company." He tried to turn his head, but it too had been immobilized. "Long time no see, Doc, and you brought the little woman. Hello, Leah. How are the kids?"

Leah managed to restrain herself for maybe a millisecond and then reached out and slapped Sida across the face with enough force that the report echoed through the nearly empty rotunda. "Did that tickle?" Her voice chased the slap through the recesses of the dome.

"No, it hurt, a lot." He still had some movement of his shoulders, but that did him little good. "You see, this is what I've had to work with for more than two thousand years. Violent, impulsive—" He never finished, as Sister Celeste waved her hand and Sida became rigid.

"Please. I've heard enough. You will speak only when spoken to, penitent." She took a half step back and looked him up and down. "Your concerns and thoughts about humanity are a matter of record, and I don't need them repeated here." She began to slowly walk around him, and I hoped she would produce a samurai sword and use it. "Is it necessary for me to list your many offenses, penitent?"

Sida's face relaxed. "My offenses? For two millennia I have done your bidding. Shepherding these foolish, self-absorbed, self-destructing creatures, always following your arbitrary set of rules, and never asking why—" He had more to say but a wave of the Sister's hand again cut him off.

"You are not now, nor have you ever been, in a position to ask why." She completed her first circuit and started a second. "Time has not diminished your arrogance, which doesn't surprise me. I was against your deferment from the beginning."

"And that doesn't surprise me," Sida answered through clamped jaws. "You've always enjoyed your role as the disciplinarian. The hard-ass." Despite all that Sida had done, he still managed to shock me with his disrespectful language. "Go ahead and send me to the final judgment. Even an eternity of damnation is better than another minute under your yoke of civility and responsibility—" Another wave of the Sister's hand and Sida choked on his final words.

"Unfortunately, I am not the final arbiter. Others still see the potential for redemption." She had finished her circuit and was once again facing Sida. She glared at him, and after a long second Sida's insolent expression dropped and he averted his eyes. Leah and I waited for him to morph back into his mortal form as Adis had, but Sida remained exactly as we had always known him. "I wish you peace," she said softly. Her hand opened and Sida vanished. A small cloud of dust swirled into the void created by his disappearance.

"What did you do with him?" I asked, a moment after Sister Celeste turned back to us. A wry smile crossed her face.

"All babies are born crying, but at this moment a seventeen-year-old girl in Somalia is giving birth to a baby boy that will not cry but scream with the realization that his plans didn't quite work out the way he wanted." She was openly pleased with herself. "Hopefully, he will do better."

I looked at Leah but neither of us knew what to say. Many months later, I still don't know how to feel. Was this justice? Or was this an opportunity for Sister Celeste and her colleagues to engineer a little irony of their own? Or perhaps it was a sincere attempt at redemption. I just don't know.

What I did know was that in almost a blink of an eye we were free of Adis and his wayward brother Sida. "Are there others like them?" I asked after a long quiet stretch.

She smiled. "More each day. Be thankful for that."

"Are they going to try this again?" Leah followed up. "Come after Mia?"

"No," she said simply. I wanted to press her, to get some assurance, but her stare tied my tongue.

"She will find her way without our help." Sister Celeste smiled broadly and my heart lightened. "I wish you peace."

And then we were back home in our garage. Standing in transmission oil.

Epilogue

The epilogue is where I'm supposed to make sense of things and create some degree of closure. Perhaps espouse a grand unifying principal or lesson that could only have been realized after months of reflection. It should come as no surprise that I don't have one. Maybe I need more time and reflection.

What is obvious (my strong suit) is that the world is far more complex than I ever imagined. That the curtain that separates us from the likes of Adis, Sida, and Sister Celeste hides a mechanism so intricate and delicate that it could only have been designed by Rube Goldberg. A mechanism that silently whirrs beyond our comprehension and imagination, whose sole purpose is to ensure the survival of our species despite the vagaries of random events and the all-too-common malignancies of human decisions. That's sort of a comforting thought.

I still believe that to a very large degree we determine our own fate, at least relative to the situation we find ourselves in. I doubt I will ever have the opportunity to cure cancer or become a great philosopher, and that's OK. My world is the small circle around me and that's what I need to focus on. I expect that over the course of my remaining years, "shit" will continue to happen, but as Adis put it, "shit happens because we keep making shit happen." (don't get upset if you realize that wasn't his exact quote; it's close enough.) All I can do is decide who I want to be when it rains down on me. I suppose that's all any of us can do. Whether or not this is profound enough to fulfill the requirements for an epilogue will be for you to judge, because this is as profound as I get.

I keep looking back at that last day thinking that I missed an opportunity to have all the great questions answered. Who and what is God? Why would He allow evil to warp our world and minds? Who and what are we? I could go on, but you get the point. But then I remember what Sister Celeste told us, that those answers are for us to find.

Enough time has passed that we have stopped looking at our now nine-year-old daughter for signs of her becoming a great thinker and leader. In all honesty, I haven't seen even the slightest inklings. She still ignores her school work and fights with her brother and sister. Maybe the torch was passed back to Amber Lee. She is making a reasonable recovery and living with her aunt now. Fortunately, they live close enough that Amber is a regular fixture around our house. For the record, I don't see any signs of great insight in Amber either (although she is far neater and organized than our Mia). I've lost track of the other three children, except that Maggie Dale and her parents are occasionally seen on the television for a variety of reasons and they look fine.

As fate would have it, John Sharpe spent a couple weeks in my hospital, which gave me the opportunity to get to know him beyond his façade of professionalism and detachment. I have found that he is a fairly reasonable guy. We've had a number of pseudophilosophical discussions about Adis, Sida, and the entire unseen pantheon, but haven't managed to answer even a single question. We seem to spend an inordinate amount of time talking about Adis's actions at the Monkey Road house. Was there any real difference between Adis directly involving himself and his indirect participation by guiding Sharpe and Nitrox? The rules do seem a little arbitrary, but I think the real reason Sharpe keeps coming back to this is that he still hasn't come to terms with shooting two men. I respect him for that.

I would like to say that I've never seriously questioned my decision or actions towards William Hartenstein, but that would be untrue. I think about it every day. I imagine him as a small child with a world of possibilities before him. I imagine his parents in their grief having similar thoughts knowing that every memory they have of their son was just a step on a path that ended in a shallow grave in Illinois. Did they blame themselves and wonder if they had done things differently he would still be with them today? I know that he was a bad man, an evil man, as Adis had described him, and I like to tell myself that in reality I never had a choice. I was not about to sacrifice my daughter for the sake of a principle, and I made the only decision I could with the information available. Still, periodically he haunts my dreams. Maybe he met Sister Celeste and for penance is now walking the earth as Adis's replacement. That's kind of a scary thought.

I never did learn the reason Sida involved me with the death of William Hartenstein. Maybe that domino is way down the road and hasn't fallen just yet, but I think it was just to be mean. An opportunity to create mischief and chaos. I think he wanted Eris to tell me everything that he had learned about Sida and his smiling brother and consequentially drive a wedge between us. I think it was also an opportunity to defile me in much the same way I had warned Mia about so long ago. Unfortunately, some nights I lay awake believing that he has.

We never saw Adis again, at least in person. Just before I started this writing project, both Leah and I watched him on *60 Minutes.* Instead of the usual twenty minutes, the producers devoted more than half the show to Adis, Northland High, and the series of strange events of 2016. Conspiracy theories abounded, but none of them even approached the truth, and for more than half an hour Adis artfully avoided it as well. He still looked extraordinarily hale for a man in his mid-seventies, but his characteristic vitality had diminished. He had been traveling around the country by bus with no specific plan. When he found a place interesting, he would get off and start walking. He had met and talked with hundreds of people along the way, and his sustained celebrity and singular presence allowed him to "really see people as they are."

Leah and I suffered through his platitudes and pseudorealizations all the way to the end, knowing that he was in fact trying to make amends, to do something right, but we aren't ready to give him any credit. Sister Celeste's words still echo in our minds, and while she was light on specifics she made it very clear that had Adis done his job our lives would have continued in uninterrupted ignorance. Intellectually, I know that in the end he tried to correct his mistake, but my heart just isn't ready to accept that.

Like with Sister Celeste, I feel I missed an opportunity to learn from Adis. As he had been a witness to the development of human society over the millennia, I would be interested in his opinions. Does our complex society bear any resemblance to those a hundred, a thousand years ago? Are we as individuals, blessed with television, electricity, and water from a tap any better than those who came before us? Have we done enough with the blessings bestowed upon us or have they made us weaker, complacent? He probably also knew who really did kill JFK? Maybe someday he will swing back around.

It bothers me that I am no smarter as a result of these experiences. If this were a movie, my hair would have turned white and I would be standing on top of a tall rock with a staff in one hand while my other directed people towards the promised land. Unfortunately, Cecile B. De Mille is nowhere to be found, which leaves Leah and me trying to sort things out alone.

I think Leah tripped to something a couple months back. It's not earth-shattering, but it's worthy of note. We had just finished watching the movie *I, Robot* (Leah has a thing for Will Smith), and she began mumbling the phrase "ghosts in the machine."[3]

"Do you remember Adis talking about the random sequences of events that lead to unintended outcomes?" she asked.

"I remember he said that it was his job to interrupt the sequence," I answered.

"Sort of like random bits of computer code that combine to create crazy, sentient robots," she mused.

"That's a bit of a reach," I said.

"After creating such a beautiful, intricate construct, in which human actions are balanced by human reactions, why do you think they would allow ghosts in their machine?" Leah didn't wait for me to answer. "I think it's allowed to create opportunities for Adis and the rest of the penitents an opportunity to redeem themselves."

This obviously brings up a whole host of difficult questions that I will leave to you, dear reader, to ponder. I've given them enough thought, and like I said at the beginning, I really am not the person for any of this. Besides it's late and I have to go run.

End Notes
X X

1. Adis's 1-Minute Primer on Irish History, Oranmore, Father Brian Liam

"Okay, here's my one-minute primer on Irish history. Ireland as
a culture is very old, going back more than 8000 years, and it's
had more than it's fair share of troubles. About 2500 years ago,
it was invaded and conquered by the Gaels, who as coincidence
would have it spoke a language called Gaelic. Fast forward half
a millennium and Irish pirates capture a sixteen-year-old boy
and sell him into slavery. He escapes a few years later and finds
his way to Rome—"

"St. Patrick," I interjected.

"That's right, and he returns to Ireland and converts the
better part of the island to Christianity. For the next five or six
hundred years the Irish live rather peaceably and practice their
own brand of Catholicism with a dash of Irish mythology. However, just after the new millennium, the pope, who happened to
be English at the time, is not really happy that Jesus has to share
center stage with wood nymphs, so he decrees that England will
have lordship over Ireland. This of course gives England the
papal right to invade and subjugate the wayward Irish, which
starts almost 900 years of oppression, starvation, and war.

"The potato arrived in Ireland from America in the eigh-
teenth century and immediately improved the diet and lives of
most of the Irish peasantry, but it brought with it a high degree
of dependence, and when in the 1840s the crop was hit by the
blight, a cycle of mass starvation and emigration began. In a
decade, the population of Ireland had been reduced by a third."

Oranmore is a small town just south of Galway city on Ireland's west coast that exists even today. In the mid-seventeenth century it was little more than a fishing village with a big castle that people had been fighting over for centuries. In Father Liam's time it was being rebuilt and fortified by the English after Irish patriots burned it down in 1667, an act which prompted a brutal reprisal from the British and was likely directly responsible for Father Liam's assignment.

The reconstruction project created the unfortunate consequence of placing English soldiers and Irish peasants in close proximity, a fact that made no one happy. The English soldiers did not want to be in Ireland, and the Irish certainly did not want the English soldiers in Ireland. That's about all they had in common. Unfortunately for the Irish, the English were the ones with all the weapons.

Brian Liam was born in 1644. His birth place is listed as Oranmore, but it is likely that Oranmore was simply the closest town to whatever unnamed hamlet witnessed his birth. He was ordained a priest at the tender age of nineteen in Dublin. History loses track of him until he took over the Sacred Heart parish in Oranmore in 1669, and was made a bishop in 1698. He lived only five more years.

He wrote extensively about his early experiences as pastor of Sacred Heart after he moved to Galway as a bishop (possibly because the diocese provided him with a scribe). He describes being in a quandary. He was fiercely patriotic and describes the British as being worse than the weather.

However, Father Liam was a sensible man and he knew that any organized resistance, or any attempt to expel or hinder the English would only add to the hardship his flock already bore. An English warship sat in Oranmore's small harbor, which meant they controlled the sea and when and if the Irish could fish. An English regiment lived outside the castle and routinely patrolled the town and farms in a none-too-subtle hint that they also controlled the land.

In the 29 years Father Liam served as pastor, Oranmore prospered. Whether Adis's story is true and the gold pieces are responsible for the improved living conditions I leave for you to decide. Personally, I think that Father Liam's practical approach to the British occupation led to a relative calm that allowed for both sides to live as best as they could.

2. Jedidiah Woodman and Kioawa—A Long Short-Story

I recount this story as Adis told it, which includes my commentary as well.

"Jedidiah Woodman lived about three hundred and fifty years ago. Which just happens to be about the time I came to the New World. It was so long ago, in fact, that New Hampshire wasn't even New Hampshire, it was just an extension of Massachusetts." Adis pushed back from the table, crossed his legs, and reclined into his chair. Actually, I owned the chair, but at that moment everything seemed to belong to Adis.

"Colonial America," I said.

Adis nodded his head. "Yes, colonial America, but it wasn't the colonial America you see on TV, where everyone wears funny hats and eats turkey and mashed potatoes with friendly Indians. The reality was that life was harsh, ugly, and hard, even for the gentry. There was nothing simple or romantic about it. For many, death came early and suddenly, and for most it was a blessing. I remember those days, and though time has softened my memory I can safely say that I would have preferred to skip them. Except for one thing." Adis raised one finger.

"What was that?" I didn't hesitate a moment, and asked the question on his cue. I had slipped about halfway down Adis's rabbit hole.

"The sense of community. Of course, that community became a necessity under the pressures of isolation, depredation, and the struggle to survive in a hostile environment. It's a fact of human nature that when threatened we pull together, but when life becomes easier we drift apart." He shook his head sadly. "But I digress." He brightened again. "Still, it's a nice segue back to Jedidiah. He was the exception to the rule, the proverbial loner. As I think about it, Jedidiah was an exception to most rules. He grew up as an only child, and instead of becoming overly dependent on his parents, as many only children do, he longed for independence, which more than a few times landed him in trouble. He was a large child that grew into a larger man, more than six feet of solid muscle and bone. By today's standards that would make him a big man, but by seventeenth-century standards that made him a mountain of a man. Which again landed him in trouble more than a few times. His father was an officer in a British shipping company and a former captain of the royal navy. He was a stern, unforgiving man that had little time for his undisciplined son, and after Jed's mother died of consumption, Captain Woodman announced that the pair would be leaving Boston and sailing back to England and civilization. Jed was sixteen at the time and responded that he had no desire to leave his adopted country and was quite capable of living independently. The two exchanged words and eventually more than words. In the end, the slightly chastened Captain sailed back to England alone."

"That's sad." Despite myself I was slipping into Adis's story and for a moment wondered what Jed's father thought as he sailed away. Did he look back as America dropped below the horizon knowing that he would never see his son again? Did he question whether he made a mistake and suddenly want to jump overboard and swim back? The thought of losing one of my children, either from hard words and stubborn attitudes or from a kidnapping, froze me inside.

Adis nodded. "As I was saying, Jed had always swum against the current, and when he found himself alone he quickly left Boston with nothing more than what he and his horse could carry. For as long as he could remember, he had heard stories of tall mountains, streams choked with fish, and a life full of adventure; stories told by the dark and dangerous men who lived on the fringes of society in the cheap shanties just outside Boston. When he was just a small boy, Jed had accompanied his father to meet such men. The unwashed, unshaven, and unruly lot supplied the furs that Captain Woodman exported back to England, and although he had a number of intermediaries to perform the menial negotiations, the Captain wanted his son to see firsthand what happened when individuals refused to abide by the rules of civilized society. But all Jed saw was freedom and independence. These men respected only themselves and were beholden to no man, including his father and some far-off king. They had the courage to venture inland to find their fortune and forge their own destiny, regardless of the risk. Although at the time Jed didn't know it, he had just met the first real Americans.

"In short order, he took up with a man named James Magraw. An Irish-Scot, Magraw had fled Ireland for the new world shortly after finding himself indentured to an English lord that held the debt Magraw's late father had left him. For thirty years he had wandered the wilds of New England, and he was one of the few who had lived to tell the tale. And tell he did, especially to a young, impressionable Jedidiah Woodman, who for years had taken every opportunity to escape his father's watchful eye and sneak over to Boston's dark side. Jed found the now-old man in a small lean-to tavern in a settlement without a name ten miles north of Boston and offered his services in return for all the older man could teach.

"Why would you want such a thing? You have a good life, an easy life. Go back to England, marry some wench, have a dozen little brats, and die a fat old man in front of a warm fire." Magraw was just as Jed remembered, dirty, with torn clothes and foul breath. He drank something he called frog's breath, which tasted more like liquid fire. "You won't survive the first winter," he said, and he went back to his frog's breath.

"You did, and I'm bigger, stronger, and smarter than you ever were." Jed was nearly a foot taller than Magraw.

"So you are." The old man put down his empty mug and inventoried the younger man from head to toe. "And you dress nicer as well. Can you shoot?" Magraw asked, eyeing Jed's musket. "Can you ride?" he added, looking over the young man's shoulder to the beautiful horse tied to a post. Jed nodded to both. "If you get killed, for any reason I keep 'em both. I'm leaving in two days. If you haven't come to your senses by then, meet me back here before sunup."

"Your story is starting to sound a little like the Jeremiah Johnson story," I interjected.

Adis tilted his head and looked momentarily confused. "I once knew a man named Jeremiah Johnson. He lived out west in the 1850s. I met him in St Louis. He was having dinner with a writer named Samuel Clemmons, who you may have heard of. Mr. Johnson was trying to sell old Sam a story about a man who goes up into the mountains to live and ends up fighting wild Indians. I assure you Jedidiah Woodman did no such thing. I will admit that I really didn't care for Mr. Johnson, and I don't think Mr. Clemmons was overly fond of him as well."

"Now you sound like Forrest Gump." I will admit that I'm not sure I really said that, but I should have.

"Anyway, our friend Jedidiah heads up into the mountains of what we will one day call New Hampshire with James Magraw and begins the life he has longed for. Like most things, it was different from what he imagined. For one thing, he had never really experienced sustained physical discomfort before. He had always been warm when it was cold outside. Always been able to stay dry when it was wet outside. Always been able to eat when he needed to. He had learned to take comfort for granted, and it took more than a year for him to unlearn it, and several more for him to inure himself to the challenges living outside civilized society posed.

"By the time James Magraw died six years later, the two had become close friends and Jed had become one of those dark, dangerous men who lived by their own rules. Magraw had been sick a full year before his death, and Jed had built him a small two-room log cabin at the foot of a mountain the two had taken to calling the Bitterroot, after some form of turnip that grew naturally in the mountain's high meadows. Jed buried his friend in one of those meadows, and over the next few years he often returned to that spot to think things over. For the most part, Jed was at peace with the world, but since Magraw's death the isolation had become progressively heavier. One late summer afternoon, Jed was sitting on his usual log, pondering the growing void in his life. The proximity of old Magraw's bones loosened Jeb's tongue and he carried on a conversation with himself. He sat and debated whether he should leave the mountains and return to the world when he caught a whiff of the thick musk of what could only be a bear.

"Now remember that Jed was a very large man, but bears are, well, bears. Even the black bears that inhabit the northeast can grow to nearly twice the size of our mountain man, and that's before we factor in the teeth and claws. Jed jumped to his feet and found the largest black bear he had ever seen crouching between where he stood and his musket. The beast was so large that for a moment Jed wondered if it could be something other than a bear. It whipped its head around and when they fixed eyes it roared loud enough to echo up and down the canyons.

"He silently cursed himself for being so foolish and then slowly backed away. The bear advanced, tossing his head and swatting the dirt in front of him in challenge. Jed retreated further, but the bear continued his advance.

"'What do you want?' he screamed. Magraw had told him years earlier that if ever he was cornered by a bear he should make himself as large and threatening as possible. Of course, he also told Jed never to allow himself to be cornered by a bear. Jed remembered asking Magraw if threatening a bear had ever really worked and he simply shrugged, saying that no one ever told him that it didn't.

"Jed had backed up to the edge of the clearing. One more step would lead to a hundred-foot fall to the rocks and trees below, but the bear didn't seem to care. Jed began to wave his arms and bellow until his throat ached, and finally the bear paused. He sniffed the air and turned his head, and although it's not really possible, Jed thought that he saw a slight smile form on the face of the giant bruin.

"His situation was desperate. He couldn't go forward and he couldn't go back. He took a step to his left, which as it turned out was the wrong thing to do. His foot slipped on some loose stones covered in grass and moss, and he nearly fell. He flailed his arms wildly and for a moment regained his balance, until the dirt beneath him gave way. He slipped to his knees and then fell forward, holding on to clumps of turf as his legs dangled over the ledge.

"Poor old Jed barely managed to get back to his knees before the big bear lunged. He tried to draw his knife but was bowled over before it cleared its scabbard. The bear's jaws almost completely encircled Jed's thigh as its teeth sunk into muscle and bone. He didn't feel pain so much as shock after being struck by a six-hundred-pound beast. He was tossed in the air like a rag doll, and the bear was on him again. Bites in the neck, shoulder, chest, and arm. They came so fast that Jed was having a hard time even registering them, and then once again he was flying, but this flight was considerably longer. He spun wildly in the air and caught a brief glimpse of a cloud floating through the blue sky, and then the cliff edge rushed passed him. He struck something hard and unyielding, then something else just as hard, and then a final impact took what little breath he had left. The white cloud still floated in the sky, but now it was so much further away."

"Very dramatic," I said. Adis had been using his hands to animate poor Jed's fall down the mountain. His face was just as animated, and I could easily see him telling stories to pre-schoolers at the library. "Story-time with Adis," they would call it. "Every Saturday at 1:00 p.m." Of course, they would have to reschedule if it conflicted with Adis's day job: cold-blooded killer of terrorists.

"Thank you," he beamed. "For two days and nights, poor Jedidiah lay on a stony outcrop sixty feet in the air, hovering between life and death. So long that crows had collected around him and begun to peck at his wounds. On the third day it began to rain. Not a nice spring rain, but a real gully washer. Water pounded Jed's outcrop from the cliff above, which did scare away the crows but also came perilously close to drowning poor Jed. The cold water revived him, and he managed to open his eyes between downpours. His thinking was fuzzy and his body felt fuzzy as well. He tried to get up and realized that he couldn't move his arms or legs. Water dripped onto his face and he could do nothing about it. His neck was broken and that meant he was going to die on this slab of stone. For the rest of the morning he watched droplets of water fall from high above and then splash around him or on him. He wondered what death would be like, and how long it would take to find him. His silent emotions swung from acceptance to anger. At times he wanted to scream. He was angry with himself for being so monumentally stupid. He was angry at Magraw for dying and leaving him here alone. He was angry with his mother for dying, and his father for being a man devoid of understanding. He tried to scream, but it was hard to breath and all he could manage was a weak moan, which only fueled his anger. His impotent rage finally gave way to exhaustion, and he let it flow through him. It cost too much to be angry. He closed his eyes and slept away the rest of the day.

"Jed woke just before sunset. There was still enough light to see that the sky had cleared, but that was about all Jed could see. The rocks bit into the back of his head and he tried to move his neck, but a pain so severe that he nearly passed out stopped him short. He would just have to live with the rocks and the limited view. He listened to the song birds in the trees below until a new sound, a rustling, alerted him. The crows had returned. He tried to move his arms without success. Same with his legs. His neck was still broken. Nothing had changed. It was harder to breath now, and Jed was glad that the end was near. The last thing he wanted was to slowly starve as the birds fed on him.

"Something large moved near him, and he heard rocks skitter off his perch (he figured that if he was going to die here and have his bones lie for all eternity on this perch then it rightfully belonged to him). His first thought was that the bear had somehow managed to crawl down the forty or so feet to finish what he had started but then realized that in most situations bears don't speak English. A leg appeared and Jed could make out a dark and well-toned calf. A leather thong wound up the lower leg and Jed knew a simple shoe of deer hide could be seen if he was able to move his head. Mohawk Indian. Whoever it was, was a little far north, but it was not unusual to find a solitary Mohawk anywhere in the White Mountains. They were great trappers and traded their furs with the Dutch, generally for muskets, hatchets, and anything made of metal. They were allies with the Dutch, and together they pushed the Hurons far back into French Canada. They were also known to be cannibals.

"I asked if you were still alive." A well-worn brown face appeared. His accent was British and his English was excellent, which perplexed poor Jed, who was now convinced that instead of the crows enjoying his mortal remains it would be the Mohawks. As a rule, the British and Mohawks didn't get along. That would change later, but in the mid-seventeenth century, in the mountains of what would later be called New Hampshire, the Mohawks were still firmly in the Dutch camp, and a Mohawk using English, and perfect English at that, was indeed a mystery worth exploring.

"Barely," Jed whispered. Breathing had grown steadily more difficult, and saying that single word made him see stars. He felt the Indian run a hand along the back of his neck and discover the step-off of bones.

"I'm guessing you already know." The Mohawk had the typical features. Black hair shaved in the traditional Mohawk fashion. Dark, intelligent eyes and an expression that spoke more of pity than opportunity.

All Jed could do was blink.

"I will stay with you," he stated in the usual stoic Mohawk fashion, and sat next to Jed. "I am Kioawa, and I will be the last face you see."

Jed's last night fell slowly. He tried to remain awake, but an all-consuming fatigue pulled at his eyes and mind. He wanted to thank the Indian for not letting him die alone. He had always imagined that his death would be a solitary affair, especially since Magraw was gone, but as the moment neared he was suddenly afraid of being alone when he drew his last breath. He tried to speak but the words wouldn't come. It was all he could do to draw small bites of air into his lungs. It would be the last of many things he would leave undone.

"Kioawa quietly sang as the stars began to appear in the fading light. Jed tried to focus on the soft chant and not the anger and fear in his heart and mind. He knew some of Kioawa's language and realized that the Indian was praying to his gods to receive his brother, a fellow hunter who braved the dangers of the mountains. Understanding dawned slowly in Jed's receding consciousness: by staying with him, Kioawa was making a promise to care for Jed's mortal remains. He finally closed his eyes, no longer having the energy to fight off the enveloping darkness in his mind. His last thought was a question: How did he get down here?

"Jed awoke in his bed early the next morning. Now, I know what you're thinking, that this was some sort of copout and that he had dreamed the entire affair, but you would be wrong."

In truth, I immediately flashed to the TV show *Dallas* and their lame return of Bobby Ewing (the nicer of the Ewing brothers). For those of you under forty, let me explain. Patrick Duffy played Bobby Ewing, and sometime in the 1980s decided to strike out on his own, so the writers killed off his character. Mr. Duffy later decided to return to the show, so those same clever writers decided to make the entire previous season all simply a dream. *Voila!* Bobby Ewing suddenly steps out of a shower and magically everything is as it was. Is there a stronger term than lame? For the record, I have never seen an episode of *Dallas*, which should tell you how much people disliked this little trick.

"He was in the very bed that his friend James Magraw had died in, and that fact was not lost on Jed. He looked around and found that his neck, while sore, was no longer broken. He flexed his fingers and toes and felt them slide beneath the blanket of bear fur that covered him. He had never seen this blanket before, and the irony of it was not lost on him. He lifted the pelt with newfound strength and discovered that he was naked, save for a small cloth undergarment. His torso and arms were covered with fresh clotted blood. He dropped the blanket and looked for his clothes and found the tattered remnants of his leather shirt and pants draped across the bedside chair. He had had them made by a tanner in Boston almost three years ago and regretted the loss of such new and fine clothes.

"He tried to sit up, and not surprisingly the world around him began to swirl. He waited a moment and then tried again. He managed to pull himself to a sitting position, where he waited for the vertigo to subside. The blanket slipped to his lap, giving Jed a better look at the extent of his injuries. He had been torn to ragged pieces and counted at least a dozen claw and bite marks from his shoulders to his waist. He had at least one more in his right thigh, which pulsed with pain. That was the one he remembered the best.

"'I should be dead,' he said. His voice was weak and raspy, but to his ear he sounded like himself. The blood loss alone should have killed him, not to mention the fractured neck, which had miraculously cured itself. The memory of not being able to move or breathe was fresh in his mind, and he took a deep breath just to prove he could. The fuzzy, nothing feeling from his neck down had been replaced with blessed pain. Every inch of him screamed, and it made him laugh with joy. And then there was the slow slip into oblivion. He hadn't dreamed that any more than he had dreamed the wounds that covered his body. He looked up into the clear light of morning utterly perplexed and found a bare-chested figure curled up on the floor just beneath the window. 'Kioawa,' he said, and the Indian stirred from sleep. He rolled onto his back and then in one fluid movement was on his feet, a knife in his hand, his eyes sweeping the room. Kioawa's expression was a mix of surprise, confusion, and fear, and if he hadn't been armed Jed probably would have laughed at his benefactor. 'It's all right, there's no one here but us.'

"'Who are you?' he demanded a moment after confirming that they were indeed alone. The large knife that Jed recognized as his own had dropped slightly but was now pointed directly at him. Kioawa's English was just as perfect as it had been the night before.

"'I am the man you helped on the ledge. My name is Jedidiah Woodman, and I am in your debt.' Jed wanted to bow as manners dictated but could only manage a simple nod of the head.

"Kioawa just stared, his knife still raised. He said something Jed could not recognize and then repeated it in English. 'I saw you die.' He took a step backward, openly suspicious of the white man. 'Are you a spirit?'

"It was a fair question, and a possibility Jed hadn't considered. How does one know if they are a spirit? When he was a boy his mother had taught him to read the Bible, so he knew that lots of people came back as spirits. Jesus returned as a spirit and He walked around like everyone else. He ate and drank; Thomas even probed his wounds (something that had left an impression on a young Jedidiah), but He never told anyone what it was like to be a spirit. 'I don't know,' Jed finally answered. 'So you didn't cure me?' Kioawa shook his head. 'No Indian magic?' The question sounded ridiculous, but he had to ask. Jed had heard so many stories about Indian magic that he had begun to believe in it, as much as he believed in anything he hadn't himself witnessed. Kioawa's faced darkened as if he had been insulted.

'Stupid white man,' he sneered, and he lowered the knife. 'Why did you bring me here?' Kioawa edged towards a roughhewn chair that Magraw had made weeks before he died and slowly sat, still eying Jed suspiciously.

"'I didn't. I couldn't. I can barely sit.' Jed tried to raise an arm to prove his point and found that his shoulder wound had begun to bleed. A small rivulet of blood tracked down past his elbow. Both men watched as the stream of blood reached his wrist and then dropped to the floor. Each man had the same thought, but it was Jed who voiced it. 'Do spirits bleed?' He felt light headed and asked himself if spirits also pass out.

"'No,' Kioawa said definitively, establishing that between the two he was the expert on spirits. The small but growing puddle of blood seemed to distress the Indian more than the possibility that a spirit had spirited him away. He continued to stare at the bloody floor even after Jed had swung back in bed. 'Spirits do not bleed. Maybe you were sent back.'

"The room had stopped spinning as soon as Jed's head hit the straw pillow. He had heard Kioawa but needed a moment to respond. His mouth was dry, and he felt his heart thunder in his chest. If he was a spirit, he was a pretty poor one; he couldn't even sit. 'Sent back from where?' he managed to say once he regained control of his body.

"Kioawa didn't answer. Instead, he got up and silently walked to the small collection of blood, dipped a finger in it, and tasted it.

"'That's disgusting,' Jed said. The Indian responded by prodding Jed's injured leg, which sent a bolt of searing pain to his brain. 'Damn you,' Jed said, kicking his good leg towards Kioawa.

"'You are a man,' he finally concluded, and he backed away from the bed, his eyes never leaving Jed. Kioawa returned to the chair in the front room and sat, but only after pointing the knife back at Jed. 'Tell me why I am here or I will kill you, again.' He awkwardly added the last word. His tone was threatening, but his countenance spoke more of fear.

"'I don't think it would take much to kill me, again or otherwise, but I assure you I have no idea why you or I am here. All I remember is slipping away into something completely black and cold. So cold,' he repeated. 'Then I woke up here in this bed.' Jed had managed to pull himself into a half-sitting position, his head resting on one of the logs that made up the wall. 'What happened after I—' he hesitated '—after I died?'

"Kioawa searched Jed's face for a trace of a lie. Experience had taught him not to trust anyone outside of his clan, especially the white men. They were master deceivers, but Jedidiah appeared sincere, and too weak to lie. 'A great sleep took me.' The night before he had watched Jed take his final gasp and then become still and cold. He had seen men die before, and this man's death had been no different. He rolled the body away from the edge of the ledge, retrieved Jed's knife, and then was overwhelmed by a sudden and unnatural heaviness. He sat beside the body as energy drained from him. He dropped the knife, thinking that it had been cursed, and then kicked it off the ledge with a final effort. That was all he remembered until now.

"'Then someone else must be responsible for our present condition.' Jed said, and he mentally added, *Someone who could fix a broken neck and bring people back from beyond the edge of death.*

"'What were you doing on the ridge?' Kioawa asked.

"'Talking to the man who built that chair, only he wasn't talking back.' Jed was trying to find the position that hurt the least and eventually found himself reclined forty-five degrees with his neck flexed, his chin almost to his chest.

"'I have seen you talk to the grave before.' Kioawa lowered the knife and then slid it back in its scabbard.

"'That's mine, you know. I'm not asking for it back, but just so you know.' Jed had painfully canted his head to look at the Indian. 'So you've been tracking me?' It was a question but clearly also an accusation.

"'No. I have never tracked you, only seen you in passing.' Without further comment, Kioawa stood and went outside.

"Jed waited for his new partner to return, but after a half hour he become concerned that the Indian had left him. He slowly worked his way back into a sitting position and finally stood. The world tilted and whirled for a moment, but he managed to stay upright and stumble to the chair by the door. He sat in it so heavily that it threatened to tumble backwards. The sun had cleared the trees outside the small cabin and a bright beam reached the threshold. Jed watched it slowly walk across the floor, and then Kioawa returned as suddenly as he had left.

"'Whoever brought us here left no tracks or signs.' Kioawa handed Jed his knife and the carcass of a fat rabbit. 'Do you know what to do with this?'

"Jed nodded his head and began to skin the animal. It took him about five minutes to do what would normally take ten seconds, but he managed to strip the carcass. He felt exhausted and hoped he could summon enough energy to walk back to the bed. He was getting the distinct impression that there was a limit to how much help he could expect from Kioawa. He tossed the fresh meat on a small, rough wooden counter next to where Kioawa stood pounding a handful of bitter roots into a paste. Jed had done the same thing many times before for James Magraw in the weeks before he died. The mash made a palatable meal, but a better poultice. Jed went back to the skin and began to carefully peel off the thick fat layer from the hide. The cabin was warm enough that the fat began to liquefy quickly. 'Here, take this.' Jed said, and Kioawa turned and scooped the glob of dripping fat from Jed's cupped hands. He mixed it with the mash of bitter roots and then kneaded it with his hands.

"'You must wait for it to thicken', Kioawa said minutes later. He used a strip of cloth that once had been a shirt of Magraw's to wipe the slimy mess from his hands. He then turned to the meat and began to strip the bones.

"'Where did you learn English?' Jed asked as he accepted a small cut of meat.

"From the Lord Constable Bryson.' Kioawa stepped to the wall next to the small fireplace and sat on the stone.

"'Of Boston?' Jed was surprised to hear a name he recognized from his youth. His father and Lord Bryson had known each other. 'I think I knew him. In fact I believe we once cele-brated Yuletide together.' Those had been better days for Jed, meaning that his mother was still alive and his father still had hopes that Jed would grow up to be someone respectable.

"'I was brought there when I was five. My people traded with the Dutch, something the civilized British found objection-able, so a group of you attacked our village in the middle of the night and killed everyone but the children. Being good Chris-tians, you couldn't offend God by letting us starve, so you sold us as slaves and displayed us as curiosities.

"Jed sat quietly, chewing the raw meat as a foggy memory about a cold Boston night and a dark-haired boy with a wild look in his eyes began to clear. It was very possible he had met Kioawa many years earlier. 'I remember seeing a boy at Lord Bryson's house.' He spoke slowly, as much out of fatigue as uncertainty and embarrassment.

"'Then it is possible we have met before.' Kioawa gnawed a small bone, unfazed by the possible convergence of their pasts.

"'Where were you going when you found me?'

"Kioawa turned his head away from the question. He flicked a small bone into the fireplace and then stared past Jed to the open door. They sat quietly for several moments before Kioawa spoke. 'I was going nowhere. I have nowhere left to go.'

"Now, normally, Jed was a fairly perceptive young man, but he could have been as dumb as a bag of hammers and still picked up on the fact that Kioawa had a story to tell. A story that he didn't seem to want to share, but considering the very strange circumstances the two found themselves in, it could very well prove to be important. Still, he hesitated. He was a private man naturally and out of necessity. The code of the mountains was not to ask questions. A man's past was his to keep. Reluctantly, Jed let the moment pass. 'I think that's ready now.' He stretched painfully and sunk his fingers into the pile of yellow-green goo and gently began rubbing it into the bites and lacerations that covered his torso, shoulders, and thighs. Kioawa continued to stare at the trees just beyond the clearing. Jed slowly stood and hobbled back to his bed and collapsed.

'It took the better part of the next week for Jed to regain his strength, which, all things being equal, was rather remarkable.

"'I do not think you will need my help much longer,' the Indian said after Jed had built a small fire in the hearth. The weather had turned, and despite it being late summer, snow had fallen the previous two nights. Jed sat down on his bed and Kioawa had settled into wooded chair, which had become their nightly routine, only the Indian, instead of staring out the open door or the window, turned his gaze on Jed.

"'I'm starting to feel my old strength return,' Jed said after several uncomfortably quiet moments, and he stretched his arms as proof. 'I can't thank you enough for all that you've done.' Kioawa continued with his penetrating stare, not even recognizing that Jed's comment had violated their unspoken agreement to avoid any discussion of the strange events that quite literally brought them to the small cabin.

"Kioawa's only answer was an occasionally tilt of the head as he continued his study of Jed. After several full minutes, he sat up suddenly as if he had finally made a decision. 'I have lived beyond these woods and mountains. I have learned your ways and your language. I have been taught to pray to your God, but none of that has made me forget who I am, and where I come from.' Kioawa began. 'I saw you die, of that I am certain. But now you live. The history of both of our worlds is shaped by men who have returned from the dead. All have a purpose. What is your purpose?'

"Jed of course had ruminated over this very question for the past several days, but despite hours of solitary contemplation he was just as lost as he had been when he first awoke. 'I don't know,' he finally said, sounding pathetically weak.

"'When I think as a white man I too find no meaning. Your Jesus Christ brought the word of God to all those who would listen. You bring no such message. What need has He of reanimating the body of a . . .' Kioawa finished his sentence with an unintelligible Mohawk phrase.

"Jed didn't know whether to ask Kioawa to explain his phrase or the definition of reanimating. 'Then if it is not my God, what of yours? Tell me why you were on the ridge. How did you find me?'

"This you will remember is the very question Jed had asked earlier only to have Kioawa respond with an answer so enigmatic that it cut off any further discussion. He continued his study of Jed and then turned his gaze to the floor. 'You told me that a giant bear attacked you.' Kioawa paused to allow Jed to nod. 'There are no giant bears in this mountain. The land is too steep for even a small bear to hunt or to forage.' Again, Jed nodded. This was something else that had consumed his thoughts. In all the years that he had lived in the shadow of this mountain, Jed had not seen a bear of any size near the meadow or on the nearby slopes. He had seen hundreds of bears elsewhere, but never here. It was one of the reasons Magraw had chosen this site for their cabin. 'I believe that it was Tawiskaron that attacked you,' Kioawa said. 'I believe that you have offended him in some way and he has brought you back.'

"Are you familiar with the Iroquois legend of the Twin Brothers," Adis asked me, and it took several seconds for me to realize that he had dropped out of the story.

"Not really," I finally answered.

"The Iroquois believed that the world above was inhabited by many gods, and that before the earth had taken shape one of those gods was split down the middle, creating Tawiskaron and Okiwirasch, and sent to earth. These brothers were constantly at odds with each other."

"Good versus evil," I interrupted.

"Not exactly. They weren't opposites, just halves of a whole so that neither was complete without the other." I slowly nodded my head. "They divided the world fifty-fifty. Okiwirasch, it is said, governed spring and summer, while his brother ruled autumn and spring. Okiwirasch was a friend to man, creating corn and flowers so humans could survive and cherish their new world. Tawiskaron created weeds and poisonous plants so that humans could begin to recognize and learn from their surroundings."

"I understand," I said a little dreamily.

"All right, back to seventeenth-century New Hampshire," Adis said.

"'Tawiskaron has brought me back to kill me a second time.' Jed finished Kioawa's thought.

"'A second, third, fourth time. He will go on so long as he is amused. It is his way.'

"'Are you are speaking from experience?' Jed asked, and it was now Kioawa's turn to nod.

"'When I was taken from my village and brought to your world, I was not alone. There were others. When the time came for the great man Lord Bryson to select his pick of the lot, he choose me and a small girl who had been a part of my clan.' Kioawa sat back and spit with the name of Bryson. 'We were little more than livestock at first, but when I learned your language he took an interest in cultivating my mind and saving my soul. When Onatah grew into a woman, Lord Bryson was found to have other, more personal interests. In the end, we escaped together. One night a man appeared in my cell. He held Onatah's hand and she told me to take his other. He led us out of the cellars, through the dark house, and the streets of Boston unseen. I never saw his face, but I knew him.'

"'It was Tawiskaron wasn't it?' Jed asked quickly. Religion had only a small place in his solitary life. He still considered himself a Christian but had never developed the disdain his fellow Europeans had for the traditions and beliefs of the Indian people. Maybe it was a reaction to his father's overbearingly pious attitude. With a quick wave of his hand, his father routinely dismissed any other belief as superstitious nonsense, but Jed had started to wonder if any religion really got it right. Couldn't God the father and the Iroquois' Sky Woman be different faces of the same being? And how would the Christian God fare if the Indians had all the guns and armies? Would Jesus and the holy trinity be dismissed with a wave of a hand as superstitious nonsense?

"'Yes, it was Tawiskaron,' Kioawa answered after a slight hesitation. I'm guessing that he didn't like to say the name out loud. 'After the last snow fall of this year, I took Onatah and our daughter downriver. It was a trip we had done a hundred times before.' He spoke slowly and softly, as if he were afraid of being overheard. 'The three of us were in a sturdy canoe in calm waters when they suddenly began to rise. I tried to reach the shore but didn't make it. We were washed away and apart. I awoke many hours later, alone. Everything around me was strange and unfamiliar. For weeks I searched those unfamiliar shores for any sign of my family, but they were gone. Taken from me.' He stood and turned towards the door. 'One morning I awoke to find our lost canoe tied to a tree next to me. Behind it was an enormous bear. He was watching me sleep, and when I awoke he reared up.' Kioawa stopped his story and for several seconds simply stared at the setting sun. Jed stood after several minutes of silence, and the movement stirred the Indian back to life. 'I ran. I ran, and ran. I was terrified.'

"'That's understandable. I would have run, I tried to run—' Jed said, but Kioawa waved a hand to silence him.

"'You ran because you saw a bear. I ran because I saw Tawiskaron. I knew him, and he knew that I knew him. He called after me but I kept running. I heard Onatah call my name but . . . I was a coward.'

"Jed stood in the cabin, not certain how to respond. This wasn't an age of hugs, so he simply watched Kioawa and waited for him to recover.

"'I haven't been back to the river since. I came here because I heard a rumor that a woman and her baby were seen wandering near here. I know it is just another trick by Tawiskaron, but I have to know. That's when I found you.' Another long pause followed. 'I—we—have to go back and face him. If you don't, he will find you again, and kill you. If I don't go back, I will never see my family again, and will never be free of him.' Kioawa's eyes began to tear, and he quickly walked out of the cabin and into the early evening.

"The next morning, the two men slowly climbed the mountain, keeping an eye out for unnaturally large bears. They walked in silence, and as they got higher Jed began to feel more like his old self. Kioawa trailed behind a few steps and walked virtually without a sound. When they finally made it to the clearing, the sun was high and the day was more than half gone. Everything seemed quiet and normal, except for the fact that James Magraw sat with his back against his own roughhewn gravestone.

"'Well, I see that you two finally figured it out," Magraw said. He then pulled a bottle from his tattered shirt and took a long draw. He climbed to his feet as deftly as Kioawa moved through the woods. He turned to Jed and said, 'You defiled this sanctuary, this refuge, with the bones of a filthy white man. My brother and I created this place with our very own hands. I carved out the side of this mountain, and leveled the ground, and he planted some of his finest creations. And now the spirit of a nonbeliever hangs over it.' He spat out something that looked like a large dark insect. It fell to the ground, sprouted thick grey wings, and then took off into the air. 'This is unforgivable.' Magraw moved into the bright sunlight and then turned to Kioawa. 'Are you here to help him, or to give yourself to me so that I might spare your wife and daughter? You are a fool and a coward. I should wipe the memory of you from their minds and give them both to a more deserving warrior. When I came to Onatah she stood fast. She made me proud.'

"'And you stole her,' Kioawa answered meekly.

"'I saved her.' Magraw had grown to twice his normal size and advanced to within a dozen feet of the pair. 'From you.'

"'You are the one who put her in peril by causing the flood.' Kioawa had stepped around Jed and his shadow and faced Tawiskaron. 'I have found you, now return them to me,' he demanded with as much threat as he could muster.

"Tawiskaron started to laugh in James Magraw's grizzly voice. 'No,' he finally said. He flopped to the ground and Jed could feel the solid rock beneath tremor from the impact. 'I will give you a chance, both of you, to win your lives back.' He paused again to take a swig from the bottle. 'No human has ever beaten me in combat. I give both of you the chance to be the first. Two against one; I will even let you work together or separately if you choose.' He lay back in the grass and closed his eyes. 'Choose or I will slaughter you both where you stand.'

"'Together,' the two men said as one.

"'I'm waiting,' the recumbent Magraw said.

"Jed withdrew his knife and circled the prostrate form from the cliff side while Kioawa circled from the forest side. In a blur, Magraw was on them both. Seconds later, Jed was disarmed and dangling over the cliff edge, hanging on by fingertips. He managed to find a foothold and clambered back up to find that Kioawa was draped across a tree limb twenty feet high. He was conscious but bleeding from a large scalp wound.

"'You called me a coward,' Kioawa spat, a moment after regaining his senses. 'Fight me as a man.' He pressed himself back up onto the branch and then swung his way to the ground. 'Prove yourself to me.' He banged his chest with a closed fist and walked back into the clearing. 'My hands are empty,' he said as a challenge. 'Are you afraid to do the same?'

"Jed walked into the midday sunlight but stopped when Kioawa raised his hand.

"'No! I want this between him and me,' he said loudly.

"Magraw began to laugh. 'Even as a man I would slaughter you in an instant.'"

"'Prove it then!' Anger poured from the Indian. 'Slaughter me, but do it as a man!'

"Jed watched as Tawiskaron changed from the supersized James Magraw to a normal size Kioawa. The mimicry was perfect, and if they hadn't been standing ten paces apart Jed wouldn't have been able to distinguish them.

"'How is this form? Now the only difference between us is what is in our hearts,' the twin god said as he began to stalk the Indian. 'You ran from me once, but this time you won't get the chance.'

"Just as Tawiskaron said those words, the world around the clearing began to lose its color and faded to a dull white. The trees that bordered the meadow became frosted and their branches began to intertwine, forming a frozen, impenetrable barrier. The only way off the cliff was down.

"Kioawa lunged at his evil double, and the two became locked in a tangle of arms and legs. In an instant, Jed had lost track of who was who as the pair wrestled to the ground. They rolled to and fro, and Jed silently cheered his colleague for lasting more than the instant that Tawiskaron boasted. After several minutes, neither could press an advantage until one of the pair slipped a hand around the other and grabbed a fistful of hair. The second man screamed briefly, but then his face was twisted into the dirt as the first man began to roll them both towards the precipice. Jed lunged for them, but the momentum of the two men easily bowled him over. They swept past him in a rush, and he would have watched them go over save for a sudden flash of light and a loud snap. Something large and dark sailed over the head of Jed and he instinctively ducked. When he recovered, he found that one of the Kioawas was standing at the edge of the cliff wiping blood and sweat from his brow. His face was a mask of fury, and he screamed in a voice that rattled the mountains. Jed covered his ears as Tawiskaron stomped past him and towards the prostrate form of the real Kioawa, who had been thrown halfway across the clearing. A knife appeared in one hand of the twin god and a tomahawk in the other. He continued his ungodly scream, but it had no effect on the unconscious Kioawa. Jed tried to decipher what Tawiskaron was saying, but his words were neither Mohawk nor English. He stood over the fallen Indian and continued his inarticulate bellowing.

"'Liar, cheat, scoundrel,' Jed screamed, convinced that he was about to witness the murder of his friend, but his human voice was no match for Tawiskaron. Jed jumped to his feet just as Tawiskaron raised the tomahawk, but before he could drive it home, Jed drove him into the ground. He pummeled the smaller man with a blur of fists that would have certainly killed an ordinary man, but unfortunately he was not hitting an ordinary man. A second flash blinded him, and he felt himself yanked from his knees and thrown into the afternoon sun. He landed on the flat of his back, and every breath of wind was knocked from his lungs. He stared into the blue sky trying to get his lungs to work, knowing that he only had moments to live. Any second, Tawiskaron would appear above his immobile form and the tomahawk would fall. Only that didn't happen. After several painful seconds, Jed was able to draw a breath and he rolled to his side. All he could hear was the blood rushing in his ears, and a small clump of grass blocked his view of the vengeful god and the fallen Indian. He heard mumbled distant sounds that could have been a conversation, but his oxygen-deprived brain couldn't sort it out. Gradually, his breath returned and the sounds began to resolve into words. Two voices spoke in the strange language Tawiskaron had been screaming earlier. One was clearly Tawiskaron; it remained angry and challenging, as the other was firm and unyielding. An impasse, or perhaps a resolution, between the two was met, and after a moment of silence a pair of rough hands seized Jed and lifted him into the sky. The face of his father stared back at Jed.

"'I know who you are,' Jed says defiantly.

"'Finish what you started when you were just a boy,' Tawiskaron said, referring to the last time Jed had seen his father, which was in fact in a street outside of their Boston home. Jed had raised his fist to his father that day, and the Captain lay bleeding and dazed in the street as a group of strangers dragged the sixteen-year-old Jed away. The guilt that Jed felt after that encounter was evenly balanced by the anger he felt whenever he thought of his father. Still, he deeply regretted striking his father; even though he was just sixteen at the time, he knew that he should have been stronger and resisted the impulse to lash out. 'Finish it boy, or are you too weak?' The voice was his father's, and so where the words which had been hurled at him countless times as he grew up. Tawiskaron dropped him to the ground. 'You must be punished for your impudence.' This also was a favorite saying of his father. Tawiskaron kicked Jed in the ribs, and for the second time in a matter of minutes Jed could not draw a breath. He kicked Jed again, which was unnecessary as the man had no air left in his chest; still the pain threatened his level of consciousness. Jed rolled into a ball while Tawiskaron, in his father's voice, berated him. Finally, he realized the futility of his physical and verbal barrage and withdrew to allow Jed to recover himself.

"After an eternity Jed was able to roll to his knees. He was bleeding again from all the bites and lacerations Tawiskaron had given him earlier when disguised as a bear. He was relieved to find Kioawa still breathing, twenty paces away. The Indian lay on his side, blood pooling around his face, which was swollen and almost unrecognizable. Still, one eye was open and it followed Jed to his feet. 'What glory do you find in killing a man already half dead? Or killing a man who bests you in combat?' Jed motioned towards Kioawa.

"'Glory? I have no need for glory. My only needs are vengeance and entertainment, and each of you supplies me with both.' Tawiskaron had his back to the frozen trees, and as he started towards Jed the branches released with a loud *Thwang!* that echoed off the surrounding mountains. 'I told you, brother, not to interfere,' Tawiskaron said as the largest elk either Jed or Kioawa had ever seen seemed to glide into the glen on long majestic legs. 'I have offered them each a fair deal in exchange for their lives. Lives they have both already forfeited. You have no authority here.'

"'Liar,' Kioawa whispered, loud enough for all to hear. The elk turned towards the fallen Indian and studied him. 'I would have destroyed you, but you broke your promise.' The elk looked from Kioawa back to Tawiskaron.

"'You are nothing more than a coward and a liar,' Jed joined in. 'Fight me in any form that pleases you, but do it as a mortal. Enough of these games.' Jed stared down the eyes of his father. The elk finally snorted something that may have contained words, and Tawiskaron laughed.

"'My brother agrees, but I am not bound by what he believes, or even by promises I make.'

"'Then I say again you are nothing but a coward and a liar and worthy not of reverence but derision,' Jed finally said the words meant for his father from so long ago. He screamed a Mohawk war cry and began to run at Tawiskaron. He bent low to tackle the man/god, but just before impact he dropped to his side as if he were sliding into second base and swept Tawiskaron's legs from beneath him. Jed rolled onto the surprised man and head butted him with enough force that Jed saw stars. Tawiskaron was stunned, but only for a second. He pushed the much larger man off of him with no more effort than if Jed were a piece of lint. He was on his feet in the blink of an eye, and Jed was once again on his back.

"'I can do this all day, every day,' he grinned and taunted Jed. 'How long do you think you can last?'

"'As long as I need to,' Jed said rather unconvincingly as he slowly climbed to his feet. He took his thick coat off and found that his tunic and pants were soaked with bright red blood.

"'Not by the looks of that,' Tawiskaron laughed in Jed's father's mocking voice. 'Why don't you just sit down for a moment?' A force knocked Jed's feet from beneath him and he landed on his butt with a thud. Just for a moment, he couldn't breathe, again. 'I still have some unfinished business with your partner.'

"Now Kioawa was just as bad off as Jed, if not worse. He climbed to a sitting position but knew that he had a number of broken ribs. He had been thrown onto an outcropping of rocks that were much more solid than his chest. He tried to say something but only managed to spit blood. The elk beside him nuzzled the back his head and then ambled away. Kioawa was left facing Tawiskaron alone and defenseless.

"'I doubt you can be much more fun, so why don't we simply finish this?' The knife reappeared in Tawiskaron's hand as he bore down on the Indian.

"Kioawa struggled to his feet. His breathing was shallow and excruciatingly painful. He regarded Tawiskaron for a moment and then spat a bloody glob onto the face of Jed's father. 'I should never have run from you. You are not worthy,' he whispered.

"'I am worthy enough to do this.' He slashed Kioawa across the chest. It wasn't a deep wound, just enough to further weaken the man. Kioawa fell painfully to his knees, striking the very rocks that had broken his ribs. After a moment, he tried to struggle to his feet but only managed to fall back onto his hands.

"'Unworthy,' he said a second time, but could only manage to mouth the words.

"A look of frustration creased the faux face of Tawiskaron. He wanted to break the Indian, to have him beg for mercy, or for death, but all he seemed to manage was defiance. 'I have an idea,' he said, and a second loud crack came from the frozen trees. A moment later, a young Indian woman holding a baby stumbled into the light as if they were being pushed by an unseen force.'

"'Kioawa,' she screamed, and she tried to run to her husband but struck an invisible wall. She wailed but was silenced by a wave of Tawiskaron's hand.

"'Say goodbye to your family. This is the way she will remember you, on your knees before me, bloody and broken.' He laughed and took a step backward to allow Onatah an unobstructed view of her husband.

"Once again, Kioawa tried to climb to his feet. After a full minute, he managed to be upright, but his wounds would not allow him to straighten. 'Never on my knees before you,' he said, and again he spat on Tawiskaron.

"The twin God was beyond furious, and the knife in his hand elongated into a saber. He started to swing it in a killing blow, but it struck something solid, and then the world began to press in on Tawiskaron. He was being crushed to the ground by a force that he could neither comprehend nor fight. Both his ankles cracked as he was forced lower, then his knees folded beneath him, the ligaments snapping audibly. His chest was pressed into the solid granite, preventing him from drawing a breath, and then he felt the vertebrae in his spine give way. His chin broke next, and finally everything stopped. He was beyond pain, and he struggled to reassume a more natural, nonmortal form, but the constricting bars of his prison prevented it.

"Kioawa watched as Tawiskaron was contorted before him, not fully understanding. He looked up and found Jed pressing a set of enormous antlers over the twisted body of Tawiskaron. The antlers immediately fused to the underlying stone and then slowly turned to stone themselves. A snort refocused his attention to the enormous elk, who had lost its magnificent set of antlers.

"'Drink and wash from the stream,' it said, and Kioawa found that a small stream had formed just past the imprisoned Tawiskaron. 'Both of you.' Kioawa dropped once more to the stones and the water began to flow over him. Jed joined him, and the pair greedily drank from the stream, which had begun to grow in size. The washed their wounds, which immediately sealed and then disappeared. Both men found that they could breathe freely and that energy began to flow back into their bodies. After several minutes, Kioawa jumped to his feet and ran to his wife and daughter.

"'Leave this place and never return. Ever!' the elk told Jed.

"'You are Okiwirasch?' Jed asked, and the elk nodded. 'But he is your brother.'

"'And you are my children. Even we are faced with difficult choices.' He turned and glided away into the now green trees.

"'We must leave,' Jed said to Kioawa and his family.

"'First you must meet Onatah,' Kioawa said, steering her towards Jed.

"The two stared at each other for a long second and Jed finally presented his hand, which Onatah accepted. 'I remember you,' she said softly. 'And your father.' Her eyes flicked to the twisted form of Tawiskaron. 'He hasn't changed much.'

"Jed held her eyes and thought about what she had said. 'I sincerely hope that he has.'

3. Ghosts in the Machine

In 1950, Isaac Asimov published a series of nine short stories under the title *I,Robot*. He reinvents the phrase 'ghosts in the machine,' which was originally coined by the British philosopher Gilbert Ryle's description of René Descartes' mind-body dualism (thanks *Wikipedia*). Essentially, it describes the fact that we are really all ghosts locked inside a biologic machine, but this definition has nothing whatsoever to do with what Asimov or the 2004 movie that starred Will Smith. Both book and movie borrowed the phrase and changed its meaning to describe random bits of excess computer code that somehow combine to create consciousness in domestic robots (who then begin to run amok).

Acknowledgments

I would like to thank Lou Aronica and the entire Story Plant team. I appreciate the opportunity to not do all the things necessary for success.

About the Author
✗ ✗

Brian O'Grady is the author of three novels, *Hybrid, Amanda's Story,* and *The Unyielding Future.* He is a practicing neurologic surgeon and, when he is not writing or performing brain surgery, he struggles with Ironman triathlons. He lives with his wife in Texas.